Karin Nordin is an author, martial artist, cosplayer, and self-proclaimed cat whisperer. Her first novel, *Where Ravens Roost*, was shortlisted for the 2022 CWA John Creasey (New Blood) Dagger award and her second novel, *Last One Alive*, was a 2022 ITW Best eBook award nominee. She has an MSc in Creative Writing from the University of Edinburgh and an MA in Scandinavian Literary Studies from the University of Amsterdam. Born in 'The Biggest Little City in the World' and raised in America's Rust Belt, she now lives in the Netherlands. *Sweet Little Lies* is her first standalone psychological thriller.

Also by Karin Nordin
Where Ravens Roost
Last One Alive

SWEET LITTLE LIES

KARIN NORDIN

ONE PLACE. MANY STORIES

HQ
An imprint of HarperCollins*Publishers* Ltd
1 London Bridge Street
London SE1 9GF

www.harpercollins.co.uk

HarperCollins*Publishers*
Macken House, 39/40 Mayor Street Upper,
Dublin 1 D01 C9W8, Ireland

This paperback edition 2023

First published in Great Britain by
HQ, an imprint of HarperCollins*Publishers* Ltd 2023

Copyright © Karin Nordin 2023

Karin Nordin asserts the moral right to be
identified as the author of this work.
A catalogue record for this book is
available from the British Library.

ISBN: 9780008601003

For my sisters, Kelly and Kristina.
Did you eat nachos today?

Sunday, October 14, 2007

1:17 a.m.

The police keep asking me where my homecoming dress is.

I can't tell them. I can't tell them that I set it on fire in order to hide the bloodstains. I can't tell them that I buried the ashes in a ditch off the side of the highway. I can't tell them who I was with or what I've done. And even if I could, I wouldn't be able to.

Because no one can ever know.

My face is streaked in mascara tears. The interrogation room is cold and I have goose bumps on my legs. They're asking me why I'm wearing shorts in the middle of October, but I don't say anything. My throat is thick from crying. Not the cute Hollywood kind of cry, but the relentless choking sobs that come with learning something so inconceivable that it strikes you at your core. Like lightning. Like hitting a brick wall at full speed without your seat belt on. Their words have turned me into an empty husk. The more I think about it, the more I feel like I can't breathe. Like the life is being sucked out of me. It can't be true. I refuse to believe it's true.

They continue to bombard me with questions.

Where were you? Did you get into a fight? Where did you go

after you left the dance? Did anyone go with you? Did you see Amber? Were you in the woods at any time this evening? When was the last time you saw Riley? People say you were arguing at the dance. What were you arguing about? Did he ever threaten to hurt you? Did he ever threaten to hurt Amber?

My eyes are burning. My hands are shaking. I can barely see anyone through my tears. If they would just give me a moment to catch my breath. A moment to think. Is this even legal? Shouldn't my parents be here?

But they don't stop.

Where's your dress, Alexandra? Why won't you talk to us? Don't you want us to find out what happened?

Of course I want to know what happened! Of course, I want to help. She's my sister, for God's sake! But I can't tell them where I was. I can't tell them about the blood on my hands.

What did you do with your dress?

I burned it.

I burned it to hide the evidence.

Chapter 1

YOU'RE NEXT.

My chest tightens, breath catching in my throat. I feel winded as my heart plummets into my belly. For a second, I'm somewhere else. Somewhere I shouldn't be. And I imagine I hear her screaming, a high-pitched wail that pierces the base of my head like a migraine. Then I blink. The memory is gone. I'm angry.

Then I realize the message isn't for me.

It's a threat from the neighboring school for the upcoming football game. Their students have been committing random acts of vandalism all week. Our students have done the same to them, no doubt. It's a time-honored tradition of riling each other up. Except they don't have to clean it up.

The words drip from the mirror in the girls' gymnasium bathroom. Red. The walls are coated in sanitary pads, leaking spray paint on the tile floors. Worse yet, someone has stuffed the toilets full of tampons. The floor is covered in an inch of water. They flushed the goddamn toilets, too. It's probably a hundred dollars' worth of sanitary products clogging up the drains. Maybe even two hundred dollars' worth. I recognize the brand name on

3

the wrapping someone tossed in the corner. Stuck-up, high-maintenance bitches. Couldn't they just teepee the end zone? That's what we used to do. We never caused structural damage. We never made a mess for somebody else.

Except for that one time someone died.

An audible sigh falls from my lips, all the exhausted impatience from the week exiting my body like an exorcised spirit. I don't have the time to deal with this today. I have to be at my mother's house in half an hour and I still haven't emptied the trash cans from the cafeteria.

I tape a note on the front of the bathroom door along with a yellow *wet floor* sign. *Closed for cleaning.* I'm going to have to call a plumber. I'll do that on the drive. Hopefully someone will be able to come and clean it up before the game on Friday. I don't know if I have enough paint remover to get rid of the stains. I don't even know if it'll come out of the mirror. Baking soda and hot water might do the trick. But there might not be enough elbow grease in the world to get it out of the floor. I suppose I should be grateful it's not actually blood.

But blood is easier to get out.

The final bell rings and students rush out of the classrooms, bottlenecking the hallway on their way to their lockers. They sound like a swarm of bees. Someone throws a football over the crowd, just barely missing Mr. Roth's head, egg-shaped with a receding hairline, exactly as one would expect an AP Calculus teacher to look. He yells at them to take it outside, but the boys just laugh. There's a hierarchy in high schools. Everyone knows it. Football coaches and principals are at the top. Math teachers at the bottom. If there was a trapdoor in the food chain leading to a subterranean level of bottom-dwellers, that's where you'd find me. Lex Wicker. Part-time custodian. Invisible emptier of trash cans. The one who didn't get out. Tainted goods. Small-town pariah. The girl whose boyfriend killed her sister.

The one who should have died.

I stand off to the side of the hallway, just behind a large bin on wheels, waiting for the mass exodus of students to subside. Someone tosses a half-open bottle of cola at the bin. It sprays when it hits the rim, but thankfully misses me. I learned a long time ago not to stand next to the bins for that exact reason.

The jocks are always the first ones out, high-fiving each other and slapping their buddies on the back. Large herds of girls—the popular ones with the perfect hair sporting the top-of-the-line fashion, the type to vandalize public property without a second thought—follow after them, huddling together, whispering and laughing. Even in the middle of ass-crack Ohio, there are kids who think they can strut the catwalks of Milan. It'll be at least ten years before they realize how stupid they look. I would know. I used to be one of them. Then come the marching band kids, lugging their tubas and trombones alongside their twenty-pound bookbags. The real MVPs of the school since the football team is shit. Lastly, everyone else. The nerds, mostly. The art students. The after-school program volunteers. And the kids from the other side of the tracks who don't have to rush to catch the buses because the buses don't go to their side of town.

The kids who remind me of Riley.

It takes me fifteen minutes to empty all of the trash cans in the school and another ten minutes to replace the toilet paper in the bathrooms. There's a night custodian who does most of the mopping, so I don't bother with the spill in the cafeteria. Normally, I would out of courtesy to my colleague—he's a decent guy—but I'm already running late. And my mother has a thing for punctuality. Which in retrospect is morbidly amusing considering the fact that she's a raging alcoholic. She could drink an entire bottle of bourbon for breakfast and still be five minutes early for her hair appointment. I could be stone-cold sober, leave my house an hour ahead of time, and somehow manage to be late. Which is all anyone needs to know to understand how unfair life is.

Once I finish up I grab my jacket out of the staff lounge and head for the exit. I never bring a bag or purse to the school. Too much risk of something getting stolen. If it doesn't fit in the pockets of my coveralls, it doesn't go with me. The only other people who seem to have figured that out are the automotive and woodshop instructors. Driver's license, credit card, phone, keys. I don't need anything else. I'm not trying to impress. Not anymore. Not that I could even if I wanted to. Everyone already knows too much about me. Braxton Falls gossip is a stigma that's impossible to shake.

They're not right, of course. But they're not wrong either.

"Lex! Hey! Wait up!"

I turn to see Principal Henson waving me down from his office door. I glance up at the clock on the wall. It's two minutes fast, but I'm already three minutes late. I stop and jog back the few steps to his door. "Yeah?"

"Just wanted to let you know that CJ is retiring at the end of the month, so if you want the full-time custodial position, it's yours."

I fight back the urge to roll my eyes. Everyone knows CJ isn't retiring. CJ has cancer. And if he's leaving at the end of the month, it's not because he's picking up and moving down to Florida like most of the snowbirds in town. It's because he's getting his affairs in order. I feel a pinch of guilt now for not mopping up that mess in the cafeteria. "Thanks, Principal Henson. I'll think about it."

I won't think about it. I'd rather die than spend the rest of my days cleaning up after snot-nosed teenagers and wandering these grief-stricken halls. The halls that Amber and I used to wander before everything went to hell. As it is, I would have left a long time ago if there'd been another opportunity that paid enough. But no one wants to hire the girl who lied. Even if there's no proof of a lie.

"How many times do I have to tell you to call me Richard?"

"Not sure. Should I start keeping count?"

He laughs. I wasn't trying to be funny. The sound echoes in the empty corridor. Principal Henson is the kind of man who most people find charming and trustworthy. Straight teeth, reasonably attractive, full head of hair for a man who is probably pushing sixty. He looks like he should be on a box of men's hair dye. *Impress the ladies with the salt-and-pepper look!*

The eyes. His smile never reaches his eyes.

Also, he used to be my history teacher when I attended Braxton Falls High. So, calling him by his first name is out of the question. That's just too weird. Even if it's been more than fifteen years since I was a student.

I give him a halfhearted smile. My mother is going to kill me. "Well, I better be going."

"Give my regards to Audrey."

Audrey. As though he and my mother were best friends. But that's how everyone talks about her. Poor Audrey. What a horrible thing to go through. How tragic it must be to be left behind. And to lose Michael last year, too. As if I didn't also lose people.

"Will do."

I head off down the hallway again.

"Oh, Lex!"

I glance back over my shoulder, impatience prickling under my skin. "Hm?"

"Are you going to the homecoming game next week?"

My pulse quickens and I clench my fist so hard the knuckles crack. Homecoming. The anniversary of Amber's death. The day someone brutally murdered my sister and left her body in the woods to be mauled by animals.

No, I'm not going to the fucking homecoming game.

Henson knows that. Everyone knows that.

But for a split second I think I see something intentional in his gaze. As though this wasn't an innocent mistake. As though he's asking because he wants to see if I'll give something away.

I shrug. "I'll think about that, too."

I won't think about that either.

I hurry off before he can say more. My entire arm has gone numb from clenching my fist. By the time I get to my car, my face

7

is hot and my heart is racing. There's an empty pit in my stomach that's churning. Not from hunger, but from hatred. From grief.

I turn on the ignition. Cold air blasts from the heater and the radio crackles the end of a Radiohead song. When I swerve out onto the main road, I just miss hitting a cement truck that came out of nowhere. It blares its horn at me and I blare back. It's my fault. I forgot to look left. But this is a twenty-mile-per-hour zone and he's going at least forty. My nerves are shaken. I inhale to a count of six and try not to think about how if my reaction time had been a little slower I might be with Amber now.

Which is probably where I deserve to be.

Chapter 2

I pick up the post: a hefty stack of letters, bills, and local magazine ads, from my mother's mailbox at the end of the drive, before I make my way to the front door. I steel myself with a deep breath and a reminder that today is no different from any other day. If I could make it through the last 417 days since my dad passed away, leaving me to care for my mom one-on-one, I could make it through today. I just had to remind myself that it was only an hour or two. Then I would be back at my place, popping in a microwave dinner, and catching up on the latest binge-drama on Netflix. Anything to avoid the resurgence of whispers in town. As if I needed a reminder that next weekend was the anniversary of my sister's death. As if I hadn't already seen the local news vans outside city hall, treating fifteen years since my family's tragedy like the lead-up to a Memorial Day parade. Like I didn't know everyone was looking at me and thinking, *There she is. There's the girl who let her boyfriend sacrifice her sister in the woods.*

Because even when the man is responsible, the woman always gets the blame.

Or is that survivor's guilt talking?

The inside of my mother's house is immaculate. It hasn't changed much since I used to live there, aside from the heavy odor of flowery perfume meant to cover the scent of booze. She still has a plastic runner in the foyer and the carpet looks clean enough to eat off. I remove my shoes at the door and hang my jacket on the coat rack. The furniture is all late Nineties. She still has the same sofa, area rug, and coffee table we had growing up. But there's a newer flat-screen TV mounted on the wall. That was my dad's last big purchase before he died. Massive heart attack while raking the leaves in the front yard. The doctor said it wouldn't have mattered if he'd been in the hospital when it happened. It was, as they call it, *the big one.*

"Mom?" I walk through the hallway, family photos decorating the walls in an eerie timeline from my birth to Amber's death. Amber's junior year photograph is the last one on the wall. Her dark brown hair falls in effortless waves over her shoulders, bright green eyes eternally unblinking. Her crooked smile and sun-soaked freckles forever immortalized behind glass. There's nothing after that. No graduation photo of me. No picture of Dad's promotion to chief of police. No family vacations with the three of us. Because nothing happened after Amber died. Time stopped inside that house. Life stopped. For all of us.

Mom is sitting at the dining room table, her hair tied back in a loose graying ponytail, stray shorter strands frizzy along the sides her face. She hasn't done her makeup and she's still wearing pajamas beneath her bathrobe. Not the new robe I bought her last Christmas, mind you, but the one she had before. She's sifting through old photo albums. I hold back the urge to give a disgruntled sigh. So, it's going to be one of those days.

I set the mail on the table and sit down across from her. "Didn't you hear me come in?"

"You're late."

"I was talking to Principal Henson."

She looks up from a page of Amber's baby pictures and for a split second I see a rare sparkle in her eyes, as though she's forgotten who we are and what our relationship has become.

"Ah, Richard. That dear man. He was always Amber's favorite teacher, you know."

"I thought Mrs. Woodrell was her favorite teacher."

"The lesbian?" Mom scoffs and turns the page in the album.

"She was married to a man from Akron." Normally I wouldn't correct my mother because it risks putting her in a mood. But sometimes I can't help myself. Besides, she's wrong. I know for a fact that Mrs. Woodrell was Amber's favorite teacher. And I hate the small-town stereotypes that people who have never left the tri-county area come up with just to dislike a person they don't know.

"She had short hair."

Those kinds of stereotypes.

"I have short hair, Mom."

"Yes, but we all know you're not into that." She says 'that' like it's something criminal. Like it's something that would prevent her from showing her face in public for the rest of her life.

She picks up her coffee mug with an unsteady hand and takes a sip. The coffee looks cold and I suspect it's composed of a higher percentage of vodka than caffeine. I guess I ought to give her credit for still being awake. Half the time I come over after work she's passed out drunk on the sofa. To be honest, I prefer when she is.

I look up at the large oak hutch behind her. When I was a child it was covered in Royal Copenhagen Christmas plates. She had every year from 1968 to 2006. Then she stopped collecting them. The plates are gone now, shoved in a box in the basement or in the cabinet with the good china, replaced by Precious Moments figurines. She has a hoard of them lining the shelves. An army of wide-eyed, innocent, porcelain collectibles. All of them little girls. All of them looking like Amber.

"Is that a new one?" I ask, pointing to one of the figurines on the edge of the lower shelf. Small talk is all Mom and I have left.

Mom glances back and rolls her eyes. "Yeah, three years ago."

She reaches over and takes it off the shelf. The figurine is wearing a raincoat and galoshes that are at least three sizes too big for her. At her side is a small puppy pulling on her umbrella. She has a sweet, but surprised look on her face. The eyes are empty though. The eyes are dead.

Mom smiles. "This one reminds me of the time we took that trip to Salt Fork and it rained all weekend. You were a grump and refused to leave the cabin. But Amber spent the entire first day running through puddles."

"And she spent the rest of the trip in bed with a cold."

Mom pretends like she doesn't hear me. Or maybe she really doesn't. She's been tuning me out for years. Amber was always her favorite, even before she died. I don't know why. Maybe because people always said that Amber was the spitting image of Mom when she was younger, which is weird because people always said that Amber and I looked so much alike. I think they just meant that Amber had more of Mom's interests and eccentricities. I remember the day she wore Mom's old cheerleader uniform to tryouts and immediately made the team. You would have thought she'd just been crowned Miss America. Whereas Mom and I never really had a lot in common. When I was younger we would always argue over the stupidest things. Now it's like I don't exist. I shouldn't complain. The silent treatment is better than being yelled at.

I'm about to begin sorting her mail when there's a flash at the window. I turn my head to see a man in the backyard with a camera. "What the hell was that?"

Mom doesn't even look up from her figurine, her tone uninterested. "Reporters."

"Reporters?"

"They've been chiming at the door all morning. They keep asking me for a statement, but I told them I refuse."

"A statement for what?"

This time she does look up and I'm surprised to see genuine concern in her face. Or is that annoyance? It's so hard to read her when she's been drinking. "Where have you been? It's all over the news. Chief Newman came by this morning. They've given that bastard a date. Less than two weeks from today. The day before the anniversary. Can you believe that? It's karma. Long-awaited karma."

"What?" I stare at her, confused. My reaction is delayed because I always knew this day would come. We all did. But I never imagined how I would feel when it finally arrived.

Surprised. That's how I feel.

"Your two-faced murdering boyfriend," Mom says through clenched teeth. The vein on the side of her forehead is throbbing, but her hands, once shaking around her coffee mug, are uncommonly still. It's as though this knowledge has slapped the liquor right out of her. "They're going to execute him next week. They're going to fry that bastard for what he did to my baby. And we've got front-row seats."

Chapter 3

Mom's words are meant to be dramatic. They don't use the electric chair anymore. They haven't for years. But now I have the image in my head and I can't get it out. I'm going to be sick. I have to stand up just to calm the somersaults in my stomach and prevent myself from dry-heaving on the dining room table.

I close the curtains on the window, blocking out the small crowd of journalists and cameramen who are trampling over my dad's azalea bushes. If he were still alive this would never happen. If he were still alive Mom would be chasing them down the driveway with a frying pan, hollering at the top of her lungs. The fact that she's so dismissive about it makes my face burn. I've always had a problem with my temper, but it's getting worse the older I get.

I thought people were supposed to become more patient and understanding with age. Maybe that's only for other people. Not us. Not me.

"Were you going to tell me?" I'm trying not to sound accusatory, but even I can't ignore the bite to my words. The fury. "Amber was my sister."

"And she was my *daughter*," Mom snaps back. We're both venomous, but no one knows quite how to hit a nerve like a mother does. And my mother is an expert in poison.

I take my phone out of my pocket and do a quick Google search. It takes less than a second for the results to pop up in the local headlines. Hell, it's even reached the national news. Of course, it has. Riley King is infamous. First teenager in the state ever to be sentenced to death. And now the first prisoner to be executed since the capital punishment stay that resulted from the state's inability to acquire the chemicals necessary for lethal injection. Funny, that. Murder? Inhumane? Who would have thought.

I should have been more prepared for this moment. Riley's conviction never sat right with me; I never saw anything in him to suggest he was capable of murder. When he was first condemned I lost it. He couldn't have done it. Nothing would have convinced me. I was obsessed with the idea that it was a stranger—a serial killer who stalked small towns and moved on before anyone could catch them. Not someone I knew. Not someone I loved. I tried to visit Riley after his sentencing, but then Mom went berserk in the kitchen while Dad urged me not to go. He said there'd be too many questions. People might assume I knew something.

Then there was the pressure from everyone else. The entire town was adamant that Riley was guilty and even though I couldn't believe it, taking his side felt like a betrayal of my sister. I began questioning my own convictions. How much of that night could I really remember? I tried so hard to forget most of it. And as the years went by I eventually accepted that I must have missed something. But I still couldn't stop myself from hoping that the police made a mistake. Not just to prove Riley's innocence, but to ease my own conscience.

I hoped this day would never come. But it was only a matter of time. I should be siding with my mother. With the town. I should feel the same anger and resolution. I should be overjoyed that justice will finally be served. That's what we've all been waiting for, after all.

I hate Riley for what he did. I'll never forgive him. But I know his death won't give me solace or retribution.

Because I loved him. And no amount of time or circumstance can take away the intensity of a person's first love. For better or worse, that feeling is eternal.

"That man deserves to die. He deserves worse than death for what he did to my baby." Mom grips the Precious Moments figurine so hard I think I can hear the porcelain cracking.

"No one *deserves* to die," I say, more to myself than to her, but when I look at Riley's photo on the top article I can't help but be blindsided by the wave of nausea in my belly. It's the same photo they've been using since his arrest. In the eyes of everyone—in *my* eyes—he hasn't aged a day. Why do people always look guilty in arrest photos? Even suspects who are later proven innocent have an incriminating gleam in their mug shots. Dark circles under the eyes, messy hair, lips turned in a downward spiral, and a terrifying emptiness in the gaze that exists somewhere between despair and malevolence. How could I not see it then? Was I so blind?

When we were kids Riley used to joke about one day making it into the *Guinness Book of World Records*. I don't think this is what he had in mind.

The doorbell rings. Mom ignores it. She doesn't even flinch. She dusts off the figurine and sets it neatly on the shelf beside the other Amber doppelgangers. Then she begins looking through her mail. I might as well not even be there. She picks up her coffee mug and takes another tentative but thirsty sip. I have the urge to snatch it out of her hands and pour it down the drain.

Or drink it myself.

I resist giving in to my anger by making my way into the attached kitchen and filling up a glass of water from the tap. Above the sink is a window with a view into the backyard. Our old metal swing set is still sitting out there, overgrown with weeds, the chains rusty. I remember when Dad installed it. It was a gift for my eighth birthday, but Mom said it was for both of us. Dad just winked at me afterwards, a reminder that it was actually for me. We used to play on it daily, Amber and me. Just the two of us testing the limits of how high we could go and who could jump the furthest. I always won at those little competitions. Not because I was the oldest, but because I didn't want anyone to think I was afraid.

When I was five I broke my arm falling off a jungle gym. While most kids would probably grow up with a permanent fear of heights or hurting themselves after that, the experience initiated an obstinance in me. I didn't want to be afraid of anything. I wanted to be untouchable. As a young girl, Amber was the opposite. She acted like she was afraid of everything. Heights, insects, dirt. She could cry at the drop of a hat. That's what started the expectations. That's why everyone blames me. They didn't know we were both putting on an act. They thought I was the strong one. They said I was supposed to protect her. But I was faking it. And that's why their question has never been answered.

Why weren't you there to protect her?

Because I was frightened.

"This one's for you," Mom says, tossing an envelope on the other side of the dining room table.

I down the glass of water and set it in the sink. By the time I make my way back to the dining room table, my mom has moved on to another page in the photo album. Toddler Amber. I wonder how long she's been sitting there. How many times has she already gone through the album, running her fingers over the images of her favorite daughter? How many cups of coffee-laced vodka is she on? Three? Four? And when would I stop caring about where all her love goes?

I pick up the envelope. There's no return address, but there are multiple ink stamps denoting that it was returned to sender on at least three occasions. When I look at it more carefully I realize it's because the address was written incorrectly. Technically the entire thing was incorrect since I no longer live with my mother. But the house number has been inverted. The sender wrote 71 instead of 17. And I know immediately who it's from.

Riley always messed up my address like that. Riley who'd fought dyslexia all the way through middle school. Riley who once swore he'd sent me a Valentine's Day card in the mail only for it to arrive eight months later in time for Halloween. I'd felt so guilty about yelling at him for forgetting.

"Who's it from?" Mom asks, but I can tell from the sound of her voice that she doesn't really care. Or maybe that's just my panic talking. My panic worrying why Riley has sent me a letter after all this time.

What could he possibly want to say? And what makes him think I would listen?

I rip the envelope open without thinking. Inside is a single sheet of loose-leaf paper that looks like it's been torn out of a spiral notebook. It's folded into an origami square like the notes we used to pass to each other in class.

I'm more tentative about opening the note inside. My hands are shaking worse than my mother's. When I see what's written inside I gasp audibly. Like being clapped on the back and having the wind knocked out of me. Mom looks up and if I knew better I would think she actually appears worried. But I can't focus on interpreting her micro-expressions right now. All I can focus on are the six little words handwritten on the center of the page.

I know what you did, Lexie.

Then the doorbell rings again.

Chapter 4

I throw open the door prepared to scream at the reporter on the other side, but a familiar face stops me in my tracks. My head physically jolts back when I look into the eyes of Jessica Hampton. My best friend. Strike that. My ex–best friend.

"Jess?"

She looks equally surprised. "Lex? What are you doing here?"

The question should sound more absurd than it does. I am at my mom's house, after all. The house I grew up in. But my thoughts are scrambled. I've just found out that my ex-boyfriend has been given an execution date for next week. And I'm still holding the letter from him in my hand like it's glued to my skin.

"I could ask you the same thing."

I haven't spoken to Jessica in years, but very little about her has changed in that time. She is, without a doubt, one of the most attractive women in Braxton Falls. Hell, she doesn't look like she even belongs in Braxton Falls. Jessica has one of those high-class, pampered appearances. I don't mean that to sound rude. She comes from a wealthy family and she's always been beautiful. Not to mention glamorous. But not in the way people think models or movie stars are glamorous. She just has one of those auras. She's the type of person who should be sitting at an exotic seaside restaurant in the Mediterranean wearing an outfit that to a layman might look like it belongs on a department store rack but comes with a designer price tag. Elegant simplicity. To be honest, it never really made sense that we were friends. And maybe we never really were. Maybe that's why it's been years since I've seen her.

But that doesn't explain why she's standing at the front door of my mom's house while a crowd of photographers and journalists crowd the sidewalk to get photos.

Or maybe that crowd is the explanation.

Before Jessica can answer my question, however, Mom's wailing voice hollers from behind me.

"Jessica, darling!"

Mom pushes past me and wraps her arms around my former friend as though she were Amber suddenly brought back from the dead. She squeezes her into a hug that I can barely even imagine receiving from my mom. Afterwards, Mom tugs Jessica into the living room, leaving me to stand in the doorway while cameras flash in the background.

It's like I don't even exist. Like I'm invisible. Maybe I am. I wouldn't be surprised if I didn't show up in any of those photographs.

"Come in, I guess," I mutter beneath my breath before closing the door.

Mom and Jessica settle themselves on the sofa. Mom clutches one of Jessica's hands with both of hers, like she's the one consoling my friend as opposed to the other way around. That's when I notice the rings. Jessica has a massive diamond-encrusted wedding ring on her left hand, but she also has two on her right. Even my untrained eye can tell they're expensive. I can't help but wonder if the three together would pay off the mortgage on this house.

"I heard on the radio and I thought I should come over right away," Jessica says. She pats Mom's hand and gives her a soft, but encouraging smile. Then she turns her attention to me. The smile loses some of its affection when our eyes meet, but I don't see any deception in her gaze. I assume she's telling the truth. I have no reason not to. After all, I don't really know her anymore.

But that's precisely why it's so weird to see her sitting in my mom's living room acting like they're best bridge buddies.

"You've always had such a good heart, Jessica. I appreciate it so much. Everything you've done for me over these years."

I scoff.

They both stare at me like I've shown up drunk to a funeral.

"What are you talking about, Mom? When have you seen Jess? She hasn't been around since we were in high school."

In fact, the last time I ever really spoke to Jessica was at Amber's funeral. And even then, we didn't really talk. What do you say when your best friend's sister is murdered? I don't think I would have been able to choke out anything if circumstances were the other way around. After that I slipped into my own world and basically ignored everyone. I suppose as far as friendships ending, ours was fairly innocuous. I shut down. And maybe, in her own way, Jessica did too.

Later, when I tried to get in touch with her, Jessica ignored me. I never did figure out why. Maybe she thought I had something to do with Amber's death. Or maybe she just wanted to avoid the stigma of being associated with me. The girl everyone thought knew more than she let on.

Which is why her being in my mom's living room is even more bizarre than Riley writing me a letter for the first time in fifteen years.

"That's simply not true." Mom's voice changes like she's speaking to a child. She's also trying to hide the animosity she was showing me not moments before Jessica rang the doorbell.

I should be angry, but this is a pattern with her. We must uphold the outward appearance at all times, after all. Wouldn't want the rest of the town knowing that we've all been permanently damaged by an unimaginable tragedy. Wouldn't want anyone to think we're guilty or that we're hiding something. Or that we're fucking traumatized.

"Jessica has been such a great support to me. Always sending gift baskets around the holidays. And last year when you helped with Mike's funeral costs—"

"What?" I can't hold back my surprise at this point. Did she just say that Jessica paid for Dad's funeral? Because I distinctly remember staying up until three o'clock in the morning with Mom going through all of her finances to find enough money to cover the cost of the casket and the service. I remember looking into getting a loan because Mom insisted that he had to be buried in a top-of-the-line casket. I even got to the point where I considered going to the police station and asking if they could assist in any way. If there was a bursary or something for full-time officers. Thankfully, it didn't come to that because the last place I wanted to show my face then—or now, for that matter—was the police station.

But all that? And then Jessica just swoops in and pays for it? And Mom never told me?

"It was the least I could do," Jessica says. "Audrey was always so kind to me when I was younger. You know my mom. Never around much. Always traveling. And then she ran off and Daddy just replaced her with mistresses who were barely old enough to be my babysitter. I always enjoyed coming over here and spending time with you guys. It always felt like more of a home than my place."

I don't know what to say. Not that I disbelieve Jessica. I don't have any reason to. But this is a woman I haven't seen in years. And then to find out that she's secretly had a close mother-daughter relationship with my mom after all this time? While maintaining *zero* contact with me? The person who used to spend every weekend with her since elementary school? My jaw could literally hit the floor.

"Is this going to change anything with the memorial service?" Jessica asks.

I blink. "Memorial service? What memorial service?"

"Didn't I tell you?" Mom shakes her head like a bad actress feigning forgetfulness. "It must have slipped my mind. I always get so emotional around this time of year and what with it being fifteen years since Amber left us. It's all so much."

Jessica gives my mom's hand an encouraging squeeze. "We understand."

"I don't mean to be rude or anything," I interrupt. "But what are you talking about?"

"Your mom wanted to do something special for Amber's memory. I've been helping her organize a community memorial service for Amber. The proceeds will be going to the local women's shelter."

I don't know what to say.

"Goodness! I'm being a horrible hostess. Would you like anything to drink?" Mom asks, standing up from the couch. "I can put on a pot of coffee."

Jessica gives a polite smile, but I wonder if it's also something of a grimace. The stench of alcohol on my mom's breath is probably overwhelming. She has to notice. I bet she's just better at pretending than Mom is.

"No, thank you," Jess says. "I should get going soon. I just wanted to stop by and see how you were doing."

"You're too kind. Really. To be thinking about me at a time like this. You stay right here. I'm going to get you something for the road."

Mom's little act isn't nearly as good as Jessica's, but I save my commentary until she's made her way into the kitchen. Then I turn a more forceful and scrutinizing glare on Jessica.

"What is going on? What are you really doing here?"

Jessica stands up and I follow her lead. "Like I said, I wanted to see how Audrey was doing."

"You wanted to check on my mom? Really? My mom? It didn't—oh, I don't know—strike you to maybe check on me?"

Jessica doesn't respond directly. Her lips purse. She's searching for the right words. I don't blame her. I probably look like a ticking time bomb. And the way I'm clenching Riley's letter in my hand, like it's my lifeline, I can't blame her for being cautious.

"I didn't know if you wanted to see me," she finally says.

"Why would you think that?"

"Well, we haven't exactly talked since . . ." She hesitates. Everybody hesitates when it comes to mentioning Amber's death. You'd think that time would make it easier to say.

Since Amber's death. Since Amber's passing. Since Amber's murder. Since we lost Amber. Since Amber was killed.

Since Amber.

Jessica flips her long wavy hair over her shoulder. It falls perfectly, like she's posing for a makeup commercial. It might seem pretentious considering the circumstances, but I recognize it as one of her tells. Jessica was always good at hiding her nervousness behind her appearance.

"I always felt weird about reaching out to you," she says after a pause. "I wanted to. I felt horrible for how our friendship ended without any real reason. How things just stopped between us. Between *all* of us. I guess I didn't know how to approach you. After Amber died, you kind of fell off the face of the planet. When you came back from Christmas break you were different. And then we graduated a few months later and all went our separate ways."

She's not wrong. I was basically a lifeless zombie the last half of the school year. I don't even remember graduation. I remember Dad insisting that I go to the ceremony, but I have no recollection of walking across the stage or getting my diploma. I never had a graduation party. I didn't go out and celebrate with friends. I didn't do anything after Amber died. Whereas the friends I did have, the ones I stopped talking to after my sister's murder, did exactly what everyone expected of them. They moved on. They left

24

Braxton Falls. They went to university. They traveled the world. In the case of Jessica, she did both. I remember hearing that she got into a school in Paris. But I couldn't tell you when she moved back. Everyone moved on. Everyone got married. Everyone had kids. Everyone had lives.

I didn't do any of that. I didn't have a life.

I lost my life the same night that Amber did.

Except I still have to wake up every morning and go through the motions.

"I'm sorry," Jessica said.

I really want to be mad at her. I want to yell at her. I want to tell her to get out of my house and stay away from my mom. But I can't. It's not like I ever really gave her a chance to renew our friendship. If it even was a real friendship. I mean—is anyone in high school ever truly friends? It's a game of survival. The key is finding a small pack of teenagers who make you feel like you belong and can protect you from the bullies for four years. No one actually expects those friendships to last. And, if they were supposed to last, wouldn't a tragedy bring true friends closer together?

Maybe it's not their fault. Maybe it's just mine. Maybe I'm just jealous and angry that they got out and I didn't.

"It's fine. I suppose I should be thanking you. My mom doesn't have a lot of advocates. And we don't exactly get along." I glance off to the kitchen. Mom is probably frantically looking for something in the fridge that she can wrap up and pretend she made from scratch. Like that frozen cherry cobbler I baked for her last week. She probably doesn't remember that I had to throw it away because she drunkenly knocked it on the floor.

"Are *you* OK?" Jessica asks.

"I don't know. I just found out right before you rang."

"Shit. I didn't know. I mean, it's been all over the news and social media. I figured everyone knew."

I fold up the letter from Riley, careful to follow the same lines he had when he folded it into that origami shape he used to do

25

in high school. I can feel Jessica watching me. She wants to ask. I'm tempted to tell her. But it doesn't feel right.

"It's no big deal. Honestly. We knew it would happen eventually. It was just a matter of time."

"Right." She doesn't sound convinced. She inches toward the door. I must be making things uncomfortable. "If you want to talk about Ri—"

"I don't." I cut her off so quickly it sounds like a snap, but that's not my intention. I'm simply not ready to hear someone else say his name. Not yet. Not out loud. I don't know how I'll react. And I don't want Jessica, or my mom for that matter, to see how vulnerable I am where Riley is concerned.

"Well, if you or your mom need anything, I hope you know you can still reach out to me. Audrey has my number."

"Thanks."

Jessica makes her way to the door, my mother's plastic floor runner squeaking under her steps. I catch her before she leaves. "Hey, Jess?"

She turns around on the heels of her ankle boots. "Yeah?"

"Are you certain Riley did it?" My voice catches in my throat. "Don't you have any doubts?"

Jessica stares at me, her expression oddly blank. Cautious. Maybe even a little sorrowful. She feels bad for me. She pities me. She's probably the only one who does.

"Yes, Lex. He did it. That's why he's in prison."

Chapter 5

The ball python locks its jaws down on the thawed mouse. There's no crunch, but there is a hesitating pause where it looks like the head of the mouse might roll out of its mouth. Then the snake momentarily unhinges its jaw to gulp the mouse's body down its throat. The python barely moves, the majority of its four-and-a-half-foot form coiled at the opposite end of the enclosure where it's made a bed out of Astroturf and shredded bark. I watch as the undigested body of the mouse bulges out of the snake's neck, elongating the ovular brown shapes on its scales. I hate feeding it, but I can't help but watch when it eats.

Spaghetti technically isn't mine, but I've had her ever since Riley received his sentence. She was Riley's pride and joy. I remember when Riley first got her. He told me how he went to some guy's house for a party and saw the snake stuffed in an empty aquarium that was less than half its size. The poor thing looked half dead. It didn't have room to stretch and its vertebrae were visible through the scales. It was shedding, but not because it needed to. Because it was unhealthy. Riley just grabbed the aquarium while the rest of the party smoked pot and he took

27

her home. Then he got her a proper vivarium meant for large snakes and nursed her back to health.

He'd only had her for a few months before Amber's death. When Riley went to prison, his father threatened to throw the snake on a fire pit. I don't know what compelled me to go over there and take a python more than half my size, but I did. I did so many crazy things in the months after Amber died. Mom was livid. She didn't want a snake in the house. Let alone one that belonged to the boy who killed her daughter. Dad never said anything about it, but he understood it was something I needed to do. Maybe he thought it would help me deal with my grief.

Regardless, I was adamant. But all these years later I still don't feel like she belongs to me. She's Riley's snake. In the beginning, I lied to myself. I'm good at that. I convinced myself that I was just looking after her until Riley got out. But I knew that would never happen. Even when I look at Spaghetti now a small voice in my mind tells me this is temporary. I watch the lump slowly move down the python's neck, the scales expanding around the shape. This isn't forever.

But it is. I think about the years immediately after Amber's death. I think about all of the arguments between Mom and me about Riley's guilt. About all the pent-up anger I felt over my own doubt. The frustration of having to choose between my first love and my sister. The defeat of recognizing that my defense of Riley was based more on feeling than fact.

I think about how much I wanted to tell my parents the truth of that night. How I wish I could tell my mom now. But I was so afraid back then and so much time has passed. And what good would it do now? No one can change what happened.

I couldn't save Amber or Riley. But I could save Spaghetti.

The microwave pings and snaps me out of my brief hypnosis.

It's been one of those days.

I arrived at the school early that morning, but the front lawn was already covered in press and media people. They'd parked their vans just beyond the drop-off point where some parents had already begun to line up, letting their teenagers out. One of them even attempted to shove a camera into the window of one of the waiting vehicles, trying to get a statement from someone. Maybe they hoped they'd accidentally come across someone who remembered the murder or was a student at Braxton Falls High School when Amber was there. But they probably didn't even care who as long as they got an interesting sound bite.

Damn vultures.

I hurried up to the main entrance with my jacket collar pulled up to hide half my face. I heard someone call out and I knew it was my attention they wanted, but I didn't give them the satisfaction of a glance. I just picked up the pace.

"There she is!"

"Hold up! Miss Wicker! Can we get a word?!"

"Just one picture, please!"

I dashed up the steps and into the building, shielding the rest of my face with my hand. Once I was inside the school I breathed a sigh of relief, but I could still feel their eyes on me. They'd be waiting when I got off, too. I knew it.

The workday lumbered by. I spent almost an hour cleaning up another graffiti mess in the second-floor girls' bathroom. Someone had spray-painted 'HAPPY HO-CUMMING' on the mirror. Thankfully I caught it early enough that it was still wet. Graffiti comes off relatively easily as long as I scrub it with a mixture of soap and paint thinner. My elbow ached by the time I was finished and the mirror still had a permanent smear on it. But I decided to leave that until tomorrow.

To be honest, it was the class changes that were even more infuriating than the vandalism. Every time the bell rang announcing the end of the period, I caught students casting quick suspicious glances in my direction. It was weird being noticed after so many years of being ignored. I saw them whispering by their lockers when I passed them at the drinking fountain. No one said

29

anything to me directly, but when I spied a teenage girl filming me I told her to delete the video or I'd make sure she got expelled. I don't have that kind of power, but she didn't know that. Not that it did any good. An hour later the social media accounts on my phone were blowing up. I rarely use them. I thought they were private. But when I opened them on my break I was inundated with pictures, tags, and memes. Gossip about me. Derogatory comments about Riley. Slander about Amber.

I spent my lunch hour turning off notifications on all of the social media apps on my phone. Out of sight. Out of mind.

I just wanted to do my job and go home.

Which is exactly what I did. Only this time I left out the back entrance to avoid the small crowd of journalists who were still hanging around the lawn. It should be illegal to film outside of a school. Maybe it is. Maybe no one cares because they think I deserve to be hounded. Because they think I had something to do with Amber's death.

I stopped by the grocery store on the way home and picked up a week's worth of microwave meals and some concentrated tropical fruit juice. When I got home, I popped a spinach and ricotta lasagna into the microwave and nuked it for almost ten minutes. Then I remove a thawed mouse from the paper bag in my fridge and place it in Spaghetti's vivarium.

In the beginning I tried feeding Spaghetti live mice because that's what Riley did. But I don't have the stomach for it. And I don't think Spaghetti cares.

The lasagna is practically steaming when I remove the plastic. I dump it onto a plate, fill a glass with water, and slump on the sofa. I turn on the television for background noise. Then I take out my phone.

Three new messages from Samara.

OMG you should see the new artist we acquired at the gallery! She's almost as good as you!

Text me when you get home! I'll be up! xx

I can't help but smile when I see her messages. Samara is my only friend. Well, sometimes I think she might be more than a friend, but she's about as long-distance as one can get. I look at the time on my phone. 6:42 p.m. That meant it was 11:42 p.m. in London.

Samara and I met online almost seven years ago. We found each other on an abstract art message board. I always wanted to be an artist, but I mostly gave up on that after Amber died. Samara liked one of the charcoal sketches I posted on the forum. It wasn't even finished. Hell, it still isn't finished. I don't even know why I posted it in the first place. I guess I just felt like it was a small step toward putting myself out there. Maybe I was trying to judge whether I had any actual talent. I've never been a very good judge of my own work. Or my own self, for that matter. But Samara loved it.

We started talking. At first it was just superficial. Shared interests. She said she was an assistant curator at a modern art museum. She said she could get one of my paintings displayed in their new artists gallery if I sent her one. It was nice to feel seen as someone else. Not as Lexie, the girl whose sister died. But as Lex, the artist.

Eventually our conversations turned into a daily thing. She's been a constant presence in my life. She knows everything. Well, almost everything. She doesn't know what happened the night Amber died and I don't think I'll ever be ready to tell her. But she's probably my most important supporter. And no one knows about her but me. Some people might think that's weird. To have this kind of secret relationship with a stranger halfway across the world. But she's safe. She can't hurt me. She cares about me in a way you can't care about someone you see in person every day. And she isn't influenced by the rumors or the gossip. She just likes me for me. Lately more than I think I even realized.

She's been pushing me to fly out to see her for the last few months. I keep telling her I can't afford to visit, which isn't a lie. But it's not exactly true either. Technically I have enough to buy a ticket, but afterwards I'd barely have anything left. The real truth is I'm afraid. Everyone around me seems to become tainted. Amber, Riley, Mom, Dad. I know it's stupid to take all the blame, but I can't help feeling like I'm at the center of everything that went wrong.

I send her a quick reply: *You're too sweet. But I haven't done anything new in months. Creative burnout!*

The telltale 'Samara is typing . . .' pops up at the bottom of the messenger app. It gives me a giddy feeling in my stomach. Literal butterflies.

Precisely why you need to get your ass over here so you can be inspired again!

I text back quickly. *And what exactly am I going to be inspired by? You said it rains all the time out there.*

The architecture. The night life. The company. ;)

I smile to myself. *In your dreams.*

Exactly!

I set my phone on the couch while I pick up the plate and fork off a corner of the lasagna. I left it in the microwave too long and the top layer of pasta is hard. It actually crunches against my teeth. The inside is soft though, so I remove the overcooked edges.

My phone dings a reply.

But only if you want. x

I don't know what I want. An online relationship is nice because it's safe. But I miss feeling something other than guilt and regret. I miss having that connection with someone. And

Samara is fantastic because while she knows about my past and what happened with my sister, she doesn't judge me. Because she isn't here. To her it's just something in my past. It has nothing to do with us. Unlike every other relationship I have, which is basically sewn together with the thread of Amber's murder.

The program that was on the television cuts to the end credits and is minimized at the corner of the screen while a local reporter announces the headlines for the upcoming news segment. The sound of Riley's name steals my attention from the text messages. When I look at the television, his face is plastered across it. Still that same photo of him as a teenager standing in a courtroom as they announced the guilty verdict. They even show the clip that has become famous across the nation. The clip of the judge ordering the death penalty. The clip where Riley collapses in the middle of the courtroom.

I remember sitting in the back with my parents when they announced it. There was palpable tension in the room. Thick enough to cut with a knife. Riley fell to the ground and in my teenage mind, someone had killed him. Then the camera panned to us just in time to catch me fainting in the bench.

My phone dings.

Did I say something wrong? You're not angry, are you??

I hesitate before responding. *No. Sorry. Just got some weird news today.*

What kind of news?

Riley got his execution date. Next week.

There's a long pause and then Samara writes back. *Are you OK?*

I don't know. He sent me a letter. I think he wants me to go see him.

Are you going to?

That's the question I've been avoiding all day. I don't want to see Riley. I don't want to get dragged back into this. Not that I was ever out of it. But then I remember the words in Riley's letter. *I know what you did, Lexie.* How could he know? And why would he tell me now?

But I'm not asking the right question. The question I should be asking is, what is he planning to do with that information?

Chapter 6

Thursday, December 18, 2008
3:13 p.m.

The heat in the courtroom has been turned up full blast. It's sweltering. Sweat drips down the back of my neck, but I'm shaking from chills. My restlessness begins the moment the jury returns to their box, filing in one at a time. I try to read their expressions, try to gauge what the verdict will be. But half of their faces are obscured by the heads of the people sitting in front of me and the rest stare down at their feet while they shuffle into their seats.

What are they thinking? I need to know what they're thinking.

I glance over at Mom. She's wringing her hands in her lap, twisting her wedding ring over and over on her finger until it becomes so slick with sweat that any unexpected jerking motion could send it flying off across the courtroom. Dad has been statue-still for the last hour. It's like he's in a catatonic state. He won't look at anyone. Not me. Not Mom. Not even the jury. He just stares forward like a guard at the Tomb of the Unknown Soldier, stoically bearing the grief of every father who's ever lost a daughter.

"Has the jury come to a verdict?" the judge asks. She has a stern face and her hair is slicked back like a fashion model from the Sixties. Big eyes. High cheekbones. She isn't what I expect of a judge. Then again, this is my first time ever sitting in on a trial. My parents wouldn't allow me to attend any of the other days. Dad didn't even want me to be here today, but Mom insisted that I be in attendance for the verdict. She said it would give me closure. That it would give us all closure.

"We have, Your Honor," the jury foreman replies.

There's a panic in my chest. It tightens. It's hard to breathe. I tug at the collar of my shirt as though that'll help me get more air. It just makes me more uncomfortable because now I can feel the wetness around my collar. I'm soaked in sweat.

"Would the defendant please rise as the jury announces the verdict?"

I watch as Riley pushes out his chair and stands up. His face is hard to read. I can only see half of it. He doesn't look scared. He looks tired. Maybe a little bored. But that could be an effect of the lights. They're very bright and yellow. They make everyone, the judge included, look sick. Riley's right hand hangs loose at his side. I can see he's picking at his middle finger with his thumbnail. I'm right. He's not scared. He's terrified.

The defense attorney clasps his hands in front of him. He looks disheveled. Public defender. Because Riley is poorer than poor.

I've got the jitters. I feel like I'm going to jump off the bench and start screaming. Why are they taking so long? Ten years pass in twenty seconds.

The judge turns her attention back to the jury. "What is your verdict?"

The foreman clears his throat. "The jury finds the defendant, Riley King, guilty of murder in the first degree."

Nothing.

No sounds. No gasps. No one moves. No one even takes a breath. I've never heard stillness like this before.

Maybe I've gone deaf.

Maybe I'm having an out-of-body experience.

Then I hear it. My mother whispering a hushed 'yes' to herself. I can't help but feel nauseous at her enthusiasm. Dad doesn't do anything. He just tenses. I can see him gritting his teeth. It causes the artery on the side of his neck to bulge.

"In the case of *The People of the State of Ohio v. Riley Anthony King*, I find the defendant guilty of murder in the first degree. As this is currently a death penalty state, sentencing will be issued at a second trial in three months' time." The judge lowers the gavel against the wooden sound block. The echo resonates throughout the room.

The silence is deafening.

No. This can't be happening. This can't be right.

A low moan reverberates through the room, cutting through my thoughts.

It's Riley. He's reeling on his feet. His eyes roll into the back of his head and he pitches himself into the counsel table. It's jarring. I can't tell if he's been pushed or if he's done it to himself. But he looks like a top, whirling on his heel. He looks possessed. His head cracks against the side of the table and he careens backward into the rail between the counsel and the public benches. Then he hits the floor.

Everyone stands on instinct. The entire room gasps, but no one reaches out to help. A delayed second later, the defense attorney crouches down beside him.

My head feels like it's trapped in a cloud. The entire room is spinning. I reach out to grab onto the bench, but I miss it. Someone says something to me. I think it's Mom. But I don't hear her. My gaze is locked. Unwavering. At the center of the court, between the two counsel tables, I see her.

I see Amber.

She raises a bloody finger to her lips and shushes me.

I scream. Blood-curdling high-pitched terror.

And then I faint into the bench.

Chapter 7

I know what you did, Lexie.

I jolt up in bed, wide awake. Riley's imaginary whisper still lingers in my ear. The room is cold, but I'm sweating. The ceiling fan rotates overhead. It clicks on every other rotation. Probably a loose screw. Or maybe there's something wrong with the electrical. I reach for the remote control on my nightstand and lower it to a slower setting. Then I sit up. My stomach is twisted in knots. The bedsheets are clammy. My anxiety has soaked through to the mattress. I glance over at the clock—2:37 in the morning. I haven't even been asleep for three hours and I know I'm never going to get back to sleep now. I can't. My mind is too busy. Thoughts of Riley, Amber, and the events of fifteen years ago are spiraling in my head. Circling like vultures. I can't stop thinking about them.

How does Riley know? What does he want?

And why now, after all this time?

He's trying to get me to see him. That's what this is about. Nothing else makes sense. He knows his time is short. He knows Mom and I have been invited to the execution. He wants to get my attention before he's gone. He wants to rattle me.

Except that doesn't feel right. That doesn't feel like the Riley I knew. The Riley I knew may have looked rough around the edges, but he was kind. He was soft. Thoughtful. The Riley I knew wouldn't have wanted me to suffer. He wouldn't have waited until the last possible moment to taunt me with a secret no one was supposed to know.

But that had always been the biggest barrier between me and everyone else, hadn't it? The Riley I knew was not the Riley everyone else knew. I saw my first love. My first kiss. My first everything. They saw a killer. I've never been able to find a compromise between what I saw—what I *believed*—and what everyone else said. Part of me still doesn't believe it's possible for those two sides of Riley to exist. Surely it has to be one or the other. A person can't be good, affectionate, and kind-hearted and also be a cold-blooded murderer. Can they? And, if he was, I would have seen something. Sure, I was young, but I wasn't stupid. I wasn't blind. If he'd been capable of such horrors I would have sensed something.

I've binge-watched every true-crime documentary on television. In almost every interview the spouse or partner admits that they felt something was off. Like a little warning bell jingling in the back of their minds. But it was never enough for them to suspect they were living with a killer. They never felt like their lives were in danger.

Until they were.

Until it was too late.

But me? I never saw anything in Riley that gave me pause. I was never afraid of him. The fear didn't come until later. Until he was locked away and I realized it could have been me instead of Amber. Because Riley didn't have a reason to murder my sister.

I know what you did, Lexie.

But how could he know?

I hang over the side of the bed and pick up my laptop from the floor. When I pull up Google, the first thing I type in is Riley's name. Just as earlier I get thousands of hits, most of which are recent news articles about the execution announcement, made possible by the state's renewed access to the chemicals required for lethal injection. Twitter is a frenzy of political science and legal know-it-alls talking about the weird position of Ohio's capital punishment cases over the last few years.

I skim through some of the local and national media posts that give quick recaps of the events fifteen years ago. *Local horror. Every parent's nightmare. Tragic death. Cold-blooded killer. Teenage terror.* They use the same words over and over. The same terminology they used when my sister died. It makes me sick to think that Amber—and Riley—have been reduced to these splashy definitions. These headline-selling slanders written by people who never even knew them. People who have never even set foot in Braxton Falls. People who just want to clickbait viewers to their channels so they can beg for a follow.

And it's not just the news. There are social media posts from all over the country. There's even a hashtag for it. #TheBraxtonButcher and #HomecomingHorror are trending on Twitter alongside debates regarding the nation's stance on death penalty repeals. It makes my head spin.

I type Amber's name into the search engine. I've never done that before. It's never struck me to do that. Maybe my subconscious always thought it was too morbid. Why would I need to see what other people had to say about Amber? I knew her. I lived with her. I was the closest person to her: it didn't matter what anyone else said or thought. And, to be honest, I don't even know why I'm looking her up now. It won't change anything. She's still dead.

The initial articles and social media posts are sentimental. Lots of people expressing their anger and frustration about her death, relating it to crimes against women and children. I come across a few TikTok compilations that have been transferred to YouTube showing teenage girls—too young to have been alive when Amber died—speaking out about their own brushes with creeps and bad boyfriends. It's not that I don't sympathize with them. But something about it feels playacted. I can guess what the next girl is going to say before she even says it. And Amber is lost in the message. She's not a person to these kids. She's just a hashtag. A trend they can hop on and mimic and hope they accidentally see fifteen minutes of fame.

When the true message of Amber's life is that you don't want that fifteen minutes of fame.

I scroll down to the second page of search results. That's when it gets weird. Lists of conspiracy websites pop up, followed by an entire page of local American legends. Somewhere near the bottom of the search results I find one titled "Midwest Monsters: The Wynwood Witch." I click it.

Almost immediately I wish I hadn't.

At the top of the website is a long essay about the Wynwood Witch legend. I skim through it. It's almost verbatim the story I remember from childhood. The essay briefly paraphrases the history of settlers moving west beyond the fort in the Hudson Valley and their struggle to survive in the unknown wilderness. Then it goes on to highlight the story of Margaret Stedman, one of the first residents of Braxton Falls, who was persecuted by her own people for witchcraft. Her fellow settlers blamed her murder on the local indigenous tribe so the village men who were actually responsible could avoid sentencing. It's the same typical Wild West bullshit that endures today. But the legend comes after her death where local records state the presence of Stedman's spirit haunting the Wynwood woods around the settlement, condemning to death anyone who desecrated the place where she was killed. Hence the birth of the Wynwood Witch.

At the end of the essay is a list of the witch's potential 'victims' over the years. It's not a long list. Only five names. Three of them are dated in the late nineteenth century. One in 1903. But it's the fifth and most recent supposed victim of this legend that causes me to pause.

Amber Wicker—maimed and murdered in Wynwood Forest, 2007.

Amber's name has a link connected to it. I click it. For the second time in less than ten minutes I regret my actions.

The link brings up a message board that appears to be wholly focused on the mysterious circumstances of Amber's death and the controversy, according to these nebulous online conspirators, surrounding her murder case. What's even more disconcerting? There are dozens of folders on this message thread. And hundreds of comments, dating back almost to the day the news of her murder was released. And the most recent? Less than an hour ago.

"What the fuck."

I open up the threads and what I find practically freezes me in my bed.

Some of the threads talk about long-winded conspiracy theories about how the Wynwood Witch murdered Amber in order to send an innocent man to jail for the crime. These ones don't make any sense at all and are debunked quickly by most of the forum writers with the contradicting theory that the Wynwood curse isn't on men but on women. That it was a dark entity brought forth by the evil male settlers who wanted to abuse women. And that same entity was still hunting the woods for young women. These people argued that the name of the legend, calling her the Wynwood Witch, was just catchy and didn't actually have anything to do with witchcraft. It was simply a convenient name for a young woman who didn't fit into society. Which wasn't Amber at all. She was a token Midwest teenager. She wasn't an outcast. She wasn't different. It was her death that separated her from the rest of us.

But those comments aren't the ones that bother me. It's the ones that follow. The comments that don't have anything to do with the legend or my sister's murder. The anonymous responses meant to arouse hatred and misogyny.

>> *She was probably a bitch. I bet she deserved it.*

>> *Who goes out in the woods on homecoming night anyway? A whore that's who.*

>> *A hundred bucks she was out there getting fucked by her sister's boyfriend.*

>> *I bet she was jealous, threatened to cry rape, and then he killed her.*

>> *The papers should call her the Homecoming Ho.*

>> *Wish I'd had the nerve to do what Riley King did. My homecoming date was a cold-ass bitch too.*

>> *slut*

>> *WHORE*

>> *Who cares? One less stuck-up bitch in the world.*

>> *He's an idiot for getting caught.*

>> *they wouldn't have caught me*

>> *Too bad he didn't do in her sister too. Heard she's even more of an ice queen than the dead one.*

>> *Fucking hilarious how she passed out in court!! I could watch that clip on repeat.*

>> *Link???*

And after almost three hundred comments in this vein? Only three of the threads have been closed to new comments for "violating community guidelines." But they haven't been erased. They're still out in the open, eternally online, for anyone to see. And that doesn't stop the comments in the other threads.

Dozens, maybe hundreds, of anonymous strangers making Amber out to be some kind of 'Nice Guy'–hating teenage narcissist while Riley was hailed as a literal king for killing her. Amber wasn't perfect, but she didn't deserve to be demeaned in death. It makes me furious. I want to put my fist right through the screen.

And then I see another thread titled 'REVENGE??'

I click on it.

There aren't many responses to the starting thread. Barely any traffic. Maybe because someone has posted it recently and no one else has seen it. Maybe they're all too busy making their TikToks and retweeting other people's vile garbage. Too busy chasing the likes and the clout and trying to go viral to notice the one comment that sent a chill down my spine.

>> *Maybe he killed her to get back at her sister.*

I could practically hear Riley's response in my mind.

I know what you did, Lexie.

He couldn't know. It was impossible. But there's only one way to find out for certain.

I'd have to visit Riley myself. I'd have to ask him.

Chapter 8

I'm sitting in a nervous sweat. The last few hours have put me on edge. The drive out to Miller's Creek Federal Correctional Institution, the safety and protocol questions at the reception, the strict security check, the repetition of the rules—*Nothing is to be passed to the inmate. No cell phones. No food. Keep your visitor's badge visible at all times*—another check to ensure that my visitor's request was properly processed; all of it makes me feel extra self-conscious about my every move and thought.

Normally visiting a condemned prisoner takes weeks to schedule, but the state's sudden turnaround on the execution stays and Riley's impending date made it easier for me to get my request accepted. It also helped that I worked for a school, which made my background check go through quickly. But I still had to go through the metal detector, the pat-down, and walk past a drug dog. So, my anxiety is at an all-time high.

The room is cold and impersonal. The walls are a bland shade of off-white and the slate-gray floor is marred with scuff marks from tennis shoes. I feel like my skin is on fire, but I have goose bumps on my arms because I had to leave my jacket in a locked cubby along with my phone and car keys. When the door on the other side of the partition opens, I'm practically in a catatonic state. I don't even see Riley until he's directly in front of me.

I don't recognize this man.

Riley King sits still as a statue. We're separated by a divider, a thick piece of glass that needs washing. There's a small counter and two paper-thin partitions in this tiny cubicle meant to separate me from any other visitors. Meant to give us privacy. But there aren't any other visitors and there isn't any privacy. There are two armed guards standing less than six feet away from Riley. Their expressions are drawn into permanent scowls, arms hanging tense at their sides as though they're waiting for something to happen. They look like they're going to pounce and I have to physically pry my eyes away from them.

But not looking at the guards means I have to look at Riley.

He picks up the phone, a clunky black handheld that looks like it should be hanging in an old phone booth. There's one on my side too, but I haven't touched it yet. I can't move. I'm frozen in place. Frozen in fear.

No, not fear.

Fury.

He has a beard, full but not long. His hair is cut short. Not stylishly. Like someone buzzed it down to his scalp two months ago and this is the resulting growth. He's too young to have gray in his hair, but he does. More than my dad had when he died at sixty-seven. His eyes are lifeless. Icy blue like a cloudless winter sky. If it weren't for that dent in his nose, the one he got from picking a fight with Billy Chandler in the third grade, I probably wouldn't recognize him. This man is a stranger to me.

A stranger I used to love.

I'm going to throw up.

A tapping sound rips me out of my thoughts and I realize Riley is ticking his knuckles against the glass to get my attention. I pick up the receiver and bring it to my ear. The plastic handle is sticky. I don't want to think about why. As soon as I leave this place I'm going to jump in the shower and scrub my skin raw.

"I didn't think you'd come."

Oh God, it's his voice. It's older, deeper. A little rougher than I remember, but it's his voice. It's Riley.

How could he do this to me?

"It's kind of hard to ignore a threat."

He flinches.

I'm surprised by the sudden venom in my tone. I don't know how I've managed to conjure that confidence. Probably a defense mechanism. Like an animal caught in a corner. But I'm not going to let it go. I'm going to cling to that fake backbone for as long as I can. Just like I used to.

"It wasn't supposed to be a threat."

"'I know what you did, Lexie,'" I repeat from memory. "How is that not a threat?"

"I just wanted to get your attention."

"Well, you've got it. Now what?"

He hesitates. Something changes in his expression. His eyes soften. There's a brokenness to him. When we were teenagers he was so carefree. So spirited. That's what drew me to him in the first place. Riley King never put on airs for anyone. He knew who he was. He knew where he came from. And he didn't care. Unlike me. I'd always been the coward between us. I wanted people to accept me. I needed to be part of the group. Because if I wasn't then I was nobody. I always thought it'd be better to be surrounded by people who hated me than to be alone.

Until I got my wish.

"I'm sorry," he says, breaking his gaze with me.

I don't want to believe him, but I do. It makes me so angry that I believe him. Then I have to remind myself that this is what manipulators do. This is how they pull you in. They're charismatic. They're kind. They're loving. Right up to the moment they're not.

I think of Amber. I think of how that beautiful image of my sister with the radiant smile and the sweet disposition is replaced by the grotesque remains of her mutilated corpse. Of crows pecking at her eyes. There was blood everywhere. The leaves were covered in it.

47

"You don't get to be sorry. Not after what you've done." I'm hissing through my teeth. They're clenched so hard I can feel the vein on my temple pulsing. I sound like my mother. Maybe she's right. Maybe she's always been right.

Riley raises his head and this time he's the one who looks like he's staring at a stranger.

I would wonder what I look like to him, but I realize I don't care. He doesn't know anything. He's just baiting me. This was a waste of time. If he's trying to get last-minute forgiveness then he picked the wrong person. I could never forgive him for what he did to my sister.

For what he did to me.

I start to take the phone away from my ear.

"Wait!"

I hesitate. Why? I shouldn't listen to him. I should leave. I never should have come here.

"I didn't do it, Lexie."

A surge of frustration fills me, pushing back my nausea. I'm so annoyed I could scream. But still I don't hang up the phone. Still I sit there, waiting.

"And I can prove it."

My certainty slips away. It drops into the pit of my stomach, replaced by a strange combination of emotions. Anticipation and fear.

"If you could prove it you wouldn't be in here."

"I tried for an appeal, but it was denied. Not enough evidence to provide a reasonable doubt."

He leans forward. He's so close to the glass I imagine I can feel his breath against my face. I want to believe him. I do. I want to believe that the last fifteen years have been a mistake. I want to believe that I couldn't be so foolish as to fall for a cruel, sadistic killer. I want to believe that all the harassment I've had to endure since that tragic day was unfounded. I'd love to be able to stare back at the faces of all those cowards who whispered about me behind my back and say, 'See! I didn't do anything wrong!' But then I hear all of their voices in my head.

48

Two-faced psycho killer.
Child murderer.
She must be blind.
I'd never be in that position.
She knows more than she's saying.
He probably did it before.
Poor stupid girl.
How could she not see it?
He would have killed her next.

I shake my head. For fifteen years I've been the subject of gossip, ridicule, and pity. I put on a strong face when I'm in public, but it's been breaking me down bit by bit. A little over a year ago I finally made a plan. I was going to leave. I was going to pack up my car, drop the key to my apartment in my landlady's mailbox, and just walk away. Not a word until I got to where I was going. I was going to start fresh. A new life. I was going to be free.

Then Dad died. Then I realized I was trapped here forever.

Or at least until I could put Amber—and Riley—behind me.

But these are just mind games. And nothing Riley can say will make a difference. I've spent years coming to terms with what happened. The police did their job. They were thorough. They questioned everyone. Went through all the evidence. I never fully accepted it because I never wanted to believe that I could be so gullible. That I was so easy to fool. Or that everyone was right. That I would have been next.

But they had to be right. If they weren't then that would mean Riley was in jail for nothing. And that I spent fifteen years convincing myself a lie was the truth.

"The real killer is still out there, Lexie."

He's bullshitting.

"I can't prove it, but you can."

This is just another trick.

"It wasn't me."

He's lying.

"But I know who it was."

49

Chapter 9

"Who?"

My pulse quickens. Have I always been so anxious? Was I like this before Amber died? Or did her death bring forth an alternate version of myself? A weak, terrified, uncertain Lex who doesn't even have the guts to get out. Sometimes I think back to the person I was before the tragedy, but the memory is all blurred. I look at photographs of myself as a child and I think, *That's when I was happy. That's when I was strong and confident and carefree.* But when I try to remember how I felt back then, the emotions are cloudy. It's like seeing myself through a haze. Now I don't know if there ever was a time before the tragedy. There was only ever the tragedy, a pinpoint moment in time that engulfed us completely and never let go.

Sometimes I hate Amber for doing this to us.

Sometimes I think I would kill her myself if she wasn't already dead.

"If you didn't do it then who did?" I clench my fingers around the phone. I know he's not going to give me an answer. Not a real one. But my heart beats faster all the same.

Riley looks at me. There's pity in his eyes, but I can't tell if it's for me or for himself. This would be easier if he looked the way he did in the newspapers. If he was still that teenage boy I thought I loved. Then it'd be easier to hate him. But this man? I barely recognize this man. How can I hate a man I don't recognize? How can I hate a man I don't know?

Riley glances over his shoulder to the guards. One of them raises a hand, showing two fingers. At first, I think it's a peace sign and it puts me off guard. Then I realize he's telling Riley how much time we have left.

Two minutes.

Riley leans closer to the glass. If there wasn't a partition between us then I might think he was moving in for a kiss. But that's absurd. And I curse myself for even thinking that in the first place. Even more so for the small part of me that wishes it were true.

"The police weren't wrong," he says. "I was in the woods that evening after the dance. When you didn't want to go to the after party I got angry. I drove out to the trailhead and had too much to drink. It was stupid, but I was pissed. I thought you were breaking up with me."

I stare at him, unblinking. I've never heard this story before. This isn't the story that was written in the papers. This isn't what Riley testified in court. Is he lying? But if he is, what's the point? What does he gain from making up stories? He only has a week left to live. What could possibly change between now and then by telling lies?

Nothing.

Unless he's telling the truth.

"But I wasn't just me out there."

He looks me dead in the eyes now. The intensity of his stare frightens me. It's a look I've never seen on him. A look that could make me believe he was capable of killing someone.

He doesn't continue. He just stares at me as though waiting for me to beg for him to tell me.

"Who did it, Riley? Who killed my sister?"

"It was your dad," he says.

I flinch. Of all the people he could have incriminated that was the last person I expected him to say. Literally anyone else in all of Braxton Falls would have made sense to me. But Dad? He'd raised Amber and me as his own. That was his condition upon marrying my mother. He wanted to be our legal father. I remember the day he signed the adoption papers and everything. We all went out to Dairy Queen afterwards and bought an ice cream cake. They didn't have any plain cakes left in the freezer so we got a birthday cake with a race car on it. He always joked that he would need that race car to keep up with us.

Dad loved Amber. He loved all of us. He was the only thing that kept us together after Amber's death. And he never stopped fighting to repair the broken relationship between Mom and me. He was never our stepdad. He was always Dad.

He was our protector.

He couldn't be a killer.

And, conveniently for Riley, Dad couldn't speak for himself anymore.

I shake my head. I refuse to believe it. "No. No. He was home with my mother that night. He never worked Saturdays."

"How can you know that for certain?"

"Because Mom said he was home the entire night."

"And you trust her?"

"They both arrived at the station together when I was there." But as soon as I say that I begin to wonder if I'm remembering correctly. Everything had been so frantic that night.

"And before that?"

"What do you mean?"

"How do you know he was at home? Did you see him there after the dance?"

The question is two-pronged, but Riley wouldn't know that. The truth is I didn't see Dad after the dance. And I didn't see Mom either. Because I didn't go home after the dance. That's what he assumes I did because that's what everyone assumes I did. Because that's what I said.

But I didn't go home. That was the first of the many lies I told

52

that evening. I didn't go home, so I couldn't know for certain if Dad and Mom were together.

But Riley couldn't know that.

How could he? There was only one person who knew where I went after the dance. And I know they'd never say anything. Least of all to Riley.

"I saw him there, Lexie."

"How can you be certain? Out in the woods in the middle of the night? Do you know how dark it is out there? Not to mention the drinking. It could have been anyone. Assuming this isn't already some kind of fucked-up lie to begin with just to mess with me."

"I'd never mess with you, Lexie."

"It's *Lex*. I haven't been Lexie since . . ." I trail off. Because we both know when I stopped going by that silly little nickname.

"It was him, Lex. He was there. I swear to it. Go to the woods. The proof is out there. I know it is. It has to be."

"Proof? It's been fifteen years, Riley. There's nothing out there." I scoff. "I'm not playing this game with you any longer."

I slam the phone back on the hook and stand up. Riley mimics my action. For the first time I can see how different he looks physically. Still tall, but not as gangly as he'd been when we were in high school. His shoulders are broader and his torso tapers to his waist. He also has a tattoo on his arm. Seeing it causes me to do a double take. It's a name.

My name.

"He was there, Lex! I swear to you!" Riley yells. He slams his fist on the glass. The partition shudders. There wasn't much separating us. If he really wanted to break it, he could.

The guards move to grab him from behind, each one taking an arm.

I'm halfway to the door when Riley's next words cut me to the bone.

"He was there! And he wasn't alone!"

53

Chapter 10

Sunday, October 14, 2007
1:39 a.m.

I can hear Dad yelling at the detectives outside the door. They've left me alone in the interrogation room. I have a cramp in my abdomen that won't go away. I want to cry, but I don't have any tears left. I've sobbed my eyes raw. One of the detectives dropped a photograph of Amber's body before my dad barged into the room and I started screaming. It felt like someone was stabbing me with a knife.

It can't be true. It can't be.

Amber, Amber, Amber.

Oh my God. What has happened? What have I done?

There's a plastic cup of water on the table and I reach for it with a shaky hand, but I accidentally knock it over and it spills on the floor. My stomach is twisted in knots. It's like someone has reached up inside of me and started carving out my insides. I'm dry-heaving. I want to go home. I want to wake up. This has to be a nightmare. This can't be true.

It can't be.

What was she doing out there? Why was she in the woods?

The door flings open and my mom comes flying in. She grabs me by the arms. She's squeezing so tight I start to lose sensation in my fingers. She's going to leave a bruise. I'm staring at her, but I don't really see her. I'm thinking about that photograph of Amber.

"Alexandra! Alexandra! Where have you been?! Where were you?! What happened?!" She's shaking me. I feel like a rag doll. I don't have any control over my body.

"Don't say anything!" Dad bellows. "Not until we call a lawyer."

"Where were you?!" Mom yells in my face. Her nails are cutting into my skin. No one is asking me how I am. I can barely breathe. Everything is caught in my throat. Is this what dying feels like?

No. I know what dying feels like.

Dying is how I felt when I dropped that match on my dress.

Oh my God. What have I done?

A hand slaps my face.

The room echoes silence.

Dad shoves Mom out of the way and reaches his arms around me, picking me up like a twig. Like I weigh nothing. I barely feel anything. I'm numb from all the pain. But I somehow manage to wrap my arms around his neck and cling to him like a buoy in the middle of the sea.

"Come. We're going home," he says.

Mom is yelling. I can't tell if she's yelling at me or at Dad or at the police officers, but it doesn't matter. Her voice is drowned out by the thoughts in my head, the memories of the evening. It's my fault. It's all my fault.

"We need a statement, Michael."

"Not now."

"You know how small the window is on these things. She may have seen someth—"

"My daughter didn't see anything," he snaps back at them.

He's right. I didn't see anything. I didn't. But I should have. I would have. If I hadn't been so selfish, I would have seen it all.

Or it wouldn't have happened in the first place.

Chapter 11

By the time I get back to Mom's house, she's already passed out on the sofa. I walk over and bend down close just to make sure she's still breathing. She smells like bourbon, sickeningly sweet. A stainless-steel coffee thermos is lying on the carpet and I pick it up. The sides are sticky. She's probably spilled it all over herself, but I can't tell from the way she's lying, like a lump of dirty clothes tossed in a corner. I set the thermos on the side table. Then I unfold the quilt on the back of the couch and drape it over her. If I'm lucky she'll stay asleep until tomorrow. The longer she sleeps the more she forgets. Maybe then I can avoid talking to her about where I was today.

My heart is still beating at a mile a minute.

I make my way into the kitchen and peer out through the window to the backyard. It's empty. No journalists crawling around looking for a morsel to spike their media accounts. I'm sure they'd love to see the inside of the house. This deranged time capsule of a family that lives in a single moment in time.

I look at the swing set, rusted and unused, and a wave of shame sweeps over me. What was I thinking going to see Riley? How could I betray Amber like that? It wasn't as though I didn't know what would happen. Anyone could have guessed that he'd try to pull some kind of trick on me. Try to get me to believe his sob story. He'd probably been doing that for years. I just hadn't received any of the other letters. Or maybe my mother had and she'd burned them. Not that it would have mattered. I never would have had the nerve to read them. My feelings have always been too conflicted when it came to Riley.

Apparently they still are.

I open the fridge. I don't drink much, but I catch myself hoping to find a beer. Fortunately, Mom only drinks the hard stuff. She drinks to forget and nothing less than twelve percent alcohol per volume will get her to that land of make-believe. I sigh and take out a can of diet soda. I pop the tab and take a sip. It's cold, but tasteless. It's probably been sitting in there past the sell-by date.

It was your dad. He was there. And he wasn't alone.

Riley's words have been rattling in my head ever since he said them. I suppose that was the point. To try to get to me. And he has. But he's always had the ability to throw me off balance. Even behind bars—even with fifteen years of silence between us—he's managed to wedge himself into my daily thoughts. Mom thinks that the execution will put an end to our suffering. That it'll free us from the binds of Amber's death. But I'm less certain. I think even in death Riley will still be in my mind. Amber, too. Both of them haunting me from beyond the grave for what I did.

And what I didn't do.

I head down the hallway to the other side of the house, pausing in front of Dad's office. I peek inside. It's musty and looks like it hasn't been vacuumed. The desk is cleaned off, leaving nothing but a laptop and a framed family photo. On the wall behind the desk is a photo of him and 'the guys.' The guys being his colleagues at the station. Most of them are still there. I see them sometimes, but I never stop to say hello. It's awkward in more ways than one. They respect me as Michael's daughter, but they don't trust me. They still think I know more about what happened to Amber than I said.

I scan the room from the doorway, stopping to stare at the closet door, which is slightly ajar. I can see some of his clothes still hanging in there. He was a baggy sweater kind of guy. He only had two dress shirts. One for church, which we only ever went to for Christmas and Easter despite Mom claiming we were good God-fearing Christians, and one for funerals. He despised wearing both. I know that if I were to open the closet completely I'd find his dress uniform from the Braxton Falls Police Department hanging in between his winter sweaters and his Hawaiian shirts. If it weren't for the odor of stuffy air and dust, I could almost imagine he was still with us.

I catch a glimpse of one of the boxes on the closet floor. I don't need to guess what those are. Amber's case files. Dad had never been completely satisfied with the case. Like me, he'd still had questions. I'm one hundred percent certain we're not allowed to have those documents. But no one from the station would have dared stop Dad from trying to figure out the one question that still eluded all of us.

Why?

Dad wouldn't have done it. Maybe I could believe that he was out in the woods that night. I could come up with any number of scenarios to explain that. But none of those scenarios ended in Amber's death.

I close the door and continue down the hall. My old bedroom is on the left. It's mostly empty now. Mom's been using it for storage ever since raccoons got into the attic last year. There's still a bed and dresser, but all of my posters and belongings are gone. Most of them were thrown out. By me, not Mom. Mom can't throw out anything.

I hesitate at the room across from mine. The door is closed, but there's no question as to who it used to belong to. Amber stenciled her name on the cross rail when she was twelve and colored it in with hot-pink fabric paint. It's faded now, but the letters are still visible. As are the outlines of the pony stickers that framed her name until she turned fifteen and decided she was too old for them.

My fingers grasp the knob. It's been fifteen years since I've been in this room. I've tried to forget that it even exists. And while I steel myself for what I'm about to see inside, I'm completely unprepared for what I find when I finally push open the door.

It's like walking through a portal back in time. Everything—and I mean everything—is exactly how I remember it. The bed is in the same position. The comforter is the same. Backpack is still on the floor, stuffed full of books. Her cheerleading uniform is on a hanger on the closet door. There's a Black Eyed Peas poster taped to the wall adjacent to the window that's beginning to curl from the sunlight through the lace curtains. Her white desk, which doubled as a dressing table with an ovular vanity mirror, is still bedazzled in plastic glitter rhinestones. Her cheerleading ribbons are strung up around the mirror alongside a collage of photographs, all of Amber and her friends. Even her framed picture of Orlando Bloom, cut out from a *Tiger Beat* magazine, still sits on the desk. Still smiling.

There's no dust. Not like Dad's office. Not like my room. This place is pristine.

It's a shrine.

I knew this is how it would look. I knew Mom wouldn't have touched anything except to clean it, but even knowing doesn't change my horror. Nor does it change the rush of emotions that hit me.

What if Riley was telling the truth? What if he didn't kill Amber? What if Dad *was* involved?

There's a feeling of free fall in my chest. Like that split second after a roller coaster tips over the edge of a hill and the gut leaps into the throat. That breathless pause before everyone starts screaming.

I sit down at Amber's desk and look at myself in the mirror. I try to see myself fifteen years ago. I try to see what Amber would

59

have seen. But my imagination isn't that good. All I can see is the empty defeat in my gaze and the dark circles under my eyes.

What happened to you, Amber? What were you doing in the woods?

In the mirror's reflection I see a flicker of color—lavender—from the closet I hadn't noticed before. I turn around and see that something has caught between the door and the frame. My heart skips a beat. I walk over to the closet and turn the knob. The door flings open from the weight of the garment on the inner hook. I stumble backwards in horror. The echo of my heart thumps between my ears. A cold sweat drips down my back.

"What the hell are you doing in here?"

I whip around so fast I nearly send my elbow through the window. Mom stands in the doorway. Her face is taut, stone-cold sober. And if I didn't know better I'd say there was murder in her eyes.

"I was just—"

She shoves me to the side with a force I don't expect her to have and I grab at the footboard of the bed to keep myself from falling over. She doesn't apologize. She doesn't even look at me. She goes straight for the closet door and the garment hanging on the inside. Amber's homecoming dress. The one she wore the night she died. The one that had been ripped apart and covered in her blood. Except this one isn't tattered or stained in dirt and death. This one is perfect. Immaculate. Never worn. It still has the tags.

Mom bought a second dress. She bought it and hung it up in Amber's room to make it look like it had in the days leading up to her murder. It was a museum. A disturbed homage to the daughter who should have lived.

"Get out of here!" she screams, her voice cracking. "GET OUT!"

And I do.

Chapter 12

The earlier chill in the air has been replaced by an eerie warm front. Thick, slate-covered storm clouds move in from the west. There's a languid rumble of thunder in the distance. Slow-moving and guttural like a death rattle. I sit on the swing in the backyard, the rusty chains creaking with each minuscule sway. The plastic seat is almost too small and my hips pinch against the chains, but I do nothing to adjust my position. The media people are gone. Maybe because it's supposed to rain. Maybe because there's a better story somewhere else. Or maybe they're just hiding in the shadows, waiting for me to do something crazy so their ratings can spike.

I can't stop thinking about Amber's homecoming dress hanging on the door. Just the thought of it sends a shiver up my spine. I'm not surprised that my mother would go this far. Not really. That's not what has my nerves rattled. That's not why I stood there, mouth gaping in shock until Mom started shouting at me. It was the horror of seeing the dress intact. Of being reminded of how it looked *before*, a stark contrast to the way it was in the police photos. It was as though the entire event had been erased. As though the presence of a new, untouched dress somehow blotted out the night it happened. Select All. Delete.

I wonder what Amber would think of it. Would she be flattered or would she be disgusted? She'd probably roll her eyes and tell us we were all being melodramatic.

She wouldn't be wrong.

I remove my phone from my jacket pocket. My social media notifications are still turned off, but I have a text message from Samara. Not just one message. Fifteen. Most of them are gifs of adorable animals, no doubt meant to cheer me up or distract me, but there are also a few selfies of her at a work shindig. She looks so put-together in her chic clothes with her stylish colleagues, the London Eye in the background lit up against the night sky. Or maybe that's just my biased American perspective. I have to admit that half of my initial interest in her was the fact that she was a million miles away in a part of the world that at least looked like it had its shit together. I know that the entire Western world is fucked up, but the grass is always greener. Especially when you live in Braxton Falls. I smile when I read her last two messages. They fill me with simultaneous excitement and grief.

When are you coming to visit?
I want to see you in person.

My heart wants to soar.

I start replying to the message, but then I remember the time change. Samara should be asleep and I know she keeps her sound on at night in case of emergencies. I'm about to slip the phone back into my pocket when it buzzes with the arrival of a new message. It's as though she's reading my mind from halfway across the world.

I'll pay.

I'm not a hopeless romantic. Not anymore. But for a fraction of a second I imagine myself melting into a puddle like that girl from the old television show on Nickelodeon. I want to say yes. I want to grab my bag and head for the airport right now. I want to step on the plane and leave my life behind me. I want to forget the last fifteen years. I want to start over. These are all the things I want to say. All the things I *should* say.

But then I think of Riley sitting on the other side of the glass begging me with those wide, pleading eyes that he didn't do it. That there was someone else out in the woods with my dad that night. That there's proof that Amber's real killer is still out there. That I could be next. And I know I can't leave until I'm certain.

Or until it's over.

It's a moment I've waited fifteen years for. I can make it one more week.

I text back a blushing smiley face because I'm an idiot.

I'm partially through composing a less vague reply when the shrieking pop of a firecracker followed by a blaring car alarm stops me.

I jump off the swing and jog around the side yard in time to see three teenage boys speed off down the street on low-rider BMX bicycles, laughing. The lights on my old sedan are flashing and I dig through my pockets for my keys as I approach the car. I click the alarm button on my key fob while I'm crossing the lawn. The car quiets, the last alarm blare cutting out like a gasping wheeze. I'm surprised it even went off in the first place.

I step onto the driveway. There's a pile of burned-out ash and cardboard from the firecracker near the front passenger side tire. I don't know if they were trying to cause any damage or just be annoying, but when I bend down to check I don't see anything obviously broken. My phone buzzes in my pocket, but I ignore it. It looks like I've gotten lucky. But when I walk around to the opposite side of the car I realize my thoughts have spoken too soon.

The entire driver's side of my car is coated in yellow spray paint, the words 'PSYCHO SLUT' dripping down the windows and doors. Rage boils inside me. I try to push it back down, but it sticks in my throat like a half-eaten piece of meat that hasn't been fully chewed. My eyes burn like I'm going to cry, but I don't. I just stand there staring at the words while the world around me becomes a dark blur.

I'm slamming my fists onto the hood of my car before I even realize it. That bottled-up fury finally reaches my mouth and I let out a long, voice-cracking howl. I should stop myself. The neighbors are probably peering out through their windows. I'm just embarrassing myself. Embarrassing my family. Embarrassing Amber. But I don't care. Let them watch. Let them think I'm crazy. Maybe I am.

It starts to rain. Thick, plonking drops speckle the driveway. When it begins to fall more heavily I use my palms to try to wipe the paint off the windows. I only make it worse. After a few minutes I'm up to my elbows in yellow and the glass is so smeared I can't even see through it.

Riley's voice interrupts my thoughts.

I didn't do it, Lexie.

I wasn't the only one in the woods that night.

I don't know how much of that first statement is a lie, but I know the second is true. Riley wasn't the only one in the woods the night Amber died. I was there, too.

I know what you did, Lexie.

How could he know? How could he know if he wasn't there?

I look up from my stained hands and see my mother staring sternly through the window at me. I blink and I imagine I see the flash of something else in that glare. Something leery and malicious.

Mom said he was home the entire night.

And you trust her?

I don't know.

Chapter 13

Against my better judgment I pull into the police department parking lot. Instinct tells me this is a bad idea. Not because it's the wrong thing to do, but because it's been years since I last stepped foot inside the station. The last time I was there things hadn't gone swimmingly.

Growing up, the old-timers at the station always treated me well. I was Mike Wicker's daughter, after all. We may not have been blood relations, but most people forgot that when they saw us together. We didn't look too similar, but people never seemed to notice. And he was the only dad Amber and I ever knew. Mom never spoke about our biological father and both of us were too young when he left to really remember him. Amber always swore she never had any memories of him at all. I had a few flashes of something. Not a face, but a feeling. Nothing I could put into words.

But it didn't matter who he was. Dad was the one who was there to take me to my first day of kindergarten. He was the one who taught me how to ride a bike without training wheels. He was the one who dressed up like Santa Claus and crept through the house on Christmas Eve leaving gifts beneath the tree. He was the one who bought me my first art set. The one who attended all of my school choir concerts and took me out for ice cream on my birthday. The one who stood beside me when the town thought I had something to do with Amber's murder. He was the one who believed me without question.

The only one, for that matter.

Most of the old-timers are gone. Those who are still around are in retirement. Chuck Newman, a younger sergeant at the time of Amber's murder, is police chief now. He took over after Dad passed away. He's never liked me. Not that I blame him. The last time I spoke to him was the day of Amber's funeral. Coincidentally, it was the same day the courts sentenced Riley to death. He made the mistake of telling us as we were walking away from the gravesite.

I made the mistake of not controlling my temper.

Thankfully I had Dad to maintain the peace. But not anymore.

I turn off the engine of my car, shove the keys in my jacket pocket, and make my way toward the entrance. The police station itself is still the same old building that's been there since the early Fifties, but the interior was recently renovated thanks to a levy passing last year. The money should have been invested in the high school, which still has lead pipes running to the drinking fountains and asbestos in the gym ceiling, but education has never been a priority in Braxton Falls.

I used to remember the station having a damp, sweaty odor to it. Like dirty socks stuffed in a gym bag alongside a wet towel and forgotten about for a week. That smell is gone now, covered up by a fresh paint job and new waiting-room chairs. These chairs have cushions with vinyl coverings. Easier to keep clean, I imagine. But I can't help but feel like I'm in the lobby of a dentist's office instead of a police station.

I walk up to the reception. A woman with bright blonde hair tied up in a tight bun, tucked neatly around one of those donuts they used to sell on TV, looks up at me from her computer screen. I don't know her name, but I recognize her as someone who was a few years behind me in school. It's clear from her expression, however, which went from a perkily pleasant customer-service smile to a deadpan glare in less than a second, that she knows exactly who I am.

"Can I help you?" she sneers. At least, I think it's a sneer, but that's what I've come to expect from most people.

Funny how my sister dies and everyone else makes it their tragedy. Like they're more of a victim than I am.

"I need to file an intentional damage report," I say. "Someone vandalized my car."

The woman shoots me a disbelieving look before reaching into a filing drawer under the desk and removing a piece of paper. She slips it under the glass partition. "If you fill it out online it'll process faster."

"I know." I take the form. "I'd also like to speak with Chief Newman."

"Do you have an appointment?"

"No."

"Is it an emergency?"

"Well, no. Not exactly."

The woman shoots me an annoyed stare.

"I'd like to talk to him about an old case."

"Are you reporting an incident or new evidence? Because then I can have you talk to one of our on-duty officers."

"No, I . . . That's not what I . . . I just wanted to talk to the chief."

"The chief is busy. He has an entire town to protect. If you'd like to speak with one of the on-duty officers then—"

"No. Never mind." I step away from the desk. My hands are shaking from nerves. What was I thinking coming here? What was I going to say to him anyway? That I went to see Riley in prison and he told me he saw two other people out in the woods that night? One of whom had been an upstanding member of Braxton Falls society? One who was dead? The chief would laugh in my face. Or worse.

Just fill out the incident report and get out, I tell myself.

I turn and walk directly into an expensive tailored suit. A suit that now has an entire cup of coffee spilled over it.

"Oh my God! I am so sor—" The apology is halfway out of my mouth before I look up and realize who I've bumped into. Cameron Ellis. My brain glitches. Neither of us says anything. We just stare at each other like we've both seen a ghost. In a way, we have.

Cameron is the one who eventually breaks the awkward silence between us. He laughs and shakes off the coffee that's spilled on his hand. "Guess I should be glad I'm the only idiot in town who buys an iced coffee in October."

He tosses the cup in a nearby trash can.

The woman behind the reception, who only moments ago was as stiff as an iron gate, comes rushing out with a box of tissues. She shoots me another glare, but I ignore it.

"Thank you," Cameron says, taking the tissues and dabbing them on his shirt. "Sadly, I don't think this is going to help. Do you?"

It takes me way too long to realize he's talking to me.

"Oh! No, I think the entire outfit is doomed. Best to just call it a day."

He laughs again. Maybe I am funny.

"Lucky for me I have another shirt in the car for just these sorts of occasions. I'm a terrible klutz, you see."

He's not. He's just trying to be nice. It's hard to tell if this is genuine politeness or a political tactic. Cameron is what you might call a local legend. Kind of like Riley, but without the stain of murder. He's running for governor. His deep brown eyes and veneer-white teeth are plastered on signs in half the yards across the county. It's his job to be everyone's best friend. Which is weird considering he used to be one of my actual best friends. But at least he's not looking at me like I'm hiding a bloody dagger in my hope chest.

"I don't think being a klutz gets you a full-ride football scholarship to a division-one school."

"Maybe not. But it does prevent you from going pro." Cameron smiles, but for an instant I think I see a flash of regret in his eyes. It's probably just my imagination. What does Cameron Ellis have to regret, after all? He has, quite literally, everything. Always has. Seeing as how his dad is the richest man in town. Probably in the entire state.

He's also Jessica's ex-boyfriend and Riley's former best friend, which is how we know each other so well. Or how we used to know each other. But that's another story.

"What are you doing here, Lex?" he asks. "Are you OK? Did something happen?"

I scrunch my face in confusion. Then it hits me. Oh, right. I'm in a police station. I'm in a police station making a complete fool out of myself.

"No, no. I'm fine. I just . . . I was hoping I could talk to Chief Newman, but it's no big deal. It's not important."

Cameron's expression is pure disbelief. As it should be. He was there at Amber's funeral when I lost my cool. "You want to talk to Chief Newman? And it's not important?"

"I just wanted to ask him a question about . . ." I hesitate. Do I really want to say anything? "I heard a rumor about something that happened *that* night and I just wanted to see if it had ever actually been reported."

"A rumor about what?"

"About there being someone else in the woods when Amber was murdered."

Cameron's face flushes in shock. "Where did you hear this from?"

". . . Riley."

"You spoke to *Riley*?"

69

It might be my imagination, but I think I see a few heads stop what they're doing and look our away. Including the woman behind the desk.

"I know. It's probably just bullshit. I bet he's just trying to fuck with me. One last hurrah before . . ." I pause. "Well, I'm sure you've heard."

"Come on," Cameron says, taking me by the elbow and leading me past the reception.

"Where are we going?"

"To talk to Chuck."

"No, no, Cameron. Really, it's not necessary. It's stupid."

He stops and fixes me with a severe stare.

"It's not stupid, Lex. Not when it's about Amber."

I don't know why, but I'm surprised by this unexpected determination in his eyes. It's not unlike the look I saw in Riley when the guards were taking him away. Defiance, but also a little bit of desperation.

I guess we all need to put this behind us. I guess we all need more of the truth.

I nod. "You're right. It's not stupid when it's about Amber."

But just because we feel that way, doesn't mean the chief will.

Chapter 14

"This is a fucking joke, right?"

Chief Newman glares from behind his desk. It's been years since I've been this close to him, but I can't help but feel that same teenage defiance I did when I struck him with a rock after Amber's funeral. He still has a scar just above his left eyebrow. Nothing big. Even from this distance it looks like an age spot. He never was intimidating, maybe because I always saw him as Dad's inferior, but time has roughened him around the edges. His hairline has receded so far back on his forehead that he would be doing himself a favor if he shaved it off completely. He has a mustache that reminds me of that one cop from *NYPD Blue*. And even though he has a belly, something he didn't have when he was a sergeant fifteen years ago, he looks strong. Or maybe that's just an illusion made by the shoulder pads in his suit.

All of that aside, the look of aggravation on his face is telling. He is not pleased to see me.

"You should hear her out," Cameron says. He's perfected that firm politician tone. If I wasn't looking at him, I might not even recognize him. Although for the life of me I can't figure out why he's helping me after all these years.

Maybe he feels guilty too.

"You sure you want to get involved in this?" Newman asks Cameron, refusing to look in my direction. "Now? With everything going on?"

Cameron shrugs. "I have a duty to my constituents. Election or no election."

"This goddamn week," Newman grumbles, slamming his laptop shut.

He finally looks at me for the first time. There's real hatred in his eyes, but I can't tell if it's directed at me personally because of what I did or to the entire situation in general. Not that many people make the distinction.

"Say whatever it is you have to say, Miss Wicker. In case you haven't noticed I have a mess of media to deal with. Not to mention all the other shit that this news has brought up."

I take a deep breath, wondering what it is I'm going to say exactly. I should have thought this through better.

Fuck it.

"Was my dad out in the woods the night Amber died?"

A palpable silence fills the office. I see Cameron flinch out of the corner of my eye. That's not what he was expecting to hear. Neither was Newman, but his expression is less obvious. He still looks annoyed. Like he's going to pop a vein.

"Excuse me?"

"Was my dad out in the—"

"Yes. I heard you the first time. What are you really asking me? Are you asking if Chief Mike was responsible for your sister's death?"

"No, I—"

"That man was the pinnacle of leadership in this community. He tore this town inside out for evidence. Even though he couldn't work on the case, he didn't stop for a second. He made sure the case was watertight. And he never stopped grieving. *Never*. And you dare come in here—in his old office—and ask me if he had something to do with her death? Where do you get off having

72

the nerve to defile your sister's memory with this bullshit? Who the fuck do you think you are?"

"Chuck," Cameron interrupts. He's holding up his hands as though that might calm him down. But the chief's face is red. And there's a fire in his eyes I haven't seen in a long time. "I don't think Lex is trying to insinuate that her father was responsible for what happened to Amber."

Cameron looks at me, questioning. "Are you?"

I don't know.

"I spoke to Riley."

The chief pushes his chair out from behind the desk and stands up. "That's it. I've heard enough. You know, I've been waiting for this. I should have known it would happen this week. You were always such a stupid, selfish girl. That man is a murderer. A killer. And I don't care how old you were, you should have seen something bad in him. Hell, I'd bet my career you did see something. If anyone is to blame for Amber's death, it's—"

I cut him off before he can finish. "I received a letter from Riley. I went to speak to him. I thought maybe it would help put all of this behind me. He told me that he saw two people out in the woods the night of Amber's death. He said one of them was my father. All I want to know is whether he's telling the truth or not. I just want to know if there's more to the story or if he's just pulling my chain."

"—And your poor mother. All these years having to put up with a brazen disappointment of a daughter."

"Was Dad out there or wasn't he?"

"No," Newman says, his tone clipped and defiant. "Mike Wicker was not in the woods the night your sister was killed. And there was no evidence of anyone else being out there either. Just your boyfriend."

"You're sure?"

The chief slams his fist on the desk. It shakes over a cup of pens and sends them toppling to the floor. "The case was clean-cut

73

from the beginning. There was evidence placing Riley King at the scene of the crime. His alibi never stood up in court. No one could verify that he was anywhere else."

"You mean the knife? But it was never confirmed that the knife was the murder weapon, was it?" Cameron asks.

The question surprises me. I didn't realize Cameron had followed the case so closely. But that's stupid of me. Of course he followed the case. Amber wasn't just my sister. She was his friend. We were all friends.

"We didn't need to confirm the murder weapon. The evidence was overwhelming. Riley King killed Amber Wicker. Period. Case closed. If he's saying anything different now it's because he's trying to create confusion. He wants to extend his time. Time which is, thankfully, running out."

I feel like an idiot. Just because I don't like the chief doesn't mean he's wrong. Riley has set me up to look like a fool and I played right into it. I can only hope this doesn't get back to Mom. The last thing I need is more of her drunken disappointment.

I stand up and make my way to the door. "I'm sorry for bothering you, Chief."

"Your alibi never stood up either."

Those words freeze me in place. I glance back, expecting to see a smug smirk or some form of self-satisfaction, but all I see is the look of a man who's been trying to work out the same jigsaw puzzle for years, unaware that he's missing some pieces.

I don't say anything. Neither does Cameron. I can feel his eyes on me, waiting, anticipating.

"I always thought you knew more about what happened than you let on. But the evidence against Riley was so convincing it didn't make sense to look in any other direction. And Mike was adamant that you couldn't have been there."

"I wasn't," I say through gritted teeth.

"But you were somewhere. And you did something." His glare looks like it could bore holes in my skull. "I've interviewed hundreds of people over the years. Those who were guilty and those who were innocent. You weren't innocent that night. I don't know what you're guilty of, but it's something. And one day I'll find out. I can promise you that."

Chapter 15

"Are you all right?"

Cameron places a hand on my shoulder and I instinctively pull away. I feel ashamed immediately afterwards. I don't want him to think I don't appreciate his concern, but I've had trouble with physical closeness ever since Riley's sentencing.

No, that's a lie. I had trouble with it before. I guess I have difficulty trusting people.

"Yeah, I'm fine," I say, trying to shrug off my wince as surprise.

I take a deep breath and look up at the graying sky. The longer I stood in the police station, the more claustrophobic I began to feel, and the openness of the outside is a literal breath of fresh air. It's cold though and I stuff my hands into the pockets of my jacket. I must look like an adolescent boy standing next to Cameron with his fancy coffee-stained suit and hundred-dollar haircut. I try not to compare myself to people that way, but sometimes I can't help myself. Even I look in the mirror and wonder if this was who I was always supposed to be. Or is this just the version of myself that exists in a world without Amber?

"Chuck is an asshole. You shouldn't listen to him. You're not the only one in town he has it out for."

"Really? Because if there's a bigger pariah in this town than me please point them out. I could use a few friends right about now."

"You have friends."

"Do I?" My response is meant to be flippant but it comes off more caustic than I intended. And Cameron isn't laughing.

Strike that earlier sentiment. Clearly, I'm not as funny as I think.

"I know we went our separate ways after high school, but I never blamed you for what happened, Lex."

I hunch my shoulders to keep warm. I should have grabbed a scarf out of my car.

"You know that, right?"

I look up at Cameron. He might not be as buff and broad-shouldered as he was in high school, but he still has that chiseled quarterback jaw and fit frame. He was never my type. I was always drawn to the dark-haired loners. But I could see why half the girls—and even some of the guys—had drawn hearts around Cameron's face in their yearbooks. Most people assumed he was just a dumb jock because he was on the football team, but he was actually quite smart. He just played up the role of the star athlete in order to keep up appearances. That's what high school is all about anyway. Maintaining your fake identity, an identity often given to you by everyone else. Jock. Cheerleader. Nerd. Bully. I never really knew where I fit in the hierarchy of high school clichés. I was something of an enigma, passing in and out of various groups, a rarity in the sense that I didn't get my cliché until Amber died. And unlike Cameron I was never able to shake it.

The Killer's Girlfriend. The Liar.

I offer a halfhearted smile, but even I'm not convinced by it. "Sure, I guess. I never thought you did. Not really. Things were just . . ."

"A little crazy?"

"Something like that."

Cameron nods. "I started seeing a therapist after that night. Well, not right away. But after I started my first semester at university, things quickly started going downhill. I couldn't stop thinking about what happened and whether I could have done anything different. You know what I mean? I would replay the entire night in my head, over and over and over, looking for anything I might have been able to change. Anything I could have noticed that might have prevented what happened. I almost flunked that first semester. Almost lost my scholarship."

"I didn't know that."

"I never talked about it. You know how quickly word travels around here. Thankfully the coach was understanding. He'd seen a lot of athletes burn out from not dealing with past traumas. He's the one who convinced me to start seeing someone. I never even told my parents."

"It's not really any of their business."

"No, but sometimes it's nice to share those things with the people close to you." He shrugs. "I couldn't face them trying to tiptoe around it though. My parents—my dad in particular—always had a plan for the person I'd become. They just wouldn't understand."

"My mom would just laugh. Then get too drunk to remember."

"You never talked to anyone about what happened?"

I glance back at the police station and think of the night I sat in that cold interrogation room. My legs were covered in goose bumps. I was shivering, but my insides felt like they were on fire. My mind was racing and my lungs were gasping. I thought the walls were going to close in on me, crush my bones into powder.

Where were you, Alexandra? Where were you when your boyfriend was murdering your sister? Why won't you tell us?

I shake my head. "Like you said, word travels too fast in this town. There was no one I could talk to."

Of course, that's not entirely true. There was one person I could talk to. The person who knows where I was. But I just wanted to forget everything about that night. I just wanted to close my eyes and make it disappear.

"I should go," I say, stepping off the pavement.

"Lex."

I stop and glance back at Cameron. "Yeah?"

"Do you think he did it?"

The question doesn't catch me off guard, but it does give me pause. Isn't that the same thing I've been asking myself every day for the last fifteen years?

I think back to the look in Riley's eyes when I saw him at the prison. He was a broken, meaningless husk of a man. There was barely anything about him that I could connect to my memories of him from before. There was the Riley King of the past, the bright-eyed enthusiastic slightly mocking boy from the other side of the tracks, and then there was Riley King, the man on death row for killing a teenage girl. No, not just killing her. Defacing her. Making a spectacle of her. Turning her into a legend. But there was a flash in his eyes when the guards began to take him away. A brief spark of life. Of fear.

And it reminded me of the boy who once loved me.

"Everyone says he did."

Chapter 16

I intend to go home after I leave the station, but instead of taking a left out of the parking lot I take a right without thinking. It's as though another consciousness has taken control of my body. Before I know it, I'm driving over the railroad tracks to the south side of Braxton Falls. As kids we used to refer to it as Saltside on account of the Braxton County Salt Mine. Large swaths of land south of the tracks have been leveled of woodland in order to drill and blast for salt to make the roads drivable in the winter. The northern side of town has done a fairly decent job of hiding the southern eyesore through careful landscaping and community planning. If you never ventured over the tracks, you might never know it was there. But once you're on the other side it's like crossing into another dimension. Goodbye, lush green oaks and turn-of-the-century buildings. Hello, gravel driveways and dismal salt storage facilities.

Needless to say, Saltside's appearance has lent itself to an unflattering stigma. But most of the area doesn't really deserve the bad reputation it receives. It's a lower rent district with a higher number of trailer park homes than on the northern side of the tracks, but we still have them even if most of us don't like to admit it.

Back when my parents were young, the kids from Saltside used to go to a different high school. But lack of funding for local education caused them to close that school in the late Eighties. The building is still there, but half of it has been turned into a VFW club and the other half is a combination community center and driving school. There was an attempt to revitalize the area in the Nineties, but it never gained any traction. Probably because no one on the 'nice' side of town wanted to invest in an area they never had any business going to and the people who lived in Saltside couldn't afford to pass any of the levies that would help clean up their neighborhoods. The result was that it looked more and more run down every year. And when the rubber factory, the only other major revenue outside of salt mining, closed its doors, there was literally no hope of ever turning it around.

I was never allowed to go south of the railroad tracks as a kid, but I did anyway. Not often, because Riley didn't like the rest of us seeing where he lived, but there were at least half a dozen times when I dropped him off after school when his car broke down. And then there were the days when Jessica wanted to pretend like she was rebelliously defying her parents by driving through Saltside in her dad's convertible, screaming at the top of her lungs to get anyone's attention. I was simultaneously embarrassed and envious of her boldness. I would always shrink into the back seat when she got into one of her boisterous moods. Or maybe I just realized earlier on that her pleas for attention made it look like she was showing off how much better she was than everyone else.

But is anyone really that self-aware when they're a teenager?

I slow my car near the curb. The sign for Greenwood Trailer Park hangs half crooked on a rusty pole. An American flag with frayed edges flops in the wind beneath it, like a drowning victim's last attempts at waving for help. I put my car in park, uncomfortably aware of how out of place I am despite the fact that my vehicle looks worse than the others that line the street. The leftover yellow graffiti paint has left streaks on my driver's side window

81

and a large stain on the door that I wasn't able to wipe off. I might have to take it to a car wash, but I doubt even a pressure washer will remove all the paint now. I've waited too long. Stupid kids. I didn't recognize them, but they looked old enough to have parents who might have been classmates of mine. Classmates who probably blame me for what happened. And when I think about it I'm surprised my car hasn't been vandalized sooner.

I turn off the ignition and climb out of the car. I lock the doors, but even though I lock them instinctively no matter where I go, I'm consciously aware of doing it now. And that makes me feel ashamed.

There aren't many people milling about. Most of the people who live in Saltside don't have specific nine-to-five working hours. They go from one job to the next, coming home just long enough to sleep a few hours before starting their next shift. A few people look at me as I walk past the trailers, doing my best to avoid eye contact. It's not quite as unkempt as the people in my neighborhood might like to imagine. I pass a double-wide with a fresh coat of paint and a neatly mown lawn. The grass is greener than the yard at my mom's house and the bright pink flamingos with the spinning wings are more welcoming than kitsch. An old lady lets out her terrier mix and she gives me a gentle smile from her porch.

They don't smile at me on the *good* side of the tracks.

I'd never been inside the trailer Riley grew up in, and as I stand outside of it now I don't have to wonder why. The yard is an eyesore of dirt, crabgrass, and garbage. There's a line of fallen beer cans that look as though they've been shot full of pellets from a BB gun. A lawn chair lies on its side, the legs broken. And a ratty old tire looks like it was being used as a fire pit, the pungent odor of burning rubber still lingering in the air long afterwards. Most uncomfortable of all, however, are the three kids sitting in the dirt. The tallest, a girl, can't be much older than nine or ten. She's holding a toddler in her lap who's trying to eat pieces of gravel off the ground. The middle one, a boy of about four, is running around in his underwear, legs scuffed up and bruised.

Riley used to be one of those barefoot gravel-eating kids.

Riley was in the foster system before he'd left his mother's belly. His real mother lost custody of him while she was pregnant because she was a crack addict. Or so the prosecution said during the trial. Another way to admonish his character and prove he was rotten from birth. He never knew his real father. He was placed with the Kings at the age of six after bouncing around from one temporary home to the next. He didn't love them, but the feeling had been mutual. At least, as far as Riley told the story. He always said the Kings were the kind of people who fostered kids for the money. And looking at the state of the place now, I can't help but believe him.

Coming here was probably a bad idea. But before I could trust Riley—before I could allow him to lead me on this breadcrumb trail concerning Amber's death—I had to know for certain. I had to eliminate any doubt.

I needed proof that the boy I once loved hadn't lied to me. That he wasn't the one who destroyed my world.

I didn't know if coming here would give me the answers I was looking for, but where else could I go? Where else but to the place that formed the basis of the person Riley had become?

I crouch down in front of the little girl to ask her if her parents are home, but before I say anything the door to the trailer flies open and a man stumbles out. Inside a woman is screaming profanities at him, but he's not paying any attention. The door slams shut and clatters against the metal frame. I stand up just as he hobbles into a pair of grungy flip-flops.

He's a big man who looks even bigger because of the beer belly that's sagging over his jeans. He's wearing a stained singlet and his arms are covered in poorly inked tattoos. I'd only ever seen him a few times when I was younger, back when he was in better shape and was more capable of giving Riley some of those bruises he had on his back and arms, but I'd never forget his face. Not after what he said to me the day they arrested Riley.

Stuck-up, high-maintenance, rich-bitch pussy.

He takes one look at me and I know he hasn't forgotten either.

"Well, well, well. If it isn't the little ho come riding in on her high horse. Come to gloat, sweetheart?"

The question takes me off guard. "Mr. King, I just wanted to—"

"Let me stop you right there. You get off my lawn and out of my neighborhood before I give you a real reason to go lying to the police."

"I didn't lie to the police."

"No? That's not what it looked like from the other side of the courtroom."

I fidget and take a step backwards so I'm no longer standing on the dead grass.

Riley's foster father kicks off the top of a cooler, half stuck in the dirt. He reaches inside and pulls out a can of cheap beer that's floating in water, the ice cubes long since melted.

"WHO THE FUCK ARE YOU TALKING TO, MITCH?" the woman's voice calls out from inside the trailer. "IS THAT ANOTHER WOMAN I HEAR?!"

"NONE OF YOUR GODDAMN BUSINESS!" He pops the tab on the can and takes a long guzzle. Some of the beer drips down his chin. He belches and the kids on the lawn laugh. "Y'all get your asses inside! Go on! Get!"

They do as he says without waiting for him to tell them twice.

Then Mitch remembers I'm still standing there. "What do you want?"

"I just . . . I wanted to give you and Mrs. King my condolences. For Riley. I heard on the news about his . . ." I can't bring myself to say it.

Mitch snorts. "*Mrs.* King hasn't lived here going on eleven years now. Not that she was ever around when she did. And why the hell would I want your condolences? For what? Because that

84

murdering son of a bitch is finally going to bite it? I don't give a rat's ass about any of that. You think coming out here and giving me your *condolences* is going to change things? Is that supposed to get rid of the shame and the stigma? Is that supposed to get me my job back?"

I don't know what to say so I say nothing.

"As soon as the cops picked up that worthless boy, I knew I didn't stand a chance. None of us did. He's a blight. That idiot goes and carves up some silly northside bitch and who has to pay for it? Me. Foreman gave me my walking papers the very next day." Mitch throws his head back and takes another long gulp from the can. This time he wipes the dribble on the back of his arm. It slicks the dark hair against the grain. "Said it was on account of my drinking and fighting. But everyone knows it's because of what that stupid son of a bitch did."

"What if he didn't do it?"

Mitch snorts. "Are you shitting me? What is this, some kind of hidden camera show? Your friends going to pop out from behind a bush like this is all a joke?"

"I just thought maybe you knew something different. Something the police didn't look into. What with you being Riley's father and all, I thought maybe—"

"I'm *not* that bastard's father. That boy belonged to the devil. Ain't nothing I could have done to stop him from what he did. He was born bad. Right down to the marrow."

I bite my lip to physically restrain myself from pointing out that the drunken beatings didn't exactly make life any easier for Riley while he was growing up. Or having to share a bed with five other kids. Or working late shifts at the bowling alley when he should have been studying for exams. If Riley had been born bad, nobody had done anything to help him become good. Least of all Mitchell King, bona fide bully. A man who would have been more likely to kill a young girl than anyone else, provided he could stand up long enough to do so.

No wonder everyone was quick to assume Riley did it. This was the role model they put him up against. This stinking, angry, vile man. This abusive drunk who couldn't keep a job and left his children to fend for themselves. Naturally everyone would presume that Riley would be the same. How could someone who'd grown up under these circumstances turn into a productive member of society? The cards had been stacked against him before anyone had even found a body.

Mitch finishes off his beer, crunches the can in his fist, and tosses it on the ground. Then he grabs another out of the cooler.

I think of my mother and wonder what the difference between them is. But that's not hard to figure out. She has a house that can't be hitched to the back of a truck. She has a lawn that's always mowed. She was the wife of a police officer. She hid her drinking under the guise of grief. Vodka doesn't smell as rank as beer. She was the victim. Someone took her daughter.

He pops the tab on the can. The sound startles me out of my thoughts. I take another step backward until I'm on the asphalt and fully off of King property.

"What'd she do?" Mitch asks out of the blue.

"Huh?"

"What did your sister do to make him want to kill her?"

I shake my head. "She didn't do anything."

"Then what did you do?"

"What do you mean?"

Mitch steps forward. A dark glower peering at me from his unblinking eyes. There's something awful in that look, as though he's remembering a haunting act he once committed. Something he doesn't feel nearly bad enough about.

"A man doesn't just kill a woman for no reason," he says. "Either she did something or you did."

"We didn't do anything."

My feet remain firmly in place, like an animal caught in the high beams on a deserted road. I can smell the rotten stench of

86

beer and cigarettes on his breath. And something sharply pungent and decaying, like a dental abscess, when he speaks. "Then what did she do to you?"

The question gives me a jolt and the look on my face causes Riley's foster father to grin, pleased that he's sparked some confusion. Or maybe he thinks he's hit a nerve.

"I don't understand."

"Like I said, a man doesn't kill a woman for no reason." The smell of Mitch's breath causes me to hold my own. He slurps the beer. When he speaks again, he accidentally sends a spray of spit on my face. "Not unless another woman convinces him to."

Chapter 17

I'm furious to the point of tears when I leave the Greenwood Trailer Park. I'm so angry that my body is shaking and I have to sit in my car for ten minutes just to settle my nerves enough to drive. Am I pissed at the way Mitch King spoke to me and what he accused me of? Yes. But I'm angrier with myself. He was just a catalyst for all the emotions I've been bottling up since I got Riley's letter. Mitch just pushed me over the edge. Maybe I ought to be thanking him for giving me the courage to do what I should have done years ago.

Find my own proof of what happened to Amber.

Riley said to go to the woods. Fine. If that's what it takes to finally put all of this behind me, then that's what I'll do.

I park my car at the trailhead of Wynwood State Forest. There aren't any other vehicles in the dirt lot. Probably because it's getting close to dinnertime. I press the lock button on my key fob, the accompanying beep from the car echoing through the trees and scaring a few sparrows out of a bush. I shove the keys in my pocket, wrap a scarf around my neck, and then head up the hiking trail into the woods, ignoring the sign warning that the park is closed between dusk and dawn.

Ohio is full of urban legends. Most people don't know it, but there's actually a very lucrative business in urban legend tours here. People drive all around the state hoping to catch a glimpse of the Lizard Man near Loveland, the mutant people of Hell Town, or the ghost of a mother and child on Cry Baby Bridge. Braxton Falls is no different, although we don't get quite as many tourists because it's the one thing in Braxton Falls that people don't want to talk about. Also, because Braxton Falls is in the middle of nowhere. Urban Legend tours always perform better when there's a Walmart within a five-mile radius. The nearest Walmart to us is almost fifteen miles away. And you can forget about Target. But we're not completely uncivilized. We do have a Starbucks.

Braxton Falls has the Wynwood Witch or the Wynwood Bride, as some people call her. Everyone knows the story. We had to do a report on the legend in sixth grade. It always inspires kids to dress up as the witch for Halloween. Granted, the entire story is only vaguely supported by census evidence. The article I found online the other day alongside all of those nasty posts about Amber wasn't entirely correct. The real legend, as I'd heard it growing up, told the story of the frontierswoman Margaret Stedman, who was brutally murdered by a band of cattle thieves on the night before her wedding. They supposedly carved up her body in symbols reminiscent of the local indigenous tribe and tied her to a tree in an attempt to frighten off new settlers from claiming the area. Some researchers believe that this was one of the events that instigated a decades-long skirmish between the settlers looking to move west from the Western Reserve region and the indigenous people who had rightful claim to the land. No one knows for certain.

But eventually the event became a kind of ghost story for people in Braxton Falls. People claimed to feel and sometimes see the vengeful spirit of Margaret Stedman in the woods, threatening to do the same to those who dare disturb her place of rest. There was even a mystery in the early Fifties involving a pig that had been butchered out in the woods, tied up to an old oak. The same oak they say Margaret Stedman was tied to. Most people say it was teenagers playing a prank. But suspicions run deep in small towns. And there are always those who believe in the supernatural explanation.

Those people came out of the woodwork when Amber died. That was the hardest part of the aftermath for me. The people who stood out front of our house with signs claiming that Amber had disturbed the sanctity of the Wynwood Witch's burial ground. It was bullshit. But people always want a scapegoat. Why it has to be the victim, however, is beyond me.

It's disgusting.

About a mile down the trail I veer off into an area of brush and fallen tree limbs. The golden-orange leaves crunch beneath my boots as I step around large mossy stones and thick branches that probably cracked off the trees during the last summer storm. The place where I'm going isn't easy to find. A tourist would never come across it by accident. But my legs lead me there as easily as though I'm walking to my own mailbox. I barely have to think about it. The location is burned into my memory. As long as I live I'll never forget this place.

The funny thing about being a kid is that you simultaneously believe and don't believe in the unexplainable. I remember clearly thinking that the Wynwood Witch was just a stupid story meant to frighten children. Lots of parents used it as a scare tactic to prevent their kids from doing things they weren't supposed to. Like going out to the woods after dark or driving at night with boys. Or staying away from the 'wrong side of the tracks' even though the woods are actually on the 'right side of town.' I knew it was nonsense, even as a kid. But there was also part of me that watched *E.T.* and kept a bag of Reese's Pieces in my bookbag in case I ever came across an alien life-form. And so even though I didn't believe there was a vengeful witch in the woods looking to murder anyone who disturbed her peace, I was prepared for it to be true.

As teenagers we would test that belief. We made a game of it. We'd come out to the woods at night, usually after sneaking a few cans of beer from our parents' secret stashes or smoking a joint (Cameron was the one who supplied that), and we'd do dumb shit to lure out the witch. Well, that's how it would start. We'd go out there with the intention of trying to call forth the spirit of the dead in the same way middle schoolers stand in front of the bathroom mirror and repeated 'Bloody Mary' three times, but it would always quickly turn into something else. Usually it would end with Cameron and Jessica making out behind a tree—although sometimes they weren't even that discreet—while Amber, Riley, and I would build a fire and talk about the teachers we didn't like or how we couldn't wait to get out of Braxton Falls. We'd laugh and share all the amazing things we would do after high school.

Some people used to think it was weird that Amber and I were so close. She was my younger sister, but only by ten months, so we did a lot together. In a way, she was also my friend. So, naturally she was friends with my friends.

I crawl over a large fallen log. My hand scrapes across a jagged section of bark and I pull it back sharply. It's bleeding, but not much. Just an abrasion. I wipe it off on a few oak leaves and continue onward. Ten minutes later I'm standing in an oddly open area of the forest. The trees stretch upwards, looming over the area like stone statutes. Their shadows crossing each other in a pattern not unlike the iron grille on a stained-glass window.

The hike has calmed my anger and it occurs to me that I'm probably wasting my time. There's nothing out here but bad memories. Still I continue onwards.

I carefully maneuver down the slick slope to the center of that open area. Someone has placed a ring of large moss-covered stones in the middle of the space. Probably bored teenagers trying to scare their friends. A few bottles of Miller Lite are scattered among the leaves and there's a dark pit of burned ashes in the dirt where there had once been a campfire. All in all, it doesn't look too different than it did fifteen years ago. The only difference is the aura. There's a breathless weight to the air that I don't remember from before. It's heavy and sits on my chest, suffocating me like summer's humidity.

I take a deep breath and try to shake it off. It's just nerves. There's nothing special about this place. There's no witch. There's no mysterious curse. Hell, the story itself is probably fabricated. The only thing cryptic about this place are the memories I have of it. And how I've contorted those memories to fit my own narrative.

But that's survivor's guilt, right?

A cold breeze whips through the glade, leaving a whisper on the air. It sounds like a voice. Not the voice of a vengeful witch, but a low whimper. Like a girl pleading for her life.

A chill creeps down my spine and I tug the scarf up over the back of my neck. I nudge some of the stones with the toe of my boot. Is there something I'm supposed to find here? Or have I just been sent on another wild goose chase?

Then I hear Riley's voice in my thoughts again. He was so frightened. So convincing. And even if I didn't believe what he said at the prison about seeing my father in the woods, I believe what I saw in court the day he was sentenced. The way his eyes rolled into the back of his head. The way his face went ghostly white. The way his body gave out beneath him like all of his bones had been ripped out through his flesh.

A person can't fake a fainting spell like that.

That was real.

That's why I'd never felt confident about his guilt. Also, because Riley loved me. And people who love you aren't supposed to hurt you.

This is stupid. There's nothing to find here.

I climb out of the glen, using a fallen limb to help keep my balance until I'm over the slippery moss. I turn back in the direction of the trail. That's when another breeze brushes past my ear.

But this time it's warm like someone's breath. I whip my head around, fully expecting someone to be right behind me.

Nothing.

Then I see the tree and my stomach ties itself in a knot.

I haven't looked at it in person. Not since Amber died. I only saw it in photographs at the police station when then Sergeant Newman was yelling at me. *Look what someone did to your sister, Alexandra! Look! Did you know about this? Were you there? Did you see him do it?* Just thinking about it makes me freeze. Like a rabbit in front of a starving badger. Hoping that if I say statue-still it won't see me.

I take a step toward the tree. Then another. I try not to look at the base of the trunk. I try not to remember what Amber looked like in those photographs. But even after all these years the image is crystal clear. There was blood on her face. Her skull had been crushed in on the left side. The coroner presumed she'd been bashed in the head with a heavy object. A rock, perhaps. Something with a jagged edge. They'd found bits of moss in the bone. 'Probably from the blunt force trauma,' they said. 'Probably unintentional. The moss, that is.' Unlike the rest of her. Strung upside down like a five-pointed star. Ankles bound by rope and stretched taut to the upper branches of the tree. Arms stretched toward the ground in jumping jack pose, heavy firepit stones smashing down her palms.

But it was the torso that I hadn't been able to look away from. She'd been stabbed multiple times in the lower abdomen, although the coroner couldn't confirm whether that had been the actual cause of death. Whoever did it also ripped the bodice of her homecoming dress, leaving her chest and abdomen bare. Across her stomach they carved a symbol that everyone in Braxton Falls was familiar with. Technically, it was supposed to be the emblem for the Wynwood Parks and Recreation department. But everyone knew the symbol dated back to the early settlement days of the area. It looked like the Nordic *ingwaz* rune, but turned horizontally so the two overlapping V-shapes formed a kind of W. The same symbol was marked on the trailheads. The mark of the Wynwood Forest.

The mark of the witch.

The coroner assured us that whoever carved the mark on her belly did so after she had already passed. They could tell by the coagulation of blood or something. I can't remember. But I do remember that it had dripped. It dripped down her chest and neck and chin. It didn't look like it happened afterwards. And in my mind, I remember imagining Amber screaming as the knife cut through her skin.

It had been Riley's pocketknife. There'd been no doubt about that. They never found whatever crushed her skull in. But they found the knife. And Amber's blood was all over it. As were Riley's fingerprints. But, of course, they would be. It was his knife.

Maybe I'd deluded myself back then. Maybe I still am.

Before I know it, I'm standing within arm's length of the tree. The air here feels still. Quiet as a grave. The sun is going down in the distance and it's cold, but I seem to have forgotten that this place is supposed to frighten me. Because I can't take my focus off what I see—off whatever force has led my eyes to this exact place.

Someone has carved a name and set of initials in the tree.

JESSI ♥ D.F.

No. Not an F. Maybe a P? I lean in close and run my fingers over the carving. It looks as though someone tried to scratch the letters of the second initials out and the rest faded over time. But the first name is clear. It's obvious, especially by the way the person has carved a heart to dot the I. I know exactly who that is.

Jessica Hampton.

My ex–best friend.

Chapter 18

Blood looks black in the moonlight.

I stand at the edge of the forest. The county highway curves between the trees less than fifty feet away, but the lack of street-lamps makes it impossible for me to be seen. Not that any cars have passed since I've been out here. The night is quiet. Silent as the grave I'm about to dig.

My homecoming dress lies in a pile of dry leaves at my feet. The blood has soaked through the skirt. It used to be a light green color. Seafoam. Dad loved it because it matched his old Ford pickup. I loved it because it reminded me of beach glass. Looking at it now makes me sick. The lambent green is tarnished by the deep stain of red and the memory of what I did. Everything is punctuated by the nauseating odor of blood and cucumber melon body spray. I would vomit, but I already did thirty minutes ago and there's nothing left in my gut but bile.

I'm freezing, too.

The oversized T-shirt I'm wearing is too big and the cargo shorts are hanging off my hips. That's no surprise. Neither belong to me. My legs are crawling with goose bumps and I can barely feel my toes. I'm wearing socks, but no shoes, and they're wet from the forest floor.

A pair of headlights sweeps around the bend and I almost hide behind a tree. Then I remember no one can see me out in the woods. No one from the road, anyway. It's too dark. And the only person in the forest is at least a mile away. At least, that's where they were when I left them.

I reach into the pocket and remove a matchbook. I run my thumb over the cover. The logo for Tanner's, the local steakhouse, is written across the top in faded lettering to make it look old. Mom and Dad took Amber and me there every year for Dad's birthday. Dad always ordered the same dish. Ribeye, well done. The rest of us would always sing a chorus of disgust whenever he ordered. We're medium-rare people. Except for that one year in the seventh grade when Amber tried to be a vegetarian. We all laughed when she ordered a steak salad and had to pick out all the pieces of meat when she realized her error.

I tear one of the matches out of the book and strike it against the strip. It snaps in half because it's a cheap piece of shit. I throw it on the ground and rip out another match. This one lights on the second strike.

The flame flickers in the darkness and I find myself hypnotized by its breathy spark. It's cold and I imagine my lips are blue. I inhale deeply and hold my breath to a count of six. There's a frigid scent of snow on the air and the match's quivering light is having trouble maintaining its burn. It's weak. Like I am.

I drop the match on the dress. At first nothing happens. Then a sheer section of tulle begins to burn, but it's too slow and fizzles out. I strike another match and press it to a corner of the skirt. The fabric lights up in a bright yellow flame, quickly engulfing the dress in a small blaze. Some of the leaves nearby catch fire and help speed along the process. The fresh air is marred by a smoky haze that I should probably wave away, but I don't. It doesn't matter now.

It doesn't matter if someone sees the smoke or finds me. It's too late. Within minutes the dress is gone. And even though I know it's not true, I imagine I can still smell the blood. Like it's permanently stained the inside of my nostrils.

Blood, smoke, and bile.

I don't know how long it takes for the dress to burn completely. Maybe it was minutes. Maybe it was hours. All I know is that by the time it's gone, I can't feel my toes and my face is numb from the cold. I don't even shed a tear. I can't. My brain is in survival mode. And the only way I can survive is if I never see this dress again.

While the ashes cool, I drop to my knees and dig my nails into the ground. Burying the remains is probably pointless, but I want to make sure it's gone forever. I dig until the ground becomes too hard to penetrate. My nails scrape against the earth until one of them breaks. It was a cheap press-on anyway. A fake French manicure covered in clay. My hands are shaking, covered in dirt. In the darkness that looks like blood, too.

I use a chunk of rotten bark to scoop the ash into the hole. It's not deep, but it's enough. Afterwards I cover it with leaves and broken branches. When I step back even I can't tell anything happened there. There's no evidence except for that lingering tickle of smoke in the air. But soon that will be gone.

I stumble away from the scene like a messy drunk. It's taken all of my energy to get through this night and suddenly the entire weight of it all hits me. I weave through the trees toward the highway. When my feet touch pavement it's like stepping into another world. Another reality. And I feel a rush of anticipation and relief.

The surge of adrenaline at having buried a terrible secret.

A secret no one would ever know.

Chapter 19

It takes me half the time to get back to my car than it did for me to find the clearing in the woods where Amber's body was found. The icy chill that brushed at the nape of my neck when I saw Jessica's name carved in the tree is still there, numbing my nerves like an ice cube left too long on the skin. Whose initials were those with her name? They weren't Cameron's. That much was certain. But Jessica had never been with anyone else. No one seriously, anyway. Not while we were in school. And I can't imagine her going back to that place after what happened our senior year. There's no way. She was just as traumatized as I was by what happened to Amber. We all were.

I fumble in my pocket, looking for my keys. My hands are shaking. I feel so stupid letting a little breeze get to me. It's nothing. There's nothing out there. No ghost. No witch. No killer.

Well, not Amber's killer, anyway. Not if the police are right. And if they are then I've just allowed myself to be sent on a wild goose chase. And not for the first time.

The keys fall out of my pocket and under the car. I crouch down, reaching into the dark shadows beneath the chassis. I feel around in the dirt until I find them. Then I stand up.

A white-eyed reflection in the driver's window stares back at me.

I gasp so hard that the muscles in my chest spasm, leaving me with the piercing sensation of heartburn. I turn around, keys gripped between my index and middle finger as every young woman is taught, and prepare to defend myself.

"I remember you."

It takes my mind a full second to process what I'm seeing. No, *who* I'm seeing. A second might seem quick, but it's actually a very long time for a reaction. If I'd been in real danger, it would all be over. Because as slow as my mind is to respond, my body is even slower. And I'm still clutching my car keys in a death grip when I realize who's standing before me.

Nell Abbott. The local witch.

Well, not really a witch. She's more of a hippy. The kind of person who took the 'return to nature' mantra from the Sixties a little too close to heart. No one knows how old she is, but she has to be approaching eighty. Maybe ninety. She has wild gray hair and a hunch over her right shoulder. From far away she probably looks like a homeless person, but up close I can tell that her baggy hippy clothes are actually quite well maintained. Except for that drop of bird poop on her shoulder. She smells like earth and incense. But it's her eye that stands out. That's why kids call her a witch. She has one white eye. Probably late-stage glaucoma or a large cataract. But even though she's most certainly blind in that eye, she looks like she can see right through me. Right into my soul.

"Jesus Christ," I mutter. My arm feels like it weighs a ton and relaxing my muscles from gripping the keys almost hurts.

Nell doesn't reply. She continues to stare at me as though she's waiting for something to happen. I half wonder if maybe she's lost. Maybe living out in the woods for all these years has finally caused her mind to go.

"Can I help you, Ms. Abbott?"

She takes a step closer to me. She used to scare the shit out of me as a kid. But I'm older now. I'm not scared, just surprised. She's shorter than me by about two inches, but she gets up on her toes in order to meet my eyes. How she manages to maintain her balance is beyond me.

"You're not supposed to be out here," she says. Her voice is raspy. Grainy like someone who used to smoke multiple packs a day.

"I know the park is closed. I was just leaving."

I move for the car door handle and she grabs me by the wrist. Her forceful grip contradicts her bony, wrinkled fingers. I can feel her cracked nails digging into my skin.

"You're hurting me, Ms. Abbott." I gently tug my arm away from her, unusually afraid that I might hurt her despite the fact that she's broken the skin on my wrist. It's bleeding.

"You're not supposed to be here," she repeats, staring at me with her dead eye.

"I'm leaving."

"Your sister isn't supposed to know you're here."

"Let me go." I tug harder, but Nell grabs my wrist with her other hand, forcing me to stay.

My temple pulses from irrational fear. She's just an old woman.

"She's going to see you!"

"My arm is bleeding!"

"If she sees you then she'll know. She'll know the truth about you. The truth about what you did!"

I rip my arm out of her grip. Nell's nails slide down the length of my forearm, leaving three bloody lines in their wake. Then I stumble around to the passenger side of the car and climb inside, arching my hips over the center console to get to the driver's seat. Nell is pounding on the window. I slam the lock down on the door and start the car.

When the engine sputters to life, Nell steps away from the door. Suddenly she's not quite so spry. She's not even looking at me or the car. She's staring off in the woods. Off in the direction of the clearing.

I back the car out of the parking spot and shift the lever into drive. But before I accelerate, Nell smacks her palms against the driver's side window, causing me to slam my foot on the brakes.

"You're not supposed to be here, Amber," she says, her one good eye boring a hole in my forehead. "You're not supposed to know what your sister is doing."

Chapter 20

Friday, September 7, 2007
12:55 p.m.

"All right, class! I'm going to need all of you to settle down so we can get started."

Fifth period American history with Mr. Henson is always a rowdy class because it's the first one after lunch. A group of band kids in the front row are being particularly disorderly because there's going to be a sixth period spirit assembly. They're already dressed up in marching attire, which, in and of itself, is distracting because of the bright colors. One of the boys grabs the old treasure-chest-looking box on Henson's desk that he claims is for an end-of-the-year assignment and shakes it. Henson points a reprimanding finger at the boy until he puts it back down. Then he firmly reminds the group that they have to remove their marching band hats while they're in class.

I sit in the second-to-the-back row beside Jessica. Riley and Cameron are behind us. Amber is in this class as well because she skipped a grade in history by taking an extra course her freshman year. She sits closer to the front next to one of the girls on the cheer squad. Normally it would bother people to have their younger sibling in the same class as them, but I don't mind. Most of the time I ignore her because history is a class I actually have to focus on. I'm a dunce when it comes to memorizing dates and I've always struggled with the concept of vast passages of time. I practically bombed world history last year. If it hadn't been for Amber helping me prepare for the exams I'd probably be redoing it. I can't wait until I can go to college and focus on what I love. What I wouldn't give to only have art classes all day every day.

The classroom is a cacophony of noise that refuses to settle down. It's not usually this bad. Henson runs a tight ship. But there's a football game against Grafton Lake this evening and half the class has already checked out for the day. And it doesn't help that Henson has brought in a guest speaker for the period.

Jessica leans toward me. "What's Amber doing talking to Danny Darnielle?"

"What?" I look up from my notebook and follow Jessica's gaze to my sister. To my surprise she is talking to Danny. Not only that, they're sitting very close to each other.

Danny is a bully. He comes from an upper-middle-class family, but he likes to pretend otherwise. He even affects a Saltside accent like Riley's in order to get attention. His parents own the local fish and tackle, which does a fair amount of business in the summer when people travel up for camping along the river. Once in the second grade he dared some kid in our class to suck a live bait worm up his nose. The kid ended up in the hospital because he couldn't figure out how to blow it out.

"They're not dating, are they?" Jessica asks.

"No! Of course not," I say with a scoff. But then Danny leans in closer to Amber, their faces mere inches from each other, and I can't help but wonder. "I'd know if they were."

Riley leans forward and sticks his head between us. "What are we whispering about?"

"None of your business, King." Jessica gives him a taunting smirk before shoving him in the shoulder.

Riley rolls his eyes. "Guh, I hate it when you call me that."

"Which is why I'm going to keep calling you that."

"Hey," Cameron interrupts. "You girls have a pen I could borrow? I forgot to bring one."

"How did you get through the first half of the day without a pen?" I ask.

"Shit, Lexie. You know I sleep through all my morning classes."

Jessica shakes her head disapprovingly.

"They let you football players get away with everything, don't they?" Riley twirls a mechanical pencil between his fingers before drawing an ugly smiley face on Cameron's notebook.

"Here," I say, handing Cameron a pen from the front pocket of my book bag. "But I want it back by the end of the day."

"Yes, ma'am."

A sharp, ear-piercing whistle cuts through the classroom. Everyone goes silent.

"Great," Henson says. "Now that I have your attention I want to remind all of you that your topics for the end of the quarter project on 'History as an Art Form' are due by the end of next week. Anyone who doesn't request a specific topic will be assigned one of my choosing. And, trust me, they will not be easy topics."

The entire class groans.

Henson holds up his hands until everyone is quiet. "With that out of the way, I want to introduce you to our guest speaker for today."

He opens the door and an older woman enters. She has disheveled gray hair that curls at the ends and long, flowing clothing that looks like she just tumbled out of the dressing room at the Goodwill. Nell Abbott.

"Witch!" a boy yells from the far side of the room.

"Keep it up, Kevin, and I'll have you in after-school detention for a week."

Jessica shoots me a weird look and mouths, *What is going on?* I shrug.

Henson clears his throat. "Many of you probably aren't aware, but Ms. Abbott is one of the members of the Braxton Falls Historical Society. She can trace her family back five generations in this area and is an expert on the history of the region, particularly in the area of legends and folklore."

"Yeah, because she was around for it," Riley whispers behind me.

I hush him.

"I want you all to give her your full and undivided attention because not only will this be on the exam, but it will also be part of your research project that's due when you return from Thanksgiving break."

Another simultaneous groan erupts from the class.

Nell steps up to the front of the class. She's a shorter woman and I can tell by her neck that she's quite thin, but she looks much larger than she is because of her baggy clothes. She doesn't give off the impression of someone who is a professional in anything, but that's just my mom's stereotypical opinion speaking in my own head. I was raised to believe that you dress for the job you want. Professionals wear suits and pull their hair back. They don't dress like they're homeless and ooze the nose-tickling odor of patchouli incense. But I can't afford to not pay attention so I set my pen at the ready.

"One of you called me a witch when I walked in," Nell says. Her voice is gritty like tires rolling over gravel. She aims her one good eye directly at Kevin as though she's preparing to curse him. "You're not wrong."

We all look at each other confused. Even Amber glances back at me with a WTF expression.

"I assume most of you are familiar with the legend of the Wynwood Witch. About the woman who was tortured by members of her own community for supposedly practicing black magic and threatening to destroy their village and bring a plague upon their crops. What isn't talked about often is that the women of this time, and in fact the women of centuries prior in most European countries, who were considered to be witches or practitioners of witchcraft were nothing more than what we would call midwives today."

I scribble down a few notes. Frontierswoman. Witches. Midwives. Persecution. I glance up and notice that Jessica isn't writing anything. She's looking at her nails. I know she'll ask me for a copy of my notes later.

"Now I'm assuming most of you were born in a hospital. Probably the one in Lancaster. So, you might not know what a midwife is." Nell slowly paces the room as she speaks. She walks with a limp and her steps make a shuffling sound as though she's dragging one foot behind her. "A midwife is a health professional who cares for mothers and newborns during childbirth. For various historical and cultural reasons, most of these women would be the ones responsible for delivering babies. They were specialists when it came to difficult labors, miscarriages, and abortions. And while doctors and nurses have taken on a lot of those responsibilities in primary care today, we still have midwives.

"But historically this was a very complicated and sometimes dangerous career path for a woman. Because while it was necessary to ensure the safety of mothers and children, particularly out here in the frontier, there was always the possibility of something going wrong. And when things go wrong, people like to have someone to blame. And it is much easier to accept that a woman is a witch than to explain a failed breeched birth or eclampsia or uterine rupture or any number of complications that can occur during childbirth. Not to mention that the medical knowledge to understand certain physical disabilities caused by traumatic births weren't widely known or accepted. If your baby was born different then a witch probably cursed it."

"This class is a curse," Cameron mumbles.

Jessica giggles.

"Mr. King!" Henson shouts, interrupting Nell's lecture. "Do you have something you want to share with the rest of the class?"

Riley looks up from his desk, confused. "What?"

"I won't have you interrupting my class."

"But I didn't say anyth—"

"Grab your bag and head down to the principal's office."

I shoot Cameron a stare because I know damn well that it was him and not Riley who spoke. Cameron refuses to look at me. Jessica doesn't either. They know that if Cameron gets sent to the principal he'll be banned from playing in tonight's football game. And the team needs their lead quarterback.

But I know that Riley is already down to the last few strikes on his record and that infuriates me.

I move to stand up, prepared to defend Riley, but before I'm more than a few inches out of my seat I feel a hand on my shoulder. It's Riley, stopping me. He doesn't want me to get in trouble, too.

"Come on, King," Henson says firmly. "I don't have all day."

Riley grabs his backpack and flings it over his shoulder.

I'm so angry I could scream. But I don't, of course.

Riley slips me a note as he walks by. I catch Danny giving a smug sneer as Riley brushes past his desk and heads out of the classroom.

"My apologies, Ms. Abbott." Henson sits back down. "Please continue."

The entire talk has lost my attention. I hunch over my desk as though I'm writing and carefully open up the note so no one around me can see it.

Riley has drawn a picture of two stick figures labeled 'you' and 'me'. The one of me has a pointy hat and is holding a broom. The drawing of him has two large hearts for eyes. Above it he's written: 'You've bewitched me!'

I hide a smile in the palm of my hand. You've bewitched me, too, Riley King.

Chapter 21

There's a double click on the other end of the line before an automated voice speaks.

"Hello, this is a prepaid call from—" Riley's tired voice states his name before it cuts back to the automated recording "—an inmate at Miller's Creek Federal Correctional Institution. To accept charges, press one. To refuse charges, press the pound key."

I remove the phone from my ear and press the '1' button on the screen. Then I lean back against my headboard and wait. There's another click. I assume that's the prison initiating the recording. Or do they listen in on calls? I probably should have googled that before allowing my number to be added to the list of Riley's contacts. The very short list. I can't begin to imagine who else might be on it. His lawyer, I suppose. Clearly none of the Kings. And I would know if he was talking to any of our old friends.

At least, I think I would know.

"You are now connected. You have ten minutes," the automated voice says.

"Lexie? Can you hear me?"

The sound of Riley's voice causes my heart to skip a beat. Not literally, of course. But I feel a tension in my chest. A rising anticipation. The sound of his breathing so close to my ear takes me back to when I was a teenager. When we used to stay up all night chatting on the phone. When I would hide under the blankets so my parents wouldn't see the light and attempt to stifle back fits of laughter in between hushed whispers. Riley was always good at phone calls. Good at making me laugh. I don't think I've laughed since high school. Really laughed, that is. I'm good at faking it now. I've perfected the art of pretending like everything is OK.

Nothing is OK.

"Yeah, I can hear you."

"I wasn't sure you would pick up."

"I wasn't sure I would either."

That's a lie. A week ago, I never would have answered his call. But ever since seeing him in person again I feel like I'm being sucked back into a world that ceased existing fifteen years ago. A world where I could be myself. With someone who accepted me for me.

There's a pause on the other end of the line and I don't know if it's because there's a delay in the call or because Riley doesn't know what to say. To be honest I don't know what to say either.

We end up breaking the silence at the same time.

"I wanted to ask about—"

"We don't have a lot of—"

I laugh uncomfortably. "You go first."

"They don't give inmates a lot of time on calls," Riley says. Is that a hint of sadness in his voice? Regret? He sounds just the way he did in high school when it was three o'clock in the morning and I told him I had to go to bed or risk falling asleep in first period precalculus. "We have to speak quickly."

"Right. Of course. I understand."

"What were you going to say?" he asks.

That's a good question. I know what I want to say, but now that I have him on the phone, I'm not sure how to phrase it. Not without sounding accusatory. But also not without sounding like I'm willing to believe his story.

"I did what you said. I went to the woods."

109

I can hear Riley inhale sharply. "What did you find?"

"What did you *want* me to find?" It's easier to be more defiant and confident on the phone. And as much as I want to figure this out, as much as I want to prove that Riley didn't kill my sister, I still feel as though he sent me on a wild goose chase. "You could have told me what to look for."

"If I told you what to look for you'd think I was just trying to cast doubt on someone else."

"Isn't that what you're doing?"

"That depends on what you saw."

"The tree," I say. The image of it flashes in front of my mind, leaving me with an eerie sensation of being watched. "The one where they found Amber. I saw it."

"You saw what exactly?"

"I saw the carving. The name."

"Whose name?"

"Jessica's. And someone else's initials. I couldn't make out the letters. They were too worn. Do you know who they belong to?"

The silence on the other end of the line lasts for a full thirty seconds before I interrupt it.

"Riley? Do you know whose initials they are?"

He clears his throat. "No, I don't. It's one of the things that I've been racking my brain about for years."

"It could just be a coincidence," I say, trying to play the devil's advocate. But even I'm not convinced. How could Jessica have a secret lover that none of us knew about? That *I* didn't know about? And what could that have to do with Amber? "We don't even really know if it's our Jessica."

"No one else signs their name like that."

The little heart above the letter I.

"It's not exactly uncommon. Teenage girls write hearts all over the place."

"But in that exact spot? On *that* particular tree? No way. That was our place."

I still have my doubts, but Riley has a way of changing the tone of his voice to sound more convincing. And I suppose it would be a very big coincidence if the name belonged to someone else.

"But what does any of that have to do with Amber?"

"You know Jessica was always jealous of your sister."

The comment takes me by surprise and I can't help but laugh. My lack of self-control embarrasses me. But then I remember I'm talking to a man who was convicted of killing the person I loved most in my life. And then I feel ashamed for feeling ashamed. "What are you talking about? That's ridiculous. Jessica and Amber were friends. Not close friends, of course, but they got along. She wasn't jealous of her. I would have known."

"Would you?"

"I've known Jessica since preschool. I would have been the first person to notice if she had a problem with Amber. That doesn't make any sense. Jessica had everything. Why would she have been jealous?"

"Maybe Amber was seeing someone."

I laugh again only this time it's more of a disbelieving scoff. "Amber never dated anyone."

"What about her homecoming date?"

I shake my head. "They weren't really dating."

"How do you know?"

"Because she was my *sister*, Riley. I would know."

"Like you knew about Jessica?"

A flush of anger hits my cheeks like a raw sunburn. I should have seen it coming. I walked right into it just as Riley knew I would. He was good at that. Good at manipulating other people's conjecture back around to his argument. Well, not good enough, obviously. But I was still falling for it.

The automated voice interrupts us, warning that we have two minutes remaining. I'm about to argue back when Riley cuts me off.

"Do you ever think about how different things could have been?"

The question catches me off guard. "What?"

111

"About what might have happened if Amber never died. Where do you think we'd be? Do you think we'd still be in Braxton Falls? Do you think we'd be married with a couple of kids?"

"I don't know. I never really thought about it." But there's a waver in my voice that says otherwise. I hate that he makes me forget what he did. Because he did do it. Everyone says he did. He was convicted. Twelve jurors were unequivocal in their decision. The evidence was overwhelming.

I'm the only one with doubts.

"I think about it all the time. About all the plans we made. The future we talked about," Riley says and I can almost imagine his eyes boring into me through the phone. I'm ashamed that the thought of it excites me a little. But also makes me sick to my stomach.

"Riley, I—" I stop myself from saying what I want to say because I don't know how to word my feelings. I don't know how to tell him that I've missed him, but I don't trust him. So I say something else instead. "I've been taking care of Spaghetti for you."

"What?" This is the first time I've heard actual surprise in Riley's voice.

"Your snake. I've had her ever since you were arrested. It just occurred to me that you probably never knew what happened to her."

"You did that? And you still have her?"

"Yeah, I . . . It was all I could do at the time. And I didn't think it was fair to leave her with your foster father."

"I don't know what to say." Riley's voice softens with what sounds like hopeful optimism.

Then we both go quiet long enough for me to hear my own heartbeat until Riley interrupts the silence.

"You should go back to the woods and look again. There's more out there. I know there is. But you need to be careful what you say to people, Lexie. You can't assume you really know anyone. You can't assume you can trust anyone. Somebody got away with murder. And if they find out what you're doing, you could be in real da—"

The call disconnects.

I slump my head back against the wall and stare up at the ceiling.

What about you, Riley? Can I trust you?

Chapter 22

The lunch bell rings and the hallways fill with students scrambling to their lockers. Metal doors slam and locks twist. The odor of bad teenage hygiene and soggy undercooked pizza fills the air. I stick to the edge of the corridor, trying to maneuver my rolling bucket and mop toward the girls' restroom. Most of the kids move out of the way without really noticing me. But a few groups see me coming and start whispering to each other. The hushed high-pitched kind of whisper that's followed by tittering laughs and surprised groans. They did the same thing when I came back from Christmas break during my last year of high school. Sometimes kids are horrible because being mean and being catty makes them feel powerful. Sometimes it's because they're scared out of their minds.

It's hard being reminded that bad shit can happen to anyone. I know. I used to be one of those kids who thought they were untouchable. I had it all. Until it was taken away from me.

A boy in a baggy football jersey stands in front of my path, wobbling back and forth like an action hero trying to avoid a rolling boulder. I pretend like I don't see him. When I'm within

114

inches of rolling over his toe he dives out of the way. A group of boys leaning against a row of blue lockers breaks out into laughter. The comic relief of the day. I ignore them, too. I ignore everyone. Until somebody shoves me from behind, causing the bucket to rock on its rusty wheels and spilling half of the water onto the floor.

"Hey!"

I whip around to see an even larger group of teens pointing and laughing. I can't tell who did it. The second warning bell rings and they all head off toward the cafeteria. Thirty seconds later, it's like a bomb went off. Total silence. And I'm the only one standing in the hallway.

It takes me twenty minutes to clean the toilets. Someone rolled out all of the toilet paper in the third stall. It's wet. Probably from water, but I still scrub my hands raw after picking it up and shoving it into the plastic trash bag hitched to the side of my mop. There's spit and snot and makeup smeared on the mirror. That only takes me five minutes to clean. Whoever says teenage girls are cleaner than boys doesn't know what the hell they're talking about. Girls can be gross. And they can be vicious. They just have the benefit of smelling nice.

I empty the trash in the industrial containers out back. When I return to the custodial closet for replacement bags I see that someone has vandalized the door by scrawling 'WYNWOOD BITCH' in bright orange spray paint at eye level. It's still dripping, which means it probably happened in the last few minutes. I glance down the hallways but there's nobody there. It makes me think of my car and I can't help but wonder if it's one of those kids who lives down the street from my mom. Not that it matters.

The flash of a camera tears me out of my daze and I turn to see a woman in a snug dress suit and a man with a large Nikon standing behind me.

"Miss Wicker?" the woman asks, stepping so close to me that I can smell her perfume. It has a choking rosy scent. Like something my grandmother would have worn.

"Who are you? What are you doing here?"

"We're from the *Ohio Gazette*. We wanted to ask a few questions about your sister and the impending execution of your boyfriend."

Any confidence I might have drains from my face. "*Ex*-boyfriend."

"Of course. But isn't it true that you went to speak to him recently? What did he say to you? Did he confess to the murder of your sister?"

I look down and realize her phone is recording the conversation.

"You can't be here. This is a school. If you aren't a parent here to pick up a child or a member of staff then you need to have a visitor's permit from the main office."

But the reporter only leans in closer. "Were you aware of Riley King's plans to murder your sister? Did he give you any indication that he might do something violent?"

"You need to leave." I turn my back to the woman and unlock the door to the custodial closet, hoping that if I ignore her she'll leave. The camera clicks another photo behind me.

The cameraman maneuvers around to the other side of the door in order to snap a picture of the graffiti.

"I said leave!" I yell at him. He takes a step back and just snaps another photo without a word.

"Will you be attending the execution? What about your mother? Will either of you be making a statement to the press?"

I want to curl up in a ball and disappear. Just sink into the linoleum and be swallowed up by the earth. I can't look at either of them because I'm so angry. Angry, but also afraid. Afraid of having my photo printed in the paper again. Afraid of having more people look at me like I did something wrong. Like I know something I shouldn't. Like it's my fault the entire town has to deal with this tragedy. Afraid that the entire world will blame me for Amber's death.

And angry because they might be right.

"Hey!" Mr. Henson's voice calls out from down the corridor. He storms toward us and I've never been so grateful to have

116

someone come to my rescue. He puts himself between me and the journalist. "This is an educational institution, not an interrogation chamber. If you want to talk to Miss Wicker or any other member of staff, it'll have to be outside school hours and off school property. We have minors here whose parents have not consented to being on camera."

"We just wanted to ask a few—"

"*After* school hours," Henson repeats. "This school is a safe space for our students and our staff. And if you don't leave right this minute I will call the police."

The reporter nods to the cameraman and they both head for the door.

I hate that I can't stand up better for myself. That I have to be saved by Henson, of all people. But I'm also glad he interrupted us before I said something that might have landed me on the five o'clock news.

Once the reporter and her cameraman have left I close the closet. Henson eyes the door with a glare.

"I'll clean the door up," I say, still refusing to look at him directly.

"Fuck the door," he says.

The harshness in his tone surprises me and I look up at him. His jaw is set like he's clenching his teeth and his face is a little more frazzled than usual. Not unlike the look most of the teachers have the day after parent-teacher conferences.

"You OK, Mr. Henson?"

"Those vultures have been calling my office all day. I told them that under no circumstances are they allowed to enter the school while classes are in session."

I flinch. "They've been calling because of me?"

"Not just you. Most of them just want shots of the inside of the building so they can put together some kind of bullshit memorial piece about what happened. One of them even had the nerve to ask me which locker belonged to your sister. I told them that the school administration would not be supporting any article that depicts this school, or this town for that matter, in a bad light. We've all been through enough. Some of us are still grieving."

Something about the way he says 'us' sticks in my mind. What was it that Riley said? Don't trust anyone? Henson had always struck me as a bit odd. A little too devil-may-care for a high school teacher. A little too handsome to be around teenage girls. But maybe that was just bias on my part. Maybe I was just looking for any excuse not to blame Riley for what happened.

"Thank you," I mumble. I'm not even sure I've said it loud enough to be heard until Henson places his hand on my shoulder. The hair stands up on the back of my neck.

His hand lingers there a few seconds longer than seems appropriate. When he finally lets go he looks me directly in the eyes. "I think maybe you should take some time off."

"I can't afford to take time off."

"I'll make sure you're still paid for the time you would be working. At least take off the week until—" he cuts himself off "—until everything is over."

Until Riley is dead, he means.

But even that was no guarantee of it all being over. Particularly if Riley is telling the truth.

"Who will cover my shifts? I can't put that responsibility on CJ right now."

"I'll hire in someone temporary. I've been fighting with the school board to let me have two full-time custodian positions, but we're underfunded as it is. Maybe I can get someone from the substitute teacher's pool. There's been a shortage of teacher absences this year and subs are always looking for work. Someone will be desperate enough to take it."

"Are you sure?"

"You should spend time with your family, Lex."

I almost laugh. My *family*. There's only one person left in my family and she doesn't want to spend time with me.

"Thank you, Mr. Henson. I appreciate that."

"I wish you'd call me Richard." He smiles. There's something slippery about the way his mouth moves. But maybe I'm just being insensitive. Richard Henson has never done anything to me. He's never done anything to anyone that I know of. Maybe he is a genuinely good person who just wants to help.

Or maybe he's just a really good liar.

I lock up the janitorial closet and am about to leave when Henson catches me by the shoulder. This time his grip is a little stronger, more urgent. I try not to react too quickly. My instinct is to rip my arm away from him. But I stand my ground and give him my attention.

"Have you given any thought to the full-time position?"

The question catches me off guard. Fortunately, my phone rings, saving me from having to answer. I look down at the name on my screen. It's my mother. She never calls me in the middle of the day. I press the green button on the screen and hold the phone up to my ear. "Mom?"

"You have to come home, Alexandra! You have to come home right this instant!"

"Why? What happened?"

I can barely hear her over her sobs. She must be drunk. But the more she wails the more I realize she's very sober. She says something, but I can't understand it. Then I hear a crash in the background like glass breaking. My mother screams into the phone loud enough that I have to tear it away from my ear.

"Help me, Alexandra! Somebody's trying to kill me!"

Chapter 23

I step through the front door and a Royal Copenhagen plate nearly misses my head. It hits the wall and leaves an indentation in the plaster before it shatters to the floor. Mom is standing behind the couch, wailing, her mascara smeared over her eyes and cheeks. She's drunk. Mad drunk.

"Mom! Calm down! It's Lex!"

She reaches for another plate. Her breathing is heavy and erratic and her gaze is glossy. She probably can't even see me through her tears. When she steps out from behind the sofa I see her feet are bleeding. That's when I notice the broken glass on the floor and the brick at the center of the room. The one that had gone right through the front window, shattering it across the carpet. The floor is a war zone—even the pristine plastic runner is covered in shards and bloody footsteps.

"Holy shit," I mumble. My boots crunch over the glass.

Mom doesn't seem to notice. She keeps walking, unaware that she's tearing up her feet with each step.

She's so trashed she doesn't even know she's hurting herself.

"Stop walking, Mom! Just . . . stay where you are! Let me help you."

By some miracle she stops moving and grabs onto a shelf against the wall in order to keep her balance. I take her by the arm and maneuver her around the glass and into the kitchen where I carefully help her into one of the chairs. She stinks of alcohol. Not her normal brand either. This is something sour, like old boxed wine.

"What happened?" I ask, making my way to the sink to grab some paper towels. I run them under the faucet to dampen them.

"He tried to kill me."

"Who tried to kill you?"

Mom shakes her head. Her hair is a frazzled mess and her skin is blanched. I kneel down in front of her and dab the wet towel on her feet, cleaning up the blood. She still has pieces of glass embedded in the soft skin of her arch. Some of them quite large. I pick them out carefully with a tweezers from the bathroom, but she doesn't seem to feel anything. I set the pieces on the kitchen table out of her reach, then I check for more.

"Did he come into the house? Did you get a good look at him?" I ask when she doesn't answer my other question.

"You're not listening to me! He tried to kill me!"

"I am listening to you, Mom." *But you're drunker than a laid-off steelworks foreman at the Irish-American festival.* That's what I want to say. But there's no point starting a fight with her when she's plastered from here to Cincinnati. It'll just make her even more incoherent. And even more belligerent when she sobers up.

I pick out the last piece of glass and wipe off the rest of the blood from her feet. Then I sweep the glass into the paper towels and throw it all in the trash.

"I'm going to call the police," I say, but Mom is back to crying again. The last thing I want is to have anyone see her like this, but I don't have a choice. I have to report the property damage or the insurance won't cover it. I don't have the money for a new bay window. And with the way Mom drinks Dad's pension away, I'm sure she doesn't either.

Twenty minutes later a paramedic finishes bandaging up my mother's feet and helps her into a pair of socks while a rookie police officer takes photographs of the living room. Chief Newman is there as well, which almost has me rolling my eyes. Once the paramedic has left, Newman pulls up a chair beside my mother and puts an arm around her. It looks weird. Not just because of the way he talked to me the other day, but because he used to work for Dad. That's probably the only reason he's here. Putting on a show for the rest of the police force: reminding them that they never forget their own.

But if that was true then why was he so quick to throw me under the bus when Amber was murdered? And where was the blue community after Dad died? I can count on one hand the number of cards we got from people in town. And Chief Newman's name wasn't on any of them. Where was that blue family support when my mom started drinking before breakfast? It's not like any of that is a secret. Everyone knows everything in this town.

Except what happened the night of the homecoming dance fifteen years ago.

"It's going to be all right, Audrey," Newman says. He pats my mom on the knee and I cringe. He hasn't even acknowledged me yet. Hasn't even said anything about the brick on the floor or the broken window. Hasn't sent anyone out to search the neighborhood for any signs of who could have done this. Not only is he inappropriate, he's also incompetent.

Dad would be rolling in his grave if he knew this man had his job.

The younger officer—Rollins, according to his name tag—removes a small pad of paper from his back pocket and begins taking notes.

"Shouldn't you be bagging the brick for evidence?" I ask, fully aware of how snide my voice sounds. "Maybe dust for finger-prints? Check for points of entry? Call in backup to canvass the neighborhood?"

Rollins gives me a deer-in-the-headlights look before clearing his throat. "It's probably just some local kids playing a prank."

"Probably some local kids playing a prank?" I scoff. "My mom says someone was in the house. She says someone tried to kill her."

But it's clear from the look on Rollins's face that he doesn't believe a word of it. I can't blame him. We can both smell the alcohol from the other side of the house. And, to be fair, Mom's story doesn't make a lot of sense. Why would someone break the front window if they wanted to get inside the house? Nothing appears to be missing. And Mom doesn't have any apparent injuries except for the glass, which she walked on herself.

Rollins was probably right. It probably was some neighborhood kids just fucking around because of all the shit about Riley on the news. And my mom probably made up the story about someone trying to kill her just to excuse the fact that she was completely plowed before lunch.

But that didn't mean that Rollins and Newman weren't doing everything wrong. Their job was to consider all of the possibilities. Their job was to protect and serve.

"Shouldn't you at least be taking a statement from my mom?"

Rollins trips over his words, but is cut off by Newman who has finally left my mother's side to pay me attention.

"Bag up the brick, Jeff. We'll take that down to the station with us," Newman interrupts.

Rollins nods, clearly glad for an escape from my questions and criticisms.

When Newman turns his attention to me, it's lacking any of the sympathy he showed my mother. I can tell he wishes I weren't there. Or, even better, that he had proof I was involved in this so he could finally be vindicated for his suspicions about me fifteen years ago.

"Did you witness anything?" he asks me.

I can't help but show my annoyance. "No. I was at work when Mom called me. By the time I got here the window was already broken and she was in hysterics."

"Was your mother inside the house when you got home?"

"What are you trying to say? You think she threw a brick at her own window?"

"I'm just trying to get an accurate account of what happened here, Miss Wicker."

"Yes, she was inside the house, hiding behind the couch and brandishing her decorative dinner plates. She said someone was trying to kill her."

"Did she say if they were ever in the house?"

I pause, remembering what my mother said when I arrived. "No. She didn't say."

Newman makes his way through the house and checks the back door. It's locked. As is the entrance from the garage. I follow him just to make sure. But my heart sinks when I realize it looks exactly like what Rollins said. Kids playing a prank. Not that I want someone to attack my mother, but it would make everything easier if her story was true. Now she just looks like a crazy drunk. And I look like her crazy daughter.

"We'll dust the brick for fingerprints. There wasn't a note or anything attached to it, was there?"

I shake my head.

"Any other disturbances recently?"

I think about the graffiti on my car, but Newman already knows I filed a report. Then there was the vandalism to my custodial closet at work, but I don't mention that. It's not like he can do anything about it anyway.

"No."

He's staring at me. I can feel the suspicion in his eyes. Or maybe the disgust? I don't know why he's always had it out for me. But Newman has never failed to make me feel like I'm guilty. Even when I haven't done anything wrong.

"You should be taking better care of your mother."

"Excuse me?"

"She's suffered a lot. Between your sister and Michael. That's a lot for a person to bear on their own."

124

"I lost my sister and my dad, too. I think I know what it means to suffer."

Newman doesn't say anything for what feels like a minute. He's looking toward the kitchen, his face drawn into a hard grimace. "You still talking to that boy?"

"Boy?"

"That killer."

"That's none of your business."

Newman turns to me so fast that it practically knocks me off balance. Then he catches me by the sleeve of my jacket. "You stay away from Miller's Creek. You stay away from Riley King. That man is just going to fill your head with nonsense. He murdered your sister. He doesn't deserve your time or anyone else's. He should spend the last few days of his life thinking about how no one gives a damn about him. Don't let him manipulate you into playing his game."

I tug away from Newman. "I think he's had plenty of time to think. I think we all have."

"Don't be stupid, Alexandra. Forget about Riley King. Take care of your mother."

"Like the police take care of her? Like you take care of her?"

"Now you listen up real good because I'm not going to say this twice. You stay away from that kid or you'll end up like your sister."

I try to bite my tongue, but I can't. "He's not a kid anymore. None of us are. We're adults. And my sister would be too if it weren't for this fucking town and its worthless police force."

Chapter 24

It takes me almost an hour and a half to calm Mom down enough to go to bed. Once she hits the mattress, fully clothed and feet double-bandaged, she falls asleep almost instantly. I pull my grandmother's handmade quilt over her, but don't bother trying to adjust the pillow. I sit on the edge of the bed for five minutes, checking her breathing every few seconds, before I leave the room, closing the door behind me.

I want to collapse myself. The weight of my own legs threatens to pull me down to the carpet, but I somehow manage to walk down the hallway. I stop at Dad's office and peer into the room. Again, I'm met with that musty smell of disuse. Old air blended with the lingering scent of his aftershave. Probably from the collar of one of his dress shirts. Maybe his uniform. I hear Mom's voice in the back of my mind telling me not to go in there. Is that what makes me step inside? Or is it the fury I've kept bottled up in my chest? That all-encompassing anger set off by Newman and Mom and work and Riley. It probably doesn't matter. It's there all the same.

I open the closet door. I'm quick to look at the floor as opposed to the hanging shirts and ties. If I look at those I'll just get nostalgic and distracted and there's no time for that. No time for sentiment. If I'm going to figure out what's going on, then I have to push my sentiment to the side. I have to focus on what I know to be true, not what I feel. If I'm to believe or disbelieve Riley, I need to know the facts.

Fact #1 – Amber left the homecoming dance and didn't go home.

Fact #2 – Someone murdered Amber in the woods.

Fact #3 – Evidence placed Riley at the scene of the crime.

Fact #4 – Amber's death was made to resemble the Wynwood Witch legend.

Fact #5 – I was in the woods the night of the homecoming dance.

Fact #6 – I didn't kill Amber.

I crouch down in front of a box that's squished between Dad's collection of threadbare leather loafers and a stack of old Louis L'Amour hardcovers. There's a thin layer of dust on top of the box, suggesting it hasn't been touched since before Dad died, but the edges are worn from having been opened multiple times in the years prior.

Amber's files.

Why did Dad pore over them every night? What was it about the case that kept him up late with his dim desk light on? What was it he refused to share with Mom? With me?

I pull the boxes out into the center of the room. There's three of them. They're lighter than I expected. I lift the first one onto the desk and remove the lid. Then I sit in Dad's chair and take out the first file.

I've never seen these before. Never seen Amber diminished to a nonpartisan third-person narrative of events and actions. It's equal parts fitting and infuriating. It's like reading about a stranger. Except she wasn't a stranger. I try to imagine Dad flipping through these pages. Was he able to disassociate himself from the emotion? Was he able to see through the memories of backyard barbecues and Barbie birthday parties? Could he put on blinders and read these words without getting a choking feeling in the back of his throat? Without feeling like he was going to tear the documents apart? Because that's how I feel. That's what I want to do. And it takes every bit of strength I have left not to do exactly that when I open up the first report and see Amber's eleventh-grade photo stapled to the top of an incident report. The entire scene described in emotionless black and white.

But it's the photographs that stop my heart.

I quickly flip them over, hands shaking as I hide the images. The blood. The gore. I can't have those photographs replace the image of Amber in my mind. I almost did once. When one of those pictures was shoved in my face while I sat hyperventilating in the cold interrogation room. I can still remember the sound of Newman's voice pressing me for an answer. I can't recall what he said. Only that he sounded like he was screaming underwater. And that the photograph of Amber, dress torn and covered in blood, was louder than anything else in the room. Save for my heart.

I move on to the next document. And the next. There are pages and pages of interviews, cell phone transcripts, and witness testimonies. Descriptions of the scene. Evidence collection. I don't know where to begin. All I know is that even if I stayed up all night for the rest of the week I'd never be able to sort through all of this before Riley's execution. If I try to read it all he'll be dead before I have an answer. And if he's right—if he's telling the truth—then I'll be too late.

What am I supposed to be looking for, Riley? What is it you want me to see? What is it Dad missed? And why can't you just tell me directly?

I find Dad's notebook at the bottom of the first box. Inside are all the notes he took based on the evidence. The pages are full of fragmentary thoughts and questions. Everything from potential suspects, motives, and avenues he thought his colleagues weren't properly investigating. One note in particular stands out to me.

Mark on Amber's face? What caused this? Weapon? Jewelry? Ring?

I return to the pile of overturned photographs and flip them over until I find the one with the close-up of Amber's face. Dad is right. There is a mark on her cheek that doesn't belong there. I squint my eyes. At first it looks like a cut. But then I notice that there's no blood. It's a bruise with a peculiar U shape. The curved lines are too perfect to be made by an organic object like a rock or a branch. I'm not an expert, but it looks like she was hit with something and whatever that something was left an indentation on her skin.

I skim through the rest of Dad's notes to see if he ever found an answer to his own question, but it doesn't look like he did. Nor does there appear to be anything on the recovered evidence list that would match that description. There is, however, one other handwritten note that stands out to me. On the final page of his notebook Dad has written 'TALK TO NELL' in capital letters.

My stomach drops. Why would he want to talk to Nell? What did he think she knew?

I turn the page but the rest of the pages are blank.

Damn.

Did Dad ever talk to her? If so, what did she tell him? Maybe it's in the transcripts.

I pull out the file of transcripts and flip through them, searching for one with Nell's name on it. I don't find one. But I do find the transcript of Riley's first interview. Curiosity gets the better of me and I read it.

Statement of Riley King – October 14th, 4:26 a.m., interviewed by Sergeant Charles Newman

Sergeant Newman: We found your pocketknife at the scene, Riley. So, let's go ahead and make this easy for everyone. Just tell us what we already know. Tell us what happened between you and Amber.

129

Riley King: Nothing happened.

Sergeant Newman: How do you explain what we found?

Riley King: I don't know what you found. A knife? Could be anyone's. Could be yours.

Sergeant Newman: When was the last time you saw Amber Wicker?

Riley King: At the dance.

Sergeant Newman: Did you talk to her?

Riley King: Sure. But I talked to a lot of people. So did she. Amber's popular. She has a lot of friends.

Sergeant Newman: Had a lot of friends.

Riley King: I didn't kill her.

Sergeant Newman: How do you account for your pocketknife being found near the body?

Riley King: I don't. Shouldn't I have a parent or guardian with me?

Sergeant Newman: You're eighteen. An adult in the eyes of the state.

Riley King: A lawyer then?

Sergeant Newman: Are you asking for a lawyer?

Riley King: I'm asking you to shut the fuck up about the knife. I didn't do anything.

Sergeant Newman: Did you and Amber have an argument at the dance? Did something happen?

Riley King: If something happened it had nothing to do with me.

Sergeant Newman: So, you weren't seen arguing with her on the dance floor?

Riley King: Who told you that? Was it Darnielle? Did someone actually say that or are you just talking out of your ass? I didn't kill anybody. And I don't know who did.

Sergeant Newman: Do you own a Buck 112 Ranger LT pocketknife?

Riley King: Maybe.

Sergeant Newman: That's a Boy Scout knife, isn't it? You a Boy Scout, Riley?

Riley King: As if.

Sergeant Newman: Where'd you get it then? Beat up some kid for it?

Riley King: It belonged to my dad.

Sergeant Newman: Mitchell King?

Riley King: Fuck that asshole. My real dad.

Sergeant Newman: Do you even know who your real dad is?

Riley King: Fuck you.

Sergeant Newman: Where's your pocketknife, Riley?

Riley King: I don't know.

Sergeant Newman: Take a guess.

Riley King: I don't know. I lost it.

Sergeant Newman: Where did you lose it?

Riley King: If I knew that then it wouldn't be lost, would it?

Sergeant Newman: When did you lose it?

Riley King: I don't know. A week ago, maybe. At the football game.

Sergeant Newman: That's awfully convenient, you know. You losing your pocketknife and then someone using it to kill your girlfriend's sister. It was covered in blood, you know. Amber's blood. Probably the blood of the person who used it, too. These kinds of crimes are always such a mess. It's almost impossible for the attacker not to get injured, too.

Riley King: You said the knife was at the scene. You didn't say it was used to kill her.

Sergeant Newman: Technically we won't know until it comes back from the lab. But there was a lot of blood. Blood everywhere.

Riley King: I think I want a lawyer now.

Sergeant Newman: Say that again?

Riley King: I said I want a fucking lawyer, dipshit.

Sergeant Newman: Yeah, I bet you do. Not that it'll do you any good.

I read that last page one more time. Something doesn't sit right. Something seems familiar. I scan over Newman's infuriating accusations—he'd already made up his mind about Riley before he even walked into the room—and focus on Riley's answers. Typical Riley. Trying to play it tough. Pretending to hold his own. There's no way to tell how nuanced the conversation actually was without watching the recording, but I can hear it all in Riley's voice. It sounds so natural in my head. And I don't hesitate to guess where he was trying to rile Newman up and where he was actually worried. I knew him so well back then. At least, I thought I did.

Then it hits me.

A week ago, maybe. At the football game.

He's telling the truth. Riley did lose his pocketknife. I remember. I also remember who might have taken it.

Chapter 25

Friday, October 5, 2007
8:15 p.m.

I shiver, shoving my hands into the front pocket of my hoodie. I wish I'd worn a winter coat, but then I wouldn't blend in with the others. I wouldn't be showing my team spirit. Freezing for a few hours is a small price to pay to feel like one of the crowd. Riley poked fun at me when I came out of the house in my jeans and the red-and-blue hooded sweatshirt—'Class of 2008' printed on the back above the image of our school mascot, the Braxton High Badger.

"You're going to freeze to death," he said.

"I won't," I insisted.

"You're not even wearing gloves."

"I'll hold your hand."

He shook his head and laughed.

Two hours later I can barely feel the tip of my nose and Riley is too busy snacking on a bag of Cool Ranch Doritos to hold my hand. He stands out in the bleachers. A lone figure in black against a sea of school spirit. He's probably the only one who isn't freezing his ass off and I wish I had the confidence to be like him.

To wear whatever I want. It's bullshit. I know. It's nothing more than a fear of standing out. Of being different. But I'm afraid that if I stand out too much someone will notice that I don't belong. In that sense, Riley has it easy. He's from the south side of town. He already has an excuse to feel like he doesn't belong. My dad is a cop. My mom is on the PTA. My sister is on the field, jumping up and down in her cheerleader uniform, bright smile and unending enthusiasm. I don't have an excuse. I should belong. But I don't.

Something happens on the field. I miss it. Jessica jumps up beside me and starts screaming about a bad call. I follow everyone's gaze to the football field. It's Cameron. He's buried under a dogpile of linemen. The referee blows a whistle. The coach is yelling. Before I can figure out what's going on, the marching band breaks into a judgmental chorus of "The Imperial March." I lean forward on the bleachers, an uncomfortable panic in my chest as I wait for the players to crawl off each other. Jessica is still yelling. Riley is elbow deep in his bag of chips. Is no one worried about Cameron? Then Cameron crawls to his feet holding the football in the air. The crowd cheers. The band stands and cuts into an upbeat rendition of Queen's "We Will Rock You." Everything is fine.

I catch a glimpse of Amber out of the corner of my eye, covering her mouth with her hand in what appears to be a sign of relief. At least I'm not the only one who realizes Cameron could have been really hurt. All it takes is one injury and goodbye, professional athletic career. Football is a really dumb sport.

Jessica slumps down beside me with an exasperated sigh. "Can you believe that? What a shit call."

"Yeah, that was total bullshit," I say, but in truth I don't know what she's talking about.

I'm not really a football fan. I don't even know the rules. Get the ball to the end of the field, score some points. Kick it through the goal posts, score some more points. Most points at the end of the games wins. That's as much as I know. That and the fact that Cameron will probably get a full-ride sports scholarship to any school he wants if he continues playing as well this season as he has the last three years. Not that he needs it. His parents are loaded. I, on the other hand, will have to rely on my grades to get me into the school I want. And then pave my way with a shit ton of student loans. The goal is NYU. Kent State in a pinch. But honestly anywhere that isn't Braxton Falls will do. I'll die if I have to stay in this town another year.

Jessica reaches across me and sticks her hand in Riley's Doritos bag.

"Hey! Those are mine!"

"Sharing is caring," she says with a smirk. There's a glance that passes between them that I try not to notice. Jessica is a shameless flirt. She always has been. I know she doesn't mean anything with Riley—she's way too obsessed with Cameron—but it bothers me. Riley is my first boyfriend. We've technically been together for almost a year and a half, but it hasn't gotten serious until the last five months. He asked me out the summer before our junior year while I was lifeguarding at the outdoor pool. I didn't really like it there. Most of my colleagues were jocks from the swim team and I didn't get on with them. But it's the only summer job in town that pays more than minimum wage. Riley used to bring his foster sister to the pool. He'd sit at the bottom of my lifeguard chair and talk to me while she played in the shallow end. That's how I got to know him better. That's how I fell in love. Granted, we've known each other since kindergarten, but that's not the same.

Our relationship has moved pretty fast over the last few months. We've already done it. At my house, not his. His dad is an awful drunk. Riley never takes me to his place. He's too embarrassed. I haven't told anyone yet. Not even Jessica. I probably should. Then maybe she'd stop shooting him those teasing glances.

Or maybe she'd just do it more.

"Oh my God! Is that Becca McBride down there with Kyle Vernon?" Jessica asks, nodding to a curly-haired girl a few rows down from us on the bleachers.

"Maybe?" I crane my neck. "I can't really see."

"I heard a rumor that her cousin was arrested for child endangerment. They said she was using drugs while she was pregnant and had a miscarriage."

"Who's they?" Riley asks, disbelieving.

"A family friend was talking about it at dinner with my parents. Her daughter goes to school with her in Lancaster."

"Can they do that?" I ask. The story doesn't seem entirely far-fetched, but it doesn't feel right either. "Is that even legal?"

Jessica shrugs. "I don't know. It's just something I heard. But crazy shit happens like that all the time. I read a story online about a woman who got fifteen years in prison for losing her baby after refusing to have a C-section. It was fucking crazy!"

"Yeah, but you can't arrest someone for having a miscarriage, right? That's not always in your control."

"You want me to go down there and ask Becca if it's true?"

"No!" I gasp. "Oh my God! That's so embarrassing."

Riley stands up abruptly, tossing the Doritos bag, practically empty, into Jessica's lap. "I'm going for a smoke."

Jessica rolls her eyes and makes an *eww* sound. I agree with her, but I don't say anything. I've convinced myself it's just one of those phases teenage boys go through. Besides, Riley doesn't do it that often. I'm convinced it's mostly a way of sticking it to the snobs. Or purposefully perpetuating the stereotype. Unlike me in this stupid school sweatshirt who actually wishes she was the stereotype.

"I'll go with you," I say, following his lead. Jessica looks at me like I'm abandoning her.

"Whatever," she says. "I'm going to get something to eat anyway. And I promised Amber I'd take a picture of the cheer squad for the homecoming wall."

"Shouldn't you wait until after the game?"

"Are you crazy? If we lose no one is going to want to smile and look excited. Besides, it's almost half-time. I'll catch you guys after the break."

I turn to head off after Riley, but he's already woven his way through the crowd on the bleachers and is skipping down the stairs. I hurry after, nearly bumping into a kid with a large soda. Then I scramble down to ground level.

The 'smoking pit,' which is only designated that by students, is a dark area beneath the older set of bleachers on the opposite end of the field. The school has a security guard who regularly patrols the grounds, making sure no one starts any fights with students from the opposing school. The smokers wait until the guard has already passed by that section of bleachers before they light up their cigarettes, most of which have been nicked from their parents' purses. It takes the guard a good fifteen minutes to do a full circle around the field. Just enough time for kids to suck down a cigarette or two before dispersing.

Not Riley though. He's patient, conservative in his drags. There's something sexy about the way he smokes that I can't explain. Like he's not afraid of getting caught. Unlike me who would be too terrified to even try a puff. I have secondhand anxiety about getting in trouble. Just thinking about Riley getting caught makes me feel guilty.

"Hey, King!"

I turn around to see Danny Darnielle and his trio of bully friends approaching. He's walking with a swagger like he's straight out of a low-budget performance of *West Side Story*. But he's not fooling anyone. Not me anyway. And certainly not Riley.

Riley has never put up with Danny's shit. Usually Danny isn't bold enough to try anything against Riley. Riley is a wild card. Teachers call him a 'loose cannon,' but I don't think that's really fair. I think they're just judgmental because of his circumstances. Because he doesn't fit the mold. Riley is fully capable of keeping his cool, but it doesn't take much to get under his skin.

Riley takes another drag on his cigarette and tosses Danny a short nod. So cool. Like he's right out of a movie. "'Sup, Darnielle."

"I saw your old man at the shop yesterday. Drunk off his ass."

"He's not my old man," Riley says. Cool as a cucumber.

"Yeah, that's what I'd tell people too if I had a lame excuse for a dad like that. Does he even let you eat with those food stamps you get or does he just hock them for dollar cans of piss water? Because I saw your sister the other day and she was looking pretty skinny."

"Lay off, Darnielle."

Danny's lips curl into a smug smirk and he shoots a knowing look to his buddies. "Except up top, that is. She's got more than a handful going on there. How much longer until she's in high school? Wouldn't mind getting a feel of that."

Goodbye, Cucumber Cool.

I place a hand on Riley's elbow, a quiet encouragement to not fall into Danny's trap, but it's too late. Riley's muscles are tensed and his face has lost all its chill. He looks like he's a second away from snapping and there's a darkness in his eyes that scares me. Scares Danny, too, by the looks of it.

"What did you say?" Riley asks.

"He's an asshole," I say. "Just ignore him. Let's get back to the game."

"I said your sister has nice tits," Danny says. He's gunning a little too hard for a fight. He's probably been drinking and thinks he can show off in front of his friends.

Riley drops the half-smoked cigarette to the ground and stubs it out with the toe of his shoe.

The rattling beat of the snare drums on the field announces the beginning of half-time. Pretty soon this entire area is going to be filled with people on their way to the toilets or the snack bar.

"Come on, Riley. Let's go back to the bleachers."

But Riley isn't listening to me. It's like he doesn't see anything but Danny and rage. His hand slips out of his pocket and he flips open his pocketknife. Usually he just plays around with it, carving words into picnic benches. I always thought of it as something he fidgeted with because he was bored. But he looks different now. There's no fidgeting. No hesitation. He's holding that knife like he's going to gut Danny with it. Was Riley always this angry? How could I have not noticed this temper before? Maybe it's just an act. Maybe he's just trying to scare Danny.

"Whoa, whoa, King!" Danny puts up his hands in defense. A sort of mocking white flag. But I can see the uncertain terror in his eyes. He's not sure if Riley is going to do anything either. "I'm just messing around with you."

"You think it's funny to make a joke about a twelve-year-old girl's breasts?"

Riley moves in closer. Danny takes a step back.

"No, man. Come on. I didn't mean anything by it."

"Yeah? Well, maybe I ought to make sure you didn't mean anything by it. Just in case you get it in your head to say that shit again."

"Jesus. You really can't take a joke, can you?"

Riley swings at Danny, the blade moving in a smooth arc that's so fast I can barely see it. At first, I think he's missed. Then Danny lets out a delayed yelp as the blood seeps through the sleeve on his sweatshirt. Before I can say anything they're both on the ground, grappling and throwing fists. Danny's guys, too cowardly to do anything else, do exactly what they were supposed to do before Danny started getting the shit beat out of him. They start egging them both on, yelling at Danny to get up off his ass and hit that low-life piece of Saltside trash.

I'll never forget that.

Low-life piece of Saltside trash.

And if I can't forget it, I know Riley won't either.

Riley loses his grip on the pocketknife and it gets kicked to the side. It clatters on the concrete, but everyone ignores it.

It's not important. Danny takes an elbow to the face. I wince, half expecting to hear his nose break, but it doesn't. And even though I'm appalled by the scene I can't help but feel a small swell of vindication at the idea of Danny having a black eye in his homecoming photos. Were my thoughts always this cruel? No. But Danny deserves it for what he said.

Danny leans close to Riley's ear and whispers something. Riley hesitates, casting me an odd disbelieving look. Danny laughs.

Then Riley grabs him by the back of the neck, shoving Danny's face into the ground, and I realize that this has gone too far. If they get caught they could get suspended. Or expelled and barred from graduation. And Riley was already on his last strike with the school administration. Not that it was his fault other kids picked fights with him. He was just an easy target.

I take a step forward. Danny is yelling into the pavement. The back of his neck where Riley is pinching his skin is redder than my school sweatshirt. "Riley, we need to go. We need to leave before—"

"King!"

There's an immediate hush among the instigating crowd followed by a quick dispersal as Danny's gang and the few straggling onlookers make a break for it. I turn around in time to see Sergeant Newman placing a hand on his hip near his holster. My face blanches. If Dad finds out I was involved in a fight . . . No, if *Mom* finds out . . .

But Riley is in a daze. He doesn't see anything or anyone else around him. He's in that dark place he sometimes disappears to. The blinding zone where the rest of the world melts away, leaving only him and his rage.

Sergeant Newman grabs Riley by the back of his jacket and pulls him off Danny. Danny scrambles to his feet. His face doesn't look as bad as I thought it would. It's just pebbled with bits of gravel. Maybe he'll have a bruise tomorrow. Maybe he won't.

"It's not what it looks like, Sergeant," I say. I sound pleading even though that's not my intention. It's pathetic. "Danny started it—"

Riley rips himself out of Newman's grip. He's seething. There's something savage in his eyes. Like a boy who's been abandoned in the wilderness his entire life without any human connection. Like an animal caught in a trap. But slowly the Riley I know returns. His face softens. His shoulders relax. And I breathe a quiet sigh of relief.

"You boys capable of settling this amicably or do I have to take you both down to the station?" Newman asks. There's a glimmer in his eye, like he's hoping they'll test his patience and his threat.

"We're good, Sergeant. Just fun and games," Danny says, his hand shaking. "No harm, no foul. Right, King?"

Riley takes a second longer than normal to respond. "Yeah. No harm, no foul."

"Good. Wouldn't want to see you kids miss out on the dance tomorrow night." Newman looks at me directly. "I expect you'll be more responsible in the future, Miss Wicker. Wouldn't want to have to tell your father about this."

"Yes, Sergeant." My voice cracks when I speak. God, I'm so timid. It's fucking embarrassing.

I rush over to Riley to give him a hug, but he shrugs me away. He's embarrassed too. That's the only time he gives me the cold shoulder. When he feels like he's failed in some way. But whether he feels like he failed at letting his temper get the better of him or at not beating Danny to a bloody pulp, I can't tell.

"I'm gonna take a piss and grab a hot dog before we go back to the bleachers. I'll meet you up there in a bit," Riley says. He's already heading off the back way to the toilets before I can reply.

Then I remember the knife.

"Wait! You forgot your—" But when I glance back at the ground, the pocketknife is gone. And Sergeant Newman is confiscating beer bottles from another group of kids at the far end of the smoking area.

Chapter 26

I scribble my thoughts on an old legal pad I found in Dad's desk drawer.

Who could have picked up Riley's pocketknife?
Danny Darnielle
Danny's friends
Newman
Riley

I pause for a moment before I add another name even though I know it's not true.

Me

I cross Danny's friends off the list because I know neither of them was close enough to have grabbed the pocketknife. Then I cross off myself because I know I didn't take it. I would have if someone hadn't beaten me to it, but they did. That leaves Danny, Newman, and Riley. There were other onlookers though. I don't remember who. The fight between Riley and Danny had attracted some attention. I rack my thoughts trying to remember who else could have been there. But did any of those bystanders have motive to plant that knife on Amber to frame Riley for her murder? Who else might have hated Riley that much?

There must have been someone else in the woods that night. Someone not connected to the situation who might have seen something. Someone who might know more about what happened to Amber. Someone who could verify that it wasn't Riley who left the knife at the crime scene. I think about that note in Dad's journal about talking to Nell Abbott. Then I remember the frenzied look in Nell's eye when she saw me at the trailhead. She lives in the woods. Was it possible that she'd witnessed the other figure Riley claims was out in the woods? Or this mysterious D.F. or D.P. that Jessica might have been seeing? I could ask her. But unfortunately, she didn't seem particularly lucid when she accosted me at my car. She didn't even recognize me. She thought I was Amber. So, even if she had seen something, would she be able to remember it now?

I idly tap my pen in thought beside Riley's name, leaving a patch of dotted ink spots. I'm practically in a daze when my phone buzzes in my pocket.

It's a message from Samara asking if I've checked my Instagram. Her gallery is looking to feature new talent and they've posted an open call for artists. I haven't seen it, of course. I haven't seen anything since I turned off my social media. But maybe I need the distraction. I log back into my Instagram, but before I see Samara's post I see a requested message in my spam.

A message from Cameron.

Hey, Lex! Didn't know how to reach you so I looked you up on here. Hope that's OK. It was great seeing you in town again today. Thought maybe we could go out sometime and catch up on old times? What do you say?

I stare at the message for an uncomfortable amount of time before I answer. Why hadn't I considered reaching out to Cameron before this? He might be able to shed some light on the initials carved into the tree. He might have a theory about what happened to Amber. Maybe I didn't think to reach out to him because I still see Cameron as being with Jessica, even though they both moved on a long time ago. It's ridiculous, of course.

I don't know, I write back. *I've got a lot going on. Not sure this is the best time to reminisce on the past.*

That sounds stupid and clichéd. But whatever. I send it anyway. Cameron's reply is lightning fast. *Actually, I was hoping to talk to you about Riley. About what he said to you. That he didn't do it. I might have something that could help you.*

Now he has my attention.

What do you mean? I reply.

I think it's better to tell you in person.

When?

Tomorrow night, 7 p.m.? Lorenzo's Steakhouse in Lancaster?

Shit. I can't afford that. But Cameron reads my mind when he adds another reply. *On me.*

Something about it still feels like a bad idea, but if Cameron knows something that could help me decide what to do about Riley then it would be worth it. And Lancaster is outside of Braxton Falls. Chances are no one we know will be out there. No one to stare at me or whisper or try to snap a picture for their gossip blogs. And Cameron was Riley's best friend. If anyone knew Riley better than me, it was him.

A notification from Samara pops up at the top of my screen asking if I've checked out the gallery submission. I swipe it away and send Cameron a response instead.

See you tomorrow.

Chapter 27

I don't consider myself to be a superstitious person. But the closer I get to Nell Abbott's cabin, the more I feel like someone—no, some*thing*—is watching me.

Everyone knows where Nell lives, but almost no one ventures out that way. It's actually easier to park near the trailhead for the forest and walk than to get there by car. Her land, or at least the land her cabin is on, is nestled up against the state park line. I don't know where the boundary is. I doubt anyone really does and I think Nell has always preferred it that way. It gives her place a semblance of mystery. Like the witch's cottage in Hansel and Gretel. It seems to manifest out of the fog and the shadows of the overhanging conifers. Like it's there one minute and gone the next.

Which is absurd. I know. It doesn't make sense. But that's how it is. It's easier to find Nell's cabin if you aren't really looking for it.

It's also much closer to the glen where Amber's body was found than I ever realized.

I knock on the door. The wind whispers along the back of my neck, causing the hairs to stand on end. There's a deep cramping sensation in my abdomen that makes me want to double over, but

146

I stand my ground. I knock again. No answer. It's late morning. Up above the trees I can see a blue sky trying to peek through the branches. But here on the ground there's an eerie mist creeping through the brush, rolling in from the dark distance where the trees are so close together that the line can't get through.

The urge to run is overwhelming. But I don't move. I feel like someone is peering over my shoulder. I try to turn my head, but I can't. I'm frozen in place for a second. Frozen by my own fear.

I pound harder on the door. It opens.

"Hello?" I peer inside. The spicy scent of cinnamon and wood-stove fills my nostrils. "Is anyone home?"

No answer.

I step inside, realizing that the force of my knocking must have pushed the door off its hinges. It's hanging askew.

"Mrs. Abbott? Are you home? It's Lex Wicker. We ran into each other a few days ago. I was hoping I could talk to you about my sister."

There's no one home.

It's a one-room cabin like the old frontiersmen used to build. The river-stone foundation is probably the only reason it's still standing today. There aren't any modern conveniences inside and it's lit up by a gas lamp set atop a tiny table that couldn't sit more than two people comfortably. A twin bed is pushed back in the corner. Looking at it causes my stomach to twist, like someone screwing a knife into my gut, and I turn away.

On the other side of the cabin is a kitchenette, which mostly consists of a sink, no plumbing, and a travel-sized camping stove. There's a fireplace, too, with a large cauldron hanging above it. The embers are still burning, telling me that someone was here not long ago. I imagine my initial thought is the same as anyone else's would be. *Witch.* But on second glance I realize it's not really a cauldron but a large soup pot. I peek inside. Chicken and wild rice. I assume it's from a can until I see the feathers on the floor near the hearth.

I shouldn't be here. I don't want to be here. But I can't stop thinking about the note in Dad's study. He suspected Nell knew something. Possibly something about that strange marking on Amber's face. And I need to know why. I need to know if she saw something.

I make my way over to an old cedar dresser. It looks like something that should be in an antique store. Claw feet with an ornately carved leaf pattern along the only iron knobs. Atop is a doily runner and a few framed photos of people I don't recognize and a bouquet of dried flowers tied with a yellow ribbon. But that's not what catches my attention. It's the jewelry box. A jewelry box with the Wynwood symbol carved into the lid. The same symbol carved into Amber's chest.

My nerves begin to panic. I remove the box from the dresser and set it on the kitchen table. My hands are unsteady. They're shaking and the taste of bile fills the back of my throat. It makes me wince. I swallow it back down. Then I open the lid.

I shouldn't be disappointed, but I am.

I was expecting a revelation. A clue. A missing piece to the puzzle. But instead I'm met with a box of women's costume jewelry. There are a few obscure pieces mixed in. A smooth quartz stone. A glass eyeball. A hearing aid with some old ear wax crusted on the edges. A pressed maple leaf. But most of the items are cheap, gaudy earrings and necklaces. I rifle through them with my finger. Nothing that reminds me of Amber. Nothing that could prove Riley was innocent. Nothing but—

Blood.

I almost don't see it at first because it's obscured by the darkness of the room. But underneath all of the weird trinkets and cubic zirconia is a ring that doesn't belong. A man's silver ring. I pick it up and hold it close to the lamplight. I've never seen it before. It has an unusual horseshoe shape that's inlaid with small diamonds. And in between those diamonds, specks of red. Blood. I think of the picture of Amber's bruised face. That odd U-shape dotted with pinprick cuts.

This was what the killer was wearing when he hit her.

And I've just touched it with my bare hands.

"Shit," I mutter to myself, quickly glancing around for something I could use to put the ring in without contaminating it any more than I already have. I should know better. This ring could have DNA on it that might point directly to the killer. Or at least provide enough proof to get Riley a stay of execution. And here I am fumbling with it in my palm while I look for a plastic bag in a house I have no business being in.

But despite the frantic worry in my head, my heart swells. This is what I need. This is what I've been looking for. This is what will prove Riley is innocent.

I'm so excited I've forgotten where I am. I don't even notice that I'm not the only one in the house anymore. And when I hear the creak on the floorboards it jolts me out of my elation and drops me into a pit of dread. I jerk my head to the door and find myself eye to eye with a man holding an axe.

"What the hell are you doing here?"

Chapter 28

I instinctively clench my fist, concealing the ring in my hand, and take a large step away from the table. I have that deer-in-the-headlights feeling all over again as the man steps into the flickering light from the lamp, his face becoming clearer. Likewise, he gets a better look at me. His expression pales as though he's seen a ghost.

"Lex Wicker?"

I blink, realization hitting me late. "Danny Darnielle?"

I'm surprised I recognize him. He has a full beard and his hair has gone gray on the sides. The last time I saw him he was throwing fists at Riley beneath the bleachers at the homecoming game. No, maybe I saw him at the dance, too. I can't remember. So much of that night is a blur. Either way, he's not that scrawny kid I saw scrambling in the dirt to avoid getting cut by Riley's blade. He's shorter than I remember, too. Or maybe I just always felt smaller than everyone else regardless of their actual height.

"Could you put down the axe? You're scaring me."

He stares at me. There's a strange mix of uncertainty and disbelief in his eyes. It's as though he's looking at me and seeing someone else. Someone who can't be seen anymore. Amber. He opened the door and thought I was Amber.

His gaze moves from me to the jewelry box and back again. Then he sets the axe on the ground, leaning it up against the doorframe.

"What are you doing here?" he asks again, albeit more politely. But there's a sternness in his eyes that suggests he would physically throw me out if he could. Or maybe that's just the scar on his face throwing me off. I didn't realize Riley had left such an ugly mark after their fight.

Just another thing I apparently missed.

I stutter to get the words out. "I was looking for Nell Abbott."

"Why?"

"I ran into her the other day. She said something peculiar to me and I just wanted to ask her what she meant."

"Nan has dementia. She was probably just ranting. She does that sometimes."

"Nan?"

"Nell Abbott is my grandmother."

My throat tightens. I don't know why this information surprises me. I guess because I'd always assumed, like most people, that Nell didn't have any connections in town. She was more a staple of an environment than an actual person in most people's minds. All those rumors about the woman who lives in the woods by herself. The gossip. The stories of her being a witch, or a descendant of the Wynwood Witch. The last remaining remnant of a coven that haunted the woods. I'm almost ashamed for believing those stupid childhood legends. But something about her had always felt ethereal. As though she'd always been there. And would be there long after the rest of us were gone.

"I had no idea."

Dan shrugs. "Most people don't. She and Dad got into an argument years ago and they never reconciled. I come up here and chop firewood for her. Sometimes bring her groceries. She doesn't like to go into town. Too much gossip."

He gives me a look. "Well, you know."

Yeah, I know. In another thirty years I could be Nell Abbott, hiding out in the woods where no one could find me. Only I wouldn't have a grandson to look after me.

"I should probably go," I say, moving toward the door.

He steps in front of it, blocking my path. "What did she say to you?"

I stop myself from walking into him. He smells smoky. Like birch fire and bourbon. "She said something about my sister. It's nothing. Like you said, she was probably just ranting."

I try to walk around him, but he puts his foot in front of the door. There's no way past him. Not without making a scene.

"What did she say about her?"

"I'm not even sure really. I was in a rush. I just remember her saying something about not telling my sister anything." That's not a lie. Not entirely. I remember exactly what Nell said to me. But I also don't feel like explaining that to Dan. I don't know him. Don't know what kind of man he is. And Riley told me not to trust anyone.

I try to cover my nerves with a laugh. "She probably just heard some people talking about Amber in town. Maybe read her name in the newspaper."

Dan fixes me with a stern stare. Then he turns his attention to the jewelry box. I slip my hand in my jacket pocket, discarding the ring there. Did he notice I was looking through her things?

"She does tend to get more confused when she's in one of her nostalgic moods." He closes up the jewelry box and puts it back on the dresser.

"Are those family heirlooms?"

"Maybe. Most of this box is just junk she's found on her hikes. She's been collecting other people's trash for years. I come in once a year and clean out the worthless items. Plastic candy machine jewelry and sometimes actual trash. She keeps bags of garbage she picks up on her hikes out back. I leave the nicer pieces. She never notices."

"That must be hard." I clear my throat with a cough. "To lose someone so slowly like that."

"We're not that close."

"Right." I look to the door. "I should really be going."

"Did you take anything?"

The question takes me off guard and I'm almost certain my expression has given me away. I can feel the ring practically burning through my pocket. Did he see me take it? I don't even know how long he was standing there before I noticed him. He must have seen.

My gaze flickers to the axe.

"No. Of course not," I lie. It doesn't sound convincing.

His stoic stare breaks into a crooked smile. Then he steps to the side, leaving access to the door. "Just messing with you. Should I tell Nan you stopped by?"

I shake my head. "No. That's OK. I wouldn't want to confuse her."

I brush past Dan and tug open the door. It swings limply on its broken hinge. A cold rush of air from outside pricks my face like tiny needles.

"You can tell him to rot in hell, by the way."

I hesitate halfway through the door, glancing back at Dan. The yellow light from the lamp shudders against the cool air. Sharp dagger shadows cut up his face like a cubist painting, accentuating the thick scar tissue around his left eye.

It's pasty gray and gnarled. Like Nell's dead eye.

"What?"

"Riley King. If he makes it to his execution, tell him I hope he rots in hell."

"What do you mean if he makes it?"

A slow smirk creeps over his lips. The shadows dance over it, creating a jagged jack-o'-lantern-esque form over his mouth. Dan's gaze breaks from mine and looks to the hearth where those last embers from the fire spark their final red-gold breaths.

153

"They say karma is a bitch. Like the legend surrounding these woods, it haunts a person. I wouldn't be surprised if it decided to take those last few days away from him out of spite."

"Karma is just another word for luck. It's an idea. It's not real. It's nothing more than what a person believes it to be. Ergo, it's not a bitch," I say in a rare form of confidence that doesn't feel like me.

"Maybe you're right," Dan says. "But your sister was a bitch. And karma got her just the same."

Chapter 29

Wednesday, September 26, 2007
3:27 p.m.

"Where are we going? The mall is on the other side of town."

Jessica slows down to stop at the red light and throws on her turn signal. "I have to make a quick stop in Lancaster first."

"Lancaster? That's like twenty minutes out of the way. What's in Lancaster that you can't get in Braxton Falls?"

"My birth control."

"I thought you used the CVS on State Road?"

Jessica shakes her head. The light turns green and she turns off onto the state highway that skirts along the Wynwood Forest. "My parents know the pharmacist in town. And they would go crazy if they found out I was on the pill. Like they would literally ground me until I'm eighty. Besides, it's cheaper to get it at Planned Parenthood."

"We're driving to the *Planned Parenthood*?"

The shock in my voice must sound comical because Jessica laughs. "Don't be such a prude. It's just a health clinic."

"It's not just a health clinic, Jess. It's Planned Parenthood. Those places have picket lines and stuff."

"Not out here they don't. That's big-city stuff. People out here have lives. They don't have time to protest outside small-town clinics. Besides, it's Wednesday. And it's still working hours for most people. There won't be anyone there. Trust me, I do this every month."

Jessica turns up the volume on the radio. Maroon 5's "Wake Up Call" blasts through the speakers. The beat would sound tinny in my old car, but Jessica's parents bought her an upgraded audio system for her new Jeep Wrangler. She's had it for a month and it still has that new car smell. I try not to be jealous, but I am.

I look out the window, watching as the forest eventually recedes to make way for Lancaster's city limits. Jessica spends the next fifteen minutes telling me about the fight her parents got into last weekend because of her mom's overspending. I mumble the occasional reply to let her know I'm listening, but I'm not really. I'm thinking about how much trouble I'll be in if someone finds out I went to Planned Parenthood. Jessica likes to joke about her parents being hard on her, but my parents actually would be. Mom, in particular. She'd kill me if she knew I was going to one of these places. Because she wouldn't understand. She'd jump to conclusions. Bad conclusions. Wrong conclusions.

The Planned Parenthood is in a small plaza off the highway next to a Domino's Pizza and an H&R Block. Jessica pulls the car into the parking lot and I slink down in the seat until I can barely be seen through the window. Not that anyone would see me. Jessica is right. There's nobody there. There aren't any protesters or picketers like I've heard about on the news. No Bible-thumping persecutors yelling at sobbing women. No one throwing rocks or tomatoes. There are a few cars in the parking lot, but from what I can see hunched in the passenger seat, they're empty.

"What are you doing?"

"I'm just going to wait out here."

"Oh my God. Are you serious? Come on, Lexie. It's no big deal. No one is going to recognize you. Trust me. People mind their own business here. But they can be really slow sometimes. I might be waiting for fifteen minutes or more." Jessica bats her lashes at me. "Please, come with me. We can talk about which shops we're going to afterwards. I was also thinking we should get our nails done later. And I want to pick up some hair products from Sally's Beauty."

I really don't want to get out of the car. It's not that I'm embarrassed. I know Planned Parenthood does more than provide abortions. I'm not an idiot. I know they're a lifesaving organization for thousands of women around the country. I know it's a place where women can receive various forms of medical care. But I'm still petrified. I just don't know that I'd have the confidence to stand up to my mom if she berated me about it. And I don't know if I'd be able to keep Jessica's secret if my mom accused me of being there for any other reason.

Jessica is giving me a look. She's annoyed. I don't blame her. I'm being dumb.

I unhook my seat belt. "Fine."

Jessica is right. They're pretty slow in the clinic because there aren't that many people working. We sit in the lobby across from a pregnant woman who never takes her eyes off the magazine she's reading until she's called into the back. Almost twenty minutes pass before the young woman behind the counter is able to finish putting together a prescription package for Jessica. I pick up a flier on how to reduce menstrual cramping while they exchange pleasantries.

"You ready?" Jessica asks as she stuffs that prescription bag into her purse.

"Yeah." I fold the flier in half and shove it in my pocket.

"See? You survived. And nobody threw rotten fruit at you or anything," she teases.

My cheeks flush with embarrassment. "I didn't think anyone was going to throw something at me."

"Yes, you did. You thought someone was going to shove a cross in your face and say you're going to hell because you want to have sex."

I give Jessica a playful shove in the arm. "That's not true. I've just never been to one of these places before. And you know how other people are."

I follow Jessica outside. The air is thick and a little too warm for late September, but the leaves on the trees have already started turning. Ohio weather is unpredictable. We could be wearing T-shirts today and snow coats tomorrow. But right now the sun is peeking out through the clouds and I wish we'd made plans to meet Riley and Cameron at the park instead of going to the mall. It seems like such a waste to spend a day like this indoors.

I walk around to the passenger side of the Jeep, but it's still locked. Jessica is fumbling in her purse for the key fob.

That's when I see Danny Darnielle walk out of the Domino's with a large pizza box and a two-liter bottle of Coca-Cola. Our eyes lock. He does a double take. Then he looks away from me to the sign above the Planned Parenthood and back to me again. I'm trying to read his expression, but it's blank. And I'm frozen in place. Then the Jeep beeps and I throw the door open, jumping inside as though that'll suddenly make me invisible.

Chapter 30

4 DAYS BEFORE THE EXECUTION

"What do you mean you lied to me?"

Cameron avoids looking me in the eyes long enough for the waiter to walk over and interrupt the answer to my question.

"What's your house red?" Cameron asks.

"It's a Malbec. From Argentina," the waiter replies.

"I'll have a glass of that." Cameron finally looks at me. "Or should we get a bottle?"

"Just a Diet Coke for me," I say. It's not that I don't drink. I do. But ever since I saw my mom in that last rage, breath stinking of liquor, the house a minefield of broken glass and porcelain, I can't stomach the idea of having a drink. I'm pretty sure I'd vomit all over the white tablecloth if I did.

"One glass then," Cameron says. "And a Diet Coke."

"Are you ready to order?" The waiter looks at me, but I'm staring at the menu. Not reading it. Just staring at it. Trying to process what Cameron said to me. That he lied about the reason he wanted to meet.

"I think we need a few minutes." Cameron and his air of authority. I can't remember if he was like that when we were kids or if that was something he gained after he left Braxton Falls. I wonder if I would wear that kind of confidence if I'd managed to get out.

But I didn't. So, I don't.

Once the waiter is out of earshot I turn my focus back on Cameron. "What did you lie about?"

"I don't have anything to show you. I don't have something from the past that might help you understand what happened between Riley and your sister. I only said that to get you to meet up with me. Not that I don't want to help. I do. But I don't know anything that can help. Nothing more than what I already believe. That Riley couldn't have killed your sister." He runs his fingers back through his hair and gives an awkward laugh.

I'm angry. I'm furious that he lied to me. But then I look beyond the fancy suit and tie and see the high school quarterback who used to be my friend. I see the boy who would take us all to the drive-in theater because he had the biggest car. The boy who would sign yearbooks like he was autographing an actor's portrait and add his jersey number as a reminder of how 'cool' he was—as if anyone could forget. I see the friend who stood beside me at Amber's funeral and didn't say a word. Not because he couldn't. Not because he wouldn't. But because he was trying to stay strong for me. For Jessica. For Amber. If this face was a lie then I believed it.

Just like I believed Riley.

I'm so fucking pathetic.

The sound of his voice interrupts my thoughts. "When I saw you at the station the other day, I felt guilty."

"Guilty?"

"About not keeping in touch. I know you and I weren't as close as we could have been, but you were one of my best friends, Lex. And I abandoned you when you needed me the most. We all did."

I shrug. "I didn't expect anything of you."

"I know. But I expected more of myself. It was your sister

160

who died and I took it personally. Like it was a weight I had to carry. With no thought as to how it must have felt to be you. And then to not be there for the aftermath? For the way everyone treated you during senior year? That wasn't right. I was a shit friend and I'm sorry."

Cameron's words are perfect. Of course they are. He's a politician. He knows how to read an audience. But something he said doesn't make sense to me. Why would he take Amber's death personally? Why would he imagine that he was more heartbroken about it than I am? I think back to what Riley said to me. At the time, I thought he was taunting me. But now I'm not so sure. Did I really know Amber as well as I thought I did?

Did I really know anyone?

I try to glean an answer from Cameron's expression, but he's looking down at the menu, avoiding eye contact again. Could there have been something between him and Amber? Was that the missing piece of the puzzle? And if so, why would she keep that from me?

More importantly, why would he?

"I might have found something. Some proof that somebody else was out in the woods the night of Amber's murder." I think about the horseshoe-shaped ring with the blood on it. That's all I have. I don't know if it's enough to clear Riley's name, but it might be enough for an appeal. The only problem is that I touched it. And I don't have any proof that I found it in Nell's cabin. If I take it to Newman alone, without anything else to back up my story or any other evidence to indicate another person's involvement, he might not believe me. Or he might think it's enough to prosecute me. Probably not for accessory to murder, but maybe unlawful entry. He still has a grudge against me, after all. And after reading the interrogation about Riley's knife, I don't know if I can trust him.

"What did you find?" Cameron asks, his interest suddenly piqued.

I slip my hand into my pocket, about to remove the ring, when an approaching face stops me.

Jessica.

"Shit," I mutter.

"What?" Cameron looks up, but Jessica is already placing a hand on his shoulder before he can turn around.

"A class reunion? And I didn't get an invitation? That's a bit rude, isn't it?" There's a playful smile on Jessica's face that makes it impossible to tell whether she's joking or trying to press a barb into an open wound. But I see Cameron's posture tense under the grip of her nails. Then she lets go and helps herself to the empty chair at our table.

She's stunning. But she always has been.

She's wearing a low-cut cocktail dress with a pair of slinky heels that I would break an ankle in. Her neck is bare, exposing her sharp collarbones. She has one of those physiques that most women would envy. Full-figured but fit. Just as gorgeous and effervescent as she was in high school. Maybe even more so because, like Cameron, she carries that confidence of someone who got out of Braxton Falls and made something of themselves. Someone who came back by choice, not necessity.

Jessica is the epitome of small-town perfection.

And she's a few drinks beyond tipsy.

"Just look at the two of you sitting here all cozy. I was over by the bar and I thought I was seeing things. I said to myself, 'There's no way that's Cameron Ellis and Lex Wicker having dinner together!' So, imagine my surprise when it *was* you." Jessica leans a little too far toward Cameron and nearly falls out of her chair. Cameron catches her by the arm and she giggles as though she did it on purpose.

I never understood why she and Cameron didn't make it work. They were supposed to be the eternal couple. They were even voted Couple Most Likely to Get Married by our high school class. I think the entire town had delusions of one day seeing them together on the steps of Air Force One. And if I hadn't seen the stumble in her walk or smelled that sweet odor of liquor on her breath, I might have been tempted to believe that could still happen one day. Even now, side by side, they look picture-perfect together.

And then there's me in my comfortable black slacks and a button-up from the GAP from five seasons ago. With my short hair and my barely there makeup. A faded image of the young woman I used to be. Or could have been.

God. How were we ever friends?

"It's good to see you, Jess," Cameron says, any sign of tension swept from his face. He's smiling at her with that politician smile. The kind that doesn't quite reach the eyes, but still exudes warmth and trust. He leans sideways and places a kiss on her cheek. Polite. Not at all sensual.

Jessica throws back her head and laughs like it's a joke. Like it's a game they're playing. Maybe it is. Maybe I just don't know the rules.

"Hi, Jess," I say.

Jessica reaches out and takes my hand. It feels fake. Like she's coddling me. But I let her. What else can I do?

"God, Lex, it's been so *long*. I feel like I haven't seen you in forever!"

She saw me last week.

"Yeah, it does seem like that sometimes," I lie. It doesn't feel like that at all.

"So, what brings you two together? I didn't realize you were still friends." The way she says 'friends' makes it sound like a crime. And I can't blame her. It probably looks that way. Or, at least, it would to anyone who knew us. But that might explain why Cameron chose a restaurant in Lancaster instead of Braxton Falls. Where nobody was supposed to know us.

Correction: where no one was supposed to know me.

Cameron is quick to respond and for that I'm grateful. Maybe it's just me, but I can't really figure out Jessica's behavior. I can't tell if she's trying to be degrading or if she's honestly oblivious. Maybe a little of both.

"We ran into each other earlier in the week," Cameron says. The waiter comes around with our drinks and gives Jessica a questioning glance.

"Oh, no, thank you. I have someone waiting for me at the bar." I glance to the bar. Maybe I'm imagining things, but no one appears to be missing her.

"And you two thought it would be nice to catch up? That's so sweet." But there's a darkness in Jessica's eyes when she looks at Cameron that says otherwise. Something has happened between them. Something I can't help but feel like they're both trying to keep from me.

But that's not what I want to know. What I wanted was the information Cameron had about Amber. About Riley. But that was nothing but a ruse. For what? To have dinner with me?

Or to have this awkward tête-à-tête with my former best friend?

For fuck's sake, am I really that bitter to think this is a setup? Maybe it wasn't Amber's death that tore us all apart. Maybe it was me.

Jessica picks up Cameron's wine glass by the stem and brings it to her nose, taking a deep inhalation. Her breath leaves a foggy mark on the brim. *That* was meant to be sensual.

"You look good, Jess," I finally say. My timing is off. It sounds forced. It is forced, but that doesn't mean it's not true.

"You think so? I've been trying that new fad diet. The one where you only eat natural seasonal foods like they used to in prehistoric times. You know, like red meats, local fruits, and root vegetables."

"And red wine?" Cameron smirks.

"Grapes grow on vines," Jess replies without missing a beat.

"Not in late October," Cameron says just as quickly.

My mouth cracks into a small smile. I can't help it. For a split second I imagined we were teenagers again, poking fun at each other and living without fear of tomorrow.

"You don't need to diet," I say, not bothering to hide my obvious jealousy. "You look like a supermodel."

"Thanks, Lexie. But you're the one with the supermodel haircut. It's so bold of you to wear it that short! Very edgy. First time I saw it I barely even recognized you. But you have one of those round faces. You know, petite. You have to have a small face to be able to pull off a pixie cut without looking like a dyke."

"Jesus, Jess." Cameron glances around as though fearful that someone might be listening. "You can't talk like that."

"What? It's not like everyone else doesn't already think the same thing."

"People *don't* think the same thing," Cameron argues. "That's how we end up with political correctness."

Jessica shrugs. "Lex knows what I mean. Don't you, Lex?"

I do, but I don't agree with it. Nor do I believe she's that oblivious. She's trying to rile me, but I don't know why. And if I weren't so timid I would tell her exactly what I was thinking. That she's a bitchy snob. But I am timid. So, I don't.

Cameron shoots me a disappointed glance that I pretend not to notice.

Then something in me stirs. I remember what Riley said about not trusting anyone. I remember those carvings in the tree. And even though the thought of confronting Jessica makes me sick to my stomach, I do it anyway.

"It's funny you should be here," I say. "We were just talking about people from high school. Remind me again who else were you dating back then? Besides Cameron, that is."

They both look at me like I just confessed to murder.

"I beg your pardon?" Jess glares.

"I was cleaning up at my mom's house. Going through old yearbooks and stuff. It got me thinking about all of us back then. About high school and who all of our friends were. And I was trying to remember the names of some of the other guys you were with."

Jessica scoffs. "I don't know. None of them mattered. They were just flings."

Cameron's lips purse.

"Did any of their names start with a D?"

"I don't think so. I don't know. Why?"

"No reason, really. I was just trying to remember if there was anyone else you were hanging out with before homecoming."

Cameron's gaze darts to Jessica, but she holds her stare firmly on me. The muscle in her upper arm tenses. She's clenching her fist under the table. Then she breaks her glare with a laugh. "Oh my God. Is this some kind of joke? Am I on camera or something? Don't tell me you two are putting together a gag reel for our next school reunion!"

Cameron looks like he's sweating.

I smile. Two can play the oblivious game. "No, I'm just being nostalgic. You know how it is. This time of year always gets to me. I was hanging up some of the homecoming dance posters at school and couldn't help myself from reminiscing."

"God, is it homecoming season already?" Cameron takes a large gulp of wine.

"Don't you pay attention to the football team anymore?" I ask.

"Not really. They've sucked since '09."

"Anyway." Jessica takes out a compact mirror from her clutch to check her makeup. She scratches off a small fleck of mascara that had smeared around the corner of her eyelid. Then she puts the compact away. When she looks at me it's with a seriousness she didn't have in her face earlier. It makes me wonder if she was ever drunk to begin with. "I just wanted to come over and tell you again that my thoughts are with you."

"What?" I blink, confused by the sudden turn in the conversation.

"About Riley. You must be feeling so . . ." She hesitates. She's searching my face for an answer. Like she can't guess how I might be reacting to the news of Riley's impending execution. Like she doesn't know whose side I'm on. His or Amber's. "So confused."

That's one way to put it.

"Something like that."

"Well, like I said before, if there's anything I can do for you. If there's any way I can help. Just give me a call."

It would have been a sweet gesture if she'd offered me her phone number. But she doesn't, which only reinforces why Jessica is my ex–best friend.

"Thanks. I will," I lie.

There's a pause and for a moment it seems as though Jess might tell me something else. There's an odd apologetic gleam in her eyes that I assume to be pity. Then she turns her attention to Cameron and the sorrowful look is gone, replaced by that fake smile she wears so well. "Don't be a stranger, Cam."

"Don't forget to vote, Jess."

She laughs, throwing her hair back over her shoulders like she's in a shampoo commercial. Then she stands up, waggles her fingers in a provocative wave, and disappears back to the bar.

"What the fuck was that?" Cameron asks.

I sip my Diet Coke, almost wishing it were a glass of wine. Or better yet, a vodka. "I went up to the place where they found Amber."

"You did *what*? Why?"

"I don't know. I've just been so confused about everything. And I saw some initials carved into the tree. I got it into my head that Jess had written them. That she might know more than she's letting on. And I thought—" I cut myself off. "Honestly, I don't know what I thought. Jess was just acting weird and maybe it set it me off a bit."

"You know how Jess is." Cameron reopens the menu.

"Actually, I don't." I sigh. "She came over to my mom's house the other day. The day they announced Riley's execution. That was the first time she's spoken to me since Amber's funeral."

"Are you serious? But you guys were always so close. Granted, people grow apart, but I always assumed you two had stayed in touch. At least for a little while."

By this point, I'm exhausted and frustrated. "No one stayed in touch with me, Cameron. No one. Amber died and everything fell apart. And not just with you guys. My dad never recovered. My mom can barely look at me. I turned down my art school acceptance. I work as a janitor at our old shitty high school, for fuck's sake. And now there's less than a week to go before Riley is executed and I've seriously been questioning whether or not he did it. I mean, I never entirely believed he did it: the whole thing felt wrong to me from the beginning, but I was so scared and everyone else was so convinced of his guilt. Eventually I accepted that I misjudged him. But I've been going through the old police files and searching the woods for any evidence they might have missed. I know it's crazy, but I'm really starting to believe Riley is innocent. *Really* innocent. Like someone framed him for Amber's murder."

Cameron's face blanches. "What?"

I shake my head. "I know it's totally insane."

"And then I went and got your hopes up by saying—" Cameron reaches forward and places a hand on mine. My instinct is to tug it away, but I don't. Not everyone is out to hurt me. I have to learn to give people the chance. Not everyone is Riley. Cameron gives my hand a gentle squeeze. "I'm sorry I lied to you. I shouldn't have done that. It was shit. I should have just been honest."

"Honest about what?"

He smiles. It's a nice smile. A really nice smile. But Riley had a really nice smile too. And the longer I look at Cameron, the more I think I see someone else. "About how good it was to see you after all this time. You know, one of my biggest regrets is not getting to know you better."

"You knew me."

"No. I mean *really* know you."

"You were with Jess."

"But Jess and I were never meant to be. I think that's obvious.

168

It sounds cruel, but you can't have a deep relationship with Jess. At least, I never could. That's something I always envied about you and Riley. You guys could actually talk with each other."

"And look how that turned out."

Cameron squeezes my hand. "I'm sorry I didn't notice you more then, Lex. But I'm noticing you now."

My entire body tenses. This is not where I saw this evening going and I suddenly become uncomfortably aware of how public this conversation is. And how it must look to have his hand on mine from across the table. It's also confusing. Like I've entered some parallel dimension where everyone else knows how the world works except me.

"I'm not sure if that's a good idea. To be fair, I haven't really been with anyone seriously since Riley and—" I think of Samara and her offer for me to visit her as soon as this is all over "—I'm kind of talking to someone."

"That's OK," he says. "I just wanted you to know."

I slowly pull my hand away from his and place it in my lap. I've lost my appetite. My stomach is in knots. If this had been any other week, I might have felt differently. Might have even been overjoyed. At the very least, flattered. But all I can see is the pained expression on Riley's face when he told me he didn't do it and Amber's body in those photographs. And all I can think about is what I did. The secret I buried in those woods fifteen years ago. And how I have to figure out what really happened that night.

My palms are itchy and I'm half about to burst out of my chair and run all the way home when the waiter returns.

"Have you decided?"

"Yes," Cameron says. His tone is back to normal. Politely upbeat, but not overbearingly so. "I'll have the salmon. With the sauce on the side, please."

"Very well. And you, ma'am?"

There's a thickness in my throat that I have to swallow down in order to talk. I can't concentrate. I look at the menu, but all of the words have blurred together. Anxiety brain is fucking with me again.

"I'll have the same," I say, realizing after the fact that I wasn't listening to Cameron and have no idea what I ordered.

Chapter 31

Friday, August 17, 2007
10:07 p.m.

I lean closer to the bathroom mirror as I apply my glossy lip balm. It's strawberry flavored. I don't like the taste: it's too artificial. But it's not mine. It's Jessica's. She gave it to me last week and said the sheen would look good on me. She's right.

I pucker my lips and then smack them together like you do when you're applying lipstick. The result is a tacky, sticky sensation on my lips and I realize that's going to be really uncomfortable when Riley kisses me. I grab a piece of toilet paper and rub it off gently, careful not to press too hard so my lips don't turn red. It's not enough. There's still a viscous residue on my mouth. I run the faucet and cup my hand under the water. Then I use it to wipe off the rest. It works, but now I can see that it's removed some of my foundation as well.

I'm so bad at this.

I take a deep breath and try to settle the jittery nerves in my stomach. He's not going to care. He's not even going to notice. Nevertheless I can't help but feel embarrassed. I mean, there's no guarantee that anything is going to happen. I have no expectations.

171

But I'm still wearing my new bra from Victoria's Secret. It's a push-up. Now that I think about it, I feel ridiculous in it. It's not me at all. Another Jessica suggestion.

"Trust me!" she said at the mall. "You'll look so hot in this. And if he slips his hand under your shirt the first thing he's going to feel is the silky cup and the lace. Girl, he will be all over you."

My cheeks flush red just thinking about it. Then I adjust my shirt. It's a scoop-neck, not particularly low cut. But after refiguring the adjusters on the bra straps and tugging the shirt down on my shoulders, it definitely gives another impression. Jessica is right. I do look hot. Or, at least, I feel hot. A surge of unfamiliar confidence moves through me, stimulating the butterflies in my stomach. I feel like another person entirely. But that's a good thing, right? That means I'm ready for this.

Assuming *this* actually happens. Which, granted, no guarantees. Riley might not actually be interested in that. He might not want that. It's not like we've talked about it or anything. But there was something different in the air between us when I invited him over.

"My parents won't be home. They're going down to Columbus to visit my aunt and uncle. And Amber is staying over at a friend's house," I told Riley at lunch.

"Cool," he said. Not in an uninterested way. There was a look in his eye that suggested he desperately wanted to come over. But sometimes I'm not sure that I read people properly. When I told Jess about it, however, she was adamant that he was going to expect *it*.

OK, Lex. Pull yourself together. He's already out there sitting on the couch, waiting for you. Just walk out there like there's nothing to be nervous about and ask him what movie he wants to watch. Offer to make popcorn. And then let the rest happen on its own.

I can almost imagine Jess's wink. She made such a big deal about it. I don't know why. She lost her virginity two years ago. At least, that's what she told me. Sometimes, though, I wonder if she isn't making things up in order to make herself look cooler. I'm a horrible friend to think that.

I wash my hands and then step out of the bathroom. It's late and the hallway is dark, but there's a dim light coming from the living room where the television is on. When I make my way to the couch, however, I realize that the room is empty. Riley isn't there.

That's when I hear it. A soft moaning sound coming from the kitchen. My heart races. I don't know why but my thoughts immediately go to burglar. Although why a burglar would be making those kinds of noises, I don't know.

I think about grabbing something to defend myself, but there's nothing around except for a lamp and I'm not going to walk into the kitchen wielding a lamp for my protection. Instead I tiptoe through to the kitchen, keeping close to the walls and within the shadows.

The lights are out in the kitchen, but that doesn't prevent me from seeing two figures pressed up against the kitchen island. The first is obvious. It's Riley. I'd recognize his outline anywhere. Even in the pitch-black dark. My eyes slowly adjust to the other person. To the one he's kissing. No, not kissing. The one he's practically choking with his tongue.

I reach across the wall and flip on the light switch. Then my worst nightmare comes into focus.

"Amber?"

Riley pulls away from my sister. He looks confused. Shocked, even. But I can barely look at him. I'm too busy staring at my sister. Her skirt is hiked up so high I can see the birthmark at the top of her thigh. Her shirt is unbuttoned to the center of her breasts. Riley jumps away from her, practically impaling himself on the corner of the kitchen countertop.

Amber looks over at me and laughs. Then she tosses her hair playfully over her shoulder, feigning an innocent expression. "Oops."

"What are you doing here? What the hell is going on?" My heart sinks into my stomach like a stone. My arms are shaking and a chill travels down my legs. I want to throw up and cry at the same time.

"I didn't know!" Riley says.

"What do you mean you didn't know?!" I yell at him.

"I thought it was you!"

"You thought it was me? Are you blind?"

"It was dark!"

Meanwhile Amber is laughing like it's all some kind of joke. But it's not a joke to me. Riley is my boyfriend. My first boyfriend. And she was practically swallowing his tongue not ten feet away from where we were going to—

Now I really do feel like I'm going to be sick.

I race over to the trash can and dry-heave into it. Nothing comes out because I haven't eaten anything all day. I was too nervous about tonight. Too excited.

"Oh, come on, Lex. It was just a joke," Amber says.

I shoot her a hard stare. "That's not a joke, Amber! That's not funny!"

"Honestly, Lexie. I thought it was you." Riley is panicked. And even though the entire situation is absurd, I believe him. I believe that blanched expression of fear and those big dark pleading eyes.

"He really did," Amber says, licking her lower lip before reaching across the island for an apple. "He was muttering your name the entire time. You must have missed that part."

"I hate you!" I yell. Raising my voice seems to be the only thing keeping me from falling over. "You're not even supposed to be here!"

Amber rolls her eyes. "It was just a spur-of-the-moment prank. I was on my way out. I only came in here to get something to eat and he just assumed I was you."

She bites into the apple. The crunch echoes through the kitchen. "Damn good kisser, though. I can see why you keep him. Even if he smells like Saltside."

"Bitch." Riley glares at her.

"Get out of here, Amber!"

"Fine, fine. You two are no fun anyway." She tosses Riley a knowing smirk. "Not anymore at least."

She grabs a can of soda from the fridge and then wanders off to her room. It isn't until I hear her door slam shut that I turn my attention on Riley.

"What the *fuck*, Riley!"

He holds his hands up defensively, as though he's afraid I'm going to hit him. As if I'd be able to do any damage if I did. He's got at least seven inches on me and despite his lithe appearance, he's strong. "I swear to you, Lexie. I had no idea. I honestly thought it was you."

"How could you think it was me? When have I ever acted like that?"

"Well, you invited me over here! You told me no one else was going to be home. I thought that meant you wanted to—" He doesn't finish the sentence, but he doesn't need to. Because he's right. I did want to.

I huff and storm out of the kitchen and into the living room. I slump down on the couch and tug one of the throw pillows into my lap and stare at the screen. The sound is muted. Nothing but images zipping across the screen. I'm watching it, but I don't actually see it. All I can see is red.

Riley sits down on the couch next to me, but I scoot away. I wipe off my eyes on my shirt sleeve, smearing my mascara. Great, now I'm not only crying but I probably look like shit. All of that hard work trying to get those perfect lashes he never would have seen in the dark anyway, and now there's a stain of black around my eyes.

"I'm such an idiot. Of course, you'd be into her. Everyone likes Amber more than me."

"I don't like her more than you," Riley insists.

He grabs me by the shoulder and turns me toward him. I refuse to look in his direction. He licks his thumb and wipes it under

175

my eye, gently trying to clean up the mascara stain. In any other circumstance I might think this was romantic. But right now, it just makes me feel like a child. Like he's pitying me.

"You've never kissed me like that."

"You've never let me kiss you like that."

"You probably won't now."

Riley lets go of my face and takes my hand. I can feel his eyes on me and I finally look up. His face is half shadowed by the dark, the other half lit up by the flashing television screen. I should hate him for kissing Amber, but I don't. Honestly, I'm not even really mad. Not at him. I believe him. It's Amber I'm mad at. If I hadn't been so shocked when I saw them I might have done something horrible. Something I would have regretted. But looking into Riley's eyes I know he's telling the truth.

He really thought it was me.

"I will if you let me," he says. Is it just me or is his voice huskier in the dark? "I want all of it with you. Everything."

My heart is pounding. "Even after kissing her?"

"She's not you, Lexie. You're the one I love. You're the one who sees me. Nobody else does."

That's when I know I'm going to give it to him. When I realize that Riley King could tell me to do anything and I would do it.

And I do.

Chapter 32

My apartment is cold and empty when I get home from the restaurant. I turn up the heat and check on the thermostat in Spaghetti's tank to ensure it hasn't dropped too low for her. I thought I'd feel better after talking to Cameron. I thought I'd feel relieved or find myself one step closer to understanding what happened all those years ago. But, in all honesty, I'm just more confused. Even worse, I feel like someone isn't telling the truth. Like someone is putting on a performance. I just don't know who.

So, I do what anyone raised on weekly episodes of *Catfish* would do in order to solve a mystery. I go to the internet, starting with Amber's Facebook. And then I regret it almost immediately.

We miss you!!

Forever in our hearts! ♥ ♥ ♥

RIP Beautiful Girl

I'll always remember the good times we had together

luv u babe!

Before I realize it, I've been scrolling the old comments on Amber's Facebook memorial page for over an hour. I don't know what I expect to find, but it's not there. There are a few recent comments. Most are from some of the women who were on the cheer squad with her in high school, talking about how they'll be at the memorial service. Others link to some articles about Riley. But the majority of the posts are from the year after she died. Hundreds of them. I don't recognize a lot of the people because even though we were born in the same year, Amber was a year behind me at school.

No one has written anything mean or malicious like those earlier forums I found. Everything is positive and sentimental, full of overbearing sympathy. Exactly what you would expect from the wall of a dead teenager. But I can't help but feel like it's all an act. Did any of these people really care about Amber? Did they really know her? Or were they just sucked into the shared mentality of a grieving town? How many of these comments are authentic and how many are merely people playing a role in order to fit in?

Maybe I'm just envious because I know that if I died there wouldn't be anywhere near this many comments on my social media accounts. If I were lucky I might get half a dozen. But in all likelihood no one would even notice I was gone. Because I'm not Amber. I'm not a—how did that person put it? I scroll back to one of the old comments.

A shining light taken from the world too soon.

Fuck these strangers. If they actually cared about Amber they would have done more to find out what really happened to her. Because after the last few days I'm certain that there's more to the story than I've been told.

The initials in the tree, Riley's missing pocketknife, the ring, Danny's veiled threat, Newman's unwavering conviction despite the contradictory evidence, Dad's suspicion that there was also something else going on. I don't know how it all fits together, but I'm going to figure it out.

But 2007 was a different time. The internet was a different place. We were a generation that knew how to hide things. If there was anything to find, it wouldn't be on Facebook. That's where everyone presented their better selves. That's not where we posted our secrets.

I pull up a new browser and type in the address for a website I haven't used in years. FriendSpace. FriendSpace was a lesser-known mash-up of more popular websites like MySpace and LiveJournal. It had the diary-styled layout of LiveJournal, but contained the private message features of MySpace. Some people used it as their own private online journal while others used it as a space to connect with people who shared similar interests that weren't music-based like MySpace was built around. And unlike the early version of some other social media platforms like Facebook, the accounts didn't require a school email address to join, which meant that it was the perfect place for anonymity. It was also local.

It was originally set up by a Braxton Falls High School student in one of the computer classes as a way to connect with friends in your classes. Of course, as with most things with teenagers, it quickly spiraled into something else. A place to make new friends and share photos with classmates, yes. But it also became a place to vent. To antagonize. To gossip. Which is what made it both comforting and disastrous.

I'm surprised to see the website is still up. I type in my old username and password as if it were yesterday. Yes, I know you're supposed to change your passwords over the years, but let's be honest—no one really does. And I've never forgotten the one I had for my account. My current passwords are variations of that original one, after all. Back before you needed to add random numbers, symbols, or capital letters in order to protect your information.

The website is slow, but it eventually pops up and immediately thrusts me back into another time and place.

Nothing on my homepage has changed. The last entry I made was the summer before Amber died. It shows a picture of Jessica and me at the local outdoor pool. The same pool where I got to know Riley better. We look so young and perfect; I can hardly believe it's me. My hair is long and flowing, halfway down to my waist. There's a radiance in my expression I haven't seen in years. That's a girl with confidence. A girl with a future. A girl who has no idea that her entire life is about to unravel.

I click on my friends page and locate Amber's old journal. She has more public posts than I do. Where most of mine are literal journal entries complaining about nonsensical things like homework assignments I don't want to do or art projects I'm working on for local shows, Amber's page is more photo-oriented. There are multiple pictures of her from the first day of school in front of her locker with the cheerleaders and at the lunch table with another group of friends. She even has some pictures with our group; with me, Jessica, Cameron, and Riley. Although most of those are outside school. Having a barbecue in Cameron's backyard, in the parking lot of the movie theater in front of the poster for the first *Transformers* movie, dancing at a sleepover at Jessica's house.

If I've seen these photos I must have blocked them from my memory because it feels like I'm looking at a time capsule of someone else's life. It's me in the pictures, but I'm completely disconnected from those moments. Looking at them is like trying to recall a half-remembered dream after the mind has already started to forget it.

But there's nothing ominous on her page. No threatening comments on any of her public threads. No strange interactions that would be visible to other users. And her posts themselves don't indicate that Amber was doing anything she wasn't supposed to be doing. Certainly nothing that would explain why someone would kill her in the woods on the night of the homecoming dance.

I check the journals of some of our other friends at the time too. Again, I find nothing.

Then I look at the group communities that both Amber and I belong to. We only have one in common. BFHSTimeCapsule. The Braxton Falls High School community journal.

I click on it.

There haven't been any new posts since 2010, which I assume is when the journal lost its popularity. Kids have more immediate and engrossing forms of social media nowadays. I scroll back to 2007 and am surprised by the number of photographs people have added from homecoming. Pictures that, judging by the dates and comments, were uploaded before the news of Amber's murder was released to the general public.

There are hundreds of pictures posted from multiple accounts. Most of the usernames I don't recognize, but that's not surprising. People were always 'BrightEyedGurl17' or 'Sk8trBoi90.' Sometimes we'd sit around after school and try to guess who people were by their posts. Amber was better at figuring it out than I was. She was a natural internet sleuth. But she also knew more people than I did. Her friend groups cast a wider net than mine.

If our circumstances had been switched—if I had been the one to die—she would have had this mystery solved in a minute.

I scroll further. That's when I see it. In the background of one of the photos is the image of Dad. I click on the picture, enlarging it on the screen. He's not facing the camera. Nor is the man he's speaking to: Richard Henson.

I return to the previous page and look at the other photos. There's another one that catches my father in the background. In this one he has a finger pointed in Henson's face as though he's admonishing him. It looks like an argument, but that's not what has me stumped in shock. It's the location of these photos. Homecoming 2007. But Dad wasn't at the homecoming dance.

He was with my mom the entire evening until they came to get me at the station. How could he be in these photographs if he was at home? No. That's not the question I need answering. What was he doing at the dance? And why did he lie about it?

Then it hits me.

Riley was telling the truth.

He did see my dad the night of Amber's murder.

I scroll up to see the name of the person who posted the photos but it's an anonymous account. That was the one downside of FriendSpace. A person didn't have to have an account in order to reply to group communities. There's no way of knowing who posted those pictures.

Chapter 33

The weight of the grocery bags causes the plastic handles to carve deep indentations on my forearms. I push open the front door to Mom's house with my hip, just barely making it over the threshold before one of the overfilled bags begins to tear. The front window is still boarded up with the plywood and cardboard I found in the attic yesterday, but the duct tape is peeling off in the corners, letting in cold air. I set the bags down in the foyer and make my way into the living room to press down the edges of the tape, hoping it'll close up the gaps.

"Lex! I'm so glad you're home! I need you to come into the dining room." Mom is fresh-faced. She's wearing clothes. Real clothes. Nice clothes. Clothes you would actually leave the house in as opposed to that wrinkled house dress she throws on every morning. The one I have to wash at least four times a week because of the smell.

"Why? What's going on?"

"Chief Newman is here."

"Since when?" My tone is spiteful. Antagonistic. And Mom shoots me the same look she used to give me and Amber when

183

our grandparents were visiting for Christmas. The look meant to remind us to be on our best behavior. I never really understood why my mom was always worried. For kids we were relatively well behaved. At least until we became teenagers.

But aren't most girls angels until then?

"He just got here a few minutes ago."

"What does he want?"

"He found the person responsible for the break-in."

I pick up all of the grocery bags at once because it's a cardinal sin in the Midwest to take two trips, and carry them into the kitchen. I quickly put away the foods that need to be refrigerated before joining my mom and the police chief in the dining room. He's sitting with his back to the hutch, Mom's army of Precious Moments figurines boring their pleading eyes into the back of his head. If this were a horror film they'd all descend on him before he could deliver the news, leaving us in perpetual suspense.

"I'm glad you could join us, Alexandra," Newman says.

As though I'd been invited. I don't say anything in response. I just stand there, waiting for the punchline.

Mom clears her throat with a cough and nudges the chair beside her. I sit down with a sigh.

"I came by to tell your mother that we've caught the perpetrator responsible for the broken window. And possibly for the damage to your automobile," Newman says.

I'm surprised he even remembered that.

Mom leans forward with her elbows on the table, hands clasped together as though she's about to break into evening prayer. That's when I notice how low cut her blouse is.

"Who was it?"

"Mitchell King."

That wasn't a name I was expecting to hear and I can tell by the look on Newman's face that he was waiting for my reaction.

Did he think I already knew?

"Mitchell?" Mom is confused, too. Good, at least I'm not the only one.

"How do you know it was him?" I ask.

"He was down at Buster's Billiards Hall blabbing about it. Half a dozen people in the bar heard him bragging. Said it was a long time coming. Said you both deserved it."

"Deserved it?" Mom's jaw looks like it's about to hit the floor. "He said that *we* deserved it? After everything his good-for-nothing son did? After that bastard kid murdered my little girl?"

"Mom . . ."

"Where is he?"

"In the drunk tank at the station cooling off. The bartender called me when Mitch started getting violent after they cut off his tab."

"And what are you going to do about it?"

Chief Newman sits forward in his chair. "That's up to you, Audrey. Do you want to press charges?"

I watch as Mom's expression goes from heated fury to breathless calm in a matter of seconds. If she'd been drunk she wouldn't have been able to compose herself so quickly. Maybe not even at all. I look at her hands again. Is she holding them together to prevent them from shaking or because she's actually praying? I can't tell.

Eventually she shakes her head. "No. I don't want anything to do with that man or his family. All I have to do is hang on for a few more days and they'll all be out of our lives forever."

Her voice wavers there at the end and for the first time in years I actually feel bad for my mom. She spends so much of her time numbing the pain with booze that I sometimes forget she's hurting too. I'm actually proud of her for deciding to let Mitch off. As much as I despise that man for the horrible things he did to Riley as a boy, I know he's a victim in this, too.

At least, I think he is.

But why drive all the way out to the other end of town just to break our window when he doesn't give a shit about Riley and never did?

"There's something else I wanted to talk to you about. Both of you actually." Newman clears his throat. "I'm concerned about the memorial ceremony for Amber."

"What do you mean you're concerned?" I ask.

"We've been getting a lot of threatening calls at the station—"

"Threats?"

"I don't understand," Mom says. "Threats about what?"

"Some of it is the usual stuff that comes up around the time of an execution. Anti-death-penalty activists planning to protest in front of the courthouse and the prison, for example."

That doesn't surprise me. I saw some blogs online tearing apart the justice system's handling of Riley's defense. More than half of them claimed the evidence would be considered circumstantial in today's courts.

"Who else has been calling?"

Newman purses his lips before he answers. "We've had a lot of crazies coming out of the woodwork since the news was released about the execution. People obsessed with the Wynwood Witch stories."

"You've got to be kidding me."

"Lex . . ." Mom places her hands in her lap. They are shaking.

"Urban legend enthusiasts? Really?"

"No one has specifically threatened to do anything, but we anticipate a large number of out-of-towners driving in for the event because it's so close to the execution. And based on some of the calls we've been getting, they might not be respectful of the memorial. They might try to turn it into a spectacle. Something that'll get them likes on social media or whatever it is those kinds of people do. They might try to harass you."

"I don't understand," Mom says. "Why would anyone want to ruin the memorial? Why would anyone want to desecrate Amber's memory?"

"These people aren't thinking about Amber. They don't see her as an actual person, Audrey."

"What do you mean? She *was* an actual person. She was my daughter!"

I place a hand on Mom's to help steady her. Then I shoot Newman a serious glare. "And what is the police department planning to do about it?"

"I was hoping I could persuade you both not to go. Or to put it off until after the execution."

"That's ridiculous!" Mom pulls her hand away from mine and stands up. She wobbles and grabs the back of the chair to catch her balance. "I've waited fifteen years to put my daughter's tragedy to rest. To finally see her at peace. We're having this memorial and Lex and I are both going. Nothing and no one is going to stop us. And I can't believe you, of all people, would try to do that."

A look passes between them. A look that suggests there's something else I don't know about. But I can't ask. Not now.

Newman nods. Then he stands up. "I had to let my concerns be known. That's my job."

"Your job is to protect the people of this town," Mom says, her tone biting. "Your job was to make sure Amber was safe."

There's a flash of guilt in Newman's eyes. Or is it regret? Either way, it's not a look I expect to see in his eyes. It's one I would have expected to see in Dad's. Whatever it is, it makes me reconsider my opinion of him.

"Maybe he's right, Mom. Maybe we should consider waiting until after the . . ." The word catches in my throat. I can't say it. I can't say *execution*. It just brings up an image of Riley standing in front of a firing squad. It's ridiculous. Ohio is a lethal-injection state. But still. Whenever I hear that word *execution* I picture him standing blindfolded in front of a blank wall, a warden shouting. *Ready! Aim!* The saliva in my mouth is cold. I swallow it quickly. ". . . until after Riley's gone. Maybe things will be calmer then."

Mom hits me with a hard stare.

If looks could kill.

"You said Mitchell King was responsible for the damage. He'll be in the drunk tank for how long? A day? Two?" Sober Mom is more commanding than I remember.

"I could probably stretch it to two. He did damage a jukebox at the bar. And he snapped a pool cue in half."

"The memorial will be over by then. And since he's the only one who has harassed us directly he's the only one we need to worry about. We're having Amber's memorial. And that's final."

Chapter 34

By the time I find what I'm looking for my macaroni and cheese has gone cold.

Chief Newman tried at length to convince my mom not to go through with the memorial service, but she stood her ground. I had to give it to them both. I don't think I've ever seen two people more stubborn about something that should have been put to rest years ago. It makes me wonder how Dad ever put up with them both.

While they continued to argue back and forth about safety and principle, I snuck away to Amber's bedroom unnoticed. Finding those photographs of Dad and Henson at the homecoming dance made me wonder what else I might not have known about that night. It made me wonder if Amber herself might be able to shed more light on the situation. Maybe I could find something that, combined with the ring, would be enough for Newman to take me seriously. Something he couldn't ignore or twist to place the blame on me. So, I took her laptop from her old backpack, and left with a halfhearted 'see you at the service', which fell on two sets of deaf ears.

Now I'm home with the prepackaged stovetop dinner I'd forgotten about and another unexpected turn in the mystery of that horrid night fifteen years ago.

Admittedly, my memory of the night Amber died is marred with confusion. I've seen people online refer to this as a trauma response. Something horribly unthinkable happens and the mind rearranges its memories and its feelings in order to cope with the pain. I guess it's a kind of survival mechanism. For example, I always assumed that the police went through all of Amber's possessions with a fine-toothed comb after her body was found. But according to the files in Dad's study, that never happened. That was just something my mind filled in the gaps with. I probably remembered that from various crime dramas on television and assumed that had also happened here. But it didn't. It wasn't necessary. The prosecution didn't need a viable reason for why Riley would murder my sister. They had enough evidence to sway the jury regardless. My sister's role in the entire event was, sadly, negligible.

Having read through Dad's notes, however, I realize this was a bone of contention for him. A part of the shoddy policework—his words, not mine—that Newman performed. And I have to agree with him. From everything I've managed to uncover, no one looked into Amber's laptop.

Until today.

Finding those unfamiliar photos of Dad and Henson at the high school got me thinking. At their cores, most people are liars. They may not always be intentionally misleading with the truth, but everyone lies. Everyone has something to hide. Secrets they keep from everyone, including their friends and family. Dad must have had one too, otherwise he and Mom wouldn't have lied about his alibi. I'd lied to the police by withholding my whereabouts after the dance. And Amber? Maybe she was lying about something, too.

It doesn't take me long to go through her old files and find what I'm looking for. A Word document of accounts and passwords. She didn't even try to hide them. Probably because she assumed no one would look at her laptop. Nestled in a folder of homework assignments and unfinished class reports was a list of all her personal accounts and how to access them. Facebook, email, instant messenger. Everything.

But it's the FriendSpace login that catches my interest. Not only because it's the one I was looking for—I had a notion she might have been receiving private messages from the person who killed her—but because she had two accounts. One of which I didn't recognize. There's the password for her normal account, CheerBear16, as well as another, WynWitchFan2. And when I log into it, I immediately know why Amber kept it hidden.

Growing up, Amber and I were unusually close. Dad always told people it was because we were born in the same year. That somehow being less than a year apart gave us more in common with each other. We were always more like friends than sisters. And Amber was a huge part of my friend group. But we weren't the only friend group she had. And when my senior year came around, she started hanging out with me less and less. No one ever expects teenage sisters to get along, but it was more than just the occasional squabble. We went from being thick as thieves to doing whatever we could to get under each other's skin. Something happened. I don't know what. But Amber changed.

I click on Amber's user profile. A list of journal editing features are on the left side of the page. On the right is a column where the user's followers would normally be listed if they were online. Unsurprisingly, the column is empty. Unlike her other FriendSpace account, this one doesn't have any actual journal entries. It's just pictures. Hundreds of pictures with dozens of comments from anonymous and unfamiliar journals. And these pictures aren't like the ones of us in the hallways at school. They're party photos. Frat party photos. With red cups, beer pong, and what appear to be hazing rituals. The strangest thing of all? With the exception of Amber, who shows up in most but not all of the pictures, I don't recognize anyone. And if I had to guess I'd say they weren't even taken in Braxton Falls.

Where in the world did these photos come from? And how was it possible that Amber was out at what appeared to be college parties without me knowing about it?

I continue scrolling through the posts. Pages and pages of pictures of Amber drinking, dancing, and posing duck face for the camera. Low-cut tops. High skirts. And they aren't all taken in the same location. I can tell from her outfits and the backgrounds. Different houses. Different parties. Different people. All posted during the summer before my senior year. In the months leading up to the day I caught her in the kitchen with Riley.

If my parents had seen these she would have been grounded for life.

The laptop pings, almost giving me a heart attack. I look at the top of the page where the journal menu is and see that someone has sent the account a direct message.

"What the hell?" I whisper to myself, an eerie tingling sensation forming at the back of my neck.

Anonymous674: *See anything you like?*

I stare at the screen, uncertain what to do. I know it's just a stranger on the internet. I know it's probably just some random spam message. But I can't help but feel like whoever it is might be watching me. Like they know I'm snooping where I shouldn't be. I almost slam the laptop shut, but then I remember I'm safe. I'm at home. The door is locked. No one knows it's me. And if by chance this is someone who knew Amber, then maybe they'll help me get one step closer to learning what happened to her.

I reply.

WynWitchFan2: *Depends on what you mean.*

They reply almost instantaneously.

Anonymous674: *The dead girl wasn't such a goody two-shoes, was she?*

WynWitchFan2: *What do you mean?*

Anonymous674: *You shouldn't be snooping.*

Anonymous674: *You might see something you can't unsee.*

WynWitchFan2: *Who are you?*

Anonymous674: *Guess.*

I stare at the screen. I have no idea who this could be, but whoever it is knows that Amber is dead. And they must be local if they're able to log into this server. I click on their profile, but there's no information other than the date that the account was created. April 2007. A month before Amber created this second account. That means it's someone from back then. Someone who probably used the website like the rest of us. Someone who probably has, or had, a normal account as well. But what would they still be doing on a website that was for all intents and purposes obsolete?

Unless they were just waiting this entire time for someone to log into Amber's account.

WynWitchFan2: *I don't know.*

Anonymous674: *You sure?*

WynWitchFan2: *What do you want?*

Anonymous674: *I want you to let it go, Lex.*

Anonymous674: *Before you end up like your sister.*

Chapter 35

I shouldn't be surprised by the number of people who turn up for Amber's memorial service, but I am. Word travels so quickly in Braxton Falls I sometimes forget that there's actually quite a few people who live there. Most of them don't know who I am, but all of them know who Amber is. Still, when I look around at the crowd, milling about with candles and teary-eyed faces, I can't help but wonder how many of them aren't from around here. And how many of these sob-soaked eyes never even knew Amber personally.

The memorial service is held on what locals affectionately refer to as The Green. It's a small park near downtown, a few blocks from the high school. It's your typically quaint Midwestern setting. A whitewashed gazebo, the highlight location of all local wedding photographers, stands at the center of a grassy square. Someone from the community board has put up a large poster-sized photograph of Amber in her cheerleading uniform on a stand. There's a microphone so various members of the community, all preselected by Chief Newman, can speak about the event.

A banner is draped above the gazebo from the local women's shelter, which I quickly learn is the actual organizing force behind the ceremony. Mom had just been playing it off as her work.

The shelter's volunteers weave through the crowd in their purple shirts passing out ribbons and asking for donations. I don't know why this strikes me as weird, but it does. Why them? Why not some other foundation? Amber wasn't the victim of domestic violence. Amber had a great life at home. A perfect life. Until she was murdered.

This entire event feels phony.

I drove on my own so I could leave whenever I wanted. I don't want to be here and I think that's probably obvious by the way I'm avoiding looking people in the eye and staying as far away from the gazebo as possible. I have a gut-wrenching fear that someone will drag me up there to talk about my sister and I might be too honest. I might say something I regret. Something about how my sister wasn't the perfect picture of innocence everyone has turned her into. How there was something more going on that year than just a teenage girl found murdered in the woods the night of the homecoming dance. How I wasn't certain that Riley was the killer. How the killer may still be out there.

Maybe they were even among us now.

"Lexie!"

I'm snatched from my thoughts by the sound of Jessica's voice. I look up just as she wraps me in a tight embrace. The action shouldn't feel awkward, but after our bizarre conversation at the restaurant the other night, I can't help but think this is all part of an act. Either that or she's tipsy again. Or she's completely lost her mind; can't rule anything out. But I don't smell any alcohol on her breath. I would know. I've become an expert at unconsciously searching for the odor of cheap liquor and old wine. A bad habit of trying to gauge how early in the day my mother started drinking.

"Jess," I say, caught off guard by the embrace.

"I'm so glad you decided to come!" she says as she pulls away from the hug. The taunting malice that was in her tone when she saw me with Cameron at the restaurant is gone. Perhaps I judged her too harshly. I might have been a little curt if it had been her and Riley, after all.

"If you need anything, just let me know," Jessica says. "I'm here to support you and Amber. And your mom, of course. Where is she?"

I glance around, realizing for the first time since I arrived twenty minutes ago that I haven't actually seen Mom in the crowd. I wonder if I should be worried about her getting here on her own. Then I remember how adamant she'd been with Chief Newman and how surprisingly sober she was when I left her at the house. She was probably somewhere behind the scenes preparing her speech. The one she'd no doubt spent the last fifteen years writing.

That was a horrible thought. I'm a terrible person.

"It's just a dog and pony show," I say.

"You're not being serious."

But I am. Amber should have had a memorial at the end of our senior year, not fifteen years after her death. Not a few days before Riley is about to be put to death. This isn't a memorial, this is a witch hunt. Except in the eyes of everyone here the witch has already been sentenced. They're all just pregaming the burning at the stake.

"It just doesn't feel appropriate."

"Because of Riley?"

I shouldn't be surprised that Jessica would make that leap, but I am. And clearly my expression doesn't hide that reaction.

"I'm not an idiot. I remember how hard it was for you during the trial. I remember you arguing with me about how he couldn't possibly have done it. About how it didn't make any sense. And I know I was a total bitch the other night at the restaurant. I didn't mean to be. I've just been going through some shit with my ex. He wants the house and—I should have been more compassionate about what you're going through with Riley." She places a hand on my upper arm and gives it a gentle squeeze. I can't tell if it's affectionate or belittling. "You were in love with him. Of course you're feeling conflicted by everything."

"I appreciate that, Jess. I do. But it's not that simple."

"Is it because you went to see him?"

I flinch. "How did you know about that?"

Jessica shrugs. "Cameron told me."

"*Cameron* told you that I visited Riley in prison?"

"It wasn't like a big conversation or anything. It just sort of came up."

"It just came up? When?"

"I don't know. A few days ago. Maybe when I saw you both at the restaurant?"

Except I know she knows it didn't come up then. Which means she's purposefully hiding the fact that she and Cameron spoke about me behind my back.

Though why I'm so angry about that, I don't know. Everyone in this town has talked about me behind my back. Why wouldn't my two former best friends be on that list as well?

"It has nothing to do with that."

"You can't trust him, Lex."

"Cameron?" I say, confused.

"Riley. He'll say anything to get out of his sentencing. You know that."

"Right, because no one has ever been charged for a crime they didn't commit."

Jessica stares at me. The concern in her eyes makes me want to scream. Where was that concern at the restaurant? Hell, where was it for the last fifteen years? Where was this Jess when I needed her? When my life was crumbling around me and I was all alone?

"You really believe he's innocent?"

"I don't know what to believe. All I know is that this is a sham. Amber wouldn't want this."

The scratchy sound of someone adjusting the microphone at the gazebo pierces through the speakers. Jessica and I both wince and turn our attention to the stage. To my surprise Cameron is standing up there. He's dressed in a sharp light blue suit, but without a tie. I imagine that's supposed to make him look casual, but he could be dressed in jeans and a hooded sweatshirt and still give off that haughty air of wealth. Granted, it doesn't help that everyone knows he's one of the richest people in town. Probably in the entire state.

"What's Cameron doing?" I whisper to Jessica.

"Just wait," she says, an unreadable smile on her lips.

"Sorry about that." Cameron clears his throat and adjusts the microphone closer to his face. "Most of you know who I am, but for those of you who don't—"

For anyone who hasn't seen one of the fifty billion campaign signs around town.

"—I'm Cameron Ellis."

I don't know why my thoughts are so bitter. I guess I'm still trying to get over the discomfort of the dinner we shared. Not that it was really Cameron who made me uncomfortable. Not until he started sharing his feelings.

Cameron composes himself by looking down at the stage floor. When he raises his attention to the crowd, I think I see his eyes glistening. But I refuse to believe he's about to cry. That's not Cameron's style. Maybe it's just a reaction to all of the candles. "Before we get started I'd like to thank you all for coming out tonight."

The crowd goes eerily silent. Everyone is staring up at the small stage in awe, clutching their candles near their chests. I feel like such an outsider among them. Like I don't belong. I should wonder what that says about me, but I think I already know. I never did feel like I belonged. Not in Braxton Falls. Not in my friend group. Not even in my family.

That was the thing that bound Riley and me together, after all. That sense of not belonging.

"Most of you know that I went to Braxton Falls High School. I was a student the year that Amber Wicker was murdered. It was my senior year. It was supposed to be the best year of my life. That's what they say, you know. That senior year is the best year of your life." Cameron pauses to take a breath. It doesn't look forced, but anyone who's ever been to the theater or watched a film could probably tell it's a beat. A moment to prepare the audience for what he's about to say. "What many of you probably don't know is that Amber was one of my best friends. And not just because she was a cheerleader while I was on the football team, although we did have that in common. But because she was a good person. A good listener. She was always upbeat and friendly. And even though she was a year younger than me, it never felt that way. She was strong-willed in her opinions. She was confident and bright. I know we always see the photos of her in her cheer uniform, but Amber wasn't just an athlete. She was smart. She wanted to be a veterinarian. She loved animals. And she would have been great at it. But above all she was good to others. Kind. And enthusiastically optimistic about the future. She had so many plans. Plans that she, sadly, never got to fulfill."

I look around and see everyone nodding in agreement. Their faces full of shared sympathy for someone lost so young. Even Jess has a gleam of agony in her eyes. But it doesn't strike me as grief or bereavement. It looks a little too forced. Like she's purposefully holding back from blinking so she can get a misty glaze over her eyes. But why would she do that? Maybe I'm just looking for something to be angry about.

Then I catch the gaze of Principal Henson, standing twenty feet away. He's not paying attention to the stage at all. Instead he's boring his eyes into me. I awkwardly turn so my shoulder blocks my view of him. I can still feel his stare. But when I glance back a few seconds later, he's gone.

"Tonight we honor Amber and her family. As we look back on this tragedy, I hope we can all think of the beautiful moments we shared with her, instead of focusing on the hurt and the suffering that her loss as brought to our community. What happened to

Amber should never have happened. And it should never happen again. That's why I've joined with the local women's chapter to set up a foundation in her name. A charity to support young women in sports who want to pursue a career in science or technology."

There's a respectful round of applause from the audience. When it dies down, Cameron continues.

"I've also decided to donate $50,000 to the local domestic violence shelter in Amber's name to be put toward outreach programs for young men and women with the hopes of preventing another horrible tragedy like this ever happening in Braxton Falls again."

More applause.

Jessica scoffs. "I wonder how much of that donation came from his father and how much came from the taxpayers."

"Surely Cameron wouldn't take money from his campaign. Is that even legal?"

"Does it matter if everyone loves you anyway?"

This response strikes me as strange, particularly after the way she was looking at Cameron at the restaurant. Did I miss something? Or was she just being drunk and flirtatious the night before? I don't know what it is, but Jessica's behavior is like a roller coaster. It's like she's two different people at the same time. Has she always been this way? Or is this just another tragic fallout from Amber's murder?

That anxious feeling of being watched tickles the back of my neck. I glance behind me, searching for Henson, but he's nowhere to be seen. And all eyes are on Cameron.

"For young people, Braxton Falls may not be the most exciting town in the world, but it's a town with a lot of heart. And all of you being here this evening is evidence of that heart. Let's spend this evening not only paying our respects to a young woman who was taken from us too soon, but also reminding ourselves of the importance of spending time with the people left in our lives. Thank you all again for coming."

Cameron steps down from the gazebo and is met by the flashing of cameras from various local and regional news stations. I'm glad they haven't found me. I don't look good on camera.

"Holy shit."

Jessica's voice catches me off guard. I turn back to her. Her face has completely blanched and her eyes are wide like saucers.

"What is it?" I ask.

"Is that your mom?"

I jerk my attention back to the gazebo. At first, I can't see who she's referring to over the crowd. Then I see who she's talking about. A woman stumbles to the microphone. She's frazzled. Her hair tied up in a scraggly bun. Eye makeup smeared over her gaunt cheekbones. She grabs the microphone for balance, but it just tips to the side and as her hand brushes over the rounded edge, a static clash surges through the speakers resulting in a chorus of cringes from everyone on the grass.

It is my mom.

And she's totally plowed.

"I wanted to thank all of you for coming out here tonight to support my Amber." She's already crying. No, not crying. Sobbing. Her voice choking up like she can't catch her breath. "It would have meant the world to her to know that you all still thought of her. That you remembered her."

Mom wipes her nose on her sleeve. "Cameron is right. My baby girl was smart and she was beautiful. And she was taken from me too soon. She was taken from all of us too soon."

"I have to get her down from there," I say to Jessica before I start pushing through the crowd toward the gazebo. Jessica doesn't follow. Like everyone else she's hypnotized by the sight of my mother. Like drivers rubbernecking on the highway. They're like onlookers who haven't seen a fatal accident before. Or real grief.

Or a public drunk.

I mumble apologies as I try to steer through the motionless crowd.

"But this isn't just about Amber," Mom says. "This is about justice. And we've been waiting for justice for too long. Fifteen years. Fifteen fucking years. But now we only have to wait a few more days. A few more days and Amber will finally be free. Her memory will finally be free of the burden of that vile piece of shit sitting in Miller's Creek."

I make it to the front of the crowd. Mom's gaze catches mine immediately. There's so much hatred in her eyes. She can barely stand and I imagine the only thing keeping her upright is pure vengeance. Cameras flash from the side. This is going to be such a fucking disaster.

Correction, this already is a fucking disaster.

"Mom, come on. Let me get you down from there."

And then it goes from a disaster to a full-blown catastrophe.

"Why couldn't it have been you?"

A simultaneous gasp sweeps through the crowd. And I know what they're all thinking. Did she really just say that?

But Mom has her blinders on. She doesn't see anyone but me. And she doesn't feel anything but fifteen years of fury, frustration, and bitter contempt.

All of which would have been avoided if I had been with Amber that night.

"Why couldn't it have been you?! Why did it have to be her?!" she yells. She's barely holding on to the microphone anymore, but it doesn't matter. She's close enough to it for everyone to hear. "Where were you? Where were you when your low-life boyfriend was cutting up my baby girl?!"

Now all eyes are on me. I don't know what to do. I stand there paralyzed with my own shock and ire. My body is shaking, held together by nothing but sheer nerve. Because there's no way in hell I'm going to fall apart in front of all the people who have treated me like shit for the last fifteen years. Certainly not while those news cameras are fixated on me, waiting for my reaction. I don't even allow that tear creeping at the corner of my eye to fall. They don't deserve it.

I lose all sense of time. An hour could have passed as I stood there refusing to break eye contact with my mother, denying her an answer to the question she's been screaming at me for the last fifteen years. In reality it's only seconds before Chief Newman climbs up the steps to the gazebo and leads my mother away from the microphone.

Now I owe him one.

Cameras flash as he walks her down to the grass. Out of the corner of my eye I catch a glimpse of Cameron and Jessica standing beside each other, staring on with their mouths gaped open. I see Henson as well, but he doesn't look surprised. On the contrary, he appears oddly content.

I cut through the crowd and hurry after Newman and my mother. I don't run, but my calves burn with tension as though I've just sprinted a mile. I resist the urge to look behind me at those stunned expressions and try not to imagine all of the whispers that'll soon be spreading throughout town or the photos that'll be posted on the internet by morning.

Instead I think of how I'm going to find out what really happened to Amber. If Riley is innocent, and I hope he is, I'll prove it. I'm going put an end to this charade once and for all. Even if it's the last thing I do.

Chapter 36

Mom and I drive home in palpable silence. I'll have to pick up her car in the morning and hope that she hasn't inadvertently parked in tow zone. I try not to think about how she even managed to get to the center of town without killing anyone. The only thing that could have made the evening worse was if we added another murder to the mix.

We make it all the way inside before the yelling starts.

I'm surprised Mom has the energy to keep the argument going, but she's clearly running on the fumes of fifteen years of fury. She's been saving this up for a long time. And today, for whatever reason, she's finally snapped.

God, I wish Dad were still here.

On second thought, no, I don't. I wouldn't want him to see Mom like this. She was bad before, but she's been worse since his death. I couldn't stand to see the heartbreak in his eyes if he realized she couldn't live a normal life anymore. Or the disappointment when he discovered that I'd failed to pick up where he left off. That I couldn't take care of my own mother.

I wish I could run away. If I didn't have so much guilt, I'd get in my car and drive until I ran out of gas. Then I'd walk until my feet bled. Anything to get away from this place. Anything not to have to feel the stain of being me.

"It's your fault! You killed Amber just as much as that sick fuck of a boyfriend you had!"

Mom's choice of profanity hits me the hardest. I've never seen her this unvarnished. Not since the day the police told her that Amber had been found. Not since she and Dad had to identify the body. Something imploded in Mom that day. Imploded and died. And this was a lingering remnant of that.

"You were supposed to look out for her. You were supposed to come home with her. Where were you when she was in the woods? How did she get out there without you knowing?" Mom grabs on to my shirt like she's going to shake me, but she doesn't have the strength.

I want to push her, but instead I tug away from her. And then I have a mini implosion of my own. One I've been waiting years for.

"What do you want me to say, Mom? You want me to say this is all my fault? You want me to apologize for not holding Amber's hand every second of the day? I wasn't with her that night! I don't know why she was in the woods. I don't know how she got there. We didn't go to the dance together. We were barely even talking to each other back then. She'd been an absolute horror for months leading up to that dance! But you never noticed. You didn't care. You were so obsessed with this image of Amber that didn't exist. You didn't even know her!"

"You have no right to talk to me like that."

"I have every right! You've treated me like shit ever since she died. I was hurting and you never made me feel like I could go to you for help. My life changed that night too and instead of opening yourself up to me or Dad you shut yourself away and drowned yourself in booze. You kept all these secrets—"

"What secrets?" Mom scoffs.

"Being chummy with Jess, for one. What's that about?"

"Jessica came to me when you wouldn't. She actually sympathized with my pain."

"But she's not your daughter, Mom!"

"She's a better one than you! She understood how much pain I was in and sympathized with my loss. She reminded me of Amber."

"She was my best friend. Why wouldn't you tell me that she was visiting you?"

"Because you ruined my memory of Amber. Because I can't even look at you without seeing *him*! Jessica has been good to me. And I didn't want you to ruin that relationship too!"

My mouth gapes open and I almost laugh. I barely know what to say. "Amber wasn't my responsibility! You talk about her like she was a child. She was sixteen, for God's sake! She wasn't some naïve little girl."

"You were supposed to keep an eye on her!"

"I wasn't her mother!"

I hear the slap before I feel it. It transports me back to that night in the police station. Everyone standing around, arguing, trying to get me to remember what happened. I don't remember everything they said. I only remember how clammy my skin was. How I was both sweating and freezing at the same time. And how much pain I felt, both in my chest and in my abdomen. Like something was sitting on my chest, suffocating me. Like someone was stabbing me slowly. No one even checked me over. No one took me to the hospital. Dad just picked me up in his arms and carried me to the car and we drove home. And we didn't talk about it again until the trial.

Shock. I was in shock and my mother had slapped me.

Talk about a fucking core memory.

My cheek stings. Normally I would back away from her, but not today. Today I stand my ground. Today I refuse to let Amber come before me.

"Amber wasn't as wonderful as you think she was," I say, my voice uncharacteristically calm considering the circumstances. "You've forgotten every bad thing she ever did."

Mom looks like I've insulted her. Maybe I have. But it's true.

Amber wasn't the picture-perfect golden child. She was just as much a fuckup as the rest of us.

"How could you say that?"

"Because it's true. Sometimes Amber could be a total bitch."

The silence cuts between us like a knife.

The rage in Mom's eyes is undeniable, but she's too stunned to say anything.

I know it's horrible to speak ill of the dead. But everyone has been speaking ill of me for as long as I can remember. And maybe I deserve it for some things. I'm not a saint. Neither was Amber. That's what everyone always forgets about victims of heinous crimes. Do any of them deserve it? No. But that doesn't mean they're perfect. That doesn't mean they never did anything wrong.

Amber didn't deserve to be murdered. She wasn't always a good person. She was a teenage girl. And teenage girls can do some pretty awful things.

"Get out of this house," Mom says through gritted teeth.

She starts to stumble and I catch her by the arm. Her muscles tense beneath my grip, but she doesn't pull away. She can't. She'd collapse without my support.

"Sit down before you fall down," I say, getting back into our same old pattern.

"I don't want you here anymore. I don't want to see you anymore." Her breath smells stale, like old vinegar. She must have finished off all the vodka and moved on to boxed wine.

I lead her to the couch and help her lie down. Then I make sure to pull the coffee table at least two feet away from the couch so there's nothing nearby that she might accidentally hit her head on if she rolls off the cushions.

"I wish I'd never had you," she says. "You've never been anything but a disappointment. You never even did anything with your life. Amber would have done something. She would have become someone important."

Those words hurt me more than anything else she's said tonight. I could probably convince myself that it's not true. That she doesn't actually believe the things she's saying. But who am I kidding? This is the only time Mom is ever honest with me. When her barriers are down and she's not hindered by sobriety. The only time she ever tells me the truth is when she's trashed.

But it's not the words themselves that sting. It's the fact that I stayed in Braxton Falls for her.

"You killed Amber. You killed my baby," she mumbles as she lies down, smashing her face into the side of a throw pillow.

By the time I build up the courage to respond, she's already out. But a small part of me hopes the words weasel their way into her subconscious. Then maybe she'd feel a fraction of the suffering I've felt for years.

"Well, if I'm to blame for Amber's death, then you're to blame for Dad's."

Chapter 37

September 2021

Dad takes a large bite out of his fried bologna sandwich and a glob of ketchup squirts out the end, running down his hand. I hold back a laugh as I grab a napkin for him off the dashboard.

"I don't know how you can eat those. They're so disgusting," I say, popping a greasy deep-fried mushroom into my mouth. It instantly burns the roof of my mouth and I almost have to spit it out because it's so hot.

This time it's Dad's turn to laugh. "And I don't know how you can eat those without waiting for them to cool off. At least dip them in ranch or something."

I wash the burning sensation down with a sip of Diet Coke. The root beer stand is one of Dad's favorite places to go on the weekend. It's been in Braxton Falls for at least fifty years. Maybe longer. It went through a few different names back when Dad was a young man, and the waitresses don't ride out to the cars on roller skates anymore because it's a safety hazard, but it still has that timeless Americana vibe. I don't know why, but fast food tastes better when you're parked in your car and the waitress clamps a tray on your window. Or maybe it's not the taste of the food at all. Maybe it's just that feeling of living in a different time. A simpler time.

"I don't like them when they're cold," I argue. "They lose their flavor."

"It's a miracle you can taste any flavor at all at the rate you're going." Dad smiles and wipes the napkin over his beard. He still has a few drops of ketchup on his chin, which I point out. He pulls down the visor to check himself in the mirror, wiping off those pesky spots on the side of his face.

My stomach gurgles from the greasy food and I roll the seat back a few inches to give my legs more room to stretch. "I always regret ordering the double patty cheeseburger, but I can't help myself. It really is the best burger in town."

"It's not the burger that makes it good. It's the—"

"Special sauce. I know, I know. You've been saying that for years, but you still haven't told me what's in it."

Dad shrugs. "They say it's a company secret. People have been trying to figure it out for years."

"And nobody knows?"

"People have their theories."

"And what's your theory?" I ask, dipping one of the mushrooms in the small container of ranch.

"Thousand Island dressing."

"Get out!"

"I'm serious. That's what makes it so good. They mix it in with mayonnaise or ketchup so you can't tell. But I'd bet the rest of this bologna that it's Thousand Island dressing. The creamy version, of course."

I laugh and shake my head. I don't know if Dad is serious or just telling another one of his tall tales, but I don't care. These moments we have together are the only things that keep me from losing my mind completely. He makes me forget that life hasn't gone the way I'd hoped. The way any of us hoped, really. It's a reminder that there still are some aspects of life worth cherishing.

210

"Do you remember when you used to bring us here as kids?"

A nostalgic smile pulls at the corner of Dad's lips. "I remember the time you and Amber decided to have a contest to see who could drink their milkshake the fastest. I was cleaning out strawberry and chocolate from the back seat for days."

"I wouldn't have been sick if she hadn't."

"You wouldn't have been sick at all if you'd just drunk it like a normal person."

I roll my eyes playfully. "Oh, who wants to be a normal person?"

Dad finishes off his sandwich and crumples up the wrapper before setting it on the window tray. "You know, it's not too late to do that."

"Do what?"

"Go and be a normal person."

"What do you mean?"

"I mean leave Braxton Falls. Go to college. Get that art degree you always wanted. You don't need to stay here just for me and Mom. We want you to be happy."

"We?" I scoff.

"It's not easy for your mother."

"It's not easy for any of us."

Dad nods. "I know."

A waitress runs out of the root beer stand, her ponytail bobbing in the air behind her. She can't be more than sixteen. The same age as Amber when she died. Dad and I both watch as she leans up against a Ford Taurus that just pulled in. She's smiling. Not that fake customer-service smile people give you at the grocery store. A real smile. She's young. She's happy. Life is good. She has everything to look forward to.

It changes the mood in the car instantly. We can both feel it. And I know without looking at Dad that we're thinking the same thing.

That's how Amber was. One day she had everything to look forward to. And the next day she was gone.

211

"I can't afford to go to college. Do you know how many loans I'd have to take out? Not to mention the cost of living off campus because I'm too old to live in the dorms. And I'd never be able to get a part-time job that would cover both tuition and living expenses. That ship has sailed." I shake my head. "I'll be stuck at that damn high school for the rest of my life."

"I never did like you working for that—" Dad cuts himself off. "You're too talented to be cleaning up after a bunch of high school kids. Listen, I have some money in savings. And I could probably take out some of my pension early."

"I can't ask you to do that," I say.

"You don't have to. I want to do it. I want you to get out of here and finally live your life. You deserve it, Lex."

"Do I?"

"You know you do."

It's like he's reading my mind. Or maybe I'm not as good at hiding my feelings as I think. I have been considering leaving town for a while now. This last year has been difficult. Mom's drinking has gotten worse, although she and Dad still pretend like neither of them has noticed. Work has become almost unbearable. There are too many memories roaming those high school hallways. Too many ghosts. As for friends, well, I don't really have any. And that's partially my fault. But being the sister of the girl who was murdered doesn't exactly give me the best first impression. Everyone has heard the gossip. Everyone knows the rumors. People unconsciously give me a wide berth because they don't know what to believe.

I want a new start. No, I *need* a new start. But no one ever talks about how challenging it is to take that first step.

I haven't even told Dad about Samara. About the woman I've been talking to for the past three years. I know he'd be thrilled. He wouldn't judge. He'd buy my plane ticket for me. But if I tell him about how I feel then it's real. And if it's real then it can hurt me if it doesn't work out. Or if something tragic happens.

And as afraid as I am of moving forward, I'm even more afraid of the past repeating itself.

"There's something I've been meaning to talk to you about," Dad says, interrupting my thoughts. His voice has lost its humor. This is his serious Dad voice. The tone that's one step away from his police chief voice. His way of letting me know this is something important.

Oh, God. He's going to divorce Mom.

"I'm thinking about putting the house up for sale."

I blink. That wasn't what I was expecting.

"Really? What does Mom say about that?"

"I haven't brought it up to her yet. I know I need to ease her into the idea. But I think it's time for a change. As much as this town and the people have meant to me over the years, I think we're all long overdue for a fresh start. Your mom, too. I don't need to tell you that the house is practically a tomb. I'm not saying we'd move far. Maybe Lancaster or Newton. Hell, I have a cousin in Canton who has a place they're thinking about putting on the market." Dad pauses. "I think we've done everything we can here. It's time to make some new memories."

"What about your career?"

Dad sips his soda. "I've saved up enough to retire a few years early. Then we could spend more time together. Maybe even travel?"

"I don't think Mom will go for it. She's . . ." I don't finish my thought because I can't think of a way to say it nicely. But Mom isn't really Mom anymore. She's whatever was left over after Amber died. She's a shell of the woman she once was. Amber was her light. And when that light was snuffed out, nothing could replace it.

"She will eventually. It won't be easy, but I think she'll come around to it."

I wish I had his optimism.

"And Amber?"

Dad looks at me, confused.

"I know you still go through her case files. I know you're still bothered by it."

Dad's expression turns pensive. It's then that I notice the wrinkles around his eyes, the gray hairs in his beard, and the belly that hangs over his belt a bit more than it ought to. He looks ten years older than he is. "I think I'm ready to put that behind me, too. It's time to accept that there will always be things in life that we don't have the answers to. But as hard as it is to accept, justice made its decision. It might not feel that way and it might not be the justice we hoped for. But we have to trust the system. That's the only way we'll be able to move on."

Trust the system. Accept that we'll never know why Riley did it.

I don't know that I'll ever feel that way. And when I look at Dad's face, I don't know if I think he will either. Despite his words, he still looks uncertain.

"I know we don't talk about it. And I know my refusal to believe Riley's guilt back then was hard for you, but I have to ask. Was there ever anyone else you suspected of Amber's murder? Is there any possibility that the jury got it wrong?"

Dad stares out the window, but I can tell from the vacant gaze in his eyes that he's not looking at anything. He's in his thoughts. He's in the past.

After a long pause, he shakes his head. "No. There was never any indication of someone else's involvement."

Dad's words are firm and solemn. Still I can't help but feel like he isn't telling me everything. It crosses my mind to finally tell him the truth about where I was that night, but I chicken out.

I know now that it wasn't my fault. Nothing I did could have prevented what happened that night. It's taken me years to accept that, but it's true. Sometimes shit just happens. Besides, too much time has passed to make a difference. And talking about it might only make a bad situation worse.

"We should go to the movies this weekend," I say, desperate to change the subject and get back the warmth of the father-daughter moment I wish I could have more of.

"Anything good playing?"

"I don't know. Does it matter? We could just go for the popcorn and the chocolate-covered raisins. I know they're your favorite."

"Actually, I've become more of a peanut M&Ms man in my old age."

"I bet the dentist will have something to say about eating hard chocolate with your teeth."

Dad laughs. "Of that I have no doubt."

I smile, glad to have Amber's ghost gone, if just for a moment.

"Or we could go tomorrow? What do you say? I'll even treat."

"Well, I promised your mom I'd do some yardwork first. But I don't see why we can't catch an evening show." Dad turns on the headlights to announce to the waitress that she can come back for the tray. "I'll give you a call tomorrow after I finish mowing the lawn."

Chapter 38

I inhale a sharp gasp of air and bolt upright in bed. My throat is half closed and I cough, the imaginary fingers from my nightmare finally releasing me from a chokehold. My eyes are watering. Was I crying in my sleep? I rub my fingers over my eyelids, reminding myself that it was just a dream. Probably sparked by that unsettling message I received on Amber's private account. No use thinking about that now. It's over. I'm awake. But a feverish chill runs through my body. I'm lying in a cold sweat. The sheets are damp, a perfect outline of my body beneath me where the perspiration sank through the mattress cover. I glance over at the nightstand, where the bloody horseshoe ring sits beside my alarm clock, which is flashing red. The power must have gone off while I was asleep. I clutch at my T-shirt, the last fragments of an ill-forgotten dream slipping away from my memory.

It's then that I realize I forgot to turn on the ceiling fan before I fell asleep. I must have been too out of it when I got home from Mom's house. Too aggravated and stressed out by the events of the day to follow my simple routine. I can't sleep comfortably without the fan on. Even in the dead of winter I need it. I don't know if it's the cool circulation of air or the constant whir of the motor, but I inevitably have nightmares when I don't turn it on.

Then again, I'd probably have nightmares this week anyway. Every time I close my eyes I see Riley in prison. Every time my mind drifts off to sleep I catch glimpses of Amber's body in the cold wet leaves of the woods, blood staining her homecoming dress, torso completely exposed. In my dream, her pale skin turns purple from lack of circulation, leaving behind dark blotchy bruises on her body. Those were real. Pre-mortem injuries the coroner called them.

It hadn't been a peaceful death.

I hear a noise. A quiet creaking. Someone has opened my storm door.

I swing my legs over the side of the bed and grab my cell phone. My finger hovers over the emergency call button as I slowly skirt along the walls to the bedroom door. I peer out into the living room, but see nothing except the jagged shadows from the window cutting across the floor.

You're imagining things, Lex. You're stressed.

Then I hear it again. A long breathy wheeze followed by the glimpse of a figure crossing in front of the main window, heading for my front door. I definitely didn't imagine that.

Whoever it is fumbles with the doorknob.

I press the emergency call button on my phone. It rings once before an operator picks up.

"Nine-one-one, what is your emergency?"

"I think someone is trying to break into my apartment," I whisper.

"Are they in your apartment now?"

"No, they're at the door. They're—hold on."

The emergency operator says something else, but I've muted the call so the person at the door can't hear them talking. I take a few more cautious steps toward the window, hoping I might be able to get a good look at whoever it is. My apartment is on the ground floor so it wouldn't be the first time that someone misread the numbers and knocked on it by accident. Sometimes package deliverers get lost in the complex at night. But it's too late for deliveries. It's strange that the automatic security light hasn't switched on. Is it burned out? Or did someone remove the bulb?

Don't be stupid. It's probably just broken.

There's a knock at the door that causes me to practically jump out of my skin. I can't get closer to the peephole without crossing in front of the window. Whoever is out there will see me. I unmute the call and bring it back to my ear.

"Ma'am? Can you hear me? Do you need us to send a uniform over to your place?"

The figure steps away from the door and disappears around the corner of the building.

"I think they're leaving."

Probably just a drunk college student who got lost coming back from the bars.

"Are you sure, ma'am? Would you like to remain on the call longer?"

"No," I say, shaking my head even though no one can see it. "No. I'm sorry for calling. I was just scared."

"If you're safe I'm going to hang up the call. Are you safe?"

"Yes, I'm safe."

The phone clicks. The call is disconnected.

I set the phone on the armrest of my shabby sofa and creep back up to the front window again. I peer out in the direction of the door, cursing the fact that I forgot to close the shades, but there's no one there. Whoever it was is gone. I can't see too far into the distance. The only lights that are lit are those from the building across the parking lot. Their security lamps are working. Must be a burned-out bulb.

I exhale a sigh of relief. I can't believe I called the police for no reason. I need this day to be over. No, I need this week to be over.

I step up to the door and check the deadbolt. It's set in place. As is the lock on the knob. I turn around, about to head back to bed, when there's a knock.

Panic nearly freezes me in place. I'm like a deer on a country road staring down the bright headlights of an SUV. I peer through the peephole catching a fishbowl view of my small porch. There's no one on the other side.

I step away only to see a face pressed up against my front window.

I scream.

Chapter 39

"What are you doing here?"

It takes a full minute for my panicked pulse to settle. But even when I look into Cameron's face and realize it's him, as opposed to some psychotic killer stalking my apartment, I can't help but feel a racing tension in my chest. Or maybe that's just leftover nerves. Stress from Amber's memorial service and trying to understand the handful of clues that haven't shed any light onto my sister's death. That doesn't account for the hairs standing up on the back of my neck though. I don't know why I've allowed myself to get so worked up or why I can't seem to take my fear down a notch. Maybe it's because I was imagining the worst. Maybe it's because when I saw his face flash in the window I thought it was someone else.

I thought it was the killer.

Cameron puts his hand up on the inside of the doorframe to steady himself, but I'm standing on the threshold preventing him from coming inside. He reeks of alcohol. Wine. He's drunk. And if the smell didn't confirm that then the glossy look in his eyes and the way his hair has matted over his forehead in sweat would have.

"Cameron?"

"Hm?" He looks up as though he hasn't heard my question.

"I asked what you're doing here. It's the middle of the night." I pause. "How did you know where I live?"

"I followed you after the memorial service," he says.

"What do you mean you followed me? From my mom's house? That was hours ago."

"I was worried."

"Have you been drinking?"

"I just wanted to make sure you got home safely."

Well, that's fucking creepy. Red flags are waving in the back of my mind. I don't believe him. Not entirely. If he was so worried about me then why didn't he stop my mom from making fools out of the both of us? He could have intervened. It probably would have been good for his political career. Might have earned him some extra sympathy votes. Look at the nice guy still there to console an old friend. What a stand-up thing to do. That's the kind of person we want representing our community. Someone who looks past old grievances and small-town gossip and does the right thing. Someone who's good so we don't have to be.

Except he didn't do that, did he? He just stood there with his mouth gaping open like a fish gulping water.

"I'm fine," I say without a hint of sarcasm or annoyance.

Cameron straightens his posture and leans closer to the door-frame. I hold my ground.

"I should have done something at the memorial service. I feel like an asshole for not helping you."

"Don't stress about it. No one expected you to do anything."

Except me. I expected him to do something. Nothing much. Something small. Especially after what he said to me at dinner about wanting to get to know me again. He gave me the impression that there could be something more between us. Not like *that*. At least, not on my part. But I had hopes that maybe I'd found a friend again. Or at the very least someone I could trust. Someone who understood.

I was wrong. Again.

But Cameron is persistent. "I expected it. I expected better of myself. This town has torn your family apart."

"Riley tore my family apart," I say, repeating the words Mom always says. What Dad used to say.

"That's bullshit and you know it."

I don't know how to respond to this retort. Nor do I know how to react to the fact that Cameron has leaned in even closer. Close enough that I can feel the heat off his body.

"Let me come in," he says. "We should talk."

"We're talking now."

"You don't believe Riley killed Amber, do you?"

I shrug, pretending like the question doesn't bring up a wealth of turmoil in my mind. "Does it matter?"

"Of course it fucking matters. He's going to be executed in a few days." Cameron sounds frantic. I didn't realize he was so concerned about what was going to happen to Riley. He sighs. "I can't imagine how that must be for you. What you're going through. What you must be feeling."

I'm sick of people saying that to me.

"The only thing I'm feeling right now is tired. And I want to go back to bed."

I make a move to close the door, but Cameron steps his foot between the threshold. There's no way to close it now. And if he wanted to come inside all he'd have to do is push through me. I wouldn't be able to stop him.

"I'm serious, Lex."

"So am I."

A silence falls between us. My pulse quickens in anticipation. I stare into his eyes without blinking. All of my senses are on high alert. This is a side of Cameron I haven't seen before. It scares me. But my body refuses to show my fear. By some miracle I've grounded myself into the doorway, my face stony and unrelenting. Not that I think he's noticed.

Who have I welcomed back into my life?

"Do you ever wonder if you made the right choice?"

The question catches me off guard.

"What?"

"I think a lot about the choices I made back then. Dating Jess. Leaving Braxton Falls. College, football, coming back home. All the decisions I made because other people wanted me to. All the opportunities I turned down to be the person someone else wanted me to be." Cameron pinches his nose.

I glance quickly to the right, searching for something heavy in the dark.

Just in case.

"I try not to think about any of that." It's a lie, but Cameron doesn't know that. And if it keeps him on the other side of the door, I don't care. "It doesn't matter. We can't change the past."

"Jess and I were never a good fit."

"I guess that's why you never got married then."

Cameron laughs, but there's a salty edge to it. Almost more of a scoff. Like he's remembering something sad. Like he's picturing the exact moment when he learned the truth about someone he thought he knew better than anyone else in the world. I know that sound all too well. It's the same laugh I made when they told me Riley killed my sister.

Cruel, biting disbelief.

And a tiny pinprick of awareness. A revelation that we only ever see what we want to see in another person. That it's impossible to ever truly see someone else for who they really are.

There's an umbrella in the corner. I try to calculate how long it would take me to grab it.

Too long.

"You should go home, Cameron. Get some sleep while you still can. You'll have your fair share of late nights when you're governor."

Cameron takes a step back from the doorway and looks me in the eyes again. This time it's him who doesn't blink. It's an endless stare that brings a shiver to my spine. He's not looking at me. He's looking through me. He's looking at someone else. Someone in his mind.

"Why would Riley do it? That's the one thing I can't work out. The one thing I can't get out of my head. What reason would he have to hurt Amber? Why would anyone want to kill her?"

"I'm closing the door now."

"Unless it wasn't her they wanted to kill." A dark flash crosses his eyes. "You two used to look so much alike."

"Goodnight, Cameron."

I close the door shut and double-lock it. Then I stand there, shaking, waiting for the sound of retreating footsteps. Once I hear them, my legs give way. I hit the floor knees first. A stunning pain sears through my thigh and up to my hip, but I barely acknowledge it. I just sit there, my entire body frozen in place. I think of how close he'd been to me. How I could practically taste the rancid wine as he spoke. The anticipatory terror of what he might do. What he could do. And the uncomfortable realization that on another day I might have let him. Had I made another decision in the past, I may have fallen for that act.

Were it not for Riley.

Were it not for Amber.

I hunch over my knees and throw up.

Chapter 40

Friday, October 5, 2007
4:47 p.m.

When I storm into Amber's room she's crouched down beside her window, a mess of homework papers and dirty clothes strewn across the hardwood floor. Her head snaps up before she grabs her bookbag and tugs it over to the area she was hiding. It's suspicious and on any other day I might have said something. But not today. Today I'm too enraged to be bothered by whatever asinine thing my sister is doing.

"Why are you in my room?!" she shouts.

"What did you do?" I yell loud enough for Amber to realize I'm not joking around but not loud enough for Mom to hear me from the kitchen.

Amber jumps to her feet. Within seconds her caught-in-the-act expression is gone, replaced by the faux teenage confidence she wears when she's around her cheerleader friends. It's so fake it makes me sick. "I don't know what you're talking about."

"You know exactly what I'm talking about."

"No. I. Don't."

"Jess saw you. She saw you doing it."

"Jess saw me doing what?" Amber crosses her arms over her chest.

"She saw you flirting with Riley after third period."

Amber scoffs. "Seriously? Why would I be flirting with your boyfriend?"

"That's what I want to know."

Amber rolls her eyes. That's something we're not allowed to do in front of our parents. Dad, especially. It's an instant grounding if he catches one of us rolling our eyes. He says it's a sign of disrespect, but it's worse than that. It's fucking annoying. And when Amber does it I have the urge to slap her across the face. I don't, however, because I know the consequences for that will be worse than not leaving my room for a few days and no extracurricular activities.

Next weekend is the homecoming dance, after all. Neither of us is dumb enough to risk not being allowed to go to that.

"You know exactly why I think you'd be flirting with Riley."

Amber grins and shakes her head. "Because of that stupid little kiss over the summer? Seriously? You still have your panties in a twist over that? Get over yourself, Lex. He's not even a catch. I wouldn't be caught dead flirting with him in public. You could do so much better."

My face gets warm and I can tell it's flushed red with anger and embarrassment.

"Besides," Amber continues, "maybe he was the one who was flirting with me."

"You're a liar."

"Am I?"

"Riley never would have kissed you if he'd known it was you."

Amber's lips twist into a pout. "Ah, baby. Is that what he told you? Is that how he convinced you to let him get inside your pants?"

Now it's my turn to look shocked. I glance back to the door, half-afraid that I'm going to see Mom standing in the hallway listening. Or worse, Dad. Thankfully, there's no one there. I shoot Amber a sharp glare.

"You don't know what you're talking about."

"Oh, please. I know what an orgasm sounds like, Lex. I'm not an idiot." She bends down to pick up her cheerleading uniform off the floor and drapes it on the bed. "Not like I care. It's your loss, not mine. You're the one who has to live with the memory of some pimply teenage dick as your first time."

"Shut up!"

"Damn. Regretting it already?"

I take a few steps further into her room.

"If you hit me I'll scream bloody murder."

"I'm not going to hit you."

Amber raises a brow. "You sure about that?"

I glance down and see that my right hand is clenched in a fist. I was completely unaware that my entire body had tensed, preparing for a fight. Unconscious of the fact that I was one smartass comment away from punching my sister in the nose. Or worse. Of strangling her.

I loosen my fist and take a step backwards. I feel like I've just had an out-of-body experience. Do I really have such a short temper? Or is this something new? Something that's happened since I started dating Riley?

"What were you talking about then?" I ask, my voice wavering.

"Did you ever consider the fact that Jess might be lying to you?"

I don't reply. I just stare at Amber in disbelief.

"Seriously? You would believe her word over mine? Over your sister?"

"Jess has never made out with my boyfriend."

"Really?"

"Stop lying, Amber! I'm serious. What did you say to Riley after third period? I know you were there. I know you were at his locker."

"I was just asking the dumbass if he remembered to get you a corsage."

"What?"

"A corsage. You know, for homecoming. Boys are idiots. They always forget that shit. And I thought since he doesn't have a lot of money he might need some help. So, I told him if he couldn't afford one that I would lend him some cash to get you one." Amber shrugged. "But to be honest it's probably too late. Normally you have to order those at the florist weeks in advance. Don't be surprised if he turns up empty-handed. But if he does have one then *you're welcome.*"

I don't know if I believe her. She doesn't sound like she's lying, but Amber's always been good at manipulating people. That's why she's Mom's favorite, after all. She always knows what to say at the precise moment to keep herself from getting in trouble. Me? I always step in trouble like fresh dog shit on a hot sidewalk. People believe Amber because she looks so sweet and innocent. Because she's never been caught doing anything wrong in her entire life.

Because they've never heard the way she talks to me when no one else is around.

Maybe she is telling the truth. Riley isn't exactly the portrait of romance. I doubt he'd ever think about getting me a corsage. A quiet uncertainty fills my thoughts as I realize I may have just accused Amber of doing something she hadn't done. It's not guilt so much as embarrassment. And exhaustion. It's tiring trying to keep up with her.

"Girls!" Mom calls from the living room. "If you want to go dress shopping before dinner then we need to be in the car in five minutes! I'm not going to the mall after six on a Friday! It's too busy!"

Amber grabs her purse and slings it over her shoulder. Her eyes dart to the pile of clothes and homework papers on the floor, then she pushes past me to the door. She stops when I don't follow directly. "What are you waiting for? Are you coming or not?"

"I thought you weren't going to the dance," I say.

Amber shrugs and flips her ponytail over her shoulder. "I changed my mind."

"Who are you going with?"

Amber smirks. "It's a surprise."

Chapter 41

Mom is still in her bedroom when I come by the next morning. She has the door closed and the lights are out, which means she's either still drunk or nursing the mother of all hangovers. Blackout curtains and a fistful of Tylenol are the only things that seem to bring her out of that state. Or more alcohol.

The number of journalists outside has increased, but I parked on the side street and snuck through Mrs. Zimmerman's backyard to get to the house so they wouldn't be able to see me. Principal Henson was right about me taking off the week from work. I drove by just before the first period bell and saw at least three news vans parked in front of the drop-off line. Nothing has changed. They're vultures. They were vultures fifteen years ago and they're vultures today. Just looking for scraps. And if they can't find that? Then any piece of flesh they can pick off the bone will satisfy them. I won't give them a statement. Not after the last time. Not after the way they made me look.

I should be more shaken after last night, but I'm surprisingly calm. After Cameron left my house I lay in bed and stared at the ceiling for a good two hours before finally falling asleep. It wasn't a restful sleep. The disarray of my bedsheets when I woke up told me that I'd spent the entire time twisting and turning. I dreamed of Amber. It was a hazy dream memory that I could barely remember. But when I woke up it left a lingering unease in my thoughts. Like my subconscious was trying to remind me of something crucial. Like it was trying to point out something I'd missed. Or something I'd forgotten.

The hallway leading to Amber's bedroom is dark. When I get to the end of the corridor I open the door without hesitation and step inside. This time I close it behind me. Not because I think Mom is going to wake up and throw me out again—I'm sure I have at least an hour, maybe two, before she's conscious enough to leave her bed—but because what I'm about to do feels like it should remain private. Like it should just be between Amber and myself.

Some people might associate dreaming about one's dead sister to be ominous. Like a premonition or an omen. But I'm not superstitious. I think it's just the stress of the week catching up to me. I think it's my mind finally putting together the missing pieces of a puzzle I'd lost a long time ago. Then again, I could be wrong. I might not find anything in Amber's room. After all, I'd already found the ring and secret journal account and neither of those had led me any closer to the truth. And with two days left before Riley's execution I'm beginning to regret not already going to the police about either of those things.

To be honest, I almost hope I don't find anything. What if I find proof that Riley killed her?

What if I find proof that he didn't?

The room smells like Amber. Like Moonlight Path and Warm Vanilla Sugar from Bath & Body Works. I don't even know if they still make those scents, but they were Amber's favorites. We used to joke that she should have worn Sensual Amber because of her name. It wasn't a very good joke, but teenagers will laugh at anything if it's dumb enough. Or to fit in.

It occurs to me then that Mom probably bought out an entire warehouse of those body sprays just to keep the memory of Amber's scent alive. I'm not sure if I should laugh or cry at the sheer desperation of it. I can't exactly imagine her clearing the shelves of gender-neutral cologne from Abercrombie & Fitch to preserve my high school memory. Then again, I'm not Amber. And I never will be.

I walk along the floor. The wooden planks creak beneath my feet. The room is too clean. Amber was never tidy. She was perfectly poised and pristine on the outside, but a disaster on the inside. Her bedroom always reflected that. Clutter everywhere. The way Mom keeps her room isn't really reflective of Amber at all. It's like a stage. A movie set made to look like her bedroom. But it lacks the tangibility of a moody, popular teenage girl living in it.

Closer to the window the sound of my footfalls against the hardwood changes. There's an echo, almost like there's an empty space beneath me. I take a step backward and tap the toe of my boot. Solid. I take a step forward. Another tap. Hollow. I crouch down and run my fingers over the planks. That's when I notice it. Close to the wall where the floorboards meet the trim, there's a plank that's been cut. The natural discoloring in the wood almost obscures it. But when I poke at the corner of the cut board, it gives. It's loose.

My nails aren't long enough to hook under the edge of the floorboard. I get up and dig through the drawers in Amber's vanity until I find a pink nail file. It slips easily into the crack and within seconds I've pulled it up, revealing a hidden space underneath. I set the board to the side and peer down into the hole. What stares back at me sends a cold shudder through my veins.

"Holy shit."

Nestled in the hiding place no bigger than a shoebox is a single Polaroid photo. I reach down into the old cobwebs and pull it out. I can barely hear my own thoughts from the pounding of my heart. The photograph is of a younger woman in the woods.

She's nude, posing in front of a large oak tree. Perhaps it's my imagination running wild, but it looks like the same tree from Wynwood park. The tree where Amber was found. But that's not even the most horrifying aspect of the photograph. It's the face of the woman.

No, not a woman.

Girl.

And not just any girl.

It's Jessica.

Chapter 42

I stare at the photograph for what feels like forever. My brain is stunned. If there were cogs in my mind then they'd be stuck, incapable of turning, in desperate need of oil. Because none of this makes any sense. Why did Amber have a naked photograph of Jessica hiding in her floor?

I look at the picture more carefully. Someone has written a year on the thin strip of white beneath the image: 2006. I don't recognize the handwriting. It's not Amber's, that's for certain. Amber always had a very specific way of writing the number two, with a big loop and curling tail. This number two has no loop. In fact, it looks more like a Z than a two. And the six is sharply angled with a disconnected circle. I flip the photograph over. On the back someone has written 'WHORE' in pink gel pen. A stark contrast to what was probably blue Sharpie on the front. This handwriting I'm certain belongs to Amber. In fact, I'm almost certain I saw that pink gel pen in her desk drawer.

But what does this mean? If Amber didn't take this photograph, then who did? And why did Amber have it? Better yet, why was she hiding it?

Maybe I'm asking the wrong questions. Maybe the question

I should be asking is why did this photograph exist in the first place? And why did it anger Amber so badly?

I stare at the image of Jessica, too shocked to feel ashamed that I was looking at such a scandalous picture of her. Not that I hadn't seen Jessica naked before. Once, the summer of sophomore year, we went skinny-dipping up at Twin Oaks Lake. I remember feeling incredibly self-conscious at first, but after admiring Jessica's exuberant devil-may-care attitude, I forgot all about my own modesty.

This was different though. This wasn't the image of a young girl running into a lake with her friends just for the fun of it. This was a posed photograph. This was pornographic. She stood face forward to the camera, her hips jutting forward while her shoulders pressed back against the large trunk of the tree. It gave her body an almost distorted posture, like her legs were monstrously longer than her torso. And despite the amateur quality of the photo itself, everything was visible. Most disturbing of all, however, was the year: 2006. The year before Amber was murdered. Jessica and I would have been juniors at the time this was taken. She couldn't have been older than seventeen. Sixteen, depending on which month the photograph was taken.

I shine the flashlight app on my phone into the hiding space, hoping to find something else. Another photograph, a diary, a note—anything that might explain where this photograph came from and why Amber had it. But there's nothing but fifteen years of dust under the floor.

I try to reconcile this picture with what I already know about my sister. Could she have been the one who took the photograph? Was it possible that she and Jessica were together? I rack my mind trying to think of any scenario of the two of them together that might explain this, but nothing comes to me. I have no reason to believe that my sister could have been in a relationship with my best friend. Nor do I have any proof. But the writing on the back of the Polaroid gives me pause.

235

WHORE.

Maybe Amber was jealous. Maybe it wasn't Jessica that she was interested in. Maybe it was the person who took the picture.

Maybe it was the person whose initials were carved in the exact same tree Jessica stood provocatively in front of, lit up to the left of Jessica's shoulder by the light of the camera flash.

The tree that less than a year later would be covered in my sister's blood.

Chapter 43

I pull my car up to the curb outside Jessica's house just as it begins to rain. The sky doesn't look angry. It's that typical murky autumn gray, warning of the inevitable snowstorm on next month's horizon. It's not cold, but the air is damp. And even though it's just a drizzle, it leaves a chill in my bones.

I pop the collar on my jacket and sprint up the driveway to her house. I wasn't exactly certain where she lived, but I pulled up her Facebook and found a photograph of her standing in front of her house. A sporty BMW in the driveway, license plate just as visible as the number on the mailbox. I guess mediocre things like identity theft and stalking are only for the lower middle class to worry about. Apparently if you're rich, you can afford to assume you're untouchable.

Once I'm under the awning of the front porch, I shake the rain out of my hair and try to make it look less shaggy and wild. Jessica lives in one of those cliché suburban neighborhoods where everyone has a long-ass driveway, picturesque shutters that serve no purpose other than to be decorative, and a wrap-around porch. The houses in this neighborhood probably go for an easy million. It's funny because one county away and the same house would be half that price. But Braxton Falls has a decent school district and a country club resort on the outskirts of town, so I guess you get what you pay for.

I press the doorbell. An elaborate chime echoes from inside the house. Two minutes later, Jessica opens the door. She's wearing a chic silk blouse and wide-leg slacks. God, she really does look like she could be one of those old-fashioned silver screen movie starlets. Even her hair frames her face like she's about to have headshots taken for a glamour magazine. And I'm wearing blue jeans rolled up at the cuffs with an old pair of Converse sneakers I've had for more than a decade.

How in the world were we ever friends?

"Lexie! Wow! I didn't expect to see you! Come in." Jessica turns to the side and holds the door open. She seems startled, but not in a bad way. More of a concerned way. Like she expected me to fall off the face of the planet after my mom's embarrassing performance at Amber's memorial. I wouldn't blame her for thinking that. I probably would have disappeared if I could. But this is a small town. There aren't very many places to hide.

"Thanks," I say, stepping inside. Her foyer has beautiful hardwood floors in herringbone style and the walls are a soft shade of blush that could easily be mistaken for white under the light of the crystal chandelier. It smells like lilacs, lavender, and professional cleaning services. For the first time in my life I realize just how jealous I am of Jessica Hampton. She really did get everything she ever wanted.

Except for Cameron, I remind myself. Although how that fell apart still eludes me. When I saw them standing side by side at the memorial, they looked so perfect for each other. The same wealthy glow. The same fashionable taste. The same look of horror when they heard what my mother said about me.

Jessica closes the door. She glances quickly at the floor where I'm making a puddle, but doesn't say anything. I think I see her skin tighten around her lips though. Or maybe I just want to see that.

"What brings you by?" she asks.

"I was hoping I could talk to you about something."

"Oh my God. Is it your mom? Is she OK? I felt horrible at the memorial, but honestly, I didn't know what to do. I mean, I know your mom has been struggling ever since Amber's death, but I had no idea it was that bad. Is she all right? Are *you* all right?" There's genuine concern in Jessica's face and I'm glad for it. Maybe I misjudged her. Maybe we'd all changed since Amber's death. Maybe we were all weird. Maybe burying herself in materialism is just how Jessica copes with trauma.

Maybe we weren't as different as I thought.

"She's fine. Thank you. It's . . . Well, it's been a challenge."

"Your mom always did play favorites."

"It wasn't hard to like Amber more than me."

"I didn't like Amber more than you."

Hearing that confession lifts my spirits. I miss how close Jessica and I used to be. We were close in ways that I wasn't with Amber, even though Amber and I had been inseparable for the longest time. But there was something about the closeness between two friends that often felt safer than the closeness between two sisters. I suppose because if a friend breaks your heart, there's less fallout. You can always walk away from a friend. You can't always walk away from family.

But if Jessica had ever really been my friend then why would she behave the way she did at the restaurant? That still sits uneasily with me, especially after learning how she's been visiting my mom all this time.

Maybe I'm taking things too personally.

"Let's go into the kitchen," Jessica says, making her way through the house.

I pass a framed photograph of two adolescent boys in the hallway. I don't recognize them. Jessica doesn't have any siblings so they can't be nephews, but I've never seen her with children. Before I can say anything, however, she calls out to me from the kitchen.

"Do you want something to drink? Coffee? Cappuccino? Wine?" She pauses. "Oh, shit. Sorry. That was dumb of me to ask."

I want to say that it's OK. I'm not an alcoholic like my mother, after all. But I chicken out.

"It's fine," I say. "A coffee would be fine."

Jessica's kitchen looks straight out of a *Town & Country* magazine. It hardly looks used. Everything, from the smooth quartz countertops to the stainless-steel appliances, is high-end. Or, at least, it looks high-end to me. Not that I'd really know. I don't even have a working oven in my apartment. It's probably the same one that was installed when the building was constructed back in 1992.

"Cream or sugar?" Jessica asks as she heads over to a built-in coffee maker. Not one of those countertop deals that require a pad and a push of a button. No, this is like a full-scale barista operation. I wonder if it foams the milk and makes those little designs on top as well.

"Cream, please. But not too much."

I take a seat on one of the barstools at the large kitchen island. A big ceramic bowl boasting an arrangement of exotic fruits and a vase of flowers sit at the center. There's a card dangling off the flowers and I nosily lean forward to get a look at the name of the person who sent them, but before I can see it, Jessica brings over two mugs and slides into one of the barstools. Not the one directly beside me, I notice. She's put one between us. Space. Because we're not best friends anymore.

"It's quiet. Are your kids at school?" I ask. It's a dumb question because it's Wednesday and all kids are in school, but I want to find out about the portrait in the hallway without coming off as rude. I realize after the fact, however, that assuming is also rude. "I saw the picture in the hall."

"Adopted. Technically they're not mine anymore. Their father has full custody, but they visit sometimes," Jessica replies. She's very nonchalant about it. There's no malice to her tone, which seems weird to me. Almost cruel. If anything, she sounds bored. "They live in Columbus with their father. And I've taken back my maiden name. Thank God. His name was horrendous."

She sips her coffee. I do the same.

"That must be lonely. Being in this big house by yourself."

"I like being by myself. And Jackson and Gerald prefer living with their father anyway. He's more of a kid-person than I am."

"I thought you always wanted to have kids," I say.

"I did. Until I had them."

I wonder if my mom ever felt the same way about me and Amber. Probably just about me.

"Listen, this is going to sound really weird. And, to be honest, I'm a little uncomfortable being here. But I found something in Amber's room and I wanted to ask you about it." I wrap my fingers around the mug, hoping that the warmth will help instill some courage in me, but I realize when I look at Jessica's face, full of suspicion, that I'm terrified of showing her the photograph.

No, I'm terrified of what she's going to tell me about the photograph.

"What is it?"

I unzip my jacket and reach into the inner pocket and remove the Polaroid.

Jessica's entire demeanor changes the moment she sees it. I haven't even turned it around and her body has tensed. Her neck strains, causing sharp lines from the tendons that stretch to her shoulders to protrude. She must be clenching her teeth. Her eyes, however, don't match the rest of the stiffness I see in her. Her eyes are blank. Almost dead. Empty.

I set the photograph on the counter.

"Where did you say you got this?" she asks. Something about her tone makes me want to believe that she's shocked, perhaps even a little angry, but it's also dismissive at the same time. It's a peculiar reaction that I can't quite put my finger on.

"I found it hidden in Amber's room."

"Hidden?"

"Under the floorboards by her window."

"Was there anything else?"

"No. Just this."

"And no one else has seen this?"

I wonder who she means by 'no one.' The phrase itself sounds broad. All-inclusive. But the way Jessica enunciates the syllables makes me think she's referring to someone specific in particular. But who? My mom? Cameron? The police? If we were closer I would ask her outright. But we're not. And I'm already afraid she's going to kick me out of her house without answers.

"I just found it this morning."

Jessica picks up the Polaroid and for a split second I think I see a flash of emotion in her eyes. Remorse? Nostalgia? Anger? It's hard to pinpoint. And it's gone almost as quickly as it came about, replaced by an instant groan and rolling of the eyes when Jessica turns over the picture and sees the slur written on the back.

"Typical," she says, dropping the photograph back on the counter as though it were a picture of someone's lunch and not a teenage nude. *Her* teenage nude.

Her indifference is too performative. It has to be an act. Why is she not freaking out? I would be having a meltdown.

"Who took the photo, Jess?"

Jess shrugs and sips her coffee. "I don't know."

"You don't know?" I don't even pretend to hide my disbelief.

"Cameron probably took it back when we were dating. Just dumb kid stuff. We did all sorts of weird things. I can't remember everything we did back then. Can you?"

"I'd remember if someone took a pornographic photo of me."

Jessica laughs. "Pornographic? Is that what you think this is? Oh, Lexie. You always were so innocent. Honestly, I thought you would have grown out of that by now. This isn't pornographic."

Jessica picks up the photograph again, looks at it briefly, and shakes her head. "This is just really bad art."

Then she drops the Polaroid in a nearby waste paper basket. The way she said 'bad art' strikes a chord with me, but I don't know why. It's a little too specific for someone who claims they don't remember who took it.

"Art?" I glance at the trash, the photo has fallen face down on the cardboard packaging for an organic smoothie mix, displaying nothing but Amber's looping handwriting.

"Nowadays people post the raunchiest shit on the internet. Teenagers with their photoshopped Instagram posts and their sexy TikTok videos. Compared to *that*? This is nothing. This is just two stupid kids with a cheap camera."

"But why would Amber have it?"

"Maybe she was jealous."

"Jealous of who?"

"Well, I think it was pretty obvious that she was into Cameron."

I laugh without thinking. The idea that Amber was into Cameron is absurd. I never witnessed anything between them that would suggest she had a crush on him. Or vice versa, for that matter. Even when Cameron and Jessica weren't together it was clear that he only had eyes for her. Amber knew that, too. In fact, she frequently commented on how annoying it was and how she knew it would never work out between the two of them. I always thought that was comical because there was no possible future I could imagine where Jessica and Cameron weren't together. No matter what happened in high school they always found their way back to each other.

I guess Amber saw things more clearly than I did.

I look up, but Jessica isn't laughing. Her face is statue-still. She's dead serious.

"Wait. Really? You really think that Amber was into Cameron?"

"I know she was," Jessica replies.

"How do you know? Did you catch her doing something?"

I think of Amber in the kitchen with Riley. Two starving figures pressed together in the dark. My stomach churns.

"I didn't need to. I could just tell. There was something about the way she looked at him with those big pouting eyes. And how she was always more intentionally dressed on the days when we would hang out." Jessica tapped her finger on the side of the mug. "She started wearing the same lip gloss as me after Cameron and I broke up for a few months junior year. Then when we were seniors she began copying my hairstyle. She was jealous. She kept trying to get his attention."

I'm shocked. I don't even know what to say in response to this. I've never heard Jessica speak so bluntly about Amber. Granted, it has been fifteen years since I've seen her, but I don't remember any of this. It's like being told that everything you've always believed to be true is a lie.

Then again, I'll never forget the way Amber laughed at me for getting upset when she kissed Riley. Like it was all a game to her. Like she didn't care. Was it so impossible to believe that she could have done the same to Jessica with Cameron?

"I'm sorry," Jessica says, getting up to open the fridge. "I know it's awful to speak ill of the dead. And it's not that I hold anything against Amber. I don't. Hell, if I thought it'd change things I'd go back in time and give her Cameron. He was never good for me either. Or I was never good for him."

While her back is turned I grab the Polaroid out of the trash and stuff it into my pocket before Jessica returns to the island with a handful of red grapes.

"Say that's true," I say. "Say that she was jealous of you and Cameron. Then why would she keep this photo?"

"Maybe she planned to blackmail me with it."

I scoff. "Blackmail you?"

"You know how my parents were always a hair's breadth from sending me to that all-girls Catholic school down in Georgia where my aunt lived. This photograph would have been perfect fuel for the fire." Jessica tucks her hair back behind her ear. The glamour is still there, but there's a weariness to it as well. Like tiny cracks in a porcelain vase that are invisible until held up close.

I do remember her parents threatening to send her away. Jessica was never really a 'bad girl,' at least I never thought so, but she was a little wild. And wild was always more dangerous for families with certain reputations. She's right, too. This photograph would have been the icing on the cake.

Still, there's something about Jessica's story that doesn't hold weight. It's believable. But it also sounds like a half-truth. Like there's a part of the story she's refusing to tell.

Or maybe I'm just shit at reading people.

"This might sound strange. But do you remember if Cameron wore a ring back in high school?"

Jessica raises a brow. "A ring?"

"Yeah. A big silver ring with a—"

My phone buzzes in my pocket before I finish my sentence. I take it out to see a blocked number. There's only one place that's ever called me from a blocked number. I press the call button and hold the phone to my ear. "Hello?"

"Hello, this is Officer Clark from Miller's Creek Federal Correctional Institution. Am I speaking to Alexandra Wicker?"

"Yes, this is she."

"I'm calling on behalf of inmate Riley King. He has you listed as his emergency contact number."

"What?"

"I'm obligated to inform you that Mr. King was involved in an altercation this morning and is currently in critical care. If you would like more information or wish to speak with someone on the medical staff you can contact—"

"But he was in isolation. How could he be injured if he's in isolation? And what do you mean critical care? Is he going to live?"

"If you wish to speak with a member of the prison medical team, I can transfer you to—"

My pulse is throbbing. The artery in my neck practically

punching against my skin. Then I remember Danny's threat back at Nell's cabin about Riley not making it to his execution date.

"It was someone on staff, wasn't it? The man has less than seventy-two hours to live and you just decided to quicken his trip, didn't you? Didn't you?!"

"I'll transfer you to—"

"The hell you will. I'm coming over there now. And you can tell me to my face why the man who murdered my sister probably won't make it to his own fucking execution."

Chapter 44

Saturday, August 25, 2007
9:47 p.m.

Riley tosses another stick on the firepit. The flames waver in intensity before burning a brighter yellow. I watch the tendrils of smoke twist upward toward the night sky, quickly vanishing in the shadows of the large oak trees. A few stars twinkle overhead, adding a romantic tenor to our campfire scene.

I slip my hands into the front pocket of Riley's hoodie. He let me wear it when he saw me shivering from the cool night air. Meanwhile, he's sitting in a T-shirt like summer isn't already slowly drifting into fall. I nudge myself closer to him until our hips touch, smiling when he instinctively leans into me. Last week's drama with Amber is behind us and I couldn't feel more confident that Riley was telling the truth. He was right. It had all been an honest mistake.

"I thought Jess and Cameron were going to join us," I say, although if I'm being honest, I'm kind of glad they're not here. It feels like we're always in the group and never alone. I like being alone with Riley. He's more himself when we're not around others. And it makes me feel special to know that he's comfortable enough around me to show who he truly is.

"I told them we weren't coming," Riley says without pause.

"Why did you do that?"

"Because I knew they'd never come up here without us and I wanted to spend time with just you. Things have been so hectic lately at home and school that I didn't want to deal with anyone else. Especially not Jess and her stuck-up opinions on everyone in our class."

If it were anyone else I would vehemently defend Jessica, but it's different with Riley. I understand where he's coming from. And Jessica can be overbearing sometimes. "I think she forgets that not everyone lives the life she does. That not everyone can be so nonchalant about their future."

Riley shakes his head, but I see a smile peeking at the corner of his lips.

"What?" I ask.

"Nothing. You're just always so . . ."

"So . . . what?"

"You're always thinking the best of people. Even when they're at their worst."

"I don't think it's my place to judge someone if I haven't lived their life, you know?"

"No one could ever judge you, Lexie. You're perfect."

My cheeks turn red with bliss and embarrassment. The compliment warms me more than the fire.

Riley picks up another stick and nudges the edge of the fuel, making sure it stays within the rock circle he set up earlier. When he stretches out his arm toward the flames I notice the dark bruise on the inside of his arm.

"Oh my God, Riley! What happened to your arm?"

He flinches, switching the stick to the other hand in order to avoid showing his skin, but I reach for his arm, turning it over to get a better look. That's when I realize it's not a bruise. It's a burn.

"It's nothing," he mutters.

"That's not nothing, Riley. This looks deep. It's probably

248

going to scar." I gently run my fingers over the thick red skin, but he doesn't wince. It looks really bad. It reminds me of the second-degree burn pictures we saw in health class. "How did this happen?"

After a long pause, Riley finally relents. "I got into it with Mitch the other day."

"He did this to you?"

"Not intentionally. He was high in the kitchen, trying to fry up some sausages while he could barely stand. I wanted to get him out of the trailer before he set the place on fire. He shoved me into the stove and I hit the burner."

"I'm so sorry." My words don't sound good enough to reflect my horror and my concern. But I don't want Riley to think I'm pitying him.

"It's not a big deal. I barely feel it anymore."

"He's an asshole. Someone should call children's services."

"You don't think we have? No one gives a shit." Riley jabs the stick into the dirt until it stands on end. "Besides, I'll be eighteen soon. Then I'll be gone. I'll find a real job, get my own place, and never look back."

"Never?"

Riley turns toward me, half his face lit up by the fire's glow. "You'll come with me, of course. We'll get married, have a family, and we'll do a hell of a lot better than Mitch ever did."

"You want to have kids?" I don't know why that surprises me. Maybe it's because I've never seen this side of Riley before. Maybe because I hadn't really thought about what I wanted in life or what I would do after high school. I love Riley, but I never thought of where we'd be after this year. Would he go with me to whatever college I was accepted to? Would he work while I studied? But there's a certainty in his eyes I can't deny. He's thought about this. And it makes me a little ashamed to realize I haven't.

"I think two or three is a good number. Not too many because I want them to be confident that they'll always have my attention, you know? I wouldn't want my kids to grow up feeling left out or ignored. I want to be the kind of dad who takes them on fishing trips and teaches them how to make a campfire. I want them to grow up feeling safe and loved. Not like last week's garbage left out on the curb."

"You're not garbage, Riley," I say, careful to sound earnest and not pitying. I smile unknowingly. Seeing this side of Riley fills me with so much joy. If he asked me to run away with him right now, I would. No hesitation. "I think you'd be a fantastic father."

"Thanks. I hope so. I mean, I can't be any worse than the Kings. No one could be. But when the time comes I want to do it right." He looks back toward the flames to hide the sadness in his eyes. I can tell he's holding back tears. I want to reach out and hug him, but again I don't want him to feel coddled. So, I just lean against his shoulder.

We sit like that in silence for what feels like forever, watching the flames lick against the blanket of darkness in the woods. Then he reaches into his back pocket, causing me to sit up.

"I almost forgot," he says, removing a Swiss army knife and handing it to me.

"What's this?"

"Look at it."

I turn the knife over in my hands and see that it's engraved with the phrase *L + R Forever*. My jaw drops in shock. "What's this for?"

"It was supposed to be for your birthday, but I didn't want to wait. So, I thought it could be for our anniversary."

"Our anniversary?"

"We've officially been together for eighteen months now."

"Eighteen months? That's a weird number."

"Do you prefer a year and a half? Five hundred and forty-seven days?"

I laugh. I can't believe he's been keeping track of the days. I'm so enamored I think my heart will burst.

"Oh, Riley. This is too much."

"Nah, I got it at an antique store for pretty cheap. And I know a guy at the scrapyards who was able to engrave it with a Dremel."

"It's beautiful," I say, running my fingers along the wooden handle.

"It's for protection. I want to know you'll be safe whenever we're not together."

There's a fierceness in his gaze that makes me shudder. Not in a bad way. In a way that makes me want him more than I've ever wanted anything else in my entire life. Maybe the legends about these woods are right. The sway Riley holds over me feels like a kind of witchcraft. I clench that knife in my hand and suddenly the stars became the least romantic thing about this evening.

I lean in closer to kiss him. He kisses me back.

Afterwards he takes the knife out of my hand and pulls out the blade, the steel gleaming against the light of the flames. "Let me show you how to use it."

Chapter 45

The guard standing outside Riley's hospital room can't be more than twenty years old. He stands at the door like he's been charged with protecting a priceless treasure, but he's lacking that seasoned confidence in his eyes that he'll no doubt gain with more experience. Right now, he's still trying to impress his superiors. But I see the way his expression falters when the nurses race to another room when a patient's alarm goes off. He's still soft around the edges. Good. That ought to make him easier to convince.

"I can't allow you to enter this patient's room, ma'am," he says. He straightens his posture, adding another inch to his height.

"Do you know who I am?"

The guard takes a good look at me, but I can't tell he doesn't recognize me. That means he's not from Braxton Falls. And that's also good for me.

"I'm Lex Wicker." I point at the door. "And the man in that room murdered my sister."

The guard's eyebrows turn upward at the center. There's pity in his face. Perfect. Pity is what I need.

"The warden called me and said he was injured badly. Really badly. He said he might not make it." I take a breath and put on the most pathetic and panged expression I can muster. I even sniffle as though I might turn on the waterworks at any moment. "That man—that *killer*—is supposed to get his just desserts on Friday. But he might not make it to his own execution. And that means I'll never get to tell him how much he hurt me."

"I wish I could help you, ma'am, but my boss will have my job if I let anyone in there."

"All I need is a few minutes. Just a few minutes to remind him of what he did. To say what my sister wasn't able to say."

"I can't—"

"Do you have a sister?"

"I have three."

"You know what he did, don't you? What if it were one of your sisters and this was your last chance to talk to him? Wouldn't you do anything to have the last word?"

There it is. The wavering stoicism. He's going to break.

"Just give me the few minutes he refused to give my sister when she begged him to stop."

The guard glances from one side of the hall to the other. "Three minutes. But keep your distance. And don't touch him."

I nod before quickly sneaking past him and into the room. It's a normal hospital room except that it's been stripped of anything distinguishing or inviting. No 'get well soon' cards on the wall. No balloons. No flowers. There's a window, but it's covered in bars. Miller's Creek Hospital is used to having patients sent over from the prison. The medical apparatuses are specifically hooked up so as not to provide a hazard in the event that a patient decides to take the 'easy way out' of their sentence. Then, of course, there are the handcuffs. And, in Riley's case, the leg shackles as well. Because he's a convicted killer. A murderer of a young girl. Definitely not to be trusted.

I step closer to the bed while still maintaining a safe distance. Riley doesn't appear to be in as bad a shape as I was led to believe on the phone. His face is bruised, deep blotches of purple around his left eye, and there's a cut on his cheek. His jaw is swollen on one side. Puffy like a chipmunk. No one told me exactly what happened, but I'm not an idiot. It's obvious he was attacked. Beaten up by more than one person. It would have to be more than one to take down Riley. He's not that scrawny kid he used to be, after all. I'm sure he put up a good fight. It makes me wonder if it wasn't the guards themselves. Maybe they saw the way my mom broke down on the news. Maybe they were at the memorial themselves. Maybe they got riled up and decided to enforce their own brand of justice. Not that it would matter. Riley will be dead in two days' time anyway.

The monitor beside the bed beeps.

Riley groans. He tries to roll onto his side but he's caught by the leg and arm irons. One eye is permanently shut from the swelling, but the other flutters open. He's surprised to see me.

"Lexie?"

"Since when have I been your emergency contact person?" I ask. The question is curt and pointed. It's not the first thing I intended to say, but it's what comes out. I guess I'm sick of being treated like I'm always on the outside of everything going on in my life. Mom, Cameron, Jessica, Amber, Riley. I'm tired of being the last one to know everything. From now on I want answers. Direct ones.

"Since we last spoke on the phone. I had the prison change it to your number. It was on file. They record the numbers of all incoming and outgoing calls."

"But why me?"

"Who else would I list? Should I keep my lawyer on it? He doesn't give a shit about me. And his job is over now." Riley's voice is gravelly. Speaking probably hurts, but I don't care.

"I am not your girlfriend, Riley. I'm not even your friend. I'm the sister of the girl you were convicted of murdering."

"I didn't do that."

"Twelve jurors said otherwise."

"I told you—"

"You didn't tell me shit. You fed me a load of lies to make me doubt. Then you led me on a wild goose chase causing me to question everyone and everything I know in my life. You're just playing games. And this?" I wave my hands to indicate the entirety of the situation in front of me. "This is just part of your game. Part of your manipulation. To let you get off on my pain."

"That's not true." Riley clears his throat with a cough. He winces. Then he turns his good eye on me. "I didn't murder Amber."

"Why should I believe you? No one else does. The only thing you're doing is making me look like a crazy person. I'm running around in the woods chasing ghosts. I'm suspicious of everyone, including my parents and my best friends. There are journalists outside my mom's house every day. They stalk me at my work. It's bad enough that the entire town has spent the last fifteen years believing I knew what you were planning. What do you think this looks like to them?"

"Did you find it?"

"Did I find what?"

"Proof."

I'm exasperated. Riley might as well have been talking in riddles. "You never even gave me a clue as to where to look. Or for what I should have been looking for."

"I told you—"

"Did you ever have a ring?"

Riley hesitates. "A ring? What kind of ring?"

"A big silver one with a horseshoe shape on it."

"That's not exactly my style."

"Do you remember anyone who might have had one? Someone at school? Your dad? Cameron? Danny Darnielle?"

"Darnielle? What does he have to do with this?"

That's one of the many questions I've been asking myself lately. I found the ring at Nell's house. Danny is her grandson. Was it such a leap to consider the possibility that he was involved

255

in Amber's murder? He was in close proximity to Riley's knife during the fight at the football game. He was also at the dance. And Dad did have a note about Nell in his papers. I don't know why I never considered him to be a suspect before. He should have been one of the first people the police interviewed.

"I don't know, but I think there might be a connection. There's blood on the ring. I think it could be Amber's blood. And maybe the real killer's. But I don't know if I can trust the police. And they might not do anything anyway. They might argue that the ring has passed through too many hands." I'm starting to get worked up. There's a heaviness in my chest that makes it hard to focus. I take a deep breath to prevent myself from crying.

I look up and expect to see anger or frustration in Riley's face, but that's not what I find. What I see is something more surprising. Acceptance.

This is the face of someone who knows they're going to die and can't do anything about it. It reminds me of the Riley I saw in the courtroom. The young man who heard the jury rule on his sentence and couldn't quite believe it. He was half in a dream when the judge declared he would receive the death penalty. So was I. It didn't seem right then. It still doesn't seem right now.

"It's OK, Lexie. You've done more than I could ever hope for. And I'm sorry for putting you through this again," he says. "I never should have written to you. I should have left you and your family in peace."

"It wouldn't have made a difference. Not really. There was never any peace to be had." These are thoughts I've had for years, but never spoken aloud. The belief that it wasn't murder that tore my family apart. It was just the emptiness. The void left by Amber. We probably still would have had it if she'd passed from something else. A car wreck. Cancer. A freak accident. She bound us all together. She completed us. Riley wasn't the one who destroyed my family. Amber was.

"You can leave. I promise I won't contact you again. Just

promise me you won't come to the execution. Promise me you won't be there."

Oh, God. I forgot all about that.

"Was Amber in love with Cameron?" I ask. The question falls from my lips without thinking.

"What?"

"Cameron was your best friend. You did everything together. You would know if he was dating someone besides Jess. You would know if something was going on with him and my sister."

"No, I don't think so. I don't remember anything between the two of them." It's hard to tell what Riley is thinking with his face so swollen and contused, but there's a far-off look in his good eye.

"What about Jess?"

"Are you asking if Amber was into Jessica?"

"I'm asking if there's anything you remember that seemed off in our group. Anything that struck you as odd. Not just before the dance. The entire year before. Was there anything going on that I didn't know about? Something someone may have wanted to hide from me?"

Riley goes quiet. The only sound in the room is the beeping on the monitor behind his bed.

"Cameron wanted to break it off with Jess. Like . . . completely. He never told me why. He just said that it wasn't working out. That he didn't see them together in the long run."

"Do you think it's because he was interested in someone else?"

"He never said. He only told me that he wasn't going to stay with her after graduation." Riley pauses. "He wasn't even going to ask her to go to homecoming with him. He didn't want to go. But she'd already bought the tickets. They had a big argument about it the week before the dance."

I thought back to the dance. Jessica had been acting strange that night. She was more high-strung than usual. More abrasive. I thought she was just in one of her moods, trying to get attention. Like the dress she wore. I couldn't believe the staff even allowed her in the door. It had been too provocative for high school, with a cut down the center torso that stopped just below her navel. I remember saying something to her about it and she laughed. But Cameron? I barely remember Cameron at the dance.

I recall that photograph I found on Amber's secret FriendSpace account. The one that featured Dad in the background talking to Mr. Henson. He shouldn't have been there. He wasn't a chaperone. And my mother's statement to the police was that he'd been with her all evening.

Then it hits me.

"Who was in the woods with my father that night? You said you saw him with somebody. Who was it?"

"I don't know, Lex. It was dark. It was late." Riley sighs. "And I'd had a bit to drink."

"If you had to guess."

"I don't know."

"Tell me who it was."

"I can't remember."

"Was it Cameron?"

"No."

"Was it Danny?"

"No, it wasn't."

"How can you be sure? Are you lying?"

"I'm not lying. I honestly don't know who—"

"My father didn't murder Amber. If you didn't kill her, then someone else did. And if there was someone else out there then they might be the one who—"

"Henson."

My jaw clenches so hard I think I hear a crack in my molar.

"It was Henson."

Chapter 46

I tear through Amber's room. Dresser drawers, closet, desk, shoeboxes. Within minutes the picture-perfect museum-quality staging is destroyed. I don't stop to think about the fuss my mom is going to throw when she sees it. My desperation is singularly focused. I need evidence. I need something substantial to back up Riley's statement. I need proof. Something that'll confirm— without a shadow of doubt—that I'm right.

That he's innocent.

I dig beneath Amber's old clothes, neatly folded in her wardrobe. Her scent is still on them all these years later. It permeates my senses and takes me back fifteen years. Even further than that. It reminds me of how things had been before we were teenagers. Back when we were inseparable. When being sisters meant being best friends. Before boys and parents and academic stressors came between us. When it was just her and me, ready to take on the world.

I rub away the tears from my eyes.

Nothing.

There's nothing.

I rip up the floorboard again, hoping to find something in her hiding place that I might have missed. But the only thing left in that space are cobwebs. I rap my knuckles on the floor, searching for another hollow nook beneath a loose board. I examine the entire room twice. I even pull everything out of the closet and feel up and down the walls. There must be something. Anything.

Still nothing.

I slump against the side of the bed. My breaths are heavy and I'm trying to hold back tears. Doubt creeps in again. Maybe this has all been a mistake. Maybe I was wrong. Maybe Riley did kill my sister. Maybe I'm just the biggest fool in the world for hoping that I'm not what everyone says I am—a stupid naïve girl who refuses to see the obvious. A girl who refuses to believe that she could fall in love with a killer. And a grown woman who desperately wishes she could escape her past and find love again.

Across the room, Amber's backpack sits cockeyed against the dresser. It's still open from when I removed her laptop the other day. A folder of papers is stuffed inside. I stretch across the floor and pull the backpack into my lap. Then I rip open the folder. A score of old homework assignments, quizzes, and reports that were merely tossed into the folder without regard for the pockets meant to secure them in place spills out. They scatter across the floor.

I pick them up one at a time, carefully tidying them together. Then I reach under the dresser for the last one. A two-page report that's been stapled together. When I pull it out, the grade at the top of the page practically paralyzes me. I stare at it unflinching for nearly a minute before my brain manages to catch up to my subconscious memory.

62/65 = 95% Well done!

I stare at the writing. Blue sharpie. A number two that looks more like a Z. And a six that doesn't fully connect.

My gaze darts to the top of the report where we were always instructed to type a heading with our name, date, and class information.

Amber Wicker
September 26, 2006
10th Grade History
Mr. Henson

Chapter 47

There's something eerie about an empty high school. It's like time has stopped. The silence in a place that's normally a din from the hordes of screaming teenagers is almost palpable. The smell is also more prominent. Not the smell of sweaty gym clothes and overcooked cafeteria food, but that telltale odor of high school. A kind of musty, metallic scent with a hint of used books and the same industrial cleaning formula that's been used across the country for the last forty years.

It takes me back to when I used to roam those halls as a student. The disarray of pushing through the crowd between classes. The chaos of keeping secrets. The fear of not being asked out to the next dance or losing a spot in the end-of-the-year musical. It's unreal how quickly the mind can transport you back to a prominent moment in your memory. And it's scary how easily your brain can be tricked into believing you're actually there.

I make my way to the custodial office at the far end of the school near the gym. As the part-time custodian I have a key to most of the rooms, but CJ is the only one with a key to all of the administrative offices. I've never used it before because cleaning the offices isn't in my job description. Even CJ has admitted that he doesn't do it often. Occasionally he'll throw out the trash and vacuum the carpet, but for the most part the secretarial staff and office workers maintain the upkeep themselves. But CJ still has the key in his personal locker, just in case.

It doesn't take me long to find it. CJ doesn't even have a lock on the door. When I open it, I push his coveralls and jacket to the side. The set of master keys is hanging on a hook at the back of the locker. I snatch the keys and close the door, then I make my way back out into the hallway.

I begin to second-guess myself almost immediately. What if I'm wrong? Lots of people have similar handwriting styles and I'm not an expert. Yes, the 2 and the 6 looked almost identical, but it could be a coincidence. I'm about to break into someone's office based on a few scribbled numbers on a test that's over fifteen years old. It's crazy. Maybe I'm crazy.

But if I'm right . . .

When I reach the school lobby I use the master key to unlock the door to the main office. I walk briskly past the front desk where the secretary takes morning absentee calls and I make my way to the office in the back. The principal's office. Henson's office.

Don't think, Lex. Just do it. Get in. Find what you're looking for. And get out.

I slip the key into the lock and turn it to the left. The door clicks and I step inside before I can change my mind.

Henson's office is exactly what one would expect. Dark brown bookshelves line the walls, full to the brim with texts. Most of them are history textbooks, but there are some educational manuals as well, alongside a few inspirational self-help texts that he probably lends out to students who are going through a rough time. I remember after Amber died when the guidance counselor at the time tried to offer me a book on grief. I don't remember if I ever took it. If I did I never read it.

The rest of the walls display his academic certificates and a cliché inspirational poster that haunts the halls of every American high school; an eagle soaring above the mountains with the word PERSERVERANCE underneath. Henson's desk is tidy and pushed close to the window, but faces the door. I step around to the opposite side and sit down in the chair. I pull out the desk drawers one at a time, digging through the pens and the documents for something.

It occurs to me then exactly how stupid this entire thing is. If Henson really is behind the photograph of Jessica—if it's possible that he's involved in Amber's murder—then he wouldn't be so stupid as to leave the evidence at his place of work. He'd hide it at home where he could always keep an eye on it. Only an idiot would leave something as incriminating as proof of a crime in their office. In a high school, of all places.

But then I think of all those serial killer documentaries on television and how all of those criminals thought they'd never get caught. How their narcissism blinded them to the fact that it would only take one mistake for someone to uncover their secrets. And how they all claimed they never thought anyone would figure it out. Because they were so fucking smart. And maybe they weren't wrong. If Henson was responsible for Amber's death, then technically he did get away with it.

At least for fifteen years.

I tug on the final drawer, anticipation creeping down my spine. Nothing. Files. Academic transcripts. Nothing to indicate a crime.

My shoulders slump as a heavy sigh falls from my lips. That's when I see it. Beneath the eagle poster is a waist-high bookshelf. The top two shelves display various awards and plaques. Teacher of the Year. National Honor Society Award for Best Administrator. There's also a framed photograph of him with the mayor receiving a donation to the school board's charity foundation for under-privileged students. But on the lowest shelf there's a box. It looks like a treasure box, with a lock on the front. It's familiar, too. Like I've seen it somewhere before.

It takes a moment for my brain to realize where I recognize it from. It almost startles me how quickly my thoughts are able to place the object in my memory. Henson's history class. It used to sit on his desk in his classroom. Students would ask what was in it during the first week of school and Henson would always joke about how it was a prop for a later chapter in the course. A chapter we never seemed to get to. Eventually everyone forgot about it. Ignored it as just another part of the scenery, like the inspirational posters.

He couldn't possibly be that stupid.

I climb out of the chair and move to the opposite side of the office. I pick up the box. It has a weight to it, but it's not heavy. It feels empty, but when I shake it I can hear something inside. I set the box on the desk and look at the padlock. A lock I don't have a key for.

But I don't need a key.

I take out the small Swiss army knife from my pocket and flip open the nail file. I try not to get distracted by my thoughts, but it's hard not to see the irony in the fact that I'm using a knife that Riley gave me to potentially prove his innocence. I push the pointed end of the nail file into the slot for the key and jiggle it around, feeling for the locking mechanism. Just like Riley taught me.

It's not budging. Then, without warning, click. I'm in.

I remove the padlock and take a deep breath, composing myself for what I might find. Then I rip off the proverbial Band-Aid.

It's as though someone has knocked my soul right out of my body.

There are dozens of photographs. *Dozens*. Horror catches in my throat as I stare down at the pile of Polaroids. And they're not just of Jessica. They're all different. Each one a different face. A different girl. But the same setting. Almost the same pose. Naked. Back against the tree. Legs partially spread.

I pick up the Polaroids one at a time without thinking. My thoughts are racing but my consciousness is slow to catch up. There must be at least fifty girls in these photos. Maybe more. But there's only one I'm looking for. Only one I care about.

I lay each one out on the desk as I go through them. I don't think I recognize any of them, but I'm not really looking hard enough. My focus is on one girl. One face. One—

I stop.

Me.

I stare at the photograph, my hand shaking in disbelief.

No. Not me. But someone who looks a lot like me.

Amber.

"It's not what you think."

The voice cuts through my panic and I look up to see Henson standing in the doorway. I freeze, Amber's photo clenched between my fingertips. Instinct should be telling me to run, but I can't move. I can't even think.

Then he closes the door halfway and takes a step closer.

Chapter 48

"Alexandra, hear me out."

I take a large step backwards, bumping into the bookshelf on the wall. It shakes and I move to the side, putting the desk between Henson and myself. He moves closer, but he's still blocking the door. If I try to run past him he'll have no trouble grabbing me. My fingers grip the photo, bending it.

"Stay away from me."

Henson takes another step forward. "I need you to listen to me."

"I don't want to hear it."

"You have to. You don't understand."

"I don't think there's much to understand. You're a sick, disgusting pervert." My pulse quickens as I speak, but I somehow manage to keep calm. Maybe it's that prey instinct. I know that if I do anything quick or erratic, he'll be on me in seconds.

"You're wrong. That's not it at all. That's not what this is."

"You have a locked box full of photographs of naked girls in your office. Naked *teenage* girls. And they're *dated*."

The earliest one I saw was 1999, but who knows how far this goes. Who knows how long he's been manipulating girls to take their clothes off for his camera. Not to mention what else he's made them do.

I always thought there was something about him. Even when I was younger and didn't quite believe it was possible that people you were supposed to trust could deceive you. Now I see how wrong I was.

"It's art."

"Art? Art?!" I laugh. I can't help it. Did Henson really believe what he was saying? Or was he just trying to distract me? But then I remember what Jessica said. 'This is just really bad art.' Is that how he convinced those girls to pose for him? By trying to make it look like something artistic and creative?

He moves closer and I reposition myself opposite him, putting both the desk and the chair between us. It's only after the fact that I realize I've cornered myself. "I'm sure the police will have a good laugh at that explanation."

"It's true."

"They're underage girls, asshole. They're *children!*"

"The age of consent in Ohio is sixteen."

I scoff, momentarily forgetting how absolutely terrified I am. "Is that supposed to make any of this OK? Is that supposed to make you any less despicable?"

"It makes it legal."

Lies.

"No, it doesn't. You're a teacher. People trust you. These *girls* trusted you."

I shake my head. I can't believe I'm having this conversation with a nude photograph of my sister in my hand. There's a fury boiling inside of me as I imagine Amber standing out in the woods, naked, back up against the tree her body was found bound to. There are leaves on the ground in the photo. Early autumn. Probably not long after I caught her in the kitchen with Riley. It must have been cold outside at night.

"Did you do it?"

"Do what?" Henson's expression is difficult to read. Almost impossible. I can see that he's worried. Worried that someone might find us? Worried that I might have already sent someone a text with a picture of the photographs? I curse myself for not thinking to do that as soon as I found them. That was stupid. Now I was standing in a small room without any leverage.

But Henson didn't know that.

"Murder my sister."

He stares at me without blinking. His eyes lose that worry and go blank.

My shoulders tense.

"Did you?!"

"No," he says. Then his expression breaks into disbelief. "Of course not."

I hold up the Polaroid. "You have a photograph of her standing in front of the exact same place her body was found!"

"I didn't kill your sister."

"I don't believe you!" That's when I realize I'm shouting. Not that it matters. It's late. After hours. There's no one else in the school. I don't even know how Henson knew I was there. But it's clear by his lack of concern for the open door behind him that he doesn't think anyone else is coming.

He steps up to the desk. He's less than two feet away from me now.

"I swear to you. I did not murder your sister. I didn't do anything to her."

"You did this!" I shake the photograph. "You manipulated her! You sick, twisted pedo—"

"I am not!" Henson yells. The sound of his voice carries in that cramped room like the boom through a speaker. It sends a jolt of shock through me, jerking me back to reality.

I'm taunting a man who could kill me. A man who probably killed my sister. A man who has done God knows what else to God knows how many other women.

"I've already texted a photo of this to the police," I lie. "They know where I am. They'll be here any minute."

"No, you haven't." He sounds more confident than I do.

"I have. They'll find you and they'll arrest you for indecency and child endangerment. For rape."

"I've never raped anyone."

"No one will believe that. They'll see all of this and they'll find out you've been mishandling young girls for years. They'll track them all down. People will come forward. And then they'll see this picture of Amber and realize the truth. That they put an innocent person on death row for a crime you committed."

"I never touched your sister." There's a hardness in his stare that shakes me to the bone. Any charm or charisma I might have seen over the years is gone. This is the look of a tiger being backed into a corner, ready to bare its claws. This is the look of a man who could kill.

And I'm the only one standing between him and the rest of the world discovering his secret.

An unexpected thought interrupts my fear.

What would Riley do?

My free hand slips down to my side, feeling inside my pocket for the Swiss army knife.

"Maybe you didn't touch her, but there are dozens of girls in this box. I bet there's at least one you couldn't keep your hands off of." I think of the picture of Jessica and that look of ecstasy on her face. More experienced than Amber's innocent, wide-eyed look. Was that why she and Cameron had been on-and-off during junior year? Then I remember the initials in the tree.

It was an H.

JESSI ❤ D.H.

D for Dick. For Richard.

Richard Henson.

Fuck. I should have seen it earlier.

"Some of them wanted it. Stupid, frivolous teenage girls with their heads full of fluff and gossip and delusions of romance. Your sister was one of them. But she wasn't my type."

270

I slowly use one hand to open the blade on the pocketknife.

"But she was good enough to take a picture of?"

"She was close enough."

"Close enough to what?"

"Close enough to you."

Nothing could have prepared me for that response. And while I hope it's just a ploy to keep me from trying to escape—or maybe he thinks that bizarre and degrading form of compliment will convince me to keep what I found to myself—I can hear a kind of honesty in his voice. Henson is a narcissist of the worst kind. The kind that believes his own twisted view of the world. A world where he can get whatever he wants just because he knows exactly what to say to trick a young girl's heart.

But I'm not a young girl.

And my heart was lost long ago.

"Get away from me," I say. There's a wobble in my voice, clear as day. And if I can hear it, so can Henson.

"You've seen the photos. You tell me. Which ones are the most beautiful?" He picks one up off the desk at random: 2004. A dark-haired girl with pursed lips leans provocatively toward the camera. "The sluts?"

He picks up another. Short curly hair. Glasses. Her face says she's shy. As do her hands, which are blurred mid-motion, like she was trying to cover her chest before the photo was taken. "Or the ones who don't know what they're doing? The girls who haven't quite figured out who they are."

Every word Henson speaks makes me sick to my stomach. The urge to gag scratches at the back of my throat. The blade of the knife opens fully in my pocket. I run my thumb along the sharp edge, reminding myself that I will not be another victim in Henson's list of terrified girls. I won't be another Amber.

"You're the one whose photo I really wanted. Even now, with your cropped hair and your futile attempt to hide yourself beneath those boyish coveralls, you'd be a beautiful addition to my collection. But you were always impossible to get to. Your sister was easy. She looked the part of the innocent girl, but she was anything but. And I think you know that."

He sweeps the photographs off the desk and moves toward the left side of the desk. I dash in the opposite direction but he twists and does the same. He grabs me by the sleeve of my jacket and tugs me toward the desk. The bony curve of my hip hits the corner of the desk sending a stinging pain through my side.

"Let go of me!"

"Give me the photograph!"

"No!" I unsheathe the knife from my pocket and slash the blade across the top of his wrist. It's sharp, rarely used. It doesn't take much pressure to cut the thick green vein that splinters off toward his fingers releasing a speedy flow of blood over his hand.

Henson hisses, releasing his grip on my arm long enough for me to round the corner of the desk and make for the door. He grabs me from behind, pulling me by the collar of my jacket. Thankfully it's a loose fit. I slip my arms out of it. The momentum sends Henson tumbling into the desk, knocking the treasure box of Polaroids on the floor.

"Bitch!" He lunges forward, arm stretched out to grab me again.

I stab the knife through the center of his palm.

For a second everything stops. We stand there in silence, both equally shocked by what I've done. Although I can't imagine Henson is more surprised than I am. Blood streams over his fingers, pooling on the floor by his shoes. He stares at his wounded hand with a weird kind of self-pity. Like a boy who's just learned his dog has died. That look almost creeps me out even more than the photographs. More than the realization that this was probably the man who murdered my sister.

Then I hear her voice. A whisper in my ear.

Get out, Lexie.

Get out before you end up like me.

I throw the door open and bolt out of the office. I don't stop to look behind me. I don't even breathe. I just run head on, sprinting down the slippery hallways that just hours before were full of laughing teenagers. When I come to the double doors that lead out to the employee parking lot I bear all of my weight into the push pad handles, shoving them open with more ease than usual. Then I make a break for my car.

It's sprinkling rain, but I can barely feel it. The jaundiced glow from the parking lot lights splays an eerie gleam on the vehicles. I see Henson's BMW parked near the front. Part of me wants to glance back and see if he's after me, but I know that if I don't keep moving forward I'll lose my momentum. And maybe my life.

When I reach my car, I break the record for getting in and speeding out of the lot. It's not until I'm on the road that I peer through my rear-view mirror. There's no one behind me, but that doesn't stop me from running every red light until I get home.

Chapter 49

Saturday, October 13, 2007
7:45 p.m.

We aren't at the dance more than five minutes when I know something has happened.

Up until the moment we walk into the gym, decorated with twinkling lights and dangling hand-cut snowflakes reflective of the winter wonderland theme, I thought everything had been going great. Jessica came over to the house early that afternoon and helped Amber and I with our makeup. Amber still refused to tell us who she was going with. I suspected she wasn't going with anyone. The cheerleading squad had a habit of going to homecoming in a group so I assumed that's what she had planned. She was just teasing us for the attention. Jessica fell for it. I didn't.

Cameron and Riley picked us up at a quarter after five. Cameron looked like he'd just stepped out of a men's fashion magazine. He wore a fitted suit that matched Jessica's dress perfectly in both cut and color. His tie was the same shade of blue as her bodice. It was the first time I looked at one of my friends and realized we were almost adults. Because he didn't look like a boy in that suit. He looked like a man. And Riley—

I didn't know Riley could be so handsome. My heart fluttered at the sight of him. I know it sounds clichéd to say I had butterflies in my stomach, but there was a kind of fairy-tale feeling I got when I saw him standing in the doorway. He wasn't as cool and confident as Cameron, but he was just as swoon-worthy. I even caught my mother giving an approving look. More importantly, Amber was wrong. He did remember to get me a corsage. And it was perfect. Everything was perfect.

Cameron drove us to Rinaldi's Restaurant downtown. His father had made reservations for us. He was footing the bill as well, which I was quietly grateful for. Rinaldi's was notoriously expensive. I never would have been able to afford dinner there on my own and I didn't dare ask my parents. Amber didn't join us. She said she was going out to eat with the cheerleaders and would meet us at the dance. Dad didn't like that. He wanted us to go together. But homecoming is one of those nights when parents ease up on their watchful eyes. They remember what it was like, after all. It's one of those coming-of-age events. Especially for a teenage girl. And there's nothing more embarrassing than an overprotective parent giving a girl's date the rules, punctuated by the subtle threat of what would happen if we weren't brought home on time. Thankfully, Dad didn't do that. He just told us to be home by eleven. And that was generous considering the dance ended at ten.

Dinner was fantastic. I'd never eaten so well in my life. But I knew early on that I wouldn't be able to order what I wanted and still be able to dance in my dress later. So, I followed Jessica's lead and ordered something light and salad-based even though I really wanted to stuff my face with ravioli. It was also the cheaper option, which made me feel slightly less guilty about not being able to contribute to the bill. No one else seemed to care about that though. Both Cameron and Riley ordered the most expensive dishes on the menu.

Riley was quiet during most of dinner. In fact, he'd been a little standoffish since last week's football game. I figured he felt uncomfortable in his stiff button-up shirt and dress slacks. He looked gorgeous, but it clearly wasn't his style. I tried to ease his discomfort by placing a hand on his thigh beneath the table. That would break him out of his daze long enough to give me a soft smile. Unspoken reassurance that everything was fine. Dances just weren't his thing. He was only doing it for me, because he knew I wanted to. And by the time the main courses came around he was more relaxed, grinning at Jessica's constant barrage of ridiculous stories about her extended family. I laughed so hard I almost smeared my mascara.

We finished dinner with more than an hour to spare before the start of the dance. That's when Jessica pulled out the liquor bottles hidden in the back seat of Cameron's car. I didn't want to drink. Not that I was a prude or anything. I'd had alcohol before: it wasn't the first time Jessica or Cameron showed up to one of our group get-togethers with booze. I just didn't want to tarnish the evening. I wanted everything to be perfect. I wanted to remember it all.

But peer pressure is a bitch. Especially when you're the odd one out. And I always was in our friend group. So, I gave in and downed two miniature travel-sized bottles of vodka in the back seat, which was practically nothing compared to my friends.

And by the time we arrive at the dance, we're all pleasantly buzzed.

But something isn't right.

We pose for our pictures immediately before entering the gym. The school has hired a professional photographer who has a photo area set up in the hallway. He snaps a photo of the four of us together first—Jessica insisted we get a group picture for the memories—before taking one of Cameron and Jess alone. They pose like they've been practicing for it and I wouldn't be surprised if they had, on Jessica's insistence of course. They're so glamorous. Definitely a shoo-in for homecoming king and queen. When it's time for Riley and me to get our picture taken, I sense a sudden stiffness in Riley's posture.

"Are you OK?" I ask as we stand side by side.

The photographer steps forward and puts our hands together, gently turning my wrist to show off my corsage.

Riley doesn't say anything.

"Riley? Is everything OK?"

"It's fine," he says. "I just don't like getting my picture taken. That's all."

The photographer raises his hand. "Look at the red light on top of the camera. Big smiles."

Riley smiles.

I don't.

"Oh my God, Lexie. Could you be any more serious?" Jessica mocks from behind the photographer. "It's homecoming! You're supposed to be happy!"

I am happy. I'm just a little lightheaded from the drinking and not having eaten enough. And Riley's sudden stiffness worries me. It makes me uncomfortable. Maybe my tipsiness is wearing off.

The photographer looks annoyed. "Let's try that one more time. Try not to blink. On the count of three. One . . . Two . . . Three!"

I smile just in time. Then I laugh. I don't know what got into me. For a moment I felt like I was somewhere else. But I shake it off and walk away, only half bumping into the draping fabric used for the photograph's background.

Jessica wraps her arm around mine and tugs me toward the gym entrance. Cameron and Riley follow behind us. The gym is dark, lit only by the glittering string of lights that the student council committee has hung up above the dance floor and the purple glow of floodlights positioned around the corners of the gym to give the space a gentler romantic atmosphere. Pillars with loose hanging crepe have been placed around the basketball court floor to give the illusion of a smaller, more inviting space. As long as I don't look to the walls where the bleachers have been pushed back, I can almost imagine that we're at an actual venue instead of a high school. Something fancy and classy. Like a hall reserved

277

for a wedding reception. Even the tissue paper decorations look ethereal. Or maybe that's just the alcohol.

"Should we dance?" Jess says, her voice practically buried beneath the beat of the DJ's music.

"I need to find Amber first," I say.

"Oh, come on! I want to dance!" Jessica leans into me with a pout. She's acting like she's more wasted than she actually is.

"I'd like a drink first," Cameron says. "What about you, Riley?"

Riley doesn't respond. At first, I think he's staring off into outer space. Then I follow his gaze and realize he's looking at the gym entrance where Amber has just walked in. Amber and her date.

Danny Darnielle.

"What the fuck is Amber doing with that douchebag?" Jessica practically spits.

Cameron gives an uncomfortable look. "I thought she was going with the cheer squad."

"So did I," I mumble.

"That son of a bitch almost got me expelled."

I glance up at Riley. He has the same look on his face as he did during the football game. He looks like he might cross the floor and rip Danny's head off.

"Maybe they're not together," I say. "Maybe she's just talking to him."

But then Danny wraps his arm around Amber's waist and she doesn't pull away. She's laughing at something one of the other girls in her group has said. She has no idea we're watching her. She has no idea how shocked we are to see her and Danny together.

"Guh," Jessica moans. "Danny is gross. She's way too good for him. He's not worth any of our time. And if Amber wants to hang out with him then she's not worth our time either."

"Jess! Don't be mean. She's my sister."

Jessica shrugs. "I'm just saying. If she wants to make the biggest fucking mistake of her life, then that's on her. Who wants to hang around a weasel that smells like bait anyway?"

Cameron snorts a laugh. Riley doesn't.

I place my hand on Riley's elbow. "Let's get a drink."

Jessica opens her clutch and removes a small pill. "And if fruit punch isn't enough, I've brought a little something to give us an extra kick."

"I could use one of those," Cameron says.

Cameron leans in close to her and she places the pill on his tongue before give him a kiss.

My jaw drops. "Oh my God, Jess. Did you bring drugs to the school dance?"

"Chill out, Lexie. No one's going to know."

"What if a teacher catches you with it?"

Jessica smirks. "No one is going to catch me. Now come on."

She places another pill on her tongue and waggles it tauntingly at me before swallowing. I desperately glance around to make sure no one is watching. Then Jessica holds out her hand, palm up. Two little pills waiting for Riley and me.

"I can't. I mean . . . This isn't our thing. Riley and I don't—"

But Riley snatches one of the pills out her hand so quickly I feel like I've been barreled over. What has gotten into him today? He's not acting like himself at all.

"Come on, Lexie. I want you to have a good time," Jessica pleads.

But I am having a good time. Or I was having a good time.

"It'll be fine, Lex." Cameron smiles. "I promise. It's just like drinking five Coca-Colas at once. It'll wear off in a few hours."

I glance over at Riley, hoping he'll side with me and tell them to back down, but he's back to staring at Danny again.

"You swear?"

Jessica draws a cross light above her bodice. "Cross my heart. May the Wynwood Witch strike me down if I lie."

I tentatively take the pill out of her palm and glance at it. I don't want to take it. But everyone else did. I don't want them to think I'm a loser. Worse than that, I don't want them to think I'm boring. I think about the day I caught Amber kissing Riley. He looked so obsessed with her. I want him to look at me like that.

I place the pill on my tongue and swallow.

Chapter 50

My apartment door is open.

I almost don't notice it at first. I'm so stressed out from the altercation with Henson that I'm not really thinking. Adrenaline rushes through me, making it impossible to focus as I jumble my fingers in my pockets looking for my keys. Then I notice that the door isn't completely shut. It's closed enough to look shut, but it's still slightly ajar.

My first thought is *did I lock the door?* But I know I did. I always do. I'm practically OCD about that kind of thing. But I have been distracted lately. Is it possible that I was so dead set on breaking into Henson's office that I wasn't thinking straight? Maybe I didn't lock it. Maybe my focus was elsewhere.

Or maybe someone broke in.

Shit.

I remove the keys from my pocket and slip them between my fingers, holding them in a death grip as I push open the door.

"Is someone in here?" It's a little late for an inspection from my landlady, but it wouldn't be the first time she stopped by unannounced. "Mrs. Campbell? Is that you?"

The lights are off. There's no response.

I step inside and flip on the switch, flooding the living room and kitchen with the glow of my obscenely bright ceiling light. It's then that I notice the mess. Not the mess of a burglar, but my own mess. Unwashed plates are strewn across the counters. My paint supplies, the ones I've ignored for the last week, haven't been put away. And I have to step over three pairs of shoes to get over the entranceway.

"Hello?" I call out.

Again, no answer.

I close the door behind me and step further into the living room. The apartment is still. Quiet. And while it doesn't look like anyone has been here, I can't help but feel like there's something in the room with me.

It's also cold as hell. I glance at the thermostat on the wall. The temperature has dropped almost fifteen degrees. It must be broken. But when I turn the dial, the screen lights up. It's working fine.

Did someone turn it down?

Don't be stupid. It's just a faulty battery.

I drop my keys back into my pocket just as a muddled clatter from one of the back rooms shakes me out of my daydream.

There is someone in the house.

I grab a knife from the kitchen and make my way into the bedroom. Dark shadows from the windows cascade across the bed. There's a form on the mattress, beneath the comforter. Panic clenches in my chest and I grip the knife, ready to stab my second person of the evening. The comforter moves. I raise the knife. It takes my eyes a second to adjust.

Then I see Spaghetti slither out from beneath the sheets and plop on the carpet beside the bed.

I exhale a heavy sigh of relief. She's gotten out of her tank again. That's all.

I feel like an idiot for getting worked up over nothing. I must have forgotten to lock the door. Just as I must have forgotten to make sure the lid on Spaghetti's tank was properly closed after I fed her the other day.

282

Spaghetti slowly curves along the floor near my foot. I set the knife down on the dresser and turn on the light.

There's blood on the floor. It's not much. Not more than what you'd expect to see from a cut. But the red is glaring against the off-white carpet, smudged by the python's slithering trail. I crouch down and gently pick Spaghetti up, careful to mind her head. She's not too heavy but she's long and agitated, fussing against my touch. That's when I see the blood smeared against the side of her scales near her mouth. She tenses her muscles and hisses at me, annoyed. Then my eyes dart to the nightstand. Empty.

Someone *was* in my apartment. Spaghetti bit them. And they took the ring.

Chapter 51

Saturday, October 13, 2007
8:34 p.m.

"Let go, Riley! You're hurting me." I tug on my arm, but Riley strengthens his grip. He has his fingers locked around my forearm, just under the elbow. I know it's going to leave a bruise, one that won't be easy to hide. But that's not the first thought that crosses my mind. The first thought is that at least we already had our pictures taken. Stupid. Even I can't believe myself when I think that. As if my senior homecoming photos are more important than the fact that my boyfriend is going to leave a bruise on my arm. Seriously, who thinks like that?

"Tell me the truth."

He pulls me into a corner of the gym. The overhead lights are off, the room lit up by dangling disco balls and the occasional strobe to give the gym a mood. It still smells like a gym though. Especially when you get close to the walls. No amount of glittery decorations and hanging streamers can make up for the fact that the basketball team was practicing in here yesterday afternoon, sweating all over the sleek floors. It's a temporary illusion. All high school dances are. And yet we all fall for the illusion. Just like I've fallen for the illusion that my boyfriend would never hurt me.

"What truth?"

"You know!"

I don't know what he's talking about. One moment we're on the dance floor, having a good time, and the next he's pulling me away from my friends and accusing me of something without telling me what that something is. I would laugh except it's not funny. This was supposed to be a fun evening. This was supposed to be perfect. But it suddenly doesn't feel very perfect. And it's far from fun.

To top it all off, I don't feel well. My head is a little dizzy and there's an ache in my belly that feels like period cramps on overload. Maybe I shouldn't have taken that pill Jessica gave me. Maybe I should have had something more than a salad to eat for dinner. But Jessica told me I'd regret it if I ate too much. Especially if Riley and I decided to do it later. And twice I'd been dumb enough to listen to her.

"I think I need to go to the bathroom," I say.

Riley's hand slides down to my wrist. He pulls me to him. Anyone who looks at us probably thinks we're just trying to find a quiet place to make out. That's how close we are. But it's far from that. Now I realize he's serious. Now I realize he might actually hurt me.

"I just need you to be honest with me."

"What are you talking about?" I ask. I stop trying to pull my arm away from him. Part of me hopes one of the teacher chaperones see us and tells him to leave, but another part of me is afraid that's exactly what will happen. Small-minded Braxton Falls bias and Riley's family situation have kept him off everyone's favorite list at school. If he gets suspended again, he'll probably get expelled. And then he won't graduate. And it would be my fault.

"Darnielle said you—" He cuts himself off, his gaze distracted by someone behind me.

I glance back and see Danny and Amber heading toward the drink counter.

"He said what?"

Riley blinks and looks back at me. "You'd never hurt me, right?"

The question takes me by so much surprise that I almost laugh. And I can tell by the angry red flush to Riley's face that I must be making the most incredulous expression.

"Are you joking? Of course, I'd never hurt you."

"And you'd never do anything that would hurt our relationship, right?"

"Riley, what's wrong? Why would you think that I'd hurt you?"

He squeezes my wrist. "Promise me, Lexie."

"I promise! I swear! Just let go! You're hurting me."

It's dark in the gym, but I can still see Riley's face clearly. There's a flash of something frightening in his eyes. Something violent. Like he might do something really bad if I can't prove that I've been faithful in our relationship. But really it ought to be me who's angry. I'm the one who should feel insulted and humiliated. How could he even think that I would do something to ruin our relationship? He should know me better.

Maybe he's just had too much to drink. We both have. I knew it wasn't a good idea, but I didn't want to ruin everyone's fun.

Riley opens his mouth to respond, but he never gets the chance. Cameron pops up out of nowhere, interrupting him.

"Have either of you seen Jess? I've been looking for her for the last ten minutes," Cameron asks.

My heart flutters. My stomach reels. I feel like I'm going to throw up all over my dress.

Cameron takes one look at my face and then down to my wrist where Riley is still clinging to it with a death grip. I've always misjudged Cameron. He acts like the dumb jock, but he's not. He pays attention. He just doesn't get involved unless he has to.

"You OK, Riley? You're looking a little pale."

Riley seems to snap out of his momentary fury. He lets go of my wrist. I automatically pull it to my chest to prevent him from grabbing it again. I also take a step backwards. He's crushed part of my corsage.

"Nah, man. I'm fine. Just a little dizzy."

"If I'd known you were such a lightweight I wouldn't have let Jess give you that pill," Cameron jokes. He's trying to calm Riley down. He's trying to protect me by pretending to be an idiot. By trying to play off that funny guy routine he's not very good at. I definitely haven't given Cameron enough credit. He's a good guy. "Come on. Let's all get something to drink. Maybe you guys can help me find Jess. She's probably in the bathroom though. You know how girls are about the bathroom. They go in herds and then you don't see them for an hour." Cameron looks at me. "What's that all about anyway?"

I offer a halfhearted smile. "Girl secrets. I'd tell you but then I'd have to kill you."

Cameron laughs. Riley doesn't.

Cameron slaps Riley on the shoulder. "Come on, man. Let's get your lady a drink. You want a Sprite, Lex?"

"Sure," I say, but I'm not thirsty. I don't need a drink. What I need is fresh air and some ibuprofen.

"It's hot as hell in this gym. I'm sweating worse than Rob Yancey after last year's state wrestling match."

"Can't even believe that kid made it to states last year," Riley grumbles.

"Right?"

Cameron leads Riley off to the beverage table. I follow along after, but each step I take feels like a knife is being plunged into my belly. I can't tell if it's actual pain or if it's just nerves. Does Riley think I've been cheating on him? Is he crazy? Drunk? And was he really going to hurt me?

I look down at my forearm. Stupid question, Lex. He already did hurt you.

But Riley didn't mean to do it. Someone must have said something to him that set him off. He does have a short temper.

287

I glance around the dance floor as I weave through the crowd of teenagers. Everyone is laughing. The music is thumping. No one appears to be paying us any attention. No one except—

Amber.

I catch her gaze from across the gym floor. She's standing with a group of cheerleaders. They're all chatting and jumping up and down. Acting like stupid teenagers. But not Amber. Amber is staring directly at me. Her face is blank. No smile: she's not even blinking. It's creepy. Like a figure out of a horror story.

"Is 7Up OK?"

I blink out of my thoughts and turn to look at Cameron who's holding out a plastic cup of 7Up. For a split second I think about all of those warnings people tell young women. Don't accept unopened drinks from strangers. But Cameron isn't a stranger. Cameron is my friend. My best friend's boyfriend. And this isn't a sleazy bar. This is a high school dance.

I take the cup. "Thanks."

Cameron smiles and I think I imagine there's a spark of understanding in his glance. Like he knows that he stopped Riley from doing something stupid. But he doesn't say anything. He just turns his back to me and continues talking to Riley.

I take a sip and scan the gym, looking for Amber again. This time I don't see her. She's gone. Lost in the crowd.

Another painful cramp in my abdomen almost makes me bend over. I finish the water and toss it in a nearby trash can. If I've started my period I'm going to lose my mind. If there was one thing that could ruin this night completely it would be an unexpected visit from Aunt Flo.

"I'm going to the bathroom," I say, but I don't think Cameron or Riley hear me.

I move through the dance like I'm in a daze. Everyone around me is like a moving blur. My wrist is throbbing. I shake it, hoping that'll somehow relax the nerves. It doesn't do anything. Off to the side of the dance floor I catch a glimpse of Mr. Henson standing near the pushed-back bleachers. His arms are crossed over his chest and he's staring out at the mass of teenagers as though looking for someone to yell at. I never realized how stern his face is. Out of the corner of my eye I catch a glimpse of Amber and Jess. Amber looks upset. No, she looks pissed. But before I can get her attention she's stormed away and Jess has moved on to talk to someone else.

A group of boys I don't recognize jump in front of me like they're trying to block my path. They reek of cheap body spray and teenage body odor. They're acting like they're drunk, but they're not. They're just being stupid. Trying to show off. I push away from them. Another cramp slows me down; I wrap my arm around my stomach. What was in that pill Jess gave me? Couldn't be anything too bad. No one else is sick. Just a little high-strung. Maybe it's food poisoning.

"Is everything all right, Miss Wicker?"

I turn around and stare up at Mr. Henson. He's looking at me like I have two heads. Did I do something wrong? Do I look upset? Maybe he saw my argument with Riley. I hope not. It wasn't that big of a deal. I don't want Riley to get in trouble.

"I'm fine," I say, but I can barely hear my own voice over the sound of the music.

Henson leans in closer. "Have you been drinking tonight?"

I laugh. "What? No! My parents would kill me."

He doesn't look convinced. He narrows his eyes and stares directly at me without blinking. It's like he's trying to see right through me.

"Shouldn't you be with your friends?" It strikes me as a weird question, but for some reason I don't question it in my mind as much as I normally would. Maybe because I'm too freaked out by how close he's standing to me. Maybe because I feel like I'm going to throw up.

"I'm just going to the bathroom."

"You swear you haven't taken anything? I could send Mrs. Collins into the bathroom, you know. If she catches any students using substances they aren't supposed to, it'll be an automatic expulsion."

"I just have to pee."

"If you're afraid to say anything because of your—" Henson is cut off by the sound of two boys fighting by the door. He averts his attention away from me. "Hey! Knock it off!"

I take that moment to slip back into the crowd. My chest is heaving. Maybe I should have bought a larger dress. The bodice is pinching me under the arms, making it hard to breathe. It's so hot in here. I can feel the sweat dripping down the back of my neck. Another stab of pain in my abdomen forces me to double over. Then I make a dash for the girls' room.

I barely make it into the bathroom before I'm sick.

Chapter 52

The drop-off zone for the high school is full of police vehicles. Their sirens are off, but the red and blue lights are flashing. My head is pounding and my brain is in full-blown hysteria. I think about last night and how I almost didn't make it out of Henson's office. Did he call the police on me? My shoulders tense at the thought. No, that's ridiculous. They wouldn't cordon off the school just to deal with a complaint. But he could have told them that I attacked him. I did stab him with a knife. No. I have to stop panicking. If Henson called the police on me then they would have shown up at my apartment. This is something else.

I pull up to the intersection nearest the school and stop at the red light. An officer is standing at the next street over directing cars in the opposite direction. The parking lot itself is practically empty aside from the few early-bird teachers and staff. I can see them all standing near the main entrance in a small crowd. It's too early for most students to be there, but a few teenagers are mingling on the sidewalk on the opposite side of the street, backpacks slung over their shoulder as they hold up their phones. Probably making TikToks or going live on their Instagram or

291

whatever it is they do to spread gossip and make the lives of other people miserable. It reminds me of how glad I am that social media was in its infancy when I was in high school. All of that information out in the open probably would have killed me.

Poor choice of words, I know.

The light turns green and I turn to park in the staff lot, which hasn't been cordoned off by the police. Then I get out and make my way over to the crowd of teachers. That's when I see CJ standing just inside the large double doors. He has one of those profiles that's impossible to miss even through double glass at fifty feet away. He's talking to Chief Newman.

"What's going on?"

Grace Abernathy, the morning secretary, gives me that typical Braxton Falls busybody expression. "Classes have been canceled."

"For the entire day?"

She nods. "Extracurriculars, too."

"Was there a fire or something?"

"They found a body."

"What?" My panic returns like a jolt of electricity. "Was it a student?"

Grace shakes her head. "We don't know. They haven't said anything yet."

"What's CJ doing here? I thought they were calling in someone off the substitute roster to cover my shifts."

"I guess they couldn't get anybody else. Poor CJ. Someone said he found the body this morning after opening. He was the only one in the building. He called the police." Grace taps her heel on the cement like she's late for a meeting. "This is why I hate living two counties over. I'm always on the way in or already in town before I find out school is closed. It's bad enough in the winter with the late calls on snow days. But this? I did not need to hear about this."

I don't understand what she's talking about. "What do you mean?"

"My teenage nephew committed suicide last spring. It's just, you know. I wish I could have been home when I found out about it."

Mr. Jeffries, the chemistry teacher, turns around. "We don't know it's a student."

"It's always a student. Especially in the beginning of the school year. That stretch between Labor Day and Thanksgiving break is the worst. That's when you hear about it the most."

Mr. Jeffries pushes his glasses up on the bridge of his nose. "Best not to be making any assumptions though. Not until we know more. The family could be around."

I tune out their conversation and stare off at the school. A few minutes later an ambulance pulls up and an officer comes out to ask us to back away. We all move like a herd, but we don't go too far.

It's then that a frightening thought crosses my mind. What if it had been one of the girls in Henson's photographs? I could have taken what I'd found and gone directly to the police last night. They could have arrested him. The girls in the photographs would have been protected. Why didn't I do that? Because I was afraid of what people would say if they found out that Amber was one of them? Because I was afraid to tell my mom? What if one of them couldn't take it any longer and killed themselves? A sort of sick-and-twisted Romeo and Juliet fantasy gone horribly wrong.

I bring a hand to my mouth to cover a gasp. Oh God. What if I'm responsible for someone else dying? What if my lack of action has killed another young girl?

I need to say something.

I start to take a step forward when the front doors open and CJ comes wobbling out. He looks older than he did the last time I saw him. His face is gaunt and his eyes are sunken. Probably an effect of the cancer meds he's taking. He shouldn't be working. I feel guilty about that. But I'm also angry that Henson would call him in knowing he's sick. The man is dying and he's still covering shifts for me, cleaning up after ungrateful teenagers. And now he's found one of them. Dead.

I know it's not my fault. Still, I can't help but feel responsible.

He walks by the group of us. Grace tries to get him to say something, but he ignores her and just keeps walking on to his car.

I hurry after him.

When he sees me, his surprise is immediate. "What are you doing here? I thought you were on leave."

"I am. I was just driving by and saw the commotion. Are you OK?"

CJ shakes his head. He reaches into his pocket for his car keys. His hand is shaking and the keys jingle together nervously. "I've been around a long time, but I ain't never seen anything like that."

"Must be horrible. I can't imagine."

Except I can. I can imagine a dead teenager perfectly well. Because I've seen one before. I see one every night in my dreams. I see my sister. There's nothing in the world more haunting than the body of someone too young to be dead.

"It'll be torture for the parents, too," I mumble.

CJ is halfway to opening the car door when he stops. "Won't be any worry for the parents. Gonna be hard on all of the young teachers though."

". . . What?"

"It wasn't a student," CJ says.

"Then who was it?"

"Dick Henson."

I feel like someone has knocked the wind right out of me.

"And from the looks of it, someone went to town on him. I don't like to start rumors, but I always had a feeling he was a bit of a cad. Probably some jealous husband."

"Wh-what do you mean?"

"I mean someone must have really had it out for him. To leave a body looking like that." CJ shakes his head. "That takes a lot of rage. Or a lot of crazy."

294

Chapter 53

It's barely fifty degrees outside, a brisk scent of impending snow on the morning air, and yet I'm sweating through two layers of clothing as I shuffle quickly to my car. CJ saying that someone murdered Henson has my brain on the fritz. I just saw him last night and he was fine. Granted, he'd taken a knife to the palm. My knife. But when I left him he was alive. Alive and screaming profanities. He certainly wasn't dead. And while I'd drawn blood a few times in fear for my own life, there'd been nothing of the scene to suggest the kind of supposed carnage that CJ had discovered while doing his morning cleanup. Which meant that someone found Henson after I left and finished the job I wished I'd had the courage to do on my own after finding that photograph of Amber in his collection.

But that's not what worries me.

What worries me is that I was there last night. I was in his office. My fingerprints are all over his desk and his bookshelves. Not to mention the fact that my jacket is still there. Ripped off my shoulders.

And the knife.

The knife Riley had engraved for me.

Fuck.

I fumble to remove my car keys from my pocket, dropping

them on the pavement. When I bend down to pick them up a dark shadow falls over my arm. I look up to see Chief Newman staring down at me through his useless sunglasses. Useless because it's overcast and the weather forecast is calling for rain. Useful because I can't see his eyes, which means I can't read his intent.

Double fuck.

I snatch up my keys and stand up a little quicker than is natural.

"You're looking a little jittery this morning, Miss Wicker," Newman says.

"Well, they say they found a body in the high school. I'd say that's grounds for a few jitters." I offer a halfhearted shrug. "Or maybe I just had too much coffee for breakfast."

"You must have picked that up from Mike. He used to guzzle a gallon of joe before breakfast."

"I guess."

"Can you inherit the behaviors of someone who isn't actually related to you?"

The question is pointed. Like it's supposed to be a subtle jibe at something else, but if it is I don't know what Newman is talking about. Sometimes it's hard to tell if he's just talking to talk or if he's trying to sound smarter than he really is. I've always assumed it's a combination of both.

"I don't know. That's not really my area of expertise."

"Me, for example. I prefer decaf. The regular stuff numbs my thoughts and gives me a headache."

I unlock the car door. "Good thing it's not a crime to be anti-caffeine."

I move to get into my car, but Newman stretches his arm out, resting his palm on the roof and blocking my entrance.

"I'd like you to come down to the station and answer a few questions."

"Questions?"

"Yeah, we're having some of the staff come in to give us a statement of their whereabouts over the last few days."

"I haven't worked much this week. I've been taking some time off to prepare for—" I avoid looking into the reflective lenses of Newman's sunglasses because I know I'll only see how poor of a liar I am "—to spend more time with my mom."

"She sure needs it. Your mom, that is. She could do with a little more support on the home front after everything she's been through."

Yeah, you've told me. Repeatedly.

"I'm doing my best."

"What were you doing here this morning?"

"What?"

"You said you haven't been working this week. But you're here now. Why would you be at the school if you aren't scheduled to work? I saw CJ up there already. There's no point in having two custodians. Especially not in the morning." Newman shifts his weight, leaning harder into the arm that's propped against my car.

"I was just driving by. Saw the crowd. Was curious."

"And you haven't been inside the school this morning?"

"No. I couldn't even if I wanted to. Your officers have the doors blocked off. They're not letting anyone in."

Newman doesn't reply right away. He turns his attention back to the high school. The caution tape they've put up across the front door has blown off in the wind and is flapping against the brick front of the building. We both watch as an officer runs out to grab it and affix it back across the entrance. Once he does, Newman looks back at me. "I'd like for you to come down to the station and answer a few questions."

"I really don't have time right now. I need to get back to—"

"I'm asking nicely on account of your mother and your late father. But it's not a request." He pats the top of my car. "I'll follow along after."

"I know where the police station is," I say, annoyed.

"I'll escort you." Newman smiles, but there's nothing warm about it. "Just in case you forget on the way."

Chapter 54

The interview room at the police station is warmer than I remember it being. The last time I was in one of these rooms was the night Amber died. In fact, I'm pretty sure it's the same room exactly. It has the same smell. The odor of concrete walls, old paper, and disinfectant. I don't touch the table or the chair any more than I have to. I remember Dad telling me about how sometimes they have to scrub down the walls because a suspect will do something disgusting just to give themselves the potential for an insanity plea. I try not to think of what sort of nasty and disturbing behavior might have occurred in that room or what secrets were locked in there, viewable through nothing more than a two-way mirror and a security camera blinking in the corner.

I'm not sitting there long before Chief Newman and a young investigator enter. Newman doesn't look that good. There's a bead of sweat across his brow and his skin is pallid. He looks like he's about to faint. The younger investigator is more composed. Her dark hair frames her face at a slanted angle that ends sharply at her jaw. She must be new because I don't recognize her. She has one of those no-nonsense expressions though so I remind myself to try and hold my tongue for when Newman inevitably pisses me off with some snide commentary. Or when he accuses me of doing something I didn't do.

Like cover for my boyfriend.

Or kill my boss.

The younger detective introduces herself as Detective Thompson. Then she turns on a recording device and states the names of everyone in the room before time-stamping the start of the interview. Afterwards she takes out a notepad and a pen and waits for Newman to initiate the conversation. Or the interrogation. I'm still not certain what to expect.

Newman clears his throat. He's been avoiding eye contact with me since he entered the room. When he finally does look at me it's not with the same vengeance he normally has. It's with weary sorrow. Like he's been chasing a ghost and he's finally on the verge of giving up the prospect that he'll ever catch it.

"Let's get the bullshit out of the way," he says. "We know you were at the high school, Alexandra."

"I—"

He cuts me off before I can say more and, in retrospect, I'm glad. He stopped me from lying.

"Before you say anything, I want you to know that we have proof."

Detective Thompson reaches under the table and places three evidence bags in front of me. The first contains my jacket, the one Henson ripped off me. The second are the contents of my jacket, including my wallet, which has my driver's license and credit cards. The third bag has the knife Riley gave to me for my birthday. And it's covered in blood.

Henson's blood.

I clench my hands together in my lap, nails digging into the skin between my fingers. There is a flurry of feelings flying through me. The foremost being the fact that all of these items were found at the scene of a crime. At the scene of a murder. And I don't have to be a detective's daughter to know what that means. That makes me suspect number one.

The last person to see a victim alive is usually the killer, after all.

Which begs the question—who was the last person to see Amber?

"I didn't do it," I say. There's a meekness to my voice that's embarrassing. Where was that fire I had when I stood up against Henson the night before? Where was that strength now?

"Didn't do what?" Newman asks.

"I didn't kill him."

"Who?"

"Henson." I push one of my nails deeper into the soft swath of skin between my middle and ring finger. Deep enough to make it bleed. "I didn't kill him."

"What were you doing in his office last night?"

I think back to the night that Amber died. I remember sitting in this room, freezing. My mind was swirling then too but not out of fear. Out of shock. I was equal parts hot and cold. Everything was hazy. I couldn't tell what was real and what was a memory. But I do remember Newman's voice repeating over and over in my head.

Where were you? What did you do? Where is your dress?

Over and over like a fever dream.

"Alexandra? What were you doing in Henson's office last night?"

I snap out of my thoughts and stare at Newman as though he were speaking a different language and I hadn't quite translated his question. But before he can repeat himself, I reply. "I was looking for proof."

"Proof of what?"

"Proof that he was responsible for Amber's death."

Thompson stops taking notes. She turns her attention to Newman, but he hasn't reacted. His face is blank, unreadable. He probably thinks I'm lying. He thinks I did it. Just like he thinks I was somehow involved in Amber's death. He's just waiting for me to say something that'll push me over the edge from innocent to guilty.

"Why would you think Henson was responsible for your sister's death?"

I scratch my nails over the back of my hand. "He was at the dance that night."

"There were a lot of people at the dance."

"And Riley said he saw him in the woods. Or . . . he thought he might have seen him." That's not enough though. I have to tell him what I found. Surely, he must already know. If Henson was murdered then the evidence would also be there. Unless the killer took the photographs. Which would make me even more culpable in Henson's murder. But telling him what I found means revealing Amber's secret. Jessica's secret. It means exposing countless young women who have clearly been keeping that darkness to themselves for years.

Is that really my place to share?

But it's not just those girls who were victimized. If Henson was responsible for Amber's death then it's Riley who's a victim too. And this might be the only way to prove his innocence.

"He had pictures."

"Pictures of what?"

"Students. Girls."

Thompson's mouth creases in disgust.

"What kind of pictures were these?" Newman asks. Again, no emotion. He's like a stone statue.

"Nude." I sigh. "They looked pornographic. Not with other people. The girls were all alone in the images, but there was a clear intention to what kind of response they were supposed to elicit."

"And where did you find these photographs?"

"In his office. In the treasure box he used to keep on his desk when he was teaching."

Detective Thompson stops taking notes to place a hand to her mouth as though she might gag. *Trust me, Detective. I'm right there with you.*

"And what made you think to look there?"

"I found one of the photographs in Amber's room."

Finally, Newman shows some semblance of surprise.

I take a deep breath and continue. "There was a hiding space under the floorboards near the window. I found it by accident the other day."

"Was it a photo of Amber?"

I shake my head. "No, it was someone else."

"Who?"

I clam up. I'm not sure what I'm supposed to say. Jessica didn't seem to care about anyone finding out about the photo. Hell, she was so blasé about it. But that was before she threw it away. She might feel differently about it now. And for some reason the idea of telling the police feels like a betrayal of the friendship we once had.

"I don't know," I lie. "Some girl. I'd never seen her before."

"What made you connect that girl's photograph to Henson?"

"There was writing on it. A date. I recognized the handwriting."

This time it's Thompson who looks up in disbelief. "You recognized the handwriting?"

I decide to tell a white lie here, although I don't know why. I guess I'm embarrassed to admit that I was rummaging around in Amber's things trying to put together a mystery that was solved fifteen years ago. "Yeah. Henson had a specific way of writing the number two. I remember it from school. And I saw it again on some paperwork in his office. When I saw the two on the photograph I realized he must have been the one who'd taken it."

"That seems like a pretty big leap," Thompson says.

I shrug. "I guess I got lucky."

"And you think that these photographs are the reason your sister was murdered?" Newman doesn't look convinced, but he does look interested.

"Why else? I mean, it's a pretty big fucking coincidence, don't you think? Henson takes all of these naked photos of teenage girls and one of them turns up dead? Maybe Amber threatened to expose him. Maybe she was going to tell someone. Even if it turned out that the photos themselves weren't a crime, that would have destroyed Henson's reputation. His career, at the very least, would be over. He'd probably never find a decent job ever again. Not to mention the blow it would have been to his ego."

"Sounds like you didn't like him too much." Thompson gives me a pointed look. She's trying to get an emotional response.

It works.

"I'm not in the business of liking pedophiles. The guy has always creeped me out."

"Creeped you out enough to want revenge?"

"No! Of course not. I just always felt like there was something weird about him. Even when I was a student. He just rubbed me the wrong way. I never would have thought—" I stop myself when I realize I've said that exact same thing before, after Amber's murder. Except back then I was talking about Riley. *I never would have thought he was capable of something like that.* And now I'm almost certain I was right. Because it never did make sense that Riley murdered Amber. But Henson? Henson I could believe.

Neither Newman nor Thompson say anything for at least a moment.

"I also found a ring."

Both Newman and Thompson give me pointed looks.

"It was in Nell's cabin. I think she might have found it out in the woods all of those years ago. The ring has a horseshoe shape that could match the bruise on Amber's face."

Newman holds back a sigh. "Nell Abbott is a sick old woman."

"The ring had blood on it! It could be Amber's. It could be the killer's!"

"Do you have this ring on you?"

My shoulders slump. "No. Someone stole it from my house."

Newman is annoyed. Thompson looks like she's trying not to roll her eyes. They don't believe me. I don't blame them. I barely believe myself.

"I didn't kill him," I say.

"We know." Newman leans forward, resting his arms on the table. "We've had the local coroner go over the scene twice. It was a suicide."

My head jerks back in surprise. "What?"

Didn't CJ say it was practically a blood bath in there?

"It was messy. It certainly looked like it could have been a homicide. But most of the wounds appeared to be self-inflicted. With a few notable exceptions. Then, of course, there was the fact that he was found hanging from a ceiling fan. And no offense, but you don't look strong enough to lift a basset hound, let alone an adult man who spent an hour at the gym every day after work."

For the first time in my life I don't take offense at one of Newman's jibes.

"Does that mean you'll look into the possibility that he was involved in Amber's death?"

This time Newman's silence is more disheartening than unnerving.

"We'll investigate the possibility. But your sister's case was cut and dry. Even with these photographs and a possible relationship between Henson and Amber, there was a lot of evidence against Riley King. And there was no proof that Henson was ever at the scene of the crime."

"But this is reasonable doubt! This could prove Riley is innocent. And he doesn't have much time left."

Newman doesn't respond.

I search his face for any sign of hope that this could overturn Riley's execution, but he doesn't look convinced. Or maybe he doesn't want to be. He always did think the worst of Riley. Most people did. He was the perfect poster child for Amber's murder, after all.

Then again, if their evidence was to be believed, so was I.

Chapter 55

Newman catches me in the parking lot before I reach my car. I could sense there was more he wanted to say to me after the interview, but I didn't want to talk to him anymore. I didn't want to talk to anyone. There was only one more day until Riley's execution and I wasn't any closer to finding the truth than I had been fifteen years ago. Nothing made sense. All of these convoluted relationships, secrets between friends, and not a single piece of concrete evidence that could tell me one way or another if Riley was involved. All I had was my gut instinct. And that told me Riley wasn't responsible; that there was something more going on. It had to do with Henson. That was too much of a coincidence to ignore. But if Henson had spent all of these years trying to avoid a death sentence, why kill himself?

"Alexandra, wait." Newman calls out to me before I step off the sidewalk in front of the police station.

I turn around, shrugging up the scarf around my neck to hold back the biting breeze. "What?"

Newman seems to have lost some of his brutality. Maybe that's too harsh of a word. But he looks less confident than usual. He looks rattled. This is not the man who has spent the last fifteen years making me feel like the prime suspect in a guilty line-up.

For the first time since I arrived at the station I notice the dark circles under his eyes and the sallow color of his skin. This is someone who hasn't been sleeping. Join the club, Chief.

"I need to ask you something off the record."

"Ask me what?"

He pauses, placing his hands on his hips. His face softens. Not in a sympathetic or a sentimental way, but in a tired way. In the way of someone who has been puzzling over one of those locked-room scenarios. Or a Rubik's cube with three sides completed.

"When you were in Henson's office, did you see anyone you recognized in the photographs?"

"Does it matter? They're lying all over his office. You can see for yourself who was in them."

Newman's face clenches. "We weren't able to retrieve them all."

"What do you mean? The desk was covered in them."

"He burned them."

My stomach drops. "What?"

"He dumped them in the waste paper basket in his office and set them on fire before he—" Newman sighs. "Before he killed himself."

"You're kidding, right? Are you saying you don't have any proof? You don't have any evidence of what he did to those girls?"

"We have people working to put together the remains of what we found. We may be able to restore the ones that weren't damaged too badly. But I don't have a lot of hope. He clearly felt guilty enough to end his life, but he didn't leave much behind for us to pin anything on him. Not unless someone happened to have one of the photographs." He looks me directly in the eyes. "They're Polaroids. We won't find negatives somewhere. Unless he took doubles and left them somewhere else. Or someone else managed to find one that didn't get destroyed . . ."

I'm a mix of emotions. The anger surges first. It fills me with an almost uncontrollable rage. My face is hot and I barely even notice the cold chill in the air. That fucking bastard. He took the evidence with him. That greedy, perverted, disgusting monster killed himself and took away any justice there might have been for those young women. For me. For my sister. For Riley.

That's why Newman didn't think there was a case to make for Riley.

Because there wasn't a case to make against Henson.

That's when the next emotion hits me. Grief. And failure. I might as well have killed Riley myself with my own stupidity. I should have brought the ring to the police as soon as I found it. I should have taken a photo of what I'd found when I found it. I shouldn't have let Henson corner me. I should have been stronger, more resourceful.

But that's not who I am. I'm not Amber or Jessica or Cameron or Riley. I don't stand up for myself. I'm a survivor not because I'm strong, but because I'm a coward. Because when it comes down to fight or flight, I flee. I flee and I survive. But at what price?

"Alexandra, if you have anything I can use . . ."

I reach my hand into my pocket and slip out the Polaroid of Amber. It's hot in my grip, the edges bent from when I clenched it earlier. It feels like a lead weight in my hand as I hold it out to Newman.

When he takes the photograph his entire demeanor changes. If I didn't know better, I'd say it looks like someone just shot him in the chest. Or like he's witnessed the death of a loved one.

Hell, he looks the way I probably did when I found that picture.

It drops out of his hand and hits the concrete, face down. We both reach for it at the same time. It's when he stretches his arm out for the photograph that I notice the bandage on his wrist. A bit of blood has seeped through the gauze.

"What happened?" I ask.

Newman snatches the photo and jerks his arm back, smoothing down his shirtsleeve to cover the injury. "Nothing. Just scratched myself in the garage."

But I swear I caught a glimpse of swelling along the edge of that bandage. Possibly from a bite. An infected bite.

Made from dozens of barbed python teeth.

Chapter 56

The house smells like liquor and the two empty bottles of bourbon on the carpet tell me why.

Mom is still in bed when I barge into her bedroom. She doesn't hear me, out cold to the world. I fling open the curtains, filling the room with the dull gray glow of early afternoon. Still, she doesn't wake up. My reptile brain is worried that something is wrong, but I forcibly suppress that instinctual fear for logic. She's not dead. Just dead drunk. I shake her shoulder and she groans, but she doesn't get up. Instead she rolls over onto her side. The sheets stick to her back with sweat. That's when I notice the vomit on Dad's old pillow.

I'm enraged.

"Mom! Get up!"

She mumbles something unintelligible in her half-conscious booze coma.

I shake her again. "Mom! Wake the fuck up!"

Normally this would snap her out of her funk. Profanity was something we were never allowed to use in her house. I remember saying 'shit' in front of her when I accidentally broke a glass, shattering it all over the kitchen floor. I was thirteen. Mom slapped me so hard she left a handprint on my face for thirty minutes.

She said profanity was a sign that someone was either uneducated or poor. And we were neither.

Of course, she never seemed to notice whenever Amber said something profane. Or maybe Amber was better at hiding it. Maybe I only thought I was the one getting caught. But when the F-word doesn't drag her out of bed with a vengeance I know she's really wasted.

So, I do something I know will wake her up.

I storm down the hall to Amber's room and snatch the snow globe off her desk. It's one of those expensive Disney snow globes with the elaborate bases. Princess Aurora is dancing on one foot on the inside, surrounded by the three fairies. There's a light feature on the bottom that makes her dress look like it changes from pink to blue when it's turned on. The thing probably weighs five pounds, but it feels like ten.

I twist the knob on the bottom until it starts playing a music-box version of "Once Upon a Dream." By the time I reach Mom's bedroom, the sound has infiltrated her senses, slowly waking her from whatever alcohol-induced daydream she was in. Then I throw the snow globe on the floor. The sound of glass and mechanics shattering into a thousand pieces jolts her out of bed like a gunshot.

"What in the world do you think you're doing?!"

"We need to talk."

She stares at the broken pieces of snow globe on the floor and her face fills with terror. There's a dazed look in her eyes. She doesn't know if she's awake or dreaming. To be fair, neither do I.

"What did you do? Is that—is that Amber's snow globe?"

Now she's awake.

She drops to the floor and begins picking up the pieces of glass and busted ceramic princess like they're made of gold. If it were anyone else, I'd feel horrible. I'd be overwhelmed with pity at seeing a woman grieve a snow globe as though it were the last memory of her daughter. But right now I don't feel anything except anger.

"Get up," I say.

"Are you crazy? What have you done? This was Amber's favorite—"

"I don't give a fuck what it is! You need to sober up and talk to me!"

"Talk to you about what?"

"About Dad! About Amber! About Henson! About whatever the hell is going on that you haven't told me about. I know you've been lying to me and I'm sick of it. I'm sick of all of it. Sick of putting up with all this bullshit and listening to you talk about Amber like she was some kind of saint when we both know that isn't true."

I'm crying, but I don't notice it until the tears hit my jaw. When Mom gets up I wait for her to hit me, but she can barely stand. She's wobbling on her feet, about to slip in the water and fall on the glass. So, I do what I always do. I bite my lip. Then I help her into the bathroom and wait for her to freshen up—probably with the bottle of vodka I know she has hiding under the sink—before I try talking to her again. I also clean up the mess I made while she's in there.

Twenty minutes later we're sitting at the dining room table. The army of Precious Moments figurines staring down at me from the hutch like a disgruntled jury, ready to take arms and judge me for the most heinous crime a daughter can commit. The crime of not loving their mother enough.

Mom is haggard in her bathrobe. She's tried to hide the odor of alcohol by gargling mouthwash, but it doesn't help. That smell is in her pores. It's part of her natural fragrance now. The only way she could get rid of it is a two-week detox in a locked clinic. But in true addict fashion she says she's not the one who has a problem. So that'll never happen.

And if it were up to her I'd be the one locked away.

I set a mug of coffee in front of her. When she looks at it her face goes green, but she takes a sip anyway. It's not much, but it's a start.

"Henson is dead." I don't bother giving her a warning. I just rip it off like a Band-Aid because I'm tired of playing these games with her.

Mom stares into the coffee mug without answering. At first, I think she hasn't heard me. Then I see her body tense like she was expecting to hear this.

"How?"

"The police say he killed himself. He was found in his office at the school."

This is where I expect Mom to freak out. To argue with me and call me a liar. But she doesn't do either of those things. She just sits there looking frail and weak. Like a woman who knows something but doesn't know what to say.

"Do they know why?" she finally asks. "Did they find anything?"

She knows.

Or, at least, she suspects. And that's enough to fill me with more anger than I felt when I found those photos in Henson's office. She knew and she didn't tell anyone.

"He tried to burn the evidence, but I think they found enough to connect the dots."

I think about telling her that I'm the one who found the evidence. That I know the truth. But I don't. I don't want to do anything that'll keep her from telling me what she knows.

"What aren't you telling me, Mom? What do you know? Does this have anything to do with Amber's death?"

"What?" She looks shocked by the suggestion. "No, this has nothing to do with Amber. Not really."

"What do you mean 'not really'?"

"I mean it started long before Amber."

"What started? What aren't you telling me?"

Mom raises the mug to her lips. Her hands are shaking and I can see that it's taking everything in her not to spill the coffee. She takes a sip but has difficulty swallowing. And when she places the mug back down it leaves a ring on the table.

311

"Your father had his suspicions about Henson. Of course, I thought it was ridiculous. Henson is—" she falters "—was such a nice man. So upstanding. So charming. It was absurd to think that he was doing anything untoward. But there was that one girl who came to the station. She wanted to file a report, but then retracted her statement at the last minute."

"What girl?"

Mom shrugs her shoulders. "I don't know. I can't remember. It was never registered. She was eighteen and didn't follow through with the report. There was nothing your father could do. But it did cause him to start paying more attention."

"He thought Henson was soliciting underage girls?"

"He wasn't sure what he thought. But he never trusted Henson. Never liked him. It was like a personal vendetta for him."

"What about his colleagues? What did they say?"

Mom winces and pinches the bridge of her nose as though to ward off a headache. "They didn't know. He didn't have any evidence. He was trying to find some on his own. Then Amber died and, well, he was consumed by that."

I try to recall how Dad was with regards to his work before Amber died, but it's difficult to remember. He was always home for dinner. Always around for the holidays and the special occasions. He never brought his work home with him from what I could remember. He was a great dad. He was perfect. Then Amber died and while Mom drowned herself in the bottle he buried himself in the case files. He never once said that he thought Riley was innocent, but it was clear that something about the case didn't sit well with him. Like there was a missing piece of the puzzle.

Was Henson that missing piece?

"The police found a picture of Amber."

Mom blinks. "What?"

"They found a picture of her in Henson's things. She was one of those girls."

Mom shakes her head violently. "No, no. That's not possible. That's not true."

"It is true. I saw it. They think it's possible that Henson was responsible for Amber's death."

"No!" she shouts. "He didn't kill my little girl."

"How do you know?"

"I know."

"Mom." I reach across the table and place my hand on hers. Her skin is thin and the veins on her hand are dark, like aging snakes trying to worm their way through a thin tunnel. Her wedding ring hangs loose, the stone crushed between her ring and middle finger because it no longer has the stability to stand upright. I've ignored how much she's aged in the years since Amber's death. And I suddenly feel ashamed for not noticing. "The night of the dance you told people that Dad was at home with you. But I remember him getting to the station before you. You drove separate cars. Why would you drive separate cars if you were together?"

Mom shakes her head.

"Where was Dad the night of the homecoming dance? Tell me. Please."

"I don't want to talk about this. I need a Tylenol."

"You can't keep avoiding this. I need to know what happened that night."

Mom's eyes well up with tears. She wipes them on the sleeve of her robe. "We promised not to say anything. It could have ruined the case."

"I know he was at the dance, Mom. I found proof. There's a photo on one of Amber's old online accounts."

She looks up in shock. "Have you shown anyone?"

"No. But I need you to be honest with me. What was he doing there? Why did you lie for him? And how do you know Henson wasn't involved? How can you be so certain?"

Mom's face clenches like she's biting down on a lemon. I can't tell if she's frightened or frustrated. Maybe both.

"Please, Mom."

"Your father followed Henson into the woods that night."

"The woods where they found Amber?"

"Henson was chaperoning the dance, but he left early. Your father followed him to the trailhead at the entrance to the park. He suspected that he might have been going up there to meet one of the students. A young girl from one of his classes." Mom takes a deep breath and groans into her sleeve, rocked by what I can only assume was the memory of the conversation she had with my dad. "They had an argument. Your father threatened Henson. He told him he was on to him and what he was doing. Told him that if he ever found proof he would see Henson put away. And he'd make sure every inmate in that facility knew what he was."

Riley's words echo in my mind. *It was your dad. I saw him there, Lexie.* He hadn't been lying. Dad had been in the woods. As had Henson. That could have turned over Riley's entire case. Most of it had been on the basis that he'd been the only one out there that night. But he wasn't.

"Why didn't either of you say that in your statements?"

"Because your father was adamant that Henson hadn't been up to the spot where Amber was found."

"But how could he know?"

"Because he followed Henson home and he waited there. He was going to wait all night, but—"

"But then the police found Amber." I pause. "And then they found me."

"Your father was absolutely certain that Henson wasn't up in the woods at the time of Amber's death. But to admit that would mean having to explain what he was doing outside of Henson's house. And he had no physical proof that Henson had done anything. But, also, there was no one there to corroborate that your dad was outside his house the entire time. If they questioned Henson, he could have lied. Your father could have been blamed for Amber's death."

314

Then it hits me, harder now than when Riley first mentioned it. "Is Dad to blame for Amber's death?"

The look mom gives me hits harder than a punch.

"Your father would never hurt Amber. He loved her. He loved you both."

But if Henson wasn't responsible for Amber's death, then I was back to the beginning. No motive. No murderer. And the only remaining evidence pointing toward the one person I'd been trying to prove innocent.

Then a horrible thought hits me. If Dad wasn't at home, then that meant Mom didn't have an alibi. She was also alone that night.

But Mom would never kill Amber.

Me, maybe. But Amber? Never.

And that still left one more person.

Chief Newman.

"Was it Newman?"

Mom's face goes white as a sheet. She doesn't say anything.

"Did Newman kill my sister?"

"No." Mom grits her teeth, but her gaze shifts to the corner of the room.

"Someone broke into my apartment last night and took something. Something that could prove Riley's innocence. Spaghetti bit them. I found blood on the carpet. And when I spoke to Newman today he had a bloody bandage on his wrist. I could get that blood tested. I could prove he was in my house. So, I'm going to ask you one more time." I lean across the table. "Is Newman responsible for Amber's death?"

"No." Mom is adamant. And that glossy hangover stare hardens on her face. "He had nothing to do with Amber's murder."

"How do you know?"

"Because Chuck is Amber's father."

Chapter 57

Saturday, October 13, 2007
8:52 p.m.

The pain is agony.

I shove my way into the last bathroom stall and slam the door behind me. I barely manage to lock the door before a stabbing spasm wells up in my abdomen. A group of girls stumbles in after me. I can hear them giggling and joking, their open-toed heels clicking on the linoleum floor.

"Did you see the way Justin was dancing with Courtney?"

"Oh my God! That was so embarrassing! I can't believe she agreed to go with him!"

"She wore the same dress as Katie too."

"No doubt she got it off the clearance rack."

"No doubt!" two of them say in unison.

I try to ignore them as I hike up the flowy skirt of my dress and use my armpits to hold it in place. A cramp hits me so hard I almost double over. It gives me a gag response that comes out as a dry cough. I pull down my panties.

Blood.

There's blood everywhere.

"Cameron was looking really good though."

"What I wouldn't do to get him to notice me. We have fifth period together, but he's always hanging out with the football guys."

"Or his girlfriend."

One of the girls groans. "She doesn't deserve him. He's way too hot for her."

"Too hot for you, you mean!"

More laughter. Then someone asks to borrow some lip gloss.

My chest is heaving. Why am I bleeding? I'm not on my period. And even if I was, I've never had cramps like this. My head is spinning. My forehead is sweating. But it's a cold sweat. Clammy. And the disorienting odor of body spray and school toilet water makes me feel sick.

Another cramp, this time just below my bellybutton, sends me into the side of the stall. My ankles are about to give out, but I don't have the strength to kick off my heels. And even if I did, I'd never be able to get them back on. And I can't run out of the school dance barefoot. Am I even really thinking about that? Leaving the dance? Yes. Yes, I am. Because something's wrong with me. Something is very *very* wrong.

I bend over. Blood trickles down my leg. My gut tells me that I should sit on the toilet. It tells me I should crouch down and let it all leak out. But panic won't let me. I cry out in pain and the background babbles of the girls in front of the mirrors stop, filling the bathroom with the low rumble of the DJ's bass.

"What was that?"

"Oh my God. Is someone making out in here?"

Someone bangs on the stall door. "Hey, are you OK in there?"

I don't respond. I can barely catch my breath. My brain feels like it's on fire. What do I do? What do I do?

"Maybe she needs a tampon."

Another knock on the door. "Do you need a tampon?"

"No," I say. My voice is meek and raspy. I clear my throat with a cough. "I'm fine."

"Are you sure?"

"I'm fine," I repeat, but I'm not certain if it's loud enough to hear.

"You're not crying, are you?"

"Did your boyfriend break up with you?"

"I'm fine!" This time I yell, my voice rasping in pain. This time I know they hear me.

"Jesus," one of them says with a scoff. "We were just trying to help."

"Bitch," another one adds.

They leave, back to their incessant cackling and gossip.

I tug on the toilet paper, ripping it out of the holder so hard that it unravels on the floor. I rip off a large chunk and wipe myself. The paper is soaked in blood. Bright red blood. Not period blood.

And then I know.

A groan catches in my throat. Stuck. Tears stream down my face. Hot, burning tears to match the contracting aches in my abdomen.

I rip off another wad of toilet paper and stuff it in my under-wear. I shouldn't have yelled at those girls. I should have asked for a pad. For help. For something. But then people would know. Then everyone would know. Better to think I was crying over a stupid boyfriend. Better to think I was drunk and throwing up. Better for them to just forget about me.

I have to get out of here.

I wipe the blood off my leg and pull up my panties. I should go to the hospital, but I can't. I'm a minor. They'll call my parents. Then I remember what Jessica said about Becca McBride's cousin.

They might call the police.

It takes all of my strength to push open the bathroom door.

I bump into Cameron. I can tell by the look in his eyes that he knows something happened. I can't even begin to imagine what he's thinking.

"Lex, what's wrong? Are you all right?"

There's blood on my hands. I clench them shut so he can't see. "I'm fine."

Then I make my way to the door.

"Where are you going?" Cameron calls after me.

"I just need some fresh air."

"Should I get Riley?"

"No!" My voice is louder than I expect and a few wallflowers look at me like I've lost my mind.

"Let me get Jess then," Cameron insists. He's following after me.

"I'm fine! Just leave me alone!"

It feels like forever before I'm at the double doors. I push one side open, the dark glitter twinkling of the room disappearing behind me as I'm washed in the bright fluorescent lights of the hallway. Then, before Cameron can catch up with me, I take a deep breath and run.

I run out of the school and into the brisk chill of night.

I keep running until I can't feel anything anymore.

I keep running until my legs give out.

I keep running until the life inside of me is gone.

Then I pass out.

Chapter 58

Saturday, October 13, 2007
10:48 p.m.

The cold dead eye of the Wynwood Witch peers into my soul.

I'm going to die. She's going to kill me.

She holds me down at the shoulders. I wrestle against her, but each movement sends a piercing stab of pain into my gut. I gasp. I want to cry, but I don't have any tears left. My eyes are dry. Numb. My vision blurry. Thick wafts of smoke surround me. The smell of incense is choking. I don't know where I am. I don't know if any of this is real. I just know that I'm going to die. Or that I'm already dead.

Help me! Somebody help me!

My voice sounds so loud in my own head. I'm screaming but no sounds come out. Only a soft whimper. My lip trembles. That's when I realize no one is pushing me down. It's my imagination. It's half of a waking dream. There is a hand on my shoulder, but it's soothing. Affectionate. A cold cloth is placed on my forehead. That's how I know I was burning up. I was hallucinating. But am I hallucinating now?

I slowly blink, willing the scene to come into focus. There's a woman staring at me. I'm fixated on one eye. White and mottled. Like it's been torn apart and glued back together backwards. The other is clear. Iris round, pupil wide.

Not the Wynwood Witch. She's not real. She's just a legend.

Nell Abbott. The woman in the woods.

"Your fever has come down some. I gave you something for the pain. Two extra-strength acetaminophen. It'll take some time for you to feel the effects. You'll have to take some more in six hours or so. But I'm afraid you're going to be hurting for a few days." Her voice is more soothing than I expect it to be. It's a far cry from the witch in the woods I imagined growing up. A little harsh around the edges. Low-pitched from being a long-time smoker. Breathy. Like the wind rushing over gravel. But it's also tender. Like she's sat at a hundred other bedsides before and had this exact same conversation.

Maybe she is a witch.

"I have to go home," I say.

"You have to rest."

My hand reaches down to my belly. I feel like I've been kicked in the gut with a steel-toed boot. The soft satin of my dress is wet and the sensation makes me recoil my hand.

"You've lost a lot of blood," Nell says.

Her words take an abnormally long time to register in my thoughts. And when I finally look at her directly I can tell from her expression that she knows. She knows I didn't know.

"I'm so sorry." She places a hand atop of mine and gives it a gentle squeeze. Her fingers are bony, but soft.

"What do I do?" I whisper.

"You should see a doctor as soon as possible."

"I can't. No one can know. I can't tell anyone. I didn't know." My eyes suddenly remember how to work. The tears hit my cheeks before I can even finish formulating my thoughts. "My family—I can't tell them. I won't."

Nell goes quiet. That's when I take in my surroundings for the first time. I'm in a one-room cabin. There's a wood-burning stove in the corner and a rickety rocking chair with a handmade quilt thrown over the arm. The kitchen is ancient, like something out of a frontier cabin. A pot of water boils on the stove, splashing over the brim.

Nell stands up and moves the pot off the heat. She fills a mug with water and steeps a small bag for two minutes. Then she brings it over to me.

"Drink this," she says.

"What is it?"

"Tea."

The frightened child inside me warns that this could be poison. That she is the witch from all those legends I heard growing up. But the older version of myself doesn't care. I already feel empty inside. And something has already died because of my stupidity.

How could I not have known? How could I not have realized? How can I live with this guilt? How can I keep this secret?

I sit up carefully and take a sip. It's bitter, but it feels warm going down my throat. There's an aftertaste of licorice and spice. Maybe cinnamon. For a split second I forget how much agony the rest of my body is in.

"What do I do?" I ask again, hoping she can give me another answer.

"You weren't far along. You should get some bed rest and minimize strenuous activity. The pain will take longer to dissipate, but you should feel better in a few days." There's a strange look in her one good eye. Not pity, but some form of unexpressed heartache. She's seen this before. Perhaps dozens of times. "But if your fever gets worse, if you feel faint, or the bleeding increases, then you need to go to the doctor."

I nod. Then I finish off the tea too quickly. I burn my tongue, but the numbness of my mouth is nothing compared to the piercing ache in my abdomen. "I have to go."

"You can't wear that."

That's right. My homecoming dress.

I glance down at it again. It's soaked in blood and sweat.

I look like a crime scene.

I think of the alcohol I drank before the dance. The pills I took. I didn't have much, but was it enough? Is that what caused this? Did I kill my own—?

Oh God.

I am a crime scene.

"I have something you can wear until you get home."

"Thank you. Thank you for helping me."

"Of course," Nell says, making her way to a small dresser to remove an oversized shirt and a pair of shorts. "What are witches for?"

Chapter 59

Chief Newman is Amber's biological father. But not mine. Mom was insistent on that.

I drive back to my apartment in a semi-conscious daze. When I reach my front door, I realize I don't remember any of the ten-minute trip between my mom's house and my own. It's like the earth has dropped out from beneath my feet and I'm hurtling through the vast void of space. Newman is Amber's father and he knows it. He's known it this entire time. I suppose that explains why he was so persistent with me in the interview room. I can understand his outrage and his fury. And I see why he was ready to proclaim me guilty in front of all his colleagues. He'd lost a daughter. Granted, not a daughter that he was technically a father to—Dad would always be the one who raised Amber—but I suppose for some people blood has more meaning than it does to others. Or maybe he and Mom had plans. Plans that never came to fruition because of Amber's death. I don't know. I didn't ask her. There were a million things I wanted to ask, but the words caught in my throat. After learning about the secret Mom kept for all these years, I couldn't bring myself to say anything. Not even anything out of anger or spite. I couldn't even cry. I was numb. I still am.

But now I'm left with a bigger mystery.

Henson didn't kill Amber. Neither did Newman. And if they didn't do it, then who did?

I close the door behind me, double-check that the deadbolt is in place, and slump onto my sofa. I glance over at the canvas that's been sitting untouched on the easel for months. Pristine. Not a mark on it. A blank slate waiting for inspiration, collecting dust like I am.

As I look at that blank canvas and the tray of ignored paints and brushes on the floor, I begin to wonder if I'll ever be myself again. Then a more horrifying thought strikes me. Have I ever really been myself to begin with? Or have I just been the person shaped by the tragedy around them? The person crafted by my father's grief, my mother's anger, the town's suspicions, society's expectations, and my friends' ambitions. Who would I be if I'd been allowed to thrive without all the character-building bullshit?

Probably a person who would grab a bag, get on a plane, and start anew.

I take out my phone and pull up my messages. I haven't received anything from Samara in a few days. She's angry with me. I can tell. And I don't blame her. There's nothing worse than trying to have a relationship with someone who has a past. And the long-distance aspect doesn't help any.

My laptop pings.

I lean forward, moving aside a few unwashed plates from the coffee table in order to pull the laptop closer. I click on the mouse and the screen lights up. The FriendSpace page is still open. I'd forgotten to log out of Amber's secret account. There's a red symbol in the top corner of the tab, indicating a message.

I click on it.

Then I freeze.

Anonymous674: *Have you figured it out yet?*

In all the commotion of the last few days I'd almost forgotten about the mysterious messages on Amber's account. But I'm no longer in the mood. There's less than twenty-four hours before Riley is to be executed.

I type a quick reply.

WynWitchFan2: *I don't have time for games.*

No response.

My leg bounces in anxious anticipation as I wait for a reply, the ball of my foot practically wearing a hole in the floor. I stand up and pace the room. I know this is a bad idea. But whoever this person is, they're my best chance at learning what truly happened to Amber.

The laptop pings.

I practically leap over the coffee table to look at the screen. Anonymous674 has sent me a picture. I click on the link to open it in a new page.

It's the ring.

What if this is Amber's murderer?

And they've been in my house.

My fingers shake as I type out a response.

WynWitchFan2: *What do you want?*

Anonymous674: *I told you. I want you to let it go.*

WynWitchFan2: *I'll never do that.*

Anonymous674: *Then you don't leave me any other choice.*

WynWitchFan2: *I won't stop until I know what happened to my sister.*

Anonymous674: *If you truly want to know what happened to Amber then meet me at the place where they found her.*

Anonymous674: *Come alone.*

Anonymous674: *And don't call the police.*

I take a deep breath and hold it in to a count of ten, trying to settle my nerves. Am I really considering this? Am I really going to meet this person alone? In the woods? My mind is racing, trying to put together who it could be or what they might be planning. All I can think of is Riley warning me that I could be next. But why now? After all this time? If somebody wanted me dead they had plenty of time in the last fifteen years to do it.

What's changed?

Me. That's what has changed. My need to know the truth. Once and for all.

WynWitchFan2: *When?*

Anonymous674: *Now.*

Chapter 60

Going alone is probably the stupidest decision I've ever made.

As soon as I park my car at the trailhead, I consider calling Cameron and asking him to meet me. He's the only one I can call, after all. Mom wouldn't be any help and I can't go to the police. There isn't anyone else. If Dad were still alive I might have asked him for his help. At the very least, I might have asked him for his advice. But he's not alive. And there's no one else around that I'm close to who would care to help me.

I'm on my own.

My car door slams shut, frightening a group of sparrows that were hiding in a nearby bush. They burst out of the hedges and fly up into the trees where they disappear in the low-hanging branches. I glance around the small parking area, but I don't see any other cars. Whoever else was out here must have hiked up on foot from one of the connecting trails. Or parked down along the old highway. I should have paid better attention while I was driving. Then I might be more prepared for whoever—or whatever—is waiting for me.

I check my pockets. Keys. Phone. Dad's buck knife I took from his office after he died. I'm hoping I won't need to use the last one, but if there's one thing I've learned since Amber's death it's better to be safe than sorry.

I start up the trail, my stomach full of anxious butterflies. I try to tick off in my mind the short list of people who could be waiting for me up in the glen, but I quickly realize that I'm drawing a blank. With Henson dead, I have no idea who could be up there.

The forest is quiet save for the sound of my boots crunching leaves and snapping twigs as I set off along the trail and make my way deeper into the thick woods. A rustle in a nearby shrub startles me. I twist around, ready to whip out the knife in my pocket, but there's nothing there. Just the wind. Maybe a rabbit.

I move on.

By the time I reach the old hangout, my heart is practically bursting through my chest. My shoulders ache from the tension I've held in them as I clench my fists in my pockets. A squirrel crawls down the trunk of the old oak tree where Amber's body was found. It stops in its tracks when it sees me, frantically shaking its tail. A warning to other critters nearby. Then it darts back into the upper limbs, concealing itself in the golden leaves that have yet to fall.

I look around.

There's no one here.

Is this a gag?

"Lex?"

The voice catches me off guard and sends a cold shiver up the back of my neck. I turn around to see Cameron walking up the small ridge on the other side of the glen. No. It can't be.

"What are— Was it you? The one sending me those messages? This entire time?" But those aren't the questions I should be asking. And as he comes closer I realize just how stupid I've been. "Did you kill my sister?"

Cameron opens his mouth to speak, but cuts himself off when something else rustles the ground behind me. I watch as his eyes shift from me to someone else.

I turn.

Jessica.

My instinct is to run. To panic. But that instinct is blocked by my own confusion and my desire to finally know the truth.

"What's going on?" I ask. My fingers wrench around the knife in my pocket, waiting.

"I could ask the same question," Cameron says. His eyes narrow. "You're not supposed to be here."

His comment doesn't make sense to me until I realize it's not me he's talking to. It's Jessica. She steps toward us, the fur of her designer coat framing her face like a lion's mane. I don't know what I've just walked into, but judging by the expressions on both Cameron's and Jessica's faces, it's not going to plan.

"Oh, please. Did you really think I was going to let you come up here alone? To be honest, I didn't think you would do it. I didn't think you'd tell Lexie the truth. I thought you'd chicken out at the last minute like you usually do," Jessica says to Cameron.

His response is a venomous glare. She's insulted his pride. Or something more.

"What is this about? Why are we up here? I was told that if I showed up here I would get the truth about Amber."

"I did it."

My heart drops into my gut as I look at Cameron.

"I'm the one who messaged you to come."

I'm dizzy from the vague back and forth. "Did you murder my sister?"

"No," Cameron says.

I breathe a sigh of relief.

Then he hits me with a bombshell.

"Jess did."

Jessica rolls her eyes.

Neither of them appears upset or ashamed. If anything, they both look irritated with each other. Worst of all, neither of them is really paying attention to me.

"Is this a joke?" I finally interrupt. "Because this isn't funny."

330

"It's not a joke," Cameron says. "I'm the one who messaged you on FriendSpace."

"But what were you doing on there?"

He doesn't answer at first. Instead he shoots a sidelong glance at Jessica, as though waiting for her to jump in. When she doesn't he returns his attention to me. "When I ran into you at the station I realized you were going to do whatever you could to prove Riley's innocence. I knew it would only be a matter of time before you started digging into Amber's personal life. I thought you might find her other account. And if you did, you'd see the old messages—"

"Messages? What messages?"

Jessica laughs. "She didn't even look. All this running around and little Lexie didn't even look at her sister's inbox. Unbelievable."

"I don't understand."

Cameron takes a deep breath. "Amber told me about Jess and Henson. She told me about the photos and how she was planning to tell your dad about it. She threatened to go to the police. I think she thought I'd be jealous."

"You weren't? Why wouldn't you be?" I'm in complete disbelief. If I'd been Cameron I would have been livid to find out my girlfriend was messing around with our teacher. Then it hits me. "You already knew. That's why Riley said you didn't want to be at the dance. Did everybody know but me?"

But then Cameron's words about Jess finally sink in and suddenly everything feels like it's spinning.

"I can't carry this weight around anymore," Cameron says. "It's been too long. I'm sick of the lies. And I can't see Riley executed for something he didn't do. I told Jess a few days ago that I was going to come clean if she didn't."

"You're a coward," Jessica hisses. "Don't be such a wuss. Tell her what you were really doing. Tell her how you were just pretending to like her in order to find out what she knew. Tell Lex how you faked wanting to rekindle your friendship just so you could see if she had any real proof of what happened."

I blink. "What?"

"It may have started that way, but that's not how it—"

"Save us your simpering, Cameron. Just admit that you're a spineless twit who's afraid of someone finding out you're not as perfect as you seem."

I turn to Cameron. "What does she mean?"

But Cameron's focus is completely on Jessica. "I warned you, Jess. I played your game for as long as I could. I gave you the opportunity to tell Lex the truth. She deserves to know what really happened."

"What do you even know about what really happened?"

"I saw it."

"You didn't see shit, Cameron."

That's when I realize none of this is a joke. This is real. One of them killed my sister. Maybe even both of them. And I'm with them alone. In the woods. And no one knows where I am.

"I've been covering for you for fifteen years, Jess! I'm done. I'm not doing it anymore. Tell Lex the truth. Tell her it was an accident."

A quiet fury darkens Jessica's eyes.

"What aren't you telling me, Jess?" I wish I didn't sound like I was pleading. I wish I could be more confident, but I don't know which one of them to trust. Or if I can trust either of them.

"Nothing. Cameron is a liar," she says.

"What reason do I have to lie?" he yells.

"Maybe because you're finally man enough to admit that you're never going to get what you want. That I'm never going to give it to you."

"You're a bitch."

"That's what this is about, isn't it? It's not about your guilty conscience. It's about the fact that I dumped you and never looked back. It's because you know you were never man enough for me."

"I protected you. I gave you an alibi!"

"I never asked you to do that."

332

"You didn't need to ask me! You never needed to ask me! I would have done anything for you. Even after I found out about you and Henson I would have done anything you wanted. I was willing to give you a second chance. But then you lied about Amber. Then Riley took the fall. At any moment over the last fifteen years, you could have implicated me in murder! Do you have any idea what it's like to live with that?"

"Pathetic."

I don't like where this is going. I back up slowly while they're arguing with each other. I'm fairly certain that if I can get enough distance between us I can give myself a good head start. Enough to make a run for it. Then all I have to do is get to my car and call the police.

Would I really do that to the two people I thought were my friends?

Yes. If it could save Riley I'd do it in a heartbeat.

But Cameron grabs me by the wrist just as I'm about to make a break for it. "You need to stay, Lex. You need to understand what happened."

"Let go of me, Cameron. I don't know what's going on here, but I don't want any part of it. I just want to know what happened to Amber."

I tug on my arm, but he tightens his grip. That's when I see it. The skin on his hand is red and swollen, blistered from an animal bite.

"That's why you were so determined to get into my house. You wanted to find out how much I knew. You wanted to know if I'd already figured out you two were involved."

"Not just that. I needed leverage! I needed proof in case Jess denied it. In case she tried to pin this on me."

"Proof?" The smug confidence slips from Jessica's face.

"The ring. The one he gave you. That cheap piece of carnival jewelry Henson used to convince you that he gave a shit." Cameron clenches my wrist harder. I don't think he means to, but he's so blinded by his anger at Jessica that he's not paying attention to me. My fingers begin to tingle.

"Cameron, you're hurting me . . ."

"It wasn't cheap!" Jessica yells. "It was an antique!"

"An antique piece of shit that you left at the scene of a fucking murder, Jess!"

I've never seen this kind of pain in Cameron's face before. He's not simply angry. He's heartbroken. And I believe him. I believe that he loved Jessica so much that he helped cover up my sister's murder.

I lose sensation in my fingers just as Cameron removes the ring from his pocket. He holds it up, taunting Jessica with it.

"That doesn't prove anything," Jessica says.

"It's covered in blood. How much you want to bet it still has some of Amber's DNA on it? Or maybe even your own. Stuck in the grooves from when you hit her."

"You didn't see that." Jessica glares.

My wrist throbs.

"But I did." Cameron loosens his grip on my arm in order to take another step toward Jessica. "I was there the entire time. I was waiting for you. Because I knew as soon as you disappeared from the dance that you'd be going to see him. I'd followed you there before."

His expression softens. He looks at me apologetically. "But I swear I didn't know that bastard had tricked Amber as well."

I rub my wrist, holding it protectively to my chest. Then a quiet fury builds in my chest. A years-long animosity I'd always tried to pin on Riley but had always felt misplaced. When I look at Jessica's face, callous and nonchalant, I understand why. It should have been directed toward her.

"Tell me what happened to my sister, Jess. Tell me now."

Jessica crosses her arms over her chest. Her face tightens in a glare and for the first time in my life I see a real ugliness in her. "Your sister was a lying, thieving bitch. And she deserved what happened to her."

Chapter 61

AMBER
Saturday, October 13, 2007
10:45 p.m.

"I knew you'd be here."

Jessica's head whips around. I expect her to be angry, but she's startled. She tugs her short, leather jacket around her as best she can, but it won't zip up because she's wearing an extra-padded push-up bra. Then she shines a flashlight in my eyes.

I wince and hold up my hand to block the bright glare of the light.

"Amber?" Clearly, she was expecting someone else.

I hike up my dress and step around the fallen branches. Not that I really need to watch where I'm walking. I practically have this entire area of the woods memorized. I should, after all. I've been here enough times. If not with Lex and our friends, then with Richard. Even in the darkness I stride as confidently as I would if I were following the path up to my front door.

"You're a bitch."

Jessica laughs. She thinks this is some kind of joke. "What are you talking about?"

"I know what you did. I know you've been with him."

"With who? Did I accidentally go out with one of your boyfriends or something?"

I don't stop until I'm a few feet in front of her. She's standing beside the old oak tree, which has always been our meeting spot. Not the meeting spot of our friend group, but the one where Richard and I meet. The one where we talk about the kinds of things that I can't talk about with my friends. With people my own age. They wouldn't understand.

An icy breeze cuts through the forest. My arms are covered in goose bumps. I should be wearing a jacket, but I didn't bring one to the dance. I didn't think I'd need one. I wasn't planning on going out to the woods, after all. Hell, I wasn't even planning on going to the dance. Richard and I were supposed to do something together. Just the two of us. But then he canceled on me. I had to get a date at the last minute just to provide a cover for myself so my family wouldn't be suspicious. I would have been angry if I hadn't seen Richard at the dance. At least he didn't lie to me. But seeing Jessica up here makes me think otherwise.

"I've seen it."

"You've seen what?" she asks. Then she looks around. Nervous. Because she's afraid someone will see us up here together.

Not just someone. Richard. The man we're both in love with.

"The photo."

Jessica's confidence fades like a wilting flower. There's an instantaneous spark of shock in her eyes that's quickly replaced by anger. "You don't know what you're talking about."

"I don't?"

"No. You have no idea what you're talking about and no idea what you saw."

"I found it."

"Where?"

I ignore her question. "And I kept it."

Her arms tighten around her chest as though she's trying to

hold herself back from doing something rash. Is she thinking about hitting me? Or maybe she's just worried that all of this standing around in the cold will make her less attractive to him. Her hair is beginning to flatten from the dampness in the air.

"What do you want, Amber?"

"I want you to leave him alone."

I'm doing pretty well up until this point. I'm holding my own. That's not easy to do against Jessica. Not that she's a pushover. She's not my sister. But she and I are a lot alike. We're not easy to frighten. And we don't back down. Pushing her like this will probably have the opposite effect of what I'm hoping, but I'm not really thinking about that. I didn't plan this. I'm too pissed.

She laughs. It's a callous, entitled sound. The kind of laugh only a person who knows they can talk their way out of anything can make.

It sets me off.

I shove her. She trips backwards and braces herself on the trunk of the tree.

"What the hell is wrong with you?" she snaps, pulling her heel out of the dirt.

"I want you to stay away from him."

"Why? So, *you* can have him?" She says this like it's a joke. Like she can't believe he could be interested in me. Then she sees the hardened mask of my face and knows that's exactly what I mean. "Oh. My. God. Are you serious?"

Jessica throws her head back with another high-pitched cackle. "Really? You? I guess I shouldn't be surprised. Not after hearing what you did with Riley over the summer. But Dick Henson? Really? Been playing the role of teacher's pet a little too much this year? Give it a break, Amber. He couldn't possibly be interested in you."

Now it's my turn to get the upper hand. I purse my lips together in a knowing smirk and cross my arms over my chest. I ignore the fact that I'm freezing and put all of my focus into the act.

The 'I know something you don't know' act. And while that is true, what I say isn't.

"We've been together."

Jessica's expression goes blank. She looks like a computer slowly trying to reboot itself and not quite managing to make a full connection to its own processing unit. She can't tell if I'm telling the truth. But that doesn't matter. What matters is that I can tell she's trying to decide if it *could* be true. That's how you tell a good lie, after all. You don't try to prove the lie. You don't insist that it's true. You just make the lie plausible. Then you let the other person weigh that plausibility in their own mind. The best lies aren't the most fabricated. They're the ones that leave the most doubt.

And her doubt tells her it could be possible. It could be possible that Richard has been with another woman. It's possible that he's been with me.

Jessica is so fast I don't have time to respond. She barrels right into me, shoving her elbow into my chest. I hit the ground hard. The wind is knocked out of my lungs completely and I gasp for air, my body panicking at the sudden tension in my muscles from clenching to breathe. Jessica is on top of me before I can catch my breath. She grabs the front bodice of my dress and uses it to lift me partway off the ground, only to shove me back down. This prevents my attempts to inhale. I try to scratch at her face but she slaps my hands away. She lands a punch on my cheek but quickly reels her arm back when her ring pinches the soft skin on her finger. I squirm beneath her, eventually jabbing my knee into her side. She groans and rolls over into the leaves.

That gives me the chance to catch my breath. Oxygen enters my lungs, relieving that empty pressure on my chest. It's like coming up from the bottom of an Olympic diving pool after trying to hold my breath for two minutes. It hurts. But at least now I can get away.

I crawl on my hands and knees at first, which is tricky because the long skirt of my dress keeps getting caught on the natural rubble of the forest floor. I eventually pull myself up to my feet. My heels aren't really tall. Not like Jessica's, but they weren't meant for scrambling through the woods. I slip them off to give myself better traction so I don't fall over and break my ankle.

That's when I hear the scream.

It's like a banshee wail, piercing through the night. I know it's Jessica, furious in a jealous rage, but my first thought is of something else. The Wynwood Witch.

I whip my head around. Jessica's hair has fallen out of its partial updo and hangs wild around the sides of her face. She's ghostly in the moonlight and for a split second I think I'm wrong. Maybe it's not her. Maybe it is the witch. Then the sharp edge of a rock hits me in the temple and I fall to the ground.

Everything is a dark hazy blur. The cold of the night is muzzled by the hot rush of wetness that flows from my forehead. I don't feel any pain. Just the groggy urge to close my eyes and sleep. The last thing I remember is the musky odor of damp earth and the shrill, ghostly sob of my killer.

Chapter 62

My brain is on fire.

This must be what they mean when they say 'seeing red.' Because when I look at Jessica, I can barely even make her out. All I can see is my own rage boiling to the surface. It's blurred out everything else. The woods, the tree, Cameron—they all fade into the background. The only thing I can focus on is the scorching shape of Jessica, misshapen by my mind into a faceless monster that took everything from me.

"You just left her there?" My voice wavers. "You killed her and just left her there? You didn't even try to help her? You didn't call an ambulance?"

But then it hits me that Jessica hasn't even told the entire story. She didn't simply leave my sister there in the woods. She cut her up. She tied her to a tree. She made a massacre of her body to cover up her tracks. To make it look like some sick ghost story.

I can't even begin to process the fact that it's probably impossible to imagine that Jessica did that all on her own. She might be jealous, but she's not clever. And she's not particularly strong. It would have taken a considerable effort on her part to arrange Amber the way she did. And Cameron did just admit to seeing it all. I should be putting two and two together. But I can't.

I'm too fucking furious.

I lunge at Jessica, throwing all of my weight at her. She stumbles backwards but doesn't fall.

"You killed my sister!" I scream. "You mutilated her!"

"No, I didn't! I never knew who did that. Probably some freak who found her body and thought it'd make a good joke! Probably someone else she tried to screw over." Jessica turns her gaze away from me long enough to peer at Cameron. "Or maybe it was someone who thought they were helping cover up a fucking accident."

"You're lying! You made a mockery of her because of what? Because of Henson?!"

"I didn't—"

My fist colliding with Jessica's jaw prevents her from finishing her sentence.

Her head whips to the side.

I throw another punch. This time she turns her head and I barely clip the side of her face, knocking back the hood of her coat.

"How could you do that to her?! How could you desecrate her body like that?!"

"I didn't!" Jessica spits a mouthful of blood on the forest floor. "Amber was your friend!"

"I was angry! I wasn't thinking!"

"You're selfish and vile! You could have just left her alone! Only a sick and twisted person would cut her up and—" The words stick in my mouth. I'm so livid that I'm shaking. All I can think of is my last image of Amber. Covered in blood. The mark of the Wynwood Witch cut into her chest.

A gust of air sweeps past my face. The hair stands on the back of my neck and I imagine an indecipherable whisper lingering in my ear. The echo of something ancient in these woods. Or maybe Amber herself reaching out from beyond the grave.

Or maybe it's just me.

Me and my own ire.

Jessica charges toward me. "I never touched her afterwards! I never—"

I shove Jessica with all of my strength. The force is so much that I nearly knock myself off balance. But Cameron grabs me from behind, preventing me from falling on top of her.

Jessica hits the ground with a crack. Her face freezes in shock, mouth open, eyes wide. She doesn't blink. She doesn't move. She stares up to the cloudy canopy above the trees. Then the blood spills out from the back of her head.

Chapter 63

The barista walks by and removes the empty dishes from our table.

I give her a small smile before turning my attention to the man across from me. "What now?"

Chief Newman clears his throat with a gravelly cough. It's strange looking at him now and knowing the truth. It's like seeing someone with a completely different set of eyes. And, in retrospect, I should be embarrassed by the horrible thoughts I had about him. Not that I didn't have reason to dislike him. He'd never really treated me well. But at least now I understand why he was so brusque and standoffish.

He was grieving the loss of a daughter he never got to know. He didn't want to get too close.

And he didn't want to believe that I could have killed my sister.

"Cameron Ellis is out on bail. We'd like to charge him as an accessory, but to be honest there isn't a lot of evidence against him. It would be damn-near impossible placing him near the original crime scene and according to the confession Jessica gave you, he wasn't involved. The best we could do is accessory after the fact. I don't think there's a doubt in anyone's mind that he's

343

been keeping her secret this entire time. But proving it? That's another thing entirely."

Which doesn't even begin to touch the political connections Cameron's made. They certainly wouldn't want their golden boy to lose his entire career over something a court can only argue he 'might have known.'

I hold the coffee mug between my hands, allowing the heat to warm my fingertips. The bell dings above the café door as another customer walks in for a to-go order.

"Something about it still doesn't sit right with me though. When the police found Amber's body it was positioned. It was set up to look like a scene from the old Wynwood Witch legend. Why? Why go through all of that effort?"

"To throw the police off the scent?" Newman frowns. "I'm sorry to admit that it worked."

"It just seems like an awful lot of work when there already wasn't much evidence to begin with."

"People do crazy things when they're cornered. Heinous things. Who's to say what was going through her mind? She was angry. She was jealous. She made a stupid decision in a blind rage." Newman sips his coffee. "The sad thing is that if she'd just come forward and told someone immediately afterwards, she probably wouldn't have gotten in much trouble. She was underage. Maybe she'd get a few years in juvenile detention. More likely she'd get community service. Her family could have afforded top-notch counsel. Hell, she may not have even seen the inside of a prison cell."

I can tell from the sound of Newman's voice that he wouldn't have been happy with that. I can't blame him. I wouldn't have been happy with that either. But he's not wrong. If Jess had been honest then maybe we could have all put this behind us fifteen years ago.

And maybe if I hadn't been so scared I wouldn't have spent years blaming myself for circumstances that were entirely out of

344

my control. Amber's death, Riley's incarceration, the miscarriage. None of those things were my fault. And there was nothing I could have done to prevent those events.

"But what about the knife?"

"There was a partial print on the knife that was never accounted for. I agree it's unlikely that she took it from Riley. That's where I think Cameron might not be telling the entire truth." There's regret in his eyes. Regret because he'd jumped to conclusions all those years ago. Of course, Riley's knife would have Riley's fingerprints on them. But that didn't mean he was the last one to use it. That didn't mean he killed Amber.

And now we know he didn't.

But I can't help feeling like something is still missing from the story. There's motive. There's circumstance. There's evidence. Cameron and I both witnessed her confession.

But it still feels wrong.

It still feels unfinished.

Before I can figure out what, however, Newman interrupts my thoughts.

"I want you to know that I've put in an appeal to the state to grant a full pardon and release for Riley. It'll take some time for the paperwork to go through, but he should be a free man by the end of the week."

There are no words to explain how I feel hearing Newman say that. Once Newman learned of Jessica's involvement in Amber's death, he made a call to the state to put an immediate stay on Riley's execution due to new evidence. I'd been holding my breath since then, waiting to find out if it would be enough. But hearing Newman say that Riley will finally be released feels like a weight has been removed from my shoulders. I'm so happy. Now I can finally move forward and live the life I couldn't live with the guilt of Amber and the miscarriage hanging over me.

"What about the guards at the prison? Are there going to be any consequences for what they did to Riley?"

"What do you mean?" Newman asks.

"They attacked him. He was beaten to a bloody pulp."

Newman gives me a strange look before sipping his coffee. "Nobody attacked Riley."

"But that's what they said when they called me. And I saw him in the hospital. He was in really bad shape."

"Whoever called you must have been mistaken. I talked to the warden myself. He assured me that nothing happened. He said that Riley did that to himself. Probably to try to postpone the execution." Newman shrugs. "Not that I can blame him. He was innocent, after all. I might have done the same thing."

So, Riley was just trying to buy himself some time. No, he was trying to buy me time. Time to figure out the truth. But it's strange he didn't tell me himself.

Oh well. It's over. The truth is out. Amber can finally rest in peace. And I can finally get the hell out of Braxton Falls and go somewhere nobody knows me. Where I can be someone new.

"Thank you, Chief," I say. I smile, too. It's small and it's bittersweet. But more importantly, for the first time in fifteen years, it's authentic.

Chapter 64

Almost no one attends Jessica's funeral.

As expected, her parents are there, but her husband and children are not. Cameron didn't show up either, but that was probably the smart move politically. Mom wanted to go. She made a big statement to the press about showing solidarity for Amber. But Chief Newman convinced her to stay home and for that I'm eternally grateful. Jessica may have done something horrible, but no one deserves my mother, drunk off her ass, slinging profanities at a casket as it's being lowered into the ground.

I'm there. As is Riley. Newman did what he said he would. He filed the paperwork and got him released only a few days after the news broke about Jessica being responsible for Amber's murder. Riley and I stand side by side. Close, but not too close. We're the only non-family members in attendance. I'd like to think that Jessica's parents appreciate that on some level, but I don't know if they've even noticed that we're there. I don't blame them. I don't remember much about Amber's funeral except staring at the hole in the ground and wondering why it was her and not me. It was like I was in another world. Like I was also dead and the entire event was a movie playing in the background on mute.

I'm more conscious today. I feel the cold wisp of raindrops misting my face. Most of the leaves have fallen, scattering the cemetery in a golden cover that groundskeepers are raking up in the background. Winter is in the air. Homecoming is over. I think about all of those Braxton Falls High School girls who scrambled to pick out a slinky dress they'd only wear once in their lives heading to school this week in their puffy coats. I almost laugh at the absurdity of it all. To think we were all that materialistic at one time. My gaze moves toward Jessica's headstone. To think that some of us always would be.

When the funeral ends, I don't stick around to offer the family my condolences. Instead, Riley and I walk silently through the cemetery and away from the crowd of photographers hoping to get a sound bite from Jessica's parents. I should be grateful that they aren't hounding me, but I know what it feels like to be in the spotlight for a helpless tragedy. I grieve for them and for the life they'll have to live with their daughter's stigma on them. That'll never go away. And it's not fair.

I slow my pace as we edge closer to Amber's grave. It's weathered some, but it still looks fresh to me. I step forward and brush the fallen leaves away from the front of the tombstone, revealing the short dates of her life. Something inside of me feels like this should be a conclusive moment. Like closing the book on a never-ending chapter. But everything is still too fresh. Too raw. I do feel like I found some answers though. Not all of them. But enough to help me move on.

"Have you given any thought to what I asked?"

I stand up and take a step away from Amber's grave before turning my attention to Riley. Shortly after he was released from prison he asked if I would give him a second chance. I told him I needed some time to think about it, but I knew immediately that the answer was no. Riley was my past. And even though I do still care for him in the way a person will always care for their first love, I know I can't go backwards. It's time to put the past behind me. It's time to finally be myself. The person I couldn't be while the ghosts of this town still haunted me.

"I can't. I love you, Riley, and I always will. But I have to move on with my life. I've let this town, my family, and Amber's murder consume everything about me. I want to get away from it. From all of it." I think about the message I'd sent Samara that morning about the plane ticket I'd bought for next week. It took a major chunk out of my savings, but it was the right thing to do. I'm done stalling.

The disappointment in Riley's face cuts me deeply, but he nods and I know he understands. His life was put on pause. For him very little has changed. He hasn't been in the real world for almost half his life.

"I guess a part of me just always hoped that if by some miracle I was released we would be together," he says. He sounds like the Riley I remember. Like the boy who used to make my heart flutter.

"I felt like that too for a long time. But it's never going to be the way it used to be. We're different people now."

"You're not that different."

"But I want to be."

We stand in silence, refusing to look at each other. This should be a joyous moment. Riley was finally free, as was I. But the cloud of everything that happened won't seem to lift. And I'm struggling to reconcile with the truth about Jessica and Cameron. Hell, even the truth about Amber and all of the secrets she kept from me. It hurts to remember how close we used to be before high school pulled us apart. It makes me wonder how different things might have been if she'd lived.

Would we be close now? Would we be the kind of sisters who called each other every week to catch up? Or would we be living two completely different lives, only to cross each other's paths during holidays and family reunions?

I guess I'll never know. But I can be optimistic in that hypothetical reality.

In this reality, however? I still have questions.

"There's just one thing that bothers me about all of this," I say. "What's that?"

"How did they get your knife?"

Riley frowns. "What do you mean?"

"The evidence placed your knife at the scene of the crime. The police swear that's what was used to carve those marks on Amber's chest. How did Jess and Cameron get that? I saw you lose it after the football game."

Riley doesn't look at me. He's staring across the cemetery where a small crowd of reporters is heading toward us. Then he shrugs his shoulders. "I don't know. Maybe one of them found it after the fight. Does it matter?"

I don't like this answer. Wouldn't he have wondered all of this time? Wouldn't that be the one thing plaguing him from inside prison?

"But they set you up. Aren't you angry about that?"

Riley gives me a soft smile. "I spent years being angry about a lot of things, Lexie. I'm ready to put all of that behind me. Just like you."

But he can tell from my expression that I'm not going to let this go.

"You know, I think I had another one. I might have lent it to Cameron once. It was so long ago. It's hard to remember."

"Right, of course." I'm not convinced, but I can tell that pushing the matter won't get me anywhere.

The reporters are getting closer.

"I should get going," I say. "I'm not in the mood to answer any of their questions and I have to go home and pack for my trip."

"When are you leaving?" Riley asks.

"Thursday."

"When are you coming back?"

"I don't know. Honestly? I might not."

He pauses. "What's his name?"

"Samara," I say, my cheeks warming in a blush.

"I always knew you were more adventurous than you let on."

Riley smiles again and this time it feels like we've made it over an awkward hurdle with each other. It's a smile that tells me friendship is still possible. And I couldn't be happier.

"We should get together before you leave," he says. There's a nervousness in his voice that he didn't have when we were younger. It's endearing. "Maybe have dinner? Just a little catch-up before we both move on."

"I'd like that."

He reaches out and takes my hand. It's an unexpected action, but not entirely unwanted. I think about giving him a hug, but the reporters are still out with their cameras and I don't want any more rumors started about me.

"Thank you for believing in me, Lexie. Thank you for not giving up."

"Of course, Riley."

"I know it's kind of a horrible thing to say considering everything that happened. Amber was your sister and I know how close you were. But I'm glad it was her and not you. It could have so easily been you, after all."

The change in tone gives me pause. "What do you mean?"

"I know it's ridiculous but I can't help but think what might have happened if it had been you out in the woods? It was dark. And you and Amber always looked so much alike. Anything could have happened."

"But anything didn't happen, Riley. Jess happened. The only mistake was that they got into an argument and it went too far."

"I know. I know." Riley is flustered. He lets go of me and slips his hands into his coat pockets. "Sorry, I'm still trying to process all of it. Or maybe I'm still a little confused after being in the hospital. I spent all of these years thinking it was a stranger or a serial killer. It's hard to believe that Jess and Cameron could do something like that."

"It's OK, Riley. It's a lot for all of us." I place a hand on his upper arm and give it a gentle squeeze. I expect it to be relaxed, but it's not. It's tense. Like he's clenching his fist in his pocket. Like he's angry. But I shake it off. It's nothing. I'm just trying to read into something that isn't there. "What about dinner at my place on Tuesday?"

"That'd be perfect."

Chapter 65

AMBER
Saturday, October 13, 2007
11:36 p.m.

The buzzing whirr of pain wakes me. Something warm trickles down my face. Blood. It feels good against the cold air of the forest. I open my eyes but the world is a blurry haze. It takes me a few breaths to realize what happened. To remember where I am.

That bitch hit me in the head with a rock.

And then she left me.

I can't believe she had the nerve.

My palm presses hard against the ground as I try to push myself up. A whoosh of vertigo hits me before I can even straighten my arm. I lie back down, cheek squished against the wet leaves. My dress must be a mess. Mom will be pissed. She'll want to know how I got it so dirty. I'll tell her I tripped in the parking lot. My heels were too high anyway. I'll tell her I slipped and scuffed the dress in the mud. Nothing the dry cleaners can't fix.

Then I hear it. Footsteps.

I clench my eyes shut, willing my focus to restore. But when I open them everything is still coated in a cloudy fog. Like I'm looking through an underwater lens. The darkness doesn't help either.

"Is that you, Jess?" I ask, pushing myself up from the ground. I manage to roll over onto my hip, but as soon as my head is higher than the rest of my body I feel like I'm going to fall over. She must have hit me harder than I realized. Everything is spinning. I'm nauseous, but I don't have anything in me to throw up. I skipped on dinner in order to fit into this damn dress. "You're a bitch for leaving me here."

Two legs step in front of my vision, a darker shadow falling over me. My head is throbbing and there's a piercing stab behind my right eye.

I feel the heat in my lower back first. Then the dampness. Then the sharp, searing pain of the blade. Confusion hits me first. Then fear. Then panic.

"This is for what you did!" the voice yells.

The words jumble in my head. Out of order. Not Jess. Someone else.

Someone trying to kill me.

The knife goes into me again. And again.

Not trying. Succeeding.

Someone killing me.

I turn my head to get a glimpse of their face in the night, but I'm pushed back down by the force of the blade sticking into me.

"I loved you, Lexie! How could you?! I *loved* you!"

What?

"Danny told me what you did! He saw you there! At the clinic! He saw you!"

I'm not Lexie, I try to say, but only a gargle of blood falls from my lips.

I'm rolled over. Two legs straddle me. I look up into my killer's face and for a brief second, I see a similar confusion to my own. A horror. I see his mistake. But it's quickly replaced with rage.

I'm not my sister.

I'm not Lexie, Riley.

I'm not her.

A Letter from Karin Nordin

Dear Reader,

Does anyone know a teenage girl better than her sister?

While writing *Sweet Little Lies* I was constantly reminded of my own relationship with my sisters. Like Lexie, I'm the oldest, and with that came a lot of responsibility and expectations. Some of those expectations were from family and society, but many of them came from myself. And expectations can put a lot of strain on siblings. On teenage sisters, in particular. Much of writing this book required me to look at the nuances between my own sisters and ask myself, "what if?"—and then follow that question to its darkest possibilities.

But despite the tragic fictional end for these sisters, the inspiration behind the emotional tie between them is very real. There's nothing quite like the bond between sisters, especially sisters who are closer in age. My middle sister was my first best friend. But even best friends have their ups and downs. As sisters we grew up doing everything together. We shared secrets in homemade tents in our bedroom, we reenacted our favorite films, we knew everything about each other. And we protected each other in ways that only sisters can. But like Lexie and Amber, even sisters don't share everything—even if we think we do.

About halfway through writing this novel I caught a clip of a documentary where a psychiatrist was discussing how siblings can grow up together, live in the same house, have the same parents, attend the same school, but not live the same shared experience. It was a revelation for me! That one observation really struck me as the crux of not only Lexie and Amber's relationship, but my own relationship with my sisters as well. As adults we have the benefit of reflection and are able to look back and see where our memories of the past differ from each other. Sadly, Lexie and Amber never got that opportunity.

Having a sister can be a beautiful thing. If you're lucky it's a bond for life. It's inside jokes, lifelong memories, and secrets we sometimes take to the grave. But being a sister also means jealousy, competition, and a rare form of heartache that isn't quite the same with anyone else.

If you have a sister, you probably know what I mean.

Thank you so much for taking the time to read *Sweet Little Lies*. I love hearing about the aspects of a book that readers connect to the most or how a character affected them. Likewise, I love answering questions about my books! If you want to get in touch with me you can find me on Instagram @karinnordinauthor or on Twitter @KNordinAuthor. And if you enjoyed this book I'd be incredibly grateful if you would consider writing a review so other readers can find Lexie's story as well.

Happy reading!

Karin

Keep Reading . . .

Where Ravens Roost

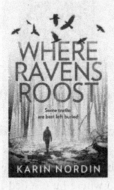

In a small town full of secrets, anyone could be a killer.

Detective Kjeld Nygaard wants nothing more than to forget
his family and Varsund, the small mining town he once called
home, even exist. But while on suspension after his last case
went disastrously wrong, his estranged father Stenar leaves a
message on Kjeld's phone claiming he's seen a murder.

But with no evidence and Stenar suffering from Alzheimer's,
the local police think he must have imagined it. Kjeld can't
stop himself from investigating what actually happened, and
soon discovers a body. But when the police start to suspect
Stenar, it's a race against time to discover the truth before it's
lost forever.

**But will uncovering the truth expose
family secrets that are best left buried?**

Last One Alive

They survived once. Can he save them this time?

When **Detective Kjeld Nygaard** is called to the discovery of a body in the burnt-out shell of a house, his heart sinks. He never wanted to see this house again. The house of a notorious serial killer. The house where he rescued **Louisa Karlsson** from being murdered.

But when they discover the body is in fact Louisa, the mystery deepens. It can't be the old serial killer. He's dead.

Then another body is found, again killed in the exact place where Kjeld saved them from another murderer. Another survivor dead.

With the clock ticking Kjeld and his partner **Detective Esme Jansson** are desperate to stop any more survivors from being murdered. But every clue they find leads to a dead end. Why is the killer picking off people Kjeld rescued? Could it be connected to another of his previous cases?

When Kjeld's daughter is kidnapped – it's a race against time to save her life. Can Kjeld stop the killer without paying the ultimate price or will he be the last one alive?

Acknowledgments

This book is a personal milestone for me and wouldn't have made it this far without the support of so many incredible people. I'll try to be brief, but I'm a chronic overwriter. So without further ado . . .

My sincerest thanks to my agent, Anne Tibbets, for taking a chance on me and my books. And my eternal gratitude to the organizers of ITW and ThrillerFest for bringing us together.

Thank you to my brilliant editor, Cat Camacho, for her enthusiasm and commitment to the story and its characters. Likewise, for catching my plethora of errors and ensuring that this book was the best it could be.

As any author knows, a novel isn't produced in a vacuum. My deepest appreciation to the entire team at HQ Stories for bringing my books to readers all over the world.

While this book is a work of fiction, it did require some research into real-world circumstances. A special thanks to James Knapp and Dave M. for answering my questions about the Ohio legal system, capital punishment, and crimes committed by authority figures. And to author James L'Etoile for providing me with information regarding the US prison system and what it's like to visit a prisoner on death row.

The majority of this book was written and edited in timed writing sprints. I'm incredibly grateful to Olivia Day for joining me on these sprints and keeping me accountable. Without her help I never would have finished this manuscript on time.

A massive thanks to Becky Youtz for helping me resolve some significant plot problems as well as providing real-world accuracy for many of the background circumstances in the story. Thanks also to Dawn Green for her overall encouragement and brainstorming sessions. And to Christy for providing me with a reader's first impression on the opening chapters when this book was still in its planning stages.

Thank you to Mika van Gelderen for inspiring the character of Spaghetti, resulting in many late nights researching how to properly care for snakes as pets—most of which didn't make it into the novel, but gave me a deeper appreciation for reptiles.

Words cannot express my gratitude for all of the wonderful booksellers, bloggers, and librarians who have supported my books from the beginning and helped readers connect with my stories.

Thanks to my family for their love and encouragement. The fried bologna sandwich is inspired by actual events. IYKYK.

As always, I am indebted to Feiko, who spent hours listening to my ramblings about the best ways to commit fictional crimes and get away with them. And to my cat, Watson, who slept beside my laptop while I wrote this entire book.

Last, but certainly not least, a book is nothing without readers. Thank *you* for taking the time to read this one.

Dear Reader,

We hope you enjoyed reading this book. If you did, we'd be so appreciative if you left a review. It really helps us and the author to bring more books like this to you.

Here at HQ Digital we are dedicated to publishing fiction that will keep you turning the pages into the early hours. Don't want to miss a thing? To find out more about our books, promotions, discover exclusive content and enter competitions you can keep in touch in the following ways:

JOIN OUR COMMUNITY:
Sign up to our new email newsletter: http://smarturl.it/SignUpHQ
Read our new blog www.hqstories.co.uk

🐦 https://twitter.com/HQStories
f www.facebook.com/HQStories

BUDDING WRITER?
We're also looking for authors to join the HQ Digital family!
Find out more here:

https://www.hqstories.co.uk/want-to-write-for-us/

Thanks for reading, from the HQ Digital team